TIME

Key Words *1000*

美國《時代雜誌》‧全球獨家授權

單挑

大師推薦

▼姜敬寬 博士
台大新聞研究所客座教授
任職美國《時代雜誌》編輯三十餘年

▼成露茜 博士
台大城鄉研究所客座教授
美國加州大學洛杉磯分校
《UCLA》永久正教授

熟讀 1048 個單字

輕鬆挑戰《時代雜誌》

經典傳訊

NOTICE

PREFACE（序）

For nearly 75 years, TIME has reported on the latest trends in world politics, science and culture for an informed audience around the world. It sets the agenda for discussion of important issues for influential citizens in every nation.

Similarly, its editors and writers have long set the standard for elegance and clarity of expression in English. Their way with words has been widely imitated but perhaps never improved upon. Much of the pleasure for TIME's most faithful readers comes from the magazine's unique way of telling a story in fresh, lively terms.

So to learn how to communicate not just clearly but elegantly, the vocabulary and expressions employed in TIME make a great place to start. We are delighted to make available to native Chinese-language readers these unique guides to the language of TIME. We are confident these will be a valuable aide to the user's understanding, not just of what is reported in TIME each week, but of all the rapid changes in the world around us.

John Marcom
Publisher - Asia, TIME
《時代雜誌》亞洲區發行人

編輯緣起

　　TIME是1923年創刊的國際性新聞雜誌，每週發行全世界180餘個國家，600萬冊，傳閱率達3000萬人次，是全球最權威、發行量最大的新聞雜誌，其報導向來深受全球菁英份子的推崇，其寫作風格之獨特、文章之優美、尤其是遣詞用字之精練，也一直深獲讀者的激賞。對於想了解國際動態、科技新知的人來說，TIME無疑是最佳的選擇，對於想提升英文能力達到世界菁英份子水平的人來說，TIME也是最佳的讀物。

　　由於TIME是一本報導性的新聞雜誌，其遣詞用字有其新聞寫作上的偏好，與課堂裡所學的英文不盡相同，若要充分了解其內容，進而品味其文章之優美，首要之務就是掌握TIME的常用字彙。

■ 電腦選字 字字珠璣

　　有鑑於此，我們繼《時代經典用字系列》政治篇、商業篇、人文篇、科技篇四冊之後，出版了這本《TIME單挑1000》，從1990年迄今TIME的所有文章中，經電腦分析篩選出1048個重要單字，作為攻克TIME常用字的入門書。這些單字的選取係根據以下四原則：

一、出現頻率較高者；

二、對文義理解具關鍵性者；

三、一般字典上解說不夠明確者，或某字出現新用法而一般字典上看不到者，如leverage(□924)一般字典上都可查到名詞義，指「槓桿作用」和「(為達某一目的而使用的)手段、影響力」，但近來在TIME也常以動詞義出現，指「使(事情)更容易、更順利」；

四、一般人很熟悉的字彙，但在TIME裡也常以另一意義出現者，如harbor(□572)一般人都知道是「海港」，但在TIME裡也以動詞的面貌出現，表示「心懷…」。

■ 由簡入難 循序漸進

　　針對讀者學習上的效果，全書編排採由簡入難、循序漸進的方式，將1048個單字分成簡易、普通、進階三級，各級單字再依詞性不同分成形容詞(副詞)、動詞、名詞三類，共三級九章。每個單字均按出現先後，排序編號。

至於這1048個單字如何分爲簡易、普通、進階三級，則是根據各單字在上述TIME文章中出現的頻率高低而定。

　　簡易字表示出現頻率在200以上，而以頻率200至500間的單字爲主。這級字有些很簡單，差不多是高中程度的單字，如abandon(□¹¹¹)，但有些字在大學英文讀本裡也不常看到，如strapped for cash(□⁹⁴)、establishment(□³⁰⁷)，會出現這種情形，是因爲就TIME文章而言，這些字出現的頻率均在上述範圍內，所以歸爲同一級。

　　普通字表示出現頻率約在90至200間。這級字出現頻率雖不及簡易字頻繁，但因數量龐大，碰到的機會也不少，以本書所收錄單字爲例，這級字數量最多，因此也是不得不熟記的。

　　進階字表示出現頻率約在50至90間。這級字出現頻率較前兩者低，但因爲對文義理解具關鍵性，若能熟記，閱讀TIME必定更爲駕輕就熟。

■ 自修留學　一舉數得

　　對有意參加出國留學考，或只是單純想提高英文字彙能力的人，這也是一本很好的工具書。從以下這個表格，你可以一目了然，熟記本書三級單字後，你的英文程度相應於托福、GRE的水準，以及在ESL(English as a Second Language)教學課程上根據使用頻率高低所選定的重要單字(core vocabulary)裡，你已達到幾千字的程度。

TIME單挑1000	在TIME出現的頻率 （1990～1997年間）	相應於 托福的程度	相應於 GRE字彙的程度	相應於 ESL字彙的程度
簡易字	高頻（200次以上）	500～550分	350～400分	2000字
普通字	中頻（90～200次間）	550～600分	400～550分	4000字
進階字	低頻（50～90次間）	600～677分	550分以上	6000字

我們堅信，由一個完整的句子來掌握單字的意義，才是學習單字的最正確途徑，因此書中每一個單字皆附有例句，所有例句絕大部分從1994年迄1997年4月的TIME文章中選出。由於例句中不免有一些生字或片語，爲了讓讀者省去查字典的麻煩，我們對此作了兩項設計：

　　一、 凡此生詞屬於本書所收錄的1048個單字之一者，即在該生詞後附上數字，說明該生詞在本書排序的編號（見次頁圖解），以利檢索。

　　二、凡此生詞不屬於本書所收錄的1048個單字之一者，即在例句中譯後加註解說。這些加註的生詞，有如另一個字彙寶庫，可讓您吸收到更多的英文字彙，其中不乏一些源自西方典故的成語，如Holy Grail(見□[168] eliminate)，以及現行字典還沒有的新字，如spinmeister (見□[108] volatile)。

　　另外，爲加深讀者對該單字的理解，部分單字下面還附上同義字及反義字。

　　因此全書實際收錄的字彙，除1048個單字外，加上同反義字及例句中加注的生詞，共計超過2000個。熟讀此書後再拿起TIME來看，你必定會對自己的英文功力刮目相看。

本書使用說明

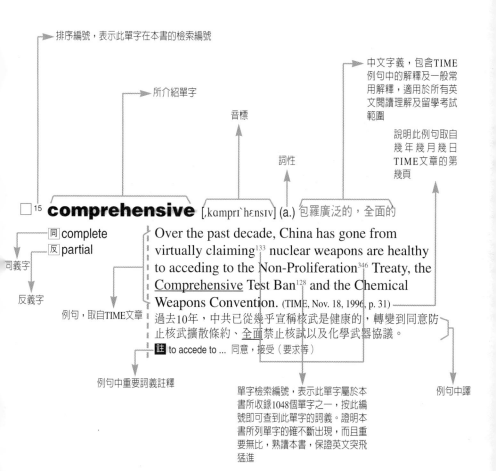

排序編號，表示此單字在本書的檢索編號

所介紹單字

音標

詞性

中文字義，包含TIME例句中的解釋及一般常用解釋，適用於所有英文閱讀理解及留學考試範圍

說明此例句取自幾年幾月幾日TIME文章的第幾頁

□ 15 **comprehensive** [ˌkɑmprɪˋhɛnsɪv] (a.) 包羅廣泛的，全面的

同 complete
反 partial

同義字

反義字

Over the past decade, China has gone from virtually claiming[133] nuclear weapons are healthy to acceding to the Non-Proliferation[346] Treaty, the Comprehensive Test Ban[128] and the Chemical Weapons Convention. (TIME, Nov. 18, 1996, p. 31)
過去10年，中共已從幾乎宣稱核武是健康的，轉變到同意防止核武擴散條約、全面禁止核試以及化學武器協議。

例句，取自TIME文章

註 to accede to ... 同意，接受（要求等）

例句中重要詞義註釋

單字檢索編號，表示此單字屬於本書所收錄1048個單字之一，按此編號即可查到此單字的詞義。證明本書所列單字的確不斷出現，而且重要無比，熟讀本書，保證英文突飛猛進

例句中譯

TIME Key Words 1000
CONTENTS

簡易字

TIME

Key Words 1000

- accustomed 習慣於
- affluent 富裕的
- ambiguous 模稜兩可，曖昧的
- anonymous 匿名的，不知名的
- appropriate 適宜的
- at stake 危急存亡關頭
- available 可取得的，買得到的
- bear 看跌的
- bilateral 雙邊的
- bland 平淡無奇的
- blunt 直言不諱的
- bull 看漲的，多頭的
- burgeoning 正快速發展的
- coherent 前後連貫的，有條理的
- comprehensive 包羅廣泛的，全面的
- compulsory 義務的，強制的
- conciliatory 有和解之意的
- conscious 意識到…的
- conventional 傳統的，一般的
- critical 重大的，居關鍵地位的
- crucial 關鍵的，重大的
- cunning 狡滑的，精明的
- dazzling 令人目眩神移的
- dedicated 專注的
- desperate 迫切的
- determined 堅定的
- disabled 殘障的
- disastrous 災情慘重的
- distinct 不易混淆的，獨特的
- dominant 主宰的，強勢的
- doomed 注定的，命定的
- drastic 劇烈的
- eccentric 特立獨行的
- elevated 崇高的
- elite 菁英的，最優秀的
- enduring 持久的

- explicit 明白表示的，直言的
- exquisite 精巧的
- extravagant 奢侈的，揮霍的
- fantastic 極大的，難以置信的
- ferocious 兇猛的
- flamboyant 顯眼的，引人注目的
- fledgling 初出茅廬的，羽毛剛長成的
- fluid 流動的，變化不定的
- formidable 難對付的，艱難的
- fragile 脆弱的，禁不起外力衝擊的
- futile 徒勞無功的，白費力氣的
- genuine 真的，非偽造的
- hefty 重大的
- hostile 帶敵意的
- immense 巨大的
- imminent 迫近的，即將發生的
- inaugural 就職的
- indifferent 漠不關心的
- intact 完好如初的
- lingering 流連不去的
- mean 卑劣的
- mutual 相互的，共有的
- namely 即，就是
- obscure 沒沒無聞的
- obsolete 落伍的，過時的
- ominous 不吉利的，不祥的
- ostensibly 表面上
- outspoken 率直的，不客氣的
- pending 審理中的，懸而未決的
- perpetual 永久的
- persistent 固執的，頑固的
- persuasive 有說服力的
- pervasive 遍布的
- phony 偽造的
- poignant 尖刻的，切中要害的
- preliminary 初步的

☐ previous 先前的	☐ sophisticated 尖端的，先進的
☐ primary 最初的，原始的，主要的	☐ staggering 令人驚愕的
☐ primitive 原始的	☐ strapped (for cash) 身無分文的
☐ profound 重大的，深刻的	☐ subject (to) 受…支配的，受…影響的
☐ prominent 著名的，傑出的	☐ substantial 大量的，重大的
☐ promising 前景看好的	☐ subtle 隱晦的，不明顯的
▨ radical 徹底的	☐ sweeping 全面的，大規模的
☐ rebel 叛軍的	▨ tangible 可觸到的，有形的
☐ reckless 鹵莽的，不顧後果的	☐ thriving 興盛的
☐ reminiscent (of) 使人想起…的	☐ tremendous 巨大的
☐ renowned 著名的	☐ tricky 棘手的
☐ rigorous 嚴格的	▨ unanimous 意見一致的
☐ rugged 崎嶇不平的，多岩石的	☐ unprecedented 史無前例的
▨ savage 野蠻的，殘暴的	☐ urgent 緊急的
☐ sensible 合理的，明智的	▨ venerable 受人尊敬的
☐ sensitive 敏感的，細膩的	☐ vigorous 精力旺盛的，充滿活力的
☐ shrewd 敏銳的，有洞察力的	☐ volatile 善變的
☐ significant 重大的，影響深遠的	☐ voluntary 志願的
☐ sluggish 遲緩的，不景氣的	☐ vulnerable 易受傷的，脆弱的

1 **accustomed** [ə`kʌstəmd] (a.) 習慣於

同 used
反 unaccustomed

Even if they are willing to make the sacrifice in dollars, whether Americans will give up long accustomed personal liberties is another question.
(TIME, May 1, 1995, p. 68)
即使美國人願意犧牲金錢上的損失，但是否願意拋棄久已習以爲常的個人自由，還是未定之天。

2 **affluent** [ə`fluənt] (a.) 富裕的

同 prosperous
   wealthy
反 poor

Leeson and his wife Lisa never really seemed to fit into the affluent, neo-colonial life-style of Singapore or into the city's multiethnic society.
(TIME, Mar. 13, 1995, p. 40)
李森和其妻子麗莎似乎與新加坡富裕的新殖民生活型態一直格格不入，也似乎一直未能融入新加坡的多種族社會。

3 **ambiguous** [æm`bɪgjuəs] (a.) 模稜兩可的，曖昧的

同 vague [veg]
反 obvious
   clear

Truman got the Korean War because he was ambiguous, and Saddam took Kuwait because Bush didn't say "No" straight out.
(TIME, Feb. 19, 1996, p. 36)
杜魯門惹了個韓戰，因爲他的立場不明確，而海珊佔領科威特，是因爲布希沒能直接了當地說「不」。
註 straight out 率直地

4 **anonymous** [ə`nɑnəməs] (a.) 匿名的，不知名的

反 known
   named

So he went on his own fact-finding mission, leaning heavily on a 49-page white paper submitted[256] last month by three anonymous high-tech firms. (TIME, Feb. 27, 1995, p. 31)
所以他繼續其真相調查工作，埋頭審閱一份厚達49頁的白皮書，這份白皮書是上個月由3家匿名的高科技公司提出的。

☐ 5 **appropriate** [ə`proprɪˌet] (a.) 適宜的

反 inappropriate

So any protein that dissolves new blood vessels may not be appropriate for younger women who have not yet entered menopause. (TIME, Jan. 9, 1995, p. 60)
因此，對於還未停經的婦女而言，任何足以分解新生血管的蛋白質或許都是不適宜的。

☐ 6 **at stake** [æt stek] 危急存亡關頭的，有可能喪失或受損的

同 at risk

At a news conference, (U.S. Undersecretary of Defense) Perry declared that the credibility[298] of the international community (NATO) was at stake. (TIME, June 5, 1995, p. 38)
在記者會上，（美國國防部次長）培里宣稱，北約這個國際組織正面臨公信力淪喪的危機。

☐ 7 **available** [ə`veləbl] (a.) （物）可取得的，買得到的；
（人有空）可見面的，可參加的

Most of the (smart) cards available in Atlanta will be worth between $10 and $50 and will be usable instead of cash at as many as 5,000 "points of purchase" throughout the city. (TIME, Jan. 8, 1996, p. 13)
於亞特蘭大出售的IC卡大部分值10-50美元，可以在全市多達5千個「指定消費點」充當貨幣使用。

☐ 8 **bear** [bɛr] (a.) （股市）看跌的

Meanwhile, pundits[1028] who do make a bear stand don't last. (TIME, Mar. 3, 1997, p. 53)
同時，那些對股市看跌的專家，也不再堅持自己的看法。

□ 9 **bilateral** [baɪˋlætərəl] (a.) 雙邊的

He would halt bilateral contact with North Korea until Pyongyang resumed[238] negotiations with South Korea. (TIME, July 8, 1996, p. 29)
他會暫停與北韓的雙邊接觸，直到平壤與南韓恢復談判。

□ 10 **bland** [blænd] (a.) 平淡無奇的

As a result news coverage tends to be bland.
(TIME, Feb. 10, 1997, p. 56)
結果新聞報導往往平淡無味。

□ 11 **blunt** [blʌnt] (a.) 直言不諱的

Clinton's summation was startlingly blunt: "It is better to have reached no agreement (on Japan's opening its domestic market) than to have reached an empty agreement." (TIME, Feb. 21, 1994, p. 41)
最後柯林頓語驚四座，直言不諱地總結說：「（在日本開放其國內市場這個議題上）與其獲致形同具文的協議，不如不要。」

□ 12 **bull** [bʊl] (a.)（股市）看漲的，多頭的

The bull market will end—but when is the question. (TIME, Mar. 3, 1997, p. 53)
多頭市場將會結束，問題是何時結束。

□ 13 **burgeoning** [ˋbɝdʒənɪŋ] (a.) 正快速發展的

Genetic information is the raw material of the burgeoning biotechnology industry, which uses human DNA to build specialized proteins that may have some value as disease-fighting drugs.
(TIME, Jan. 16, 1995, p. 54)
遺傳訊息是目前正蓬勃發展的生物科技工業的原料；此工業利用人類DNA製造特化蛋白質，而這些蛋白質或許可作為治病藥物之用。

□ 14 **coherent** [ko`hɪrənt] (a.) 前後連貫的，有條理的

反 muddled
incoherent

Curry ... impressed Clinton with his ability to fashion a <u>coherent</u> policy message that synthesized the often conflicting[295] interests of the party's traditional and moderate wings.

(TIME, June 5, 1995, p. 22)

克利就是有這個本事，能夠把黨內保守派、溫和派往往都各不相讓的利益結合在一起，做出一份<u>有條有理的</u>政策宣告，令柯林頓大為激賞。

註 fashion (v.) 製作；synthesize (v.) 綜合，合成

□ 15 **comprehensive** [ˌkɑmprɪ`hɛnsɪv] (a.) 包羅廣泛的，全面的

同 complete
反 partial

Over the past decade, China has gone from virtually claiming[133] nuclear weapons are healthy to acceding to the Non-Proliferation[346] Treaty, the <u>Comprehensive</u> Test Ban[128] and the Chemical Weapons Convention. (TIME, Nov. 18, 1996, p. 31)

過去10年，中共已從幾乎宣稱核武是健康的，轉變到同意防止核武擴散條約、<u>全面</u>禁止核試以及化學武器協議。

註 to accede to ... 同意，接受（要求等）

□ 16 **compulsory** [kəm`pʌlsərɪ] (a.) 義務的，強制的

同 mandatory

In 1919 while serving a <u>compulsory</u> stint in the military, Nurmi entered a 20-k march carrying a rifle, a cartridge belt and a knapsack filled with 5 kg of sand. (TIME, June 24, 1996, p. 66)

1919年，當他在軍中服<u>義務</u>役的時候，努爾米帶著一隻步槍，腰上繫著彈帶，背上背著裝有5公斤沙子的背包參加20公里行軍。

註 stint (n.)（在某處從事某事的）那段時間

☐ 17 **conciliatory** [kən`sɪlɪəˌtorɪ] (a.) 有和解之意的

有枝的/溫和的

The executive director of the Christian Coalition told a prominent[77] Jewish audience, in a conciliatory speech, that calling the U.S. a "Christian nation" is wrong .... (TIME, Apr. 17, 1995, p. 13)
在一場<u>有意化解對立的</u>演講中，基督教聯盟的執行長告訴台下那群猶太名流說，將美國叫做「基督教國家」是不對的。

☐ 18 **conscious** [`kɑnʃəs] (a.) 意識到…的

同 aware

Times Books recently announced that it will publish a book of socially-<u>conscious</u> poetry by former President Jimmy Carter. (TIME, July 18, 1994, p. 9)
時代圖書公司最近宣布，將出版一本由前總統卡特所寫、<u>關心社會的</u>詩集。

☐ 19 **conventional** [kən`vɛnʃənl] (a.) 傳統的，一般的，普通的

同 traditional
反 unconventional

The voice-recognition technology will not be on <u>conventional</u> desktop computers only; it will be available[7] in any sort of electronic information-processing device. (TIME, July 17, 1995, p. 44)
聲音辨識技術不只將運用於<u>一般的</u>桌上型電腦，任何電子資訊處理裝置都用得上。

☐ 20 **critical** [`krɪtɪkl] (a.) 重大的，居關鍵地位的

同 crucial

"We have only the foggiest idea," the independent daily *Segodnya* complained last week, "who is actually at the helm in this country, who is making the <u>critical</u> decisions." (TIME, Jan. 9, 1995, p. 50)
立場獨立的《塞戈尼亞日報》上週抱怨說，「誰是真正的國家領導者？誰下<u>重大</u>決策？我們所知甚少。」
註 foggy (a.) 模糊的，朦朧的

□ 21 **crucial** [ˋkruʃəl] (a.) 關鍵的，重大的

同 critical

Understanding social cues, creating works of art and spawning[953] inventions are all <u>crucial</u> mental tasks that bear little relationship to how well a person can fill in a printed test form.

(TIME, Sept. 11, 1995, p. 60)

許多<u>重要的</u>心智活動，像理解一些社交上的暗示，創造藝術品，創造新發明，其實都和填測驗卷的能力沒什麼關係。

□ 22 **cunning** [ˋkʌnɪŋ] (a.) 狡滑的，精明的

同 crafty

Perhaps the most <u>cunning</u> Disney trick is to take fairy tales in the public domain and reinvent them as corporate property. A billion-dollar example is *Beauty and the Beast* .... (TIME, May 2, 1994, p. 72)

迪士尼公司最<u>精明的</u>盤算，或許就是將童話故事搬上大眾舞台，且將其改頭換面，成為公司資產。耗資10億拍成的《美女與野獸》就是個例子。

□ 23 **dazzling** [ˋdæzlɪŋ] (a.) 令人目眩神移的

同 stunning

With computers doubling in speed and power every couple of years, and with genetic engineering's <u>dazzling</u> feats[994] growing more and more routine, the battered American faith in technological progress has been growing stronger and giddier[420] of late. (TIME, May 27, 1996, p. 67)

隨著電腦的速度與功能每兩年就增加一倍，基因工程上<u>驚人的</u>成就變得司空見慣，美國人在科技進展上備受打擊的信心，近年來已漸趨堅強，並有異常樂觀的趨勢。

註 batter (v.) 連番猛擊，毒打

□ 24 **dedicated** [ˋdɛdəˌketɪd] (a.) 專注的

In Singapore, <u>dedicated</u> Net users are planning to maintain unfettered[861] access[273] by jumping borders and dialing services in neighboring Malaysia. (TIME, Sept. 23, 1996, p. 27)

新加坡的網路<u>迷</u>正計畫跨越國界，使用鄰國馬來西亞的撥號服務，以確保網路上的自由使用權。

☐ 25 **desperate** [ˈdɛspərɪt] (a.) 迫切的

Bereft of patrons, <u>desperate</u> to rescue his economy, Fidel Castro turns to an unusual solution: capitalism. (TIME, Feb. 20, 1995, p. 50)

由於資助斷絕，而又急於挽救該國經濟，卡斯楚轉而求助於一項罕見的解救之道：資本主義。

註 to be bereft of 喪失（希望、喜悅等）

☐ 26 **determined** [dɪˈtɜmɪnd] (a.) 堅定的

Author Joe Kane came across a <u>determined</u> priest, a Spaniard who had spent years teaching a tribe of hunter gatherers, the Huaorani, how to survive outside their rainforest habitat.

(TIME, Mar. 25, 1996, p. 70)

作者喬‧卡內遇到一名性格堅毅的西班牙籍教士，這名教士花了好幾年時間教導華歐拉尼族人離開世居的雨林區之後的生存之道。華歐拉尼族以狩獵、採集為生。

☐ 27 **disabled** [dɪsˈeb]d] (a.) 殘障的

同 handicapped

Seven years ago, Dole spoke about the need to "provide care and assistance for the hungry and the homeless and the <u>disabled</u>." Nothing resembling[233] that was heard last week.

(TIME, Apr. 24, 1995, p. 52)

7年前，杜爾談到有必要「為飢民、游民、殘障人士提供照顧與援助」這樣的話上個星期不復聽到。

☐ 28 **disastrous** [dɪˈzæstrəs] (a.) 災情慘重的

同 terrible

The Kobe quake was only slightly bigger than the Northridge tremor but more <u>disastrous</u>.

(TIME, Jan. 30, 1995, p. 34)

神戶地震的規模僅稍大於諾斯里基地震，造成的災情卻更嚴重。

29 **distinct** [dɪ`stɪŋkt] (a.) 不易混淆的，獨特的

Many scientists consider the Khoisan a <u>distinct</u> race of very ancient origin. (TIME, Jan. 16, 1995, p. 54)

許多科學家認爲〔南非〕柯伊桑人是一支<u>獨特的</u>民族，淵源非常久遠。

30 **dominant** [`dɑmənənt] (a.) 主宰的，強勢的

同 pre-eminent

Now as then, the splintering of a Saddam-less Iraq would leave Iran the <u>dominant</u> gulf power, an unpalatable solution. (TIME, Sept. 23, 1996, p. 35)

現在的情況和當時相同，沒有海珊的伊拉克會四分五裂，波斯灣就屬伊朗<u>稱霸</u>，這種解決方案令人無法接受。

註 splinter (v.) 使分裂；unpalatable (a.) 不好吃的，令人不快的

31 **doomed** [dumd] (a.) 注定的，命定的

He started at the top, of course, but the fact that he is staying there has frustrated[183] the popular wisdom that an early front runner is <u>doomed</u> to fall. (TIME, June 5, 1995, p. 29)

他一開始就領先，這是想當然爾的事，但讓一般人跌破眼鏡的是，他此後一直保持領先，因爲一般人都認爲剛開始當選希望最濃的人最後<u>必定</u>會敗下陣來。

註 wisdom (n.) 看法；front runner 比賽中最有可能奪標的人

(a.) 注定要失敗或毀滅的，劫數難逃的

At the beginning of May 1945 it was clear to even the most zealous of Hitler's followers that his "Thousand Year Reich" was <u>doomed</u>.

(TIME, May 15, 1995, p. 52)

1945年5月初，即使是希特勒最狂熱的支持者，也都清楚瞭解到「千年帝國」已是<u>劫數難逃</u>。

☐ 32 **drastic** [ˋdræstɪk] (a.) 劇烈的

同 radical

The New Deal welfare safety net installed[198] in the 1930s and augmented in the Great Society programs of the 1960s has been hauled off for the kind of <u>drastic</u> restitching that France, Germany, Italy and Sweden have been laboring over for the past year or more. (TIME, Aug. 12, 1996, p. 25)

「新政」在1930年代大張社會福利安全網，到了1960年代又因「大社會」的各項計畫而更形擴大，如今這張安全網已經取下，準備<u>大肆</u>縫補，就像一年多來法國、德國、義大利與瑞典這些國家大費周章所做的修改一樣。

註 augment (v.) 擴大，加強；to haul off 撤下；restitching (n.) 重新縫補

☐ 33 **eccentric** [ɪkˋsɛntrɪk] (a.) 特立獨行的

同 odd

The <u>eccentric</u>, fact-based best seller *Midnight In the Garden of Good and Evil* sparks[247] a rush to see where it all took place. (TIME, Apr. 3, 1995, p. 79)

這本<u>風格特異</u>、根據真人實事改編的暢銷書《午夜的善惡花園》，激起一股人潮湧向故事的發生地一探究竟。

☐ 34 **elevated** [ˋɛləˌvetɪd] (a.) 崇高的

It turns out, however, that not every man who reached the pinnacle[755] of American leadership was a gleaming example of self-awareness, empathy, impulse[320] control and other qualities that mark an <u>elevated</u> EQ. (TIME, Oct. 9, 1995, p. 30)

然而，結果是，並非每個攀登到美國領導階層巔峰的人都是具有自覺、有同理心、能克制衝動，及其他<u>高</u>EQ特質的閃亮典範。

□ 35 **elite** [ɪˋlit] (a.) 菁英的，最優秀的 (n.) 菁英

Ideally, the U.N. should have a small, <u>elite</u>, standing rapid-deployment force ... trained and ready to go at once to a trouble spot that the Security Council has decided to become involved in. (TIME, Oct. 23, 1995, p. 30)
理想的作法是聯合國建立一支小而<u>精</u>、訓練有素的快速部署部隊，一旦某地發生動亂，安理會決定涉入，即可派上用場。

□ 36 **enduring** [ɪnˋdjʊrɪŋ] (a.) 持久的

The plain, undecorated object, representing the <u>enduring</u> role art has played throughout China's history, takes pride of place in the sumptuous Splendors of Imperial China, which opened last week at New York City Metropolitan Museum of Art. (TIME, Apr. 1, 1996, p. 47)
這塊樸實、毫無雕琢的物件，代表藝術在中國歷史上扮演的<u>歷久不衰</u>的角色。上週在紐約大都會博物館開幕的「中國帝國瑰寶展」豐盛的展出中，這塊物件展示在最主要的位置。
註 to take pride of place （在一組事物中）被視為最重要的；
　　sumptuous (a.) 豪華的，昂貴的

□ 37 **explicit** [ɪkˋsplɪsɪt] (a.) 明白表示的，直言的

But they won't be able to filter the Internet. They're <u>explicit</u> about that. (TIME, Feb. 17, 1997, p. 46)
但是網際網路無法過濾，這點他們已<u>明白表示</u>。

□ 38 **exquisite** [ɛkˋskwɪzɪt] (a.) 精巧的

The show also includes an <u>exquisite</u> Seurat seascape, some notable Cézannes and considerable paintings by Courbet, Gauguin, Van Gogh and others. (TIME, Apr. 3, 1995, p. 64)
這次展出的作品，包括一幅秀拉的<u>出色海景畫</u>，數幅塞尚名畫，及庫爾貝、高更、梵谷等人的不少畫作。

☐ 39 **extravagant** [ɪk`strævəgənt] (a.) 奢侈的，揮霍的

Could this fate befall James Cameron, Hollywood's most daring and <u>extravagant</u> auteur?

(TIME, July 18, 1994, p. 55)

這個惡運有可能降臨柯麥隆這位好萊塢最大膽、<u>最敢花錢的</u>大導演身上嗎？

註 befall (v.)（惡事）降臨；
auteur (n.) 法文，指具有強烈個人風格的大導演

☐ 40 **fantastic** [fæn`tæstɪk] (a.) 極大的，難以置信的；
（口語）極好的，了不起的

Because of its <u>fantastic</u> capacity to see all possible combinations some distance into the future, the machine (Deep Blue) , once it determines that its own position is safe, can take the kind of attacking chances no human would.

(TIME, Feb. 26, 1996, p. 42)

「深藍」電腦因為具有透視未來所有可能組合的<u>驚人</u>能力，一旦認定自己的位置安全，便敢冒人類不敢冒的險而進擊。

☐ 41 **ferocious** [fə`roʃəs] (a.) 兇猛的

This puts Clinton in something of a no-win situation: he is unlikely to gain much credit if the bailout[281] succeeds, but will catch <u>ferocious</u> flak if it fails. (TIME, Mar. 6, 1995, p. 34)

融資案如果成功，柯林頓不會因此博得美名，如果失敗，則會遭來<u>猛烈的</u>抨擊，由此看來，柯林頓有些像是吃力不討好。

註 flak (n.) 高射砲火；抨擊，指責

☐ 42 **flamboyant** [flæm`bɔɪənt] (a.) 顯眼的，引人注目的；奢華的

He is probably the least <u>flamboyant</u> of the Republican contenders. (TIME, Mar. 13, 1995, p. 86)

共和黨各角逐者中，他大概是最不<u>受矚目的</u>。

□ 43 **fledgling** [ˋflɛdʒlɪŋ] (a.) 初出茅蘆的，羽毛剛長成的

Early in this century, a <u>fledgling</u> effort at behavioral genetics divided people into such classes as mesomorphs—physically robust[454], psychologically assertive—and ectomorphs—skinny, nervous, shy. (TIME, Mar. 10, 1997, p. 41)
本世紀初，在行為遺傳學方面的一項<u>初步</u>研究將人分為運動型體格（身材壯碩，好堅持己見）以及清瘦型體格（身材瘦削，神經緊張，個性害羞）。
註 assertive (a.) 武斷的，過分自信的

□ 44 **fluid** [ˋfluɪd] (a.) 流動的，變化不定的

同 changeable

Information ... is now too <u>fluid</u> to control. It flows in over airways, via satellites, through microwave relays to cellular phones, faxes, televisions, radios, beepers, modems. (TIME, Aug. 19, 1996, p. 52)
今日的資訊<u>流動</u>性太大，已經不可能管制。資訊傳送方式很多，可以經由空中、衛星、微波轉接，也可以透過行動電話、傳真機、電視、收音機、呼叫器與數據機。

□ 45 **formidable** [ˋfɔrmɪdəbl] (a.)（敵人）難對付的，（工作）艱難的

"Perot as kingmaker," he says tactfully, "is a more <u>formidable</u> proposition than Perot as candidate."
(TIME, Mar. 13, 1995, p. 91)
他刻意不傷人地委婉說到：「培洛替人抬轎助選，要比自己出來選更難纏。」
註 kingmaker (n.) 有權使人當選者；
proposition (n.)（口語）要對付或注意的事物

□ 46 **fragile** [ˋfrædʒəl] (a.)（情勢）脆弱的，禁不起外力衝擊的

同 unstable

A revenue-generating[187] franchise[704] is the most <u>fragile</u> thing in the world ... No matter how good your product, you are only 18 months away from failure. (TIME, June 5, 1995, p. 32)
世界上最<u>不可靠的</u>，莫過於權利金的收入。產品再好，也只有18個月免於淘汰的安全期。

□ [47] **futile** [ˋfjutl] (a.) 徒勞無功的，白費力氣的

同 pointless

Indeed, for all the world's governments, ... attempts to control the global flow of electro-information are not only <u>futile</u> but counter[152] productive as well.

(TIME, Spring 1995 Special Issue: Welcome to Cyberspace, p. 80)

試圖控制電子資訊的全球流動，不僅<u>枉然</u>而且會招致反效果，對世界各國政府而言，這是無庸置疑的事。

□ [48] **genuine** [ˋdʒɛnjʊɪn] (a.) [1] 真的，非偽造的；[2] 真誠的，非偽裝的

同 [1] real
[2] sincere
反 fake

It is a challenge to portray a forsaken woman in a way that evokes[561] <u>genuine</u> sympathy; but Stevens manages. (TIME, Feb. 6, 1995, p. 75)

把棄婦描寫得令人<u>由衷</u>生起惻隱之心，不是件易事，但史蒂文斯做到了。

□ [49] **hefty** [ˋhɛftɪ] (a.) 重大的

Chow Yun Fat is angling for Hollywood stardom; this time next year he could be in any of three <u>hefty</u> action films. (TIME, June 29, 1996, p. 40)

周潤發正設法到好萊塢摘星，明年此時，他可能已在拍3部動作<u>鉅</u>片中的一部。

註 angle (v.) 釣魚；
to angle for ... 指（用暗示、手段、詭計等）謀取，博取；
stardom (n.) 明星的地位或身份

□ [50] **hostile** [ˋhɑstɪl] (a.) 帶敵意的

同 antagonistic
反 receptive

Unlike most baseball-playing countries, Cuba has no professional league to cream off its top talent, and <u>hostile</u> relations with Washington keep its elite[35] from migrating to the U.S. major leagues.

(TIME, Feb. 5, 1996, p. 13)

古巴與大部分棒球國家不同，它沒有職棒聯盟，所以不愁頂尖高手被挖角。它與華盛頓交<u>惡</u>，所以棒球菁英也不會移民去打美國大聯盟。

註 to cream off ... 挑出（最好的部份），提取（精華）

51 **immense** [ɪˋmɛns] (a.) 巨大的

同 enormous

His influence in the 1980s was so <u>immense</u> that Taiwanese distributors once asked a Hong Kong director if there was a role in a film for Chow Yun-fat, and if there wasn't, they requested that one be written in before they'd commit to a deal.

(TIME, May 6, 1996, p. 62)
周潤發在80年代的影響力非常<u>大</u>，過去台灣的片商曾問某香港導演，某部電影中有沒有周潤發，如果沒有，他們要求替他寫一個角色進去，否則生意免談。

註 to commit (oneself) to ... 答應，保證

52 **imminent** [ˋɪmənənt] (a.) 迫近的，即將發生的

International headlines warn of <u>imminent</u> Chinese military exercises on the coast of China's nearby Fujian province and even a possible Chinese invasion of Taiwan. (TIME, Feb. 19, 1996, p. 21)
國際媒體的頭條新聞警告說，中共<u>即將</u>在臺灣附近的福建省沿岸舉行軍事演習，甚至可能犯台。

53 **inaugural** [ɪnˋɔgjurəl] (a.) 就職的

After the oath, he gave an <u>inaugural</u> address designed to reach out to all Americans, to rally[766] the nation to work together for a great common future. (TIME, Jan. 16, 1995, p. 24)
宣誓後，他發表了以全體美國人爲對象的<u>就職</u>演說，呼籲全體國人團結起來，爲大家偉大的未來一起努力。

54 **indifferent** [ɪnˋdɪfərənt] (a.) 漠不關心的

反 concerned

Chechen militiamen hiding around the corner are <u>indifferent</u> to the Russian's fate.

(TIME, Jan. 16, 1995, p. 46)
潛伏附近的車臣民兵對俄羅斯的命運一點<u>也不關心</u>。

註 around the corner 在近處的；即將發生的

55 **intact** [ɪnˋtækt] (a.) 完好如初的

同 in one piece

But psychologists, psychiatrists and other scientists are bitterly divided over the idea that the memory of repeated abuse can be completely wiped out and then recovered, virtually intact. (TIME, Apr. 17, 1995, p. 54)

但一再受虐的遭遇是否可自記憶中完全排除，進而完全復原，與受害前幾乎沒有兩樣，這一點在心理學家、精神學家和其他科學家中引發尖銳的對立。

56 **lingering** [ˋlɪŋgərɪŋ] (a.) 流連不去的

What remains largely unspoken is the lingering hope that such a mission might experience, somewhere beneath the desolate Martian surface, a close encounter[304] with organisms that are alive today. (TIME, Aug. 19, 1996, p. 44)

而尚未說出口的那個宿願，就是希望這一項任務可以在火星荒蕪的地表下，與現在還活著的生物進行近距離接觸。

57 **mean** [min] (a.) 卑劣的

This bill is mean. It is downright low-down. What does it profit a great nation to conquer[143] the world, only to lose its soul? (TIME, Aug. 12, 1996, p. 25)

這個提案太卑鄙了，簡直是沒格。這麼大的國家如果失去了靈魂，就算征服了全世界又有什麼用？

註 downright (adv.) 十足地，徹頭徹尾地；
low-down (a.)（口語）低賤的，卑鄙的

58 **mutual** [ˋmjutʃʊəl] (a.) 相互的，共有的

"That audience was amazing," he says. "They were so sweet. They were bathing us in affection." To prove the feeling is mutual, he heads back out into the spotlight. (TIME, Nov. 11, 1996, p. 16)

「那些觀衆眞是令人驚訝。」他說道：「他們太可愛了，讓我們沐浴在熱情中。」爲了表示這種熱情是共有的，他轉身走回聚光燈下。

□ 59 **namely** [ˋnemlɪ] (adv.) 即，就是

同 that is

<u>Namely</u>, he fails to take into account Quittner's Law, which says: It is impossible to pay less than $3,000 for this year's computer.

(TIME, Nov. 11, 1996, p. 26)

這個錯誤<u>就是</u>，他沒有把奎特納定律考慮進去，這條定律就是：3千美元以下的價錢買不到今年出廠的電腦。

□ 60 **obscure** [əbˋskjʊr] (a.) 沒沒無聞的

同 unknown

He'd met Marc Andreessen, who as an undergraduate programmer had helped create the then <u>obscure</u> browsing software Mosaic, which made it easy to navigate[209] the World Wide Web.

(TIME, June 17, 1996, p. 16)

他和馬克・安德里森見了面，安德里森在大學讀電腦時，幫忙設計了當時尚<u>沒沒無聞的</u>「馬賽克」導覽軟體，讓網路族可在全球資訊網中輕鬆尋找資訊。

□ 61 **obsolete** [ˋɑbsə͵lit] (a.) 落伍的，過時的

同 outdated

Indeed, your average computer is virtually <u>obsolete</u> by the time it is shipped from the factory to the retail[356] store. (TIME, Nov. 11, 1996, p. 16)

實際上，一般的電腦從工廠送到零售店的時候，可以說已經<u>過時</u>了。

□ 62 **ominous** [ˋɑmɪnəs] (a.) 不吉利的，不祥的

同 menacing

Observers are not surprised that business is flourishing[181] despite the <u>ominous</u> political situation. (TIME, Feb. 12, 1996, p. 18)

儘管政治情勢<u>惡劣</u>，觀察家對經貿如此蓬勃發展並不意外。

63 ostensibly [ɑsˋtɛnsəblɪ] (adv.) 表面上

At 3:33 a.m., it touched down at Marseilles, <u>ostensibly</u> for a refueling stop. (TIME, Jan. 9, 1995, p. 54)
凌晨3點33分，這艘船停靠馬賽港，<u>表面上</u>是爲了添加燃料。

64 outspoken [ˈautˋspokən] (a.) 率直的，不客氣的

同 forthright

When he (Magic Johnson) tried to make a comeback in the fall of '92, the fears of some <u>outspoken</u> N.B.A. players forced him to call it off. (TIME, Feb. 12, 1996, p. 39)
1992年秋季魔術強森想重返N.B.A.，但由於一些<u>直言無諱的</u>球員〔怕被染上愛滋病〕，使他打消了這個念頭。
註 comeback (n.) 東山再起，捲土重來

65 pending [ˋpɛndɪŋ] (a.) 審理中的，懸而未決的；即將發生的

According the chairman, there are dozens of suits <u>pending</u> against the company. (TIME, June 5, 1995, p. 46)
根據該總裁的說法，該公司現有數十個正<u>審理中的</u>官司纏身。

66 perpetual [pɚˋpɛtʃuəl] (a.) 永久的

同 permanent
continual

California, locked in a <u>perpetual</u> automotive smog, requires that by 2003, 10% of the cars offered for sale in the state produce zero emissions .... (TIME, Sept. 23, 1996, p. 41)
爲<u>永久不散的</u>汽車污染煙霧所苦的加州，強制要求在公元2003年前，10%在州內銷售的汽車必須完全不排放廢氣。

☐ 67 **persistent** [pə`sɪstənt] (a.) 固執的，頑固的

A small but <u>persistent</u> group of critics, many of them supported by the oil and coal industries, still don't buy it. (TIME, July 8, 1996, p. 41)
有一群人數不多但<u>固執己見</u>的批評者，還是不信這一套，這些人中有很多受到石油業者和煤礦業者的支持。

☐ 68 **persuasive** [pə`swesɪv] (a.) 有說服力的

Could it be that religious faith has some direct influence on physiology and health? Harvard's Herbert Benson is probably the most <u>persuasive</u> proponent[348] of this view. (TIME, June 24, 1996, p. 40)
宗教信仰是不是對生理和健康有直接的影響？哈佛的哈柏特‧班森大概是這理論最<u>具說服力的</u>提倡者。

☐ 69 **pervasive** [pə`vesɪv] (a.) 遍布的

The local U.S. attorney, Eddie Jordan, has called corruption in the (police) department "<u>pervasive</u>, rampant[450] and systemic." (TIME, Mar. 20, 1995, p. 45)
當地的美國律師喬丹就曾說過，該警察局內「貪污<u>成風</u>，非常猖獗，而且整個警局已成貪污共同體。」
註 systemic (a.)（毒物、疾病等）影響全身的

☐ 70 **phony** [`fonɪ] (a.) 偽造的

A police raid on a Tokyo trading company netted 2,000 pieces of counterfeit Nike merchandise[331], including <u>phony</u> Air Maxes. (TIME, Oct. 7. 1996, p. 12)
警方突擊東京一貿易公司，搜出2千件耐吉產品的贗品，其中包括Air Maxes運動鞋的<u>仿冒</u>品。
註 net (v.) 捕獲；counterfeit (a.) 偽造的

☐ **71 poignant** [ˈpɔɪnənt] (a.) 尖刻的，切中要害的；辛酸感人的

同 moving

That's sort of a <u>poignant</u> irony. (TIME, Feb. 20, 1995, p. 38)
那段話有點<u>尖刻</u>的諷刺味。
註 to be sort of 有幾分，有點…

☐ **72 preliminary** [prɪˈlɪməˌnɛrɪ] (a.) 初步的

The American Society of Travel Agents said in a <u>preliminary</u> estimate that as many as 10,000 of its 25,000 members could be put out of business.
(TIME, Feb. 27, 1995, p. 47)
美國旅行社協會<u>初步</u>研判，該社2萬5千名會員中可能有1萬名得關門大吉。

☐ **73 previous** [ˈprivjəs] (a.) 先前的

But it is known that Senator Kennedy gave a toast more poignant[71] than the one the <u>previous</u> evening. (TIME, Oct. 7, 1996, p. 42)
但聽說甘迺迪參議員的敬酒辭比<u>前一</u>晚更加辛酸感人。

☐ **74 primary** [ˈpraɪˌmɛrɪ] (a.) 最初的，原始的，主要的

Sigmund Freud dismissed[162] religious mysticism as "infantile helplessness" and "regression to <u>primary</u> narcissism." (TIME, June 24, 1996, p. 39)
弗洛依德曾將宗教神祕主義斥為「幼稚的無能」和「退化到<u>最原始的</u>自戀」。
註 regression (n.) 倒退，退化

☐ **75 primitive** [ˈprɪmətɪv] (a.) 原始的

The chances that a <u>primitive</u> creature secreted in this rock may survive such a journey are beginning to look surprisingly good.
(TIME, Aug. 19, 1996, p. 42)
藏在這塊岩石中的<u>原始</u>生物，在歷經這樣的旅程後仍存活的機率，看來是越來越高。

76 **profound** [prə`faʊnd] (a.) ¹·重大的，深刻的；
²·（理念、作品、人）深奧的，思想淵博的

同 ¹· great
²· deep
反 ²· shallow

By creating breakthroughs in agriculture and disease-fighting, the manipulation of DNA should lead to profound improvements in human health.

(TIME, July 17, 1995, p. 40)

透過在農業與疾病防治方面的突破，DNA的操控應能大幅改進人類健康。

77 **prominent** [`prɑmənənt] (a.) 著名的，傑出的

同 well-known

Abe Lincoln was a prominent railroad lawyer in 1860, but he campaigned[285] for the White House as the simple Midwestern rail-splitter.

(TIME, June 10, 1996, p. 58)

1860年，林肯已是代理鐵路訴訟案的名律師，卻仍以單純的中西部劈木頭工人的身份，出馬競選總統。

78 **promising** [`prɑmɪsɪŋ] (a.) 前景看好的

反 unpromising

On the horizon are the remedies that may prove more promising. (TIME, Apr. 3, 1995, p. 62)

有一些可能更被看好的療法即將問世。

註 on the horizon 即將來臨的

79 **radical** [`rædɪkl] (a.) ¹·徹底的；²·根本的，基本的；³·激進的

同 ²· fundamental
反 ³· conservative
reactionary

More than at any other time in the past 25 years, men are living in a state of radical disconnection from the women-and-children part of the human race. (TIME, May. 6, 1996, p. 53)

過去25年來，男人完全脫離女人和小孩而離群索居的情形以目前最為嚴重。

☐ 80 **rebel** [ˋrɛbl] (a.) 叛軍的　(n.) 叛軍　(v.) 反叛

Yeltsin ruled out direct peace talks with rebel leader Jokhar Dudayev. (TIME, Jan. 30, 1995, p. 15)
葉爾欽決定不與叛軍領袖杜達耶夫舉行和平談判。
註 to rule out 拒絕考慮，排除

☐ 81 **reckless** [ˋrɛklɪs] (a.) 鹵莽的，不顧後果的

Sports equipment designed to make football safer encouraged more reckless moves and ended up making the sport more dangerous than unpadded, unhelmeted rugby. (TIME, May 27, 1996, p. 67)
美式足球的護具本在保護球員，反而鼓勵球員更不顧後果橫衝直撞，結果使得美式足球比起不用護墊與頭盔的橄欖球更危險。
註 to end up 結果變成

☐ 82 **reminiscent (of)** [ˌrɛməˋnɪsṇt] (a.) 使人想起…的

At Guantanamo Bay Naval Base, Cuban refugees cavort happily on the beach in a scene reminiscent of a Club Med. (TIME, May 22, 1995, p. 50)
在關達納摩灣海軍基地，古巴難民在沙灘上歡騰跳躍，恍如置身「地中海俱樂部」渡假中心。
註 cavort (v.)（喧鬧、興奮地）跳躍

☐ 83 **renowned** [rɪˋnaund] (a.) 著名的

With his boyish face and slender build, he (David Ho) could more easily pass for a teenager than for a 44-year-old father of three—or, for that matter, for a world-renowned scientist.
(TIME, Dec. 30, 1996/Jan. 6, 1997, p. 24)
娃娃臉和瘦瘦的身材，使何大一看起來更像是個青少年，而不像一位44歲、育有3名子女的父親，更不像是世界知名的科學家。
註 build (n.) 體格，體形；to pass for 被視為，被當做

□ 84 **rigorous** [ˈrɪɡərəs] (a.) 嚴格的

The work component of the legislation is <u>rigorous</u>. Within two months of offering benefits, states can require recipients to perform community service. (TIME, Aug. 12, 1996, p. 25)
此立法中有關就業的規定十分<u>嚴格</u>。州政府在開始支付福利金的頭兩個月內,就可以要求領取福利金者從事社區服務工作。

□ 85 **rugged** [ˈrʌɡɪd] (a.) 崎嶇不平的,多岩石的;
　　　　　　　　(人)體格粗壯的,個性堅毅的

The men had previously completed (Army Ranger) training in <u>rugged</u> forest, desert and mountain terrains. (TIME, Feb. 27, 1995, p. 11)
這些人先前已在<u>崎嶇不平的</u>森林、沙漠和山區受完陸軍突擊部隊的訓練。

□ 86 **savage** [ˈsævɪdʒ] (a.) 野蠻的,殘暴的

同 vicious

And the old soldiers, rows of military medals pinned to their civilian clothes, are reminiscing about the war, the friends they lost and the <u>savage</u>, tragic history of the country they saved.

(TIME, May 8, 1995, p. 78)
而這些老兵,便服上別了一排排的軍事獎章,正在追憶戰爭、失去的友人,以及他們所拯救的這個國家一頁頁<u>殘暴的</u>苦難史。

註 reminisce (v.) 回想,追憶

□ 87 **sensible** [ˈsɛnsəbl] (a.) 合理的,明智的

"<u>Sensible</u>" is not the criterion for a placard.

(TIME, Mar. 13, 1995, p. 31)
「是否<u>合理</u>」並非是評判宣傳標語好壞的標準。

註 criterion (n.) (批評,判斷,檢驗事務的) 標準

□ 88 **sensitive** [ˈsɛnsətɪv] (a.) 敏感的，細膩的

The following year, Woo's *A Better Tomorrow* ... introduced Chow Yun-fat as the sullen, brutal antihero and Cheung as his <u>sensitive</u> counterpart. (TIME, Jan. 29, 1996, p. 40)

第2年，在吳宇森的《英雄本色》中，周潤發以鬱鬱寡歡、凶殘的反英雄形象出現，相對的，與他演對手戲的張國榮則扮演性情<u>敏感的</u>角色。

註 sullen (a.) 慍怒的，陰鬱的；counterpart (n.)（劇中）對立角色

□ 89 **shrewd** [ʃrud] (a.) 敏銳的，有洞察力的

Mailer's research and his <u>shrewd</u> eye lead him to believe ... that Oswald did kill Kennedy and that ... he acted alone. (TIME, May 1, 1995, p. 94)

梅勒經過研究，加上<u>敏銳的</u>觀察，認為奧斯華的確是殺了甘迺迪的凶手，而且凶手只他一人。

□ 90 **significant** [sɪgˈnɪfəkənt] (a.) 重大的，影響深遠的

同 important
反 insignificant

The President's ambition to stand taller in the world faces one <u>significant</u> U.S. made handicap[715]: brutal cutbacks in funding[185] American foreign policy. (TIME, Nov. 18, 1996, p. 30)

柯林頓總統雄心勃勃想在世界舞台上更有自信地昂首闊步，卻面臨美國自己製造出來的一個<u>重大</u>障礙：國會不留情面，刪減了美國外交經費。

□ 91 **sluggish** [ˈslʌgɪʃ] (a.) 遲緩的，不景氣的

The Paris-based OECD predicted a <u>sluggish</u> rate of growth in 1994 for the G-7 leading industrialized countries. (TIME, Jan. 3, 1994, p. 17)

總部設在巴黎的經濟合作開發組織預測，1994年七大工業國的經濟成長率會趨於<u>遲緩</u>。

92 **sophisticated** [sə`fɪstɪˌketɪd] (a.) 1.（技術，產品）尖端的，先進的；
2.（人）老於世故的；
3.（人）精通的，老練的

同 1.advanced
2.refined

反 1. 2.unsophisticated

Once the calling of wild-eyed Cassandras and 19th century writers and social scientists on the radical[79] fringe, long-range forecasting has become a <u>sophisticated</u> and quite profitable industry. (TIME, July 15, 1996, p. 38)

這種「長遠預測」的工作，從前專屬於眼神狂亂的預言家，以及19世紀激進的非主流作家和社會學家，如今則成爲<u>先進</u>工業，而且利潤相當高。

註 calling (n.) 職業；Cassandra 對凶事提出預警，但不見信於人者。Cassandra為希臘神話中特洛伊國王之女，阿波羅為取得她的芳心，賦予她預言的能力，後因求愛不遂又下令人們不准信其預言；fringe (n.)（處於）邊緣，遠離核心的位置，較不受重視的地位

93 **staggering** [`stægərɪŋ] (a.) 令人驚愕的

同 astounding

The Pope's literary output is <u>staggering</u>. His letters, sermons and speeches fill nearly 150 volumes. (TIME, Dec. 26, 1994, p. 60)

教皇的著作多的<u>令人吃驚</u>，信件、講道詞、演講共計近150卷。

94 **strapped (for cash)** [stræpt] (a.) 身無分文的，阮囊羞澀的

Because of reduced oil prices and Gulf War debt, Saudi Arabia is so <u>strapped for cash</u> that it barely met the deadline for its latest $375 million payment on its U.S. weapons contracts.
(TIME, Mar. 14, 1994, p. 21)

由於油價下跌，加上波斯灣戰爭時所背負的債務，沙烏地阿拉伯已是<u>國庫空虛</u>，幾乎無力按照與美國簽訂的購武合約，如期支付最新一期的3億7,500萬美元錢款。

☐ 95 **subject (to)** [ˋsʌbdʒɪkt] (a.) 受⋯支配的，受⋯影響的

Quemoy ... and, along with Matsu, 280 km to the north, was <u>subject to</u> a grueling 44-day artillery bombardment in 1958 by communist troops trying to gain control over what Beijing regards as its sovereign territory. (TIME, Feb. 19, 1996, p. 21)

1958年中共軍隊試圖收回北京當局認爲擁有主權的金門和其北方280公里的馬祖時，金、馬曾<u>遭受</u>中共軍隊44天讓人消受不了的砲擊。

註 grueling (a.) 累垮人的，令人吃不消的

☐ 96 **substantial** [səbˋstænʃəl] (a.) 大量的，重大的

同 significant
反 insubstantial

True, China could seriously damage Taiwan's economy with a naval blockade or sporadic[462] missile strikes, but it would also suffer by losing foreign support, particularly the <u>substantial</u> Taiwanese investment on the mainland.

(TIME, Mar. 25, 1996, p. 16)

當然，中共可以海上封鎖台灣，或只是發射零星的飛彈攻擊，就能夠對台灣經濟造成嚴重破壞，可是中共本身也會受害，因爲會失去外援，尤其是台灣對大陸<u>龐大的</u>投資。

☐ 97 **subtle** [ˋsʌtl] (a.) 隱晦的，不明顯的，難以捉摸的

反 blatant
　obvious

Even when it seems beyond the reach of any one government, electronic information can be controlled, in ways both <u>subtle</u> and obvious.

(TIME, Aug. 19, 1996, p. 52)

表面上看來電子資訊好像任何政府都管不了，可是還是可以管制，管制的手法有些<u>看不太出來</u>，有些則很明顯。

☐ 98 **sweeping** [ˈswipɪŋ] (a.) 全面的，大規模的，影響深遠的

同 far-reaching

A House subcommittee ... will vote next week on the Smoke-Free Environment Act, perhaps the most <u>sweeping</u> antismoking legislation Congress has ever seriously considered. (TIME, Apr. 18, 1994, p. 58)
衆院一分組委員會將於下週就無菸害環境法案進行投票，這項法案是國會有史以來最看重的拒菸法案，也可能是最<u>大規模的</u>拒菸法案。

☐ 99 **tangible** [ˈtændʒəbl] (a.) 可觸到的，有形的

In fact, compared with more <u>tangible</u> assaults[280] on the President's character—namely[59] Paula Jones' pending[65] sexual-harassment lawsuit and the federal investigation into Whitewater—words in a book can barely hurt him. (TIME, Feb. 13, 1995, p. 27)
事實上，比起那些對總統人格更<u>具體的</u>抨擊（如寶拉‧瓊斯所提、正審理中的性騷擾案和聯邦著手調查的白水案），一本書的紙上批評對他幾乎不具殺傷力。

☐ 100 **thriving** [ˈθraɪvɪŋ] (a.) 興盛的

Most countries offer few opportunities for female soccer players, but Norway has a <u>thriving</u> women's professional league, and the U.S. a burgeoning[13] co-ed youth soccer movement.
(TIME, June 3, 1996, p. 17)
大部分國家的女子足球員比賽機會不多，但挪威有<u>蓬勃的</u>女子職業聯盟，而美國的青年男女混合足球運動正快速發展。
註 co-ed (a.) 男女皆收的，為coeducational之略

☐ 101 **tremendous** [trɪˈmɛndəs] (a.) 巨大的

同 enormous

Some 65 million years ago, a comet or asteroid at least five miles wide struck the earth and blasted[498] out a <u>tremendous</u> crater.
(TIME, Jan. 9, 1995, p. 59)
6,500萬年前左右，一顆寬至少5英哩的彗星或小行星撞上了地球，並在地表炸出一個<u>大</u>洞。

□ 102 **tricky** [ˈtrɪkɪ] (a.) 棘手的

同 awkward

Getting in and out of the fast lanes is always <u>tricky</u> even today. It will be even <u>trickier</u> when you have to change lanes and hand off control to the computer at the same time. (TIME, Nov. 4, 1996, p. 53)
即使在今天，進出快車道仍然<u>需要技巧</u>；<u>更棘手的</u>是，變換車道的同時還得把車子的控制權交給電腦。

□ 103 **unanimous** [juˈnænəməs] (a.) 意見一致的

The 1993 Supreme Court decision was not <u>unanimous</u>. (TIME, Feb. 6, 1995, p. 66)
1993年最高法院的判決並非在各大法官<u>意見一致的</u>情況下做出。

□ 104 **unprecedented** [ʌnˈprɛsə,dɛntɪd] (a.) 史無前例的

In an <u>unprecedented</u> move, Zedillo chose a member of the opposition party as Attorney General. (TIME, May 29, 1995, p. 40)
塞迪約<u>破天荒</u>挑選了一位反對黨人士出任司法部長。

□ 105 **urgent** [ˈɜdʒənt] (a.) 緊急的

同 pressing

All this suggests that sumo, the institution, is in <u>urgent</u> need of its own purification.
(TIME, Sept. 30, 1996, p. 28)
這一切都表示，相撲界<u>亟</u>需自清。

□ 106 **venerable** [ˈvɛnərəbl] (a.) 受人尊敬的

You could almost say this <u>venerable</u> institution with its great credibility[298] and history has been infiltrated slowly by the type of people it was not intended to deal with. (TIME, Dec. 12, 1994, p. 64)
甚至可以這麼說，這個極受信賴、擁有光榮歷史而<u>備受尊崇的</u>機構，已遭到它所不願與之打交道之流人物的慢慢滲入。
註 infiltrate (v.) 使滲入，滲透

□ 107 **vigorous** [ˈvɪɡərəs] (a.) 精力旺盛的，充滿活力的

同 dynamic

It's a signal as well that the U.S. economy may be starting to slacken after one of its most <u>vigorous</u> years in a decade. (TIME, Feb. 6, 1995, p. 49)

這也顯示，美國經濟在歷經10年來相當繁榮的一年之後，可能正開始衰退。

註 slacken (v.) 減緩，減弱

□ 108 **volatile** [ˈvɑlətl] (a.) 善變的

同 unstable

When properly combined, three <u>volatile</u> elements generate[187] American celebrity[680]: the media, the public and the spinmeisters who manipulate them. (TIME, June 26, 1995, p. 30)

下面這3個善變的因素，如果搭配得好，就可以讓人在美國聲名大噪，這3個因素就是媒體、大眾及操弄媒體與大眾於股掌間的形象包裝高手。

註 spinmeister (n.) spin加meister的複合字。spin指（對某著作、政策、情勢或事件）給予新的解讀或扭曲（以營造對作者或政治人物有利的局面，如良好的公眾形象）；meister是德文，同英文的master（高手，能手）。兩個字合起來就是指善於利用媒體以塑造良好公眾形象的人，類似spin doctor（政黨對媒體的發言人，替政治人物等處理媒體問題的顧問）。

□ 109 **voluntary** [ˈvɑlənˌtɛrɪ] (a.) 志願的

反 obligatory

It has been 16 months since Australia's Northern Territory became the first place in the world to legalize <u>voluntary</u> euthanasia. (TIME, Oct. 7, 1996, p. 39)

自從澳洲的北領地成為世上第一個將志願安樂死合法化的地方，至今已有16個月了。

□ 110 **vulnerable** [ˈvʌlnərəbl] (a.) 易受傷的，脆弱的

The long time lag between the weapons' arrival and the Bosnians' training would leave them extremely <u>vulnerable</u> to snap[460] Serb offensives .... (TIME, Oct. 10, 1994, p. 44)

在武器運達之後和波士尼亞人受訓熟悉裝備之前，有一段長長的空檔，這期間他們根本禁不起塞爾維亞人的突襲。

註 lag (n.)（事件之間的）空檔

簡易字動詞(111～272)，共162字

- ■ abandon 拋棄
- □ abolish 廢除
- □ abuse 濫用
- □ acknowledge 承認
- □ acquire 獲取，取得
- □ adapt 適應
- □ address 處理
- □ affect 影響
- □ amount (to) 等於
- □ appeal 呼籲
- □ appreciate 喜歡
- □ arouse 引起
- □ assemble 組合
- □ assert 主張，斷言
- □ assign 指派
- □ associate 將…聯想在一起
- □ assure 保證
- ■ ban 禁止
- □ betray 背叛
- □ boast 誇耀
- ■ champion 提倡
- □ characterize 有…特徵
- □ claim 聲稱
- □ collapse 崩潰，倒塌
- □ collide 碰撞
- □ command 博得（尊敬）
- □ compel 逼迫
- □ compromise 妥協
- □ concede 承認
- □ condemn 譴責
- □ conduct 經營，處理
- □ confront 面對，對抗
- □ conquer 征服，克服
- □ constitute 構成
- □ contemplate 考慮，思索（是否要…）
- □ contend 競爭，對抗
- □ contribute 貢獻，出力
- □ convert 轉變
- □ convey 表達，傳達
- □ convince 說服
- □ cope 妥善應付
- □ counter 反駁
- □ credit 褒獎
- □ curb 限制，規範
- ■ demonstrate 顯示
- □ deprive 剝奪
- □ detect 發現，偵測到
- □ deteriorate 惡化
- □ devastate 徹底破壞
- □ devote 致力於，獻身於
- □ diagnose 診斷
- □ dismiss 輕視，忽略
- □ displace 撤換，強迫遷居
- □ distinguish 區別，分辨
- □ document 用文件或文獻紀錄
- □ duplicate 複製
- ■ echo 回響
- □ eliminate 消除
- □ embrace （欣然）接受，採取
- □ endorse 背書，贊同，支持
- □ engage 從事於
- □ enhance 增強
- □ ensure 保證（進展順利），確保（地位）
- □ evade 躲過
- □ exceed 超越
- □ exhibit 顯示，顯露
- □ expand 擴張
- □ explode 爆炸性成長
- ■ fascinate 使著迷
- □ file 提出（控訴）
- □ flourish 興盛，繁榮，蓬勃發展
- □ forge 製造出
- □ frustrate 使挫折
- □ fuel 添加燃料，助長
- □ fund 資助
- □ fuss 煩惱，煩擾
- ■ generate 發（電）
- ■ halt 停止
- □ herald 作先鋒，預告
- □ host 主辦
- □ hug 擁抱
- ■ identify 指認

☐ ignore 忽視	☐ resemble 像
☐ implement 實行	☐ resent 憤恨
☐ impose （將義務、懲罰）加於…	☐ reside 居住
☐ infect 使感染	☐ resort (to) 訴諸，動用
☐ inspire 引發，導致	☐ restore 恢復
☐ install 安裝，設立	☐ resume 在中斷之後重新開始
☐ institute 設置	☐ revive 復興
☐ invade 侵略	☐ rush 匆促行事
☐ issue 發行	■ sabotage 破壞
■ justify 證明…為合理	☐ scatter 散播，散布
■ launch 發動，展開（攻擊等）	☐ shed 使瀉出，散發
☐ levy 課徵	☐ shrink 減少，變小
☐ lift 撤除，解除	☐ slash 大幅削減（經費）
■ maintain 堅稱	☐ soar 升高，（價格）暴漲
☐ merge 合併	☐ spark 刺激，鼓舞
☐ muster 召集	☐ split 分裂
■ navigate 航行於，行進於	☐ stage 推出，舉辦
■ negotiate 談判；通過談判達成	☐ stall 使停止，阻擋
■ observe 遵守，舉行	☐ steer 引導，帶領
☐ outrage 使…憤慨	☐ stem 源自；遏止
☐ overhaul 翻修	☐ stimulate 刺激，激勵
☐ oversee 監督	☐ strain 拉緊，過度使用
☐ overwhelm 壓倒	☐ stun 使…震驚
■ perceive 把…視為	☐ submit 提出
☐ plague 使…困擾，使…煩惱	☐ sue 控告
☐ ponder 思索	☐ suppress 壓制，阻止…的生長、發展
☐ pose 造成，引起	☐ surrender 交出；放棄；投降
☐ preserve 保存	☐ sustain 維持，養活
☐ prevail 勝過，占優勢	■ tap 輕按（電腦鍵）
☐ promote 促進，鼓勵	☐ testify 作證
☐ pursue （繼續）進行，推行，追求	☐ threaten 揚言，放話
■ reassure 使…安心，再向…保證	☐ tolerate 容忍
☐ reduce 簡化，減少，降低	☐ track 追蹤
☐ reflect 思索著說道	☐ transcend 超越
☐ refrain 抑制，避免	☐ transfer 轉移，轉帳，轉變
☐ register 登記，註冊	☐ transform 改變
☐ reinforce 強化，加強	■ undergo 採用；執行
☐ release 發行，放映	☐ undermine 損壞，破壞
☐ render 提供（援助、服務）	☐ undertake 採用；執行
☐ replace 取代	■ wrship 崇拜，崇敬

□[111] **abandon** [ə`bændən] (v.) 拋棄

同 give up
反 stay with

Then ... the nationalists under Chiang Kai-shek abandoned the mainland for Taiwan and took along the art that is the basis of the present-day collection at the National Palace Museum.
(TIME, Apr. 1, 1996, p. 48)

後來，蔣介石的國民黨放棄大陸，移往台灣，並且帶走了這些藝術品，形成今日故宮的基本收藏。

□[112] **abolish** [ə`bɑlɪʃ] (v.) 廢除

Man holds in his mortal hands the power to abolish all forms of human poverty and all forms of human life. (TIME, Feb. 17, 1997, p. 64)

生命有限的人類，手中握有權力，可以滅絕人類一切的匱乏，也可以滅絕人類一切的生命。

□[113] **abuse** [ə`bjuz] (v.n.) 濫用；虐待

The term is much abused lately: in its strictest sense, virtual reality means creating an artificial environment so convincing[150] it can't be distinguished[164] from the real thing.
(TIME, July 17, 1995, p. 38)

虛擬實境一詞近來常被濫用，若嚴格加以定義，虛擬實境表示創造一個人工的環境，而其接近真實的程度，令人真偽難辨。

□[114] **acknowledge** [ək`nɑlɪdʒ] (v.) 承認

同 admit

Johnson acknowledged that he has in the past taken AZT, the antiviral drug typically administered[485] when a person's helper T-cell count drops to 500. (TIME, Feb. 12, 1996, p. 40)

強森承認他曾服用AZT，這種藥物一般開給體內輔助性T細胞數量少於500的人服用。

□ [115] **acquire** [ə`kwaɪr] (v.) 獲取，取得

Even very young children learn by imitation; by watching how others act when they see someone in distress, these children <u>acquire</u> a repertoire of sensitive[88] responses. (TIME, Oct. 9, 1995, p. 29)
即使非常小的孩童也能透過模仿來學習。他們觀察別人對傷心者的反應，從中<u>學習</u>到很多情緒反應，並存在記憶中。

註 distress (n.) 痛苦，悲痛；a repertoire of 許多的，多方面的

□ [116] **adapt** [ə`dæpt] (v.) 適應

同 adjust

John Woo believes the communists are too smart to kill a cash cow like the Hong Kong movie business, and that local moviemakers will <u>adapt</u>. (TIME, Jan. 29, 1996, p. 42)
吳宇森相信中共不至於笨到殺掉香港電影業這隻金雞母，而香港電影業本身也會<u>適應</u>。

□ [117] **address** [ə`drɛs] (v.) 處理

反 ignore

Scientists first raised alarms about climate change in the late 1980s, but the international community has taken few concrete steps to <u>address</u> the problem. (TIME, July 8, 1996, p. 41)
科學家首先在1980年代末期提出對氣候改變的警示，但是國際社會未採取什麼具體行動<u>處理</u>這個問題。

□ [118] **affect** [ə`fɛkt] (v.) 影響

They insist that the issue (work-family dilemma[693]) be seen as <u>affecting</u> both men and women. (TIME, May 6, 1996, p. 52)
他們堅持認為，（工作與家庭難以兼顧）這個問題應該被視為對男性與女性都<u>有影響</u>。

簡易字
動詞

□ [119] **amount (to)** [ə`maʊnt] (v.) 等於

That morning in Seattle, addressing hundreds of analysts and media, Gates hit a rare rhetorical high, offering up what <u>amounted to</u> his new digital gospel. (TIME, Sept. 16, 1996, p. 40)

那天早上在西雅圖，蓋茲對數百名分析師與媒體人士，以罕見的慷慨激昂措詞，發表了一篇聲明，<u>等於</u>揭示了他對於數位時代的新信條。

註 hit (v.) 達到（某一水平）；rhetorical (a.) 措辭的；high (n.) 高水準

□ [120] **appeal** [ə`pil] (v.) 呼籲

In a letter released[230] after his death, Dent <u>appealed</u> to those who attacked his decision: "If you disagree with voluntary euthanasia, then don't use it, but don't deny me the right to use it if and when I want to." (TIME, Oct. 7, 1996, p. 39)

在鄧特死後所公開的一封信中，他<u>呼籲</u>那些攻擊他所作決定的人：「若你不贊成自願性的安樂死，那就不要採用它，可是如果我想採用，以及決定什麼時候採用，也請尊重我的權利。」

□ [121] **appreciate** [ə`priʃɪˌet] (v.) 喜歡

Patients <u>appreciate</u> the service, and the physicians seem to enjoy providing it. (TIME, Sept. 23, 1996, p. 43)

病患<u>喜歡</u>這項服務，醫生似乎也樂意提供。

□ [122] **arouse** [ə`raʊz] (v.) 引起

Any stranger who wanted to buy a large amount of ANFO (ammonium nitrate and fuel oil) would immediately <u>arouse</u> suspicion. (TIME, May 1, 1995, p. 54)

凡是想大批購買硝酸氨和燃料油的來路不明之人，都將立即令人<u>生</u>疑。

123 **assemble** [əˋsɛmb]] (v.) 組合

同 gather

Prosecutors sought to <u>assemble</u> a detailed chronology of the murder night with a parade of witnesses .... (TIME, Feb. 20, 1995, p. 9)
檢察官陸續訪談了多名證人，以<u>組合</u>出謀殺案當晚的詳細過程。

註 chronology (n.)（事件）發生過程的記載

124 **assert** [əˋsɜt] (v.) 主張，斷言，宣稱

同 declare

Finally, since quantum physics <u>asserts</u> that matter and energy are interchangeable, we are not individual beings at all but merely local expressions of an infinite, universal field of energy. (TIME, June 24, 1996, p. 48)
最後，既然量子物理<u>主張</u>物質和能量可以互換，那麼我們根本不是獨立的個體，只不過是宇宙間無限能量場的局部表現而已。

125 **assign** [əˋsaɪn] (v.) 指派

The new top officer of the Navy ... promised to speed up plans to <u>assign</u> women to all surface vessels and perhaps even allow them aboard submarines, the Navy's last all-male bastion.
(TIME, May 10, 1994, p. 31)
這位甫上任的海軍高階官員承諾，加速推動<u>派遣</u>女兵登上各艦隻服務的計畫，甚至可能讓女兵進駐潛水艇——這個抗拒女性進入海軍的最後據點。

註 bastion (n.) 強力護衛某習俗或觀念的體制或組織，堡壘

126 **associate** [əˋsoʃɪ‚et] (v.) 將…聯想在一起

Comets have long been <u>associated</u> with war, upheaval[792] and disaster. (TIME, Apr. 7, 1997, p. 44)
長久以來，人們總<u>把</u>彗星與戰爭、動亂和災難<u>扯在一塊</u>。

□ 127 **assure** [əˋʃur] (v.) 保證

同 guarantee

But even such battle-hardened successes do not <u>assure</u> victory for AmEx in its quest to reclaim[615] the top standing it lost in 1989 in the $562 billion credit-card industry. (TIME, Sept. 12, 1994, p. 60)

這是歷盡艱苦奮戰才得到的成功，即使如此，也不表示美國運通公司<u>必能</u>在營業額達5,620億美金的信用卡業務中，如願重登龍頭寶座。美國運通公司於1989年失去這項寶座。

□ 128 **ban** [bæn] (v.n.) 禁止

同 (v.) prohibit
bar

Beijing <u>bans</u> overseas exhibits of pre-Ming dynasty paintings and calligraphy because of the extreme vulnerability of the ancient brocade, silk and paper. (TIME, Apr. 1, 1996, p. 47)

北京當局<u>禁止</u>明朝以前的書畫出國展覽，因爲年代久遠的錦緞、絲綢與紙張極爲脆弱。

註 vulnerability (n.) 脆弱，易受傷害

□ 129 **betray** [bɪˋtre] (v.) 背叛

They take a soap-opera plot—betrothed teenager falls for a stranger, perfect mother is <u>betrayed</u> by her neighbors, ex-prostitute tries to live an honorable life .... (TIME, Jan. 29, 1996, p. 44)

他們採用通俗的肥皂劇劇情；如已訂親的少年愛上了陌生人；賢妻良母遭鄰居<u>出賣</u>；從良的妓女想過有尊嚴的生活。

註 plot (n.) （小說等的）情節，構想；betrothed (a.) 已訂婚的

□ 130 **boast** [bost] (v.) 誇耀

<u>Boasts</u> Mayor Bill Campbell: "During the Olympics Atlanta will be the safest city in this country, certainly, and on the globe, probably." (TIME, June 3, 1996, p. 17)

市長坎貝爾<u>誇口</u>說：「奧運期間，亞特蘭大將是全國，甚至可能是全世界最安全的地方。」

□ 131 **champion** [ˋtʃæmpɪən] (v.) 提倡

同 advocate

Psychiatrist Brian Weiss is perhaps the most exotic. He champions reincarnation therapy.
(TIME, June 24, 1996 p. 46)
心理醫生柏萊安・魏斯可能是最特異的一位，他提倡輪迴療法。

□ 132 **characterize** [ˋkærəktəˌraɪz] (v.) 有…特徵

同 typify

In his inaugural[53] address last month, Lee continued to hit the high notes, promising a "new culture" and a "new society" to characterize his four years in office. (TIME, June 17, 1996, p. 50)
在上個月的就職演說中，李登輝仍然慷慨激昂，高唱建立「新文化」和「新社會」，作為他往後4年的施政特色。

□ 133 **claim** [klem] (v.) 聲稱

同 maintain

In fact, authorities claim that one-third of Taiwan's more than 1200 known "black societies" were dissolved[545] during the amnesty.
(TIME, Mar. 17, 1997, p. 19)
事實上，政府當局聲稱，台灣已知的1,200多個黑社會幫派中，有三分之一在這次特赦中解散。

□ 134 **collapse** [kəˋlæps] (v.) 崩潰，倒塌

As baby boomers save for retirement, colleges for the kids or a rainy day (say, when the U.S. Social Security system collapses), their investment rates will soar[246]. (TIME, Sept. 30, 1996, p. 44)
嬰兒潮人口正在存錢以備養老、兒女的教育基金或是不時之需（例如一旦社會安全制度崩潰時），所以他們的投資比例會大幅增加。

註 a rainy day 將來可能有的苦日子

□ ¹³⁵ **collide** [kə`laɪd] (v.) 碰撞

同 crash into

Traveling at speeds of 130,000 m.p.h., mountain-size fragments of the comet Shoemaker-Levy 9 tore huge holes in Jupiter's atmosphere throughout the week, giving astronomers a glimpse[316] of the titanic forces released when celestial objects <u>collide</u>. (TIME, Aug. 1, 1994, p. 11)
這整個禮拜，「鞋匠李維9號」彗星的眾多碎片，以龐大如山的身軀，13萬哩的時速，將木星的大氣層衝出數個大洞，讓天文學家得以一窺星體<u>相撞</u>時所釋放出的巨大力量。
註 titanic (a.) 巨大的

□ ¹³⁶ **command** [kə`mænd] (v.) 博得（尊敬）

Along with enthusiasm, sumo <u>commands</u> a large measure of reverence. (TIME, Sept. 30, 1996, p. 28)
除了狂熱之外，相撲還<u>得到</u>民眾相當的崇敬。

□ ¹³⁷ **compel** [kəm`pɛl] (v.) 逼迫

They tried to push me, a Russian general, to shoot my own people in the capital of my own state. No such force exists that would <u>compel</u> me to do this. (TIME, Feb. 27, 1995, p. 26)
身為俄國將領，他們敦促我在祖國的首都射殺同胞，但世上任何力量都不能<u>逼</u>我這麼做。

□ ¹³⁸ **compromise** [`kɑmprə,maɪz] (v.) 妥協

If they think I am prepared to <u>compromise</u>, they're in fantasy[310] land. (TIME, Feb. 27, 1995, p. 58)
如果他們以為我打算<u>妥協</u>，那他們是在作夢。

□ **139 concede** [kən`sid] (v.) 承認

同admit
acknowledge

After three decades of spraying fire-ant territory with the killer compounds, however, the U.S. government was forced to <u>concede</u> defeat.
(TIME, May 27, 1996, p. 67)
然而，在火蟻分布地區用殺蟲劑噴灑了30年，結果美國政府不得不<u>承認</u>失敗。
註 compound (n.) 化合物

□ **140 condemn** [kən`dɛm] (v.) 譴責

同denounce
反praise
endorse

Washington has been urging Arafat to <u>condemn</u> the terrorism. (TIME, Feb. 6, 1995, p. 32)
華盛頓當局一直在敦促阿拉法特<u>譴責</u>恐怖主義。

□ **141 conduct** [kən`dʌkt] (v.) 經營，處理，進行

同carry out

The project, called the New Economic Equation, <u>conducted</u> focus groups around the U.S. with men and women on all rungs of the socioeconomic ladder. (TIME, May 6, 1996, p. 52)
這個稱為「新經濟等式」的計畫，鎖定美國國內一些特定團體來<u>進行</u>，研究這些來自各個社會經濟階層的男男女女。
註 rung (n.)（社會上的）階層

□ **142 confront** [kən`frʌnt] (v.) 面對，對抗

同face

It's hard to love someone who we see as an enemy, someone who kills children for profit. But God says we must love our enemies. Loving them means we must <u>confront</u> them with the truth of their sin. (TIME, June 26, 1995, p. 23)
要我們爲眼中的敵人，以及爲利而殺死孩童的人付出愛心，是不容易的事，但上帝說我們必須愛敵人，愛他們意謂我們必須如實<u>面對</u>他們的罪行。

簡易字
動詞

□ 143 **conquer** [ˋkɑŋkə] (v.) 征服，克服

Conquering the light-speed computer industry means leaping ahead one cognitive generation and landing in the right place. (TIME, June 17, 1996, p. 16)
征服光速般突飛猛進的電腦業，意謂著洞見下一世代，並做下正確的決策。
註 cognitive (a.) 認識（力）的

□ 144 **constitute** [ˋkɑnstə‚tjut] (v.) 構成

Among other things, such studies help doctors determine what constitutes a safe dose of a drug before trying it out on people. (TIME, July 8, 1996, p. 39)
別的不提，這類實驗至少幫醫生了解一種新藥的安全劑量是多少，然後才試用在人身上。

□ 145 **contemplate** [ˋkɑntɛm‚plet] (v.) 考慮，思索

同 consider

Congress is contemplating hearings on the advertising of alcoholic beverages.
(TIME, Feb. 17, 1997, p. 53)
國會正在思索是否就含酒精飲料的廣告舉行聽證會。

□ 146 **contend** [kənˋtɛnd] (v.) 競爭，對抗

Of all the infectious diseases humans will have to contend with as the world gets warmer, malaria may be the worst. (TIME, July 8, 1996, p. 41)
隨著世界變得愈來愈暖，人類所必須對抗的所有傳染性疾病當中，瘧疾可能是最屬害的。

(v.) 堅稱，力辯

These attempts to undermine[270] their country and its culture, the authors contend, "have made the Chinese people, particularly the youth, sick and full of aversion." (TIME, July 22, 1996, p. 37)
這些作者堅稱，那些企圖破壞中國及其文化的舉動，已讓中國人，尤其是中國青年，心生厭惡，激起強烈的反感。
註 aversion (n.) 嫌惡，反感

☐ [147] **contribute** [kən`trɪbjʊt] (v.) 貢獻，出力

同 donate

French officials, who regularly complain about the American refusal to <u>contribute</u> ground troops, tried again to persuade Washington to take part.

(TIME, June 12, 1995, p. 50)

對於美國不願<u>派出</u>地面部隊迭有怨言的法國官員，再次試圖說服華盛頓當局出兵。

☐ [148] **convert** [kən`vɝt] (v.) 轉變

Using a strategy Arthur calls "target, leverage[924], link and lock," Microsoft proceeded to <u>convert</u> DOS users to Windows users, Windows users to Word users and so on down the product line.

(TIME, June 5, 1995, p. 32)

利用亞瑟所說的策略「設定目標，主導潮流，連結商品，鎖定市場」，微軟公司陸續將DOS用戶轉換成Windows用戶，將Windows用戶變成Word用戶，按此方式將原用戶轉成該公司後續產品的用戶。

☐ [149] **convey** [kən`ve] (v.) 表達，傳達

同 communicate

Its report, released[230] early this month, <u>conveys</u> guarded optimism. (TIME, Oct. 7, 1996, p. 40)

該小組在本月初所公布的報告，<u>表達</u>了審慎的樂觀態度。

☐ [150] **convince** [kən`vɪns] (v.) 說服

同 persuade

If the CIA is not interested, that's their business. I am <u>convinced</u> that we should continue the research. (TIME, Dec. 11, 1995, p. 29)

如果中情局不感興趣，那是他家的事，我可是<u>相信</u>我們應該繼續這方面的研究。

□ 151 **cope** [kop] (v.) 妥善應付

同 manage
contend

Struggling to <u>cope</u> with last December's staggering[93] $1.7 billion bankruptcy, officials in California's Orange County announced plans to sell off area assets[672] such as libraries, courts and a juvenile-detention facility. (TIME, Mar. 20, 1995, p. 13)

去年12月加州橘郡因17億美元的鉅額負債而宣告破產，為應付此問題忙得焦頭爛額的該郡官員宣布，擬出售該郡資產，包括數棟圖書館、數棟法院及一處少年拘留所。

□ 152 **counter** [ˈkaʊntə] (v.) 反駁

The defense will call Nobel laureate Kary Mullis ... to testify[262] that the (blood) samples used by the prosecution were too small to ensure[173] reliable results. But deputy district attorney Lisa Kahn is an expert on DNA testing, and will be expected to <u>counter</u> such objections. (TIME, Feb. 6, 1995, p. 56)

辯方將請來諾貝爾獎得主穆里斯，以證實檢方所用的血跡採樣數量太少，構不成足夠的證據。但該地的副檢察官坎恩是DNA測定專家，想必對上述異議提出<u>反駁</u>。

□ 153 **credit** [ˈkrɛdɪt] (v.) 褒獎

DIA <u>credited</u> psychics with creating accurate pictures of Soviet submarine construction hidden from U.S. spy satellites .... (TIME, Dec. 11, 1995, p. 29)

國防部情報局<u>褒獎</u>靈媒可精確的畫出連美國間諜衛星都查不出來的蘇俄潛艇建造基地。

註 psychic (n.) 靈媒

□ 154 **curb** [kɝb] (v.) 限制，規範，克制

同 check
restrain

When a company gets to be big enough, it either <u>curbs</u> its youthful ways or it invites the kind of scrutiny[364] Microsoft is now getting.

(TIME, June 5, 1995, p. 32)

一個公司成長到相當大的時候，要不就是<u>收斂其銳氣</u>，或者像現在的微軟公司一樣，引起普遍的注目。

☐ 155 **demonstrate** [ˋdɛmən͵stret] (v.) 顯示

同 show

The fossil <u>demonstrates</u> that brooding behavior evolved long before there were birds.
(TIME, Jan. 8, 1996, p. 38)
這化石顯示，早在鳥類出現之前，孵蛋的行為就已經演化出來。

☐ 156 **deprive** [dɪˋpraɪv] (v.) 剝奪

Those who have escaped the region [Haiti] claim[133] the army has conducted[141] a scorched-earth policy in an attempt to <u>deprive</u> [the ousted President] Aristide's allies[275] of their food and livelihood. (TIME, July 18, 1994, p. 20)
逃出海地的人士聲稱，海地軍方已實施焦土政策，企圖讓〔流亡總統〕亞里斯提德的同志斷炊，無以維生。
註 scorch (v.) 使燒焦；oust (v.) 逐出

☐ 157 **detect** [dɪˋtɛkt] (v.) 發現，偵測到

More important, over the past four years the scientists have not been able to <u>detect</u> even a trace of HIV in the child's system. (TIME, Apr. 10, 1995, p. 62)
更重要的是，過去4年裡科學家一直未從這小孩身上測出任何HIV病毒的跡象。

☐ 158 **deteriorate** [dɪˋtɪrɪə͵ret] (v.) 惡化

反 improve

"The paranoia is so deep," says Jay Printz, sheriff of Ravalli County, Montana, another hotbed of militia activity. "I just hope it doesn't <u>deteriorate</u> into armed confrontations." (TIME, Mar. 20, 1995, p. 46)
蒙大拿州拉瓦里郡是另一個民兵活動猖獗的地方，該郡警長普林茲說：「被迫害妄想症已很嚴重，我只希望不會惡化為武裝衝突。」
註 hotbed (n.)（罪惡等的）溫床

☐ 159 **devastate** [ˋdɛvəsˏtet] (v.) 徹底破壞

同 ravage
wreck

Damming rivers for hydropower plants has <u>devastated</u> river systems, submerged farmland and displaced[163] thousands of people.

(TIME, Mar. 25, 1996, p. 46)

攔河築壩,建立水力發電廠,<u>破壞</u>了河川生態體系,淹沒農田,並使數千人被迫遷居他鄉。

註 submerge (v.) 淹沒

☐ 160 **devote** [dɪˋvot] (v.) 致力於,獻身於

同 dedicate

In 1902, Alfred Stieglitz, Edward Steichen and other now venerated American photographers formed a group <u>devoted</u> to convincing[150] doubters that photography was a worthy form of artistic expression.

(TIME, Spring 1995 Special Issue: Welcome to Cyberspace, p. 14)

1902年,史提格利茨、史提琛和一些當今甚受敬重的美國攝影大師組織了一個團體,<u>致力於</u>讓人們相信攝影是值得一爲的藝術表達方式。

註 venerate (v.) 尊敬,崇拜

☐ 161 **diagnose** [ˏdaɪəgˋnoz] (v.) 診斷

<u>Diagnosed</u> with prostate cancer in 1991, Dent began his journey to death several weeks ago.

(TIME, Oct. 7, 1996, p. 39)

1991年鄧特經<u>診斷</u>患有攝護腺癌,數週前他開始了死亡之旅。

☐ 162 **dismiss** [dɪsˋmɪs] (v.) 輕視,忽略

同 discount

Some educators <u>dismiss</u> as simplistic[458] and overdone the notion that girls eagerly await such "feminine" software as barbie CD-ROMs.

(TIME, Nov. 11, 1996, p. 37)

「女孩子渴望像芭比這種『女性化』的軟體光碟出現」,有些教育界人士<u>認</u>爲這種觀念太單純,而且太誇大,而<u>不值一顧</u>。

註 overdone (a.) 太過火的,太過度的

☐ 163 **displace** [dɪs`ples] (v.) 撤換，強迫遷居

Knight, however, does not believe empires last forever. Business cycles will <u>displace</u> front-runners, even Nike. (TIME, June 17, 1996, p. 47)

但耐特知道帝國並不是永恆的。景氣循環會<u>換掉</u>領先者，即使是「耐吉」。

註 front-runner (n.) 比賽中最有希望奪標的人

☐ 164 **distinguish** [dɪ`stɪŋgwɪʃ] (v.) 區別，分辨

同 tell apart
differentiate

Although this antibody treatment cannot <u>distinguish</u> between normal and misbehaving T cells, the gambit[999] has proved successful.

(TIME, Oct. 28, 1996, p. 70)

雖然這種抗體療法無法<u>分辨</u>T細胞的正常與否，但結果證明這一招相當成功。

☐ 165 **document** [`dɑkjə,mɛnt] (v.) 用文件或文獻紀錄

There's no <u>documented</u> evidence it had any value to the intelligence community. (TIME, Dec. 11, 1995, p. 29)

並<u>無紀錄證明</u>此計畫對情治單位有任何價值。

☐ 166 **duplicate** [`djuplə,ket] (v.) 複製

The suspicion that there were subversives in the atomic weapons program was encouraged by the Soviets' ability to produce their own atom bomb four years after Oppenheimer's success at Los Alamos, then to <u>duplicate</u> the H-bomb a mere nine months after the first thermonuclear explosion by the U.S. (TIME, Apr. 25, 1994, p. 64)

歐本海默在洛斯阿拉莫斯〔原子能研究中心〕成功研製出原子彈後四年，蘇聯即自行製造出原子彈，然後在美國進行第一次熱核爆炸後僅九個月，蘇聯也<u>複製</u>出氫彈，蘇聯這種能耐使人們更加懷疑，原子武器計畫中是否潛伏有內奸。

註 subversive (n.) 破壞者，顛覆份子

□ ¹⁶⁷ **echo** [ˋɛko] (v.) 回響

同 resound
reverberate

"If there is no tree, how will the soil hold the water?" The question underlines echoes across a subcontinent. (TIME, Mar. 25, 1996, p. 46)
「沒有樹，土地如何涵養水源？」這個問題在整個印度次大陸激起回響。

□ ¹⁶⁸ **eliminate** [ɪˋlɪmə,net] (v.) 消除

In just six months, Gates has refocused the work force onto Net-related projects, mercilessly eliminated a dozen others that were Holy Grails a year ago, and geared up an Internet-content group that will spend tens of millions of the dollars this year. (TIME, Sept. 16, 1996, p. 41)
僅僅6個月內，蓋茲已經把全員工作的重點轉向與網路相關的計畫，毫不留情砍掉了12個一年前還是當紅的計畫，又成立一個網路內容小組，這將會使微軟在今年花掉數千萬美元。

註 Holy Grail 傳說為耶穌最後晚餐時所用的聖杯，因此成為中世紀武士一生追尋的聖物，引申為最崇高神聖的目標；to gear up 準備就緒

□ ¹⁶⁹ **embrace** [ɪmˋbres] (v.)（欣然）接受，採取

In the end, Dole and Dominici are likely to embrace at least some tax cuts to go along with deep cuts in spending. (TIME, May 22, 1995, p. 30)
最後，杜爾和多明尼奇可能至少會接受某些減稅案，以配合某些大幅削減支出的案子順利通過。

□ ¹⁷⁰ **endorse** [ɪnˋdɔrs] (v.) 背書，贊同，支持

By paying Jordan and other athletes millions to endorse his shoes, the chairman and chief executive of Nike has helped turn them into household names and shaped sports to his liking. (TIME, June 17, 1996, p. 47)
耐吉董事長兼總裁付給喬丹與其他運動員數百萬元，請他們替他的球鞋作背書，從而讓這些運動員成爲家喻戶曉的人物，並且依他的喜好塑造了各項運動。

☐ 171 **engage** [ɪnˋgedʒ] (v.) 從事於

Like so many promising[78] HIV treatments, Ho's strategy could fail. It could even backfire[494] if it is mistakenly touted[958] as a kind of "morning after" treatment that allows people to relax their guard and <u>engage</u> in risky sexual behavior.
(TIME, Dec. 30, 1996, p. 26)

與其他許多前景看好的HIV治療方式一樣,何大一的療法也可能會失敗,甚至還可能收到反效果——如果這種方法被人們錯誤地當成是一種「事後補救」的治療方法來宣揚,導致人們放鬆警戒而<u>從事</u>危險的性行為的話。

☐ 172 **enhance** [ɪnˋhæns] (v.) 增強

In the largest study, almost 40% of those who took the placebo reported <u>enhanced</u> sexual function. (TIME, May 20, 1996, p. 60)

在一次最大規模的研究中,服用了並無藥效的「安慰劑」的人中,有將近40%的人聲稱性能力有<u>增強</u>。

註 placebo (n.) 指給病人服用、不具藥性,但會產生心理治療作用的藥

☐ 173 **ensure** [ɪnˋʃʊr] (v.) 保證(進展順利),確保(地位)

In a controversial new book called *Blindside*, journalist Eamonn Fingleton argues that these firms help <u>ensure</u> that Japan will overtake the U.S. as the world's leading economy by the year 2000. (TIME, Apr. 24, 1995, p. 58)

在Blindside這部頗具爭議的新書中,記者芬格頓辯稱,這些公司應有助於<u>確保</u>日本在2千年之前超越美國,成為世界首屈一指的經濟大國。

註 overtake (v.) 超過

☐ [174] **evade** [ɪˋved] (v.) 躲過

Chen is working in a Tokyo editing room,
finishing *Temptress Moon*. He may hope that a
film that is set before the '49 revolution will
<u>evade</u> the censors but he won't count on it.

(TIME, Jan. 29, 1996, p. 46)

陳凱歌正在東京剪輯《風月》，他希望這部時空設定在1949
年以前的電影能<u>逃過</u>電檢，但也沒十足的把握。

註 censor (n.)（出版物、電影等的）審查員

☐ [175] **exceed** [ɪkˋsid] (v.) 超越

Toy manufacturers pray for a product's sales to
double after the launch of TV ads and for demand
to <u>exceed</u> supply temporarily ....

(TIME, Nov. 11, 1996, p. 36)

玩具廠商期盼電視廣告打出去之後，銷售量能漲一倍，並且
有一段時間能供不應求。

☐ [176] **exhibit** [ɪgˋzɪbɪt] (v.) 顯示，顯露

同 demonstrate
show

Infants as young as three months old <u>exhibit</u>
empathy when they get upset at the sound of
another baby crying. (TIME, Oct. 9, 1995, p. 29)

才3個月大的嬰兒聽到別的嬰兒哭時，會感到難過，<u>表示</u>他
們也有同理心。

☐ [177] **expand** [ɪkˋspænd] (v.) 擴張

For his part, Yeltsin fears pressure from a NATO
that is likely to <u>expand</u> closer to Russia's western
border. (TIME, May 6, 1996, p. 21)

對葉爾欽來說，來自北大西洋公約組織的壓力令他害怕，因
為該組織的<u>擴張</u>，可能會更逼近俄羅斯西部邊界。

□ **178 explode** [ɪk`splod] (v.) 爆炸性成長

Gates in April 1994 called an off-site meeting of his top staff to talk about a technology that had been around for 20 years but had suddenly exploded. (TIME, June 5, 1995, p. 32)

1994年4月，蓋茲召集高層幕僚開了一場與會者散居各地的遠距會議，談論這項已有20年歷史、最近才大放異彩的技術。

□ **179 fascinate** [`fæsə,net] (v.) 使著迷

Young, who is fascinated by technology, has started a company that makes devices for the disabled[27], as well as high-tech toys.

(TIME, July 3, 1995, p. 46)

對科技深為著迷的楊格開了一家公司，除了生產高科技玩具，也製造殘障用品。

□ **180 file** [faɪl] (v.) 提出（控訴）

In response, the cult's leaders had its lawyers file suit. (TIME, Apr. 3, 1995, p. 26)

該教派領袖叫其律師提出控訴作為回應。

□ **181 flourish** [`flɝɪʃ] (v.) 興盛，繁榮，蓬勃發展

同 thrive
反 decline

Malaria, for example, has been flourishing in recent years owing to unusually hot weather.

(TIME, July 8, 1996, p. 40)

比方說最近幾年，由於異常的高溫，使得瘧疾非常盛行。

☐ **182 forge** [fɔrdʒ] (v.) 製造出

Taiwan is aggressively pursuing[223] a technological edge[699], working to <u>forge</u>, in the words of one defense expert, a flexible, fast and hard-hitting defense. (TIME, Aug. 28, 1995, p.14)

台灣正大力追求科技優勢，致力於<u>建構</u>某國防專家口中機動、迅捷、予敵迎頭痛擊的國防武力。

☐ **183 frustrate** [`frʌstret] (v.) 使挫折

For the Republicans in the House, the past two months have been a <u>frustrating</u> lesson in the meaning of checks and balances.

(TIME, Mar. 20, 1995, p. 35)

對眾議院的共和黨議員而言，過去兩個月在「權力制衡」上一直很<u>不如意</u>。

☐ **184 fuel** [`fjuəl] (v.) 添加燃料，助長

同 feed

The shocking 1995 rape of a 12-year-old Okinawan girl by U.S. servicemen <u>fueled</u> deep-seated resentment felt by residents toward the continued presence of 47,000 U.S. troops ....

(TIME, Nov. 18, 1996, p. 32)

沖繩居民對4萬7千名美軍長期駐紮當地，夙懷不滿，1995年令人震驚的12歲沖繩女童被美軍強暴事件，使不滿更爲<u>高漲</u>。

註 resentment (n.) 不滿，憤恨

☐ **185 fund** [fʌnd] (v.) 資助

S. Fred Singer, president of the industry-<u>funded</u> Science and Environment Policy Project, argues that Epstein and his colleagues fail to note the positive health benefits of warmer nights and winters. (TIME, July 8, 1996, p. 41)

辛格是企業界<u>資助</u>的「科學與環境政策計畫」的負責人，他辯解說，艾普斯坦和他的同僚未能注意到較暖和的夜晚和暖多所帶來正面、有助健康的好處。

□ [186] **fuss** [fʌs] (v.) 煩惱，煩擾

同 flap

Selling goods abroad has been such a vital part of the Asian miracle that the region <u>fusses</u> over export statistics the way other cultures follow sports scores. (TIME, Aug. 5, 1996, p. 42)

長久以來，貨物外銷一直是亞洲經濟奇蹟中極重要的部分，因此這地區的國家<u>斤斤計較</u>出口統計數字，就如同其他文化圈的國家密切注意運動成績一樣。

□ [187] **generate** [ˋdʒɛnəˌret] (v.) 發（電）

同 produce

The energy of the flywheel is stored in this rapid rotation, which <u>generates</u> electricity on demand. (TIME, Sept. 23, 1996, p. 41)

飛輪的能量就儲存在快速的旋轉中，要用的時候就可以<u>產生</u>電力。

□ [188] **halt** [hɔlt] (v.) 停止

One official told former U.S. Assistant Secretary of Defense Charles Freeman last year that Beijing had a plan to fire a missile a day for 30 days at Taiwan if Lee did not <u>halt</u> his campaign[285] for international recognition. (TIME, Feb. 12, 1996, p. 16)

某官員曾在去年告訴美國前任國防部次長傅利曼說，如果李登輝不<u>中止</u>他爭取國際承認的活動，中共計畫連續30天每天向台灣發射一枚飛彈。

□ [189] **herald** [ˋhɛrəld] (v.) 作先鋒，預告

In 1985 Chen's *Yellow Earth*, in a sensational debut[299] at the Hong Kong Film Festival, <u>heralded</u> the emergence of a pristine, passionate intelligence in cinema from the People's Republic. (TIME, Jan. 29, 1996, p. 38)

1985年陳凱歌的《黃土地》在香港電影節首映，造成轟動，<u>預示</u>一種純樸、熱情的大陸電影誕生了。

註 sensational (a.) 轟動的；pristine (a.) 質樸的，未受玷污的

190 **host** [host] (v.) 主辦

CyberCash launches[203] CyberCoins with a respectable roster of partners: some 30 Web <u>hosting</u> companies will offer CyberCash to their client sites, and by year's end CyberCash expects about 100 Web sites to take them up on it.

(TIME, Oct. 7, 1996, p. 40)

網路現金公司發行網路銅板時,其合作廠商的名單相當可觀;大約有30家<u>提供網路服務的</u>公司將提供網路現金服務給他們的客戶,同時網路現金公司預期年底之前會有約100個網站加入。

註 respectable (a.)(數量等)可觀的;roster (n.) 登記簿,名冊

191 **hug** [hʌg] (v.) 擁抱

同 embrace

Reading to a child while touching, <u>hugging</u> and holding him or her can be a wonderful antidote[669] to the impersonal tendencies of the information age .... (TIME, Feb. 24, 1997, p. 37)

對小孩唸故事的同時,摸摸他們,<u>擁抱</u>他們或把他們抱起來,可能是一劑神奇的解藥,可以消弭當今資訊時代情感越來越淡的趨勢。

註 impersonal (a.) 無人情味的

192 **identify** [aɪˈdɛntəˌfaɪ] (v.) 指認

A single mother receiving state welfare who won't help <u>identify</u> the father of her child will lose at least 25% of her benefits.

(TIME, Aug. 12, 1996, p. 25)

領受州政府福利金的未婚媽媽,若不幫助政府<u>指認</u>孩子的生父,福利金至少會被扣減25%。

193 **ignore** [ɪgˈnor] (v.) 忽視

同 disregard
overlook

No traditional toy company today can <u>ignore</u> computer technology. (TIME, Nov. 11, 1996, p. 37)

如今沒有一家舊式玩具公司可以<u>忽視</u>電腦科技。

□ [194] **implement** [ˈɪmpləˌmɛnt] (v.) 實行

同 carry out

U.S. Secretary of State Madeleine Albright referred ominously[62] to "the importance of implementing" a half-forgotten 1995 auto trade agreement. (TIME, Mar. 10, 1997, p. 28)

美國國務卿歐布萊特提到「執行」已快被淡忘的1995年美日汽車貿易協定「非常重要」，話中透露出不祥的訊息。

□ [195] **impose** [ɪmˈpoz] (v.)（將義務、懲罰）加於⋯

Moving through the U.S. Congress right now is a telecommunications-reform bill that would impose fines of as much as $100,000 for "indecency" in cyberspace. (TIME, Jan. 15, 1996, p. 51)

此刻美國國會正在審理一電訊改革法案，該法案對於在網路上傳播「粗鄙」內容者將處以高達10萬美金的罰款。

□ [196] **infect** [ɪnˈfɛkt] (v.) 使感染

Doctors at UCLA announced that a five-year-old boy, infected with HIV at birth, has been symptom[787]-free ever since. (TIME, Apr. 10, 1995, p. 62)

南加大的醫生宣布，一名出生即染上人體免疫缺陷病毒的5歲男孩，卻一直沒有症狀出現。

□ [197] **inspire** [ɪnˈspaɪr] (v.) 引發，導致

None of the contenders can afford to look soft on an issue as vital as Taiwan. The problem with such posturing is that it might inspire riskier behavior than Beijing really intends.

(TIME, Feb. 12, 1996, p. 18)

爭奪接班位子的人沒有一個敢在像臺灣這麼重要的議題上示弱，但是這種強硬立場的表達可能會擦槍走火，導致出乎北京本意之外的冒險行動。

註 posturing (n.) 態度，立場

198 install [ɪnˋstɔl] (v.) 安裝，設立

The fastest international link ever <u>installed</u>, this pipeline could be the first step toward laying a permanent network that will eventually hardwire every nation in the world into the Internet.

(TIME, Mar. 11, 1996, p. 35)

這條通訊線路是目前所<u>裝設</u>傳輸速度最快的國際線路，而這也可能是朝向舖設一個永久性網路，將全球各國都連上網際網路的起步。

199 institute [ˋɪnstəˌtjut] (v.) 設置

Mindful of the burnout suffered by child prodigies ... , the W.T.A. has <u>instituted</u> new age restrictions: players 14 and under are barred[496] from tour events, and players 15 to 17 will be gently introduced to topflight competition.

(TIME, Sept. 16, 1996, p. 49)

有鑑於天才小球員遭揠苗助長的惡果，女子網球聯盟已<u>制定</u>新的年齡限制：14歲及14歲以下的球員禁止參加巡迴比賽，15歲到17歲的球員將循序漸進地參加高級網賽。

註 to be mindful of 留心…的；to suffer burnout 由於太快走紅或太早成功導致在生涯初期就已油盡燈枯、江郎才盡；
topflight (a.) 一流的，最高級的

200 invade [ɪnˋved] (v.) 侵略

In 1950, when North Korea <u>invaded</u> the South, the Truman Administration sent the Seventh Fleet into the Taiwan Strait to keep the communists from seizing the island. (TIME, Feb. 12, 1996, p. 18)

1950年北韓<u>入侵</u>南韓，杜魯門政府立即派遣第七艦隊至台灣海峽，防止中共奪取台灣。

□ 201 **issue** [ˋɪʃjʊ] (v.) 發行

同 release

On Nov. 21, *Free as a Bird* will be <u>issued</u> as part of *The Beatles Anthology Volume 1.*
(TIME, Nov. 20, 1995, p. 50)
《自由翱翔》11月21日就要<u>上市</u>，收錄在兩張一套的專輯《披頭四精選第一集》中。

□ 202 **justify** [ˋdʒʌstə͵faɪ] (v.) 證明⋯為合理

According to a White House source, the Clinton Administration doesn't feel the changes in Cuba have been substantial[96] enough to <u>justify</u> a diplomatic rapprochement .... (TIME, Feb. 20, 1995, p. 50)
根據白宮一消息人士的說法，柯林頓當局覺得古巴的改變還不夠大，<u>不足以</u>讓兩國就此復交。

註 rapprochement (n.) 建交或復交

□ 203 **launch** [lɔntʃ] (v.) 1.發動，展開（攻擊等）；2.發售，推出（新產品）

同 1. start

Democrats too have <u>launched</u> a guerrilla operation to snag women in this presidential election. (TIME, May 6, 1996, p. 53)
在此次總統選舉當中，民主黨也<u>發動</u>了一波游擊戰攻勢，企圖拉攏女性選民。

註 snag (v.) （口語）攫取

□ 204 **levy** [ˋlɛvɪ] (v.) 課徵

Talabani claims[133] Barzani is pocketing cash from customs fees the Kurds <u>levy</u> on the 10,000 bbl. of diesel fuel Iraq secretly ships through Kurd territory to Turkey every day. (TIME, Mar. 27, 1995, p. 36)
塔拉巴尼宣稱伊拉克每天把1萬桶柴油經庫德族領土偷運至土耳其，而庫德族人就此柴油所<u>徵</u>的關稅被巴札尼中飽私囊。

☐ 205 **lift** [lɪft] (v.) 撤除，解除

It is an article of faith in Havana that if only Washington would <u>lift</u> the 33-year-old trade embargo, a vast infusion of American cash would rescue Cuba's economy. (TIME, Feb. 20, 1995, p. 52)

只要華盛頓當局<u>撤除</u>對古巴33年之久的貿易禁運措施，大筆美國資金將湧入解救古巴經濟，在哈瓦納，這已是大家都認同的事。

註 an article of faith 信條；embargo (v.) 禁運；infusion (n.) 注入

☐ 206 **maintain** [men`ten] (v.) 堅稱

同 claim

The key to success, Akimoto and other cable executives <u>maintain</u>, is to provide customers with local telephone service practically free of charge, a come-on that has worked well for cable companies in Britain. (TIME, Mar. 6, 1995, p. 66)

Akimoto和其他有線電視主管<u>堅稱</u>，提供顧客實用性的市內電話免費服務是成功的關鍵，英國有線電視公司用這個服務招攬顧客就非常成功。

註 come-on (n.) 招攬顧客的方式

☐ 207 **merge** [mɝdʒ] (v.) 合併

Viacom, Paramount's preferred suitor, announced an agreement to <u>merge</u> with video-rental giant Blockbuster Entertainment. (TIME, Jan. 17, 1994, p. 15)

Viacom公司是派拉蒙公司最中意的合併對象，卻宣布已同意和影帶出租業巨人Blockbuster Entertainment公司<u>合併</u>。

註 suitor (n.) 求婚者

☐ 208 **muster** [ˈmʌstɚ] (v.) 召集

同 summon
gather

But all he could <u>muster</u> on the House floor were 30 votes, mostly from congressional nobodies like himself. (TIME, Feb. 27, 1995, p. 18)

但他在議會所能<u>爭取到</u>的支持者只有30人，且大部分是和他一樣的小角色。

209 **navigate** [ˋnævəˏget] (v.) 航行於，行進於

Once their link to the Net is established, viewers will, in theory, be able to <u>navigate</u> Websites with their trusty remotes as easily as they now surf[642] TV channels. (TIME, Aug. 12, 1996, p. 26)
一旦與全球資訊網連線，理論上，這些觀眾用他們信賴的遙控器就能<u>漫遊</u>各處網站，就好像看電視轉台一樣容易。

210 **negotiate** [nɪˋgoʃɪˏet] (v.) 談判；通過談判達成，談成

Veterans[373] can <u>negotiate</u> their own contracts as free agents, while young players must accept what their team pays them as long as it meets the minimum salary. (TIME, Aug. 22, 1994, p. 68)
老球員可以以自由經紀人的身分和球團<u>談成</u>和約，菜鳥球員對於球隊給的薪水，只要符合最低薪資水平，就只有接受的份。

211 **observe** [əbˋzɝv] (v.) 遵守，舉行

同 honor

After obtaining the three signatures required—from his own doctor, a cancer specialist and a psychiatrist—and <u>observing</u> the nine-day cooling-off period, Dent was free to choose the time of his own passing. (TIME, Oct. 7, 1996, p. 39)
得到了3個必要的人——他的醫生，一位癌症專家及一位精神醫師——的簽字後，再<u>經過</u>規定的9天冷靜期，鄧特就可以自由選擇他自己的死亡時間。

註 cooling-off period 做重大決定前用來冷卻激情的一段時間

☐ 212 **outrage** [ˈaʊt͵redʒ] (v.) 使…憤慨

<u>Outraged</u> cyberpurists responded by deluging[894] Siegel and Canter with angry E-mail messages, following them with a steady stream of abuse as they fled from one electronic home to another. (TIME, Aug. 19, 1996, p. 52)

主張保持網路純淨的人<u>勃然大怒</u>，用憤怒的電子郵件回敬西格和坎特，讓他們的信箱垃圾成災。他們兩人不斷更換網址，可是辱罵的信件一直如影隨形，擺脫不掉。

註 abuse (n.) 辱罵，謾罵

☐ 213 **overhaul** [͵ovəˈhɔl] (v.) 翻修

Gore has also shouldered thankless but meaty tasks that give him something to attend to besides foreign funerals: reinventing government, <u>overhauling</u> telecommunications law, smoothing relations with Moscow. (TIME, June 17, 1996, p. 30)

高爾也接下一些沒有掌聲卻很吃重的工作，讓他在出國參加喪禮之外有事可做，如改造政府，<u>檢修</u>通訊法規，改善對俄關係。

註 shoulder (v.) 負起（責任），擔任（工作）；
thankless (a.) 吃力不討好的，有功無賞的；
meaty (a.) 角色吃重的，內容豐富的；smoothe (v.) 使平滑，使順利

☐ 214 **oversee** [ovəˈsi] (v.) 監督

同 supervise

"My emphasis now," says Anwar Ibrahim, the Deputy Prime Minister and Finance Minister who is <u>overseeing</u> the financing for all the projects ... "is on the financial services and foreign media." (TIME, Dec. 4, 1995, p. 16)

負責監管所有計畫的資金調度的副總理兼財政部長安華說：「我現在的重點擺在金融服務業及外國傳媒上。」

□ 215 **overwhelm** [ˌovɚˈhwɛlm] (v.) 壓倒

同 overpower

China has many more planes than Taiwan, but they would need several days to <u>overwhelm</u> Taiwan's interceptor force with its superior aircraft and pilots. (TIME, Aug. 28,1995, p. 16)

中國戰機的數量比台灣多得多，但台灣擁有優良戰機與飛行員，中國必須花幾天時間，才能<u>壓過</u>台灣的攔劫武力。

□ 216 **perceive** [pɚˈsiv] (v.) （把…）視爲

A major problem, say nutrition experts, is that most people <u>perceive</u> their diets as temporary restrictions imposed[195] from outside.

(TIME, Jan. 16, 1995, p. 58)

營養學家說，有個大問題是，大部分人都把節食<u>看作</u>是外力所施加的暫時性束縛。

□ 217 **plague** [pleg] (v.) 使…困擾，使…煩惱

Growing inventories have <u>plagued</u> retailers too since they stocked up in anticipation of a strong Christmas season. (TIME, Feb. 6, 1995, p. 49)

存貨漸多也讓零售商<u>頭痛不已</u>，因爲他們原本期待聖誕節前後會是個銷售旺季，因而進了不少貨。

註 inventory (n.) 存貨清單

□ 218 **ponder** [ˈpɑndɚ] (v.) 思索

同 contemplate
reflect upon

During a break in filming *Broken Arrow*, ... Woo casts his eye over the hundreds of technicians and <u>ponders</u> the contrasts in movie-making between Asia and America. (TIME, Jan. 29, 1996, p. 38)

在《斷箭》拍片空擋，吳宇森看著上百的工作人員，<u>思考</u>在亞洲與美國拍片的不同。

☐ 219 **pose** [poz] (v.) 造成，引起

The new legislation <u>poses</u> huge problems for some states, such as California ....

(TIME, Aug. 12, 1996, p. 25)

這項新法給某些州<u>造成</u>很大的問題，例如加州。

☐ 220 **preserve** [prɪ`zɝv] (v.) 保存

同 conserve
　　maintain
反 destroy

Today, a handful of dedicated[24] naturalists are giving time, money and even the occasional home mortgage to help <u>preserve</u> a different kind of horse—the seahorse. (TIME, Jan. 13, 1997, p. 42)

今天有一群一心奉獻的自然主義者獻上他們的時間與金錢，甚至於有時還得抵押房子去貸款，爲的就是要<u>保存</u>另一種馬——海馬。

☐ 221 **prevail** [prɪ`vel] (v.) 勝過，占優勢

同 triumph
　　be victorious

Microsoft could still <u>prevail</u>, in court and in the market, but it will not escape unscathed.

(TIME, June 5, 1995, p. 46)

在法庭與市場上，微軟都可能<u>占上風</u>，但無論如何都不可能毫髮無傷，全身而退。

註 unscathed (a.)（肉體上、名譽上）未受傷的

☐ 222 **promote** [prə`mot] (v.) ¹促進，鼓勵；²促銷，推銷（商品）

同 ¹ encourage
反 ¹ discourage

In Bangkok he will <u>promote</u> the seven-member Association of South East Asian Nations, which Washington considers increasingly influential.

(TIME, Nov. 18, 1996, p. 31)

到曼谷時，他將會<u>促進</u>由7個會員國所組成的東南亞國協的發展，華盛頓方面認爲東協的影響力與日俱增。

☐ 223 **pursue** [pɚ`su] (v.)（繼續）進行

Eventually, he dropped out of school to <u>pursue</u> his education in the online world—the poor man's university. (TIME, Jan. 23, 1995, p. 61)
最後他中途退學，到網路世界這個窮人大學<u>繼續</u>他的學業。

同 carry out

(v.) 推行，實行（計畫、調查、研究）

Another problem is that government officials often <u>pursue</u> self-serving agendas[274].
(TIME, Mar. 6, 1995, p. 66)
另一個問題在於政府官員通常<u>推行</u>對自己有利的計畫。
註 self-serving 自私的，利己的

同 strive for

(v.) 追求，追尋（目標等）

Given our history, these are extremely hard tasks, and we are forced to <u>pursue</u> both goals at the same time. (TIME, May 8, 1995, p. 74)
從我們的歷史來看，這些是非常艱鉅的任務，而且我們被迫同時<u>追求</u>兩項目標。

☐ 224 **reassure** [ˌriɚ`ʃʊr] (v.) 使…安心，再向…保證

He could see how anxious I was and he spent some of his last hour or two <u>reassuring</u> me, reminding me that this was an act of love and that I should see it as such. (TIME, Oct. 7, 1996, p. 39)
他看出我是多麼的不安，在他生命即將結束之際，還花了一、兩個小時<u>一再要我放心</u>，提醒我這是愛的舉動，並且勸我也該如此看待。

☐ 225 **reduce** [rɪ`djus] (v.) 簡化，減少，降低

反 increase

IBM made a map of the world at one ten-trillionth scale from tiny blobs of gold, while Stanford scientists <u>reduced</u> the first page of *A Tale of Two Cities* 25,000-fold. (TIME, July 17, 1995, p. 44)
IBM用黃金微粒做出一幅十兆分之一比例的世界地圖，而史丹佛大學的科學家則把《雙城計》的第一頁<u>縮小</u>了2萬5千倍。

226 **reflect** [rɪ`flɛkt] (v.) 思索著說道

"I've always believed in simplicity," Klein <u>reflects</u>. "I've never been one to see women in ruffles and all kinds of fanciful apparel. To me it's just silly." (TIME, June 17, 1996, p. 18)

克萊思索著說道:「我一向信仰簡單的風格,從來不喜歡女人衣服上有一大堆褶子和花俏的裝飾,那種衣服讓我覺得可笑。」

> **註** ruffle (n.) 褶邊;fanciful (a.)(設計等)新奇的,別出心裁的;
> apparel (n.)(華麗的)衣服

227 **refrain** [rɪ`fren] (v.) 抑制,避免

Presenters and recipients at the next Academy Awards would be advised to <u>refrain</u> from rambling thank-yous and unentertaining political proclamations. (TIME, Jan. 23, 1995, p. 63)

下一屆奧斯卡頒獎典禮上,頒獎者和得獎者都將受到規勸,避免拉拉雜雜的感謝詞和乏味的政治宣言。

> **註** rambling (a.)(談話、文章)漫無邊際的,拉拉雜雜的;
> unentertaining (a.) 無趣的

228 **register** [`rɛdʒɪstə] (v.) 登記,註冊

Here's how the system works; starting this week, you'll visit the CyberCash Web site, download an empty electronic wallet onto your hard drive and <u>register</u> it with the company. (TIME, Oct. 7, 1996, p. 40)

這套系統的運作方式如下:從本週開始,你可以進入網路現金公司的網站,把一個空的電子皮夾下載到你的硬式磁碟機上,同時向該公司註冊。

□ 229 **reinforce** [ˌriɪn`fɔrs] (v.) 強化，加強

同 strengthen

If, on the other hand, the feelings they begin to express are not recognized and <u>reinforced</u> by the adults around them, they not only cease to express those feelings but they also become less able to recognize them in themselves or others.

(TIME, Oct. 9, 1995, p. 29)

另一方面，小孩開始表達感情時，若沒有受到周遭成人的肯定和<u>鼓勵</u>，他們不但會停止再作表達，而且對自己或他人情感的感受力也會降低。

□ 230 **release** [rɪ`lis] (v.)（錄影帶、唱片等）發行，（影片）放映

It's been another hot year for consumer electronics, one that saw Toshiba <u>release</u> an impressive desktop PC, Sony take a first crack at a personal computer and a swarm of companies come out with hand-held devices ....

(TIME, Nov. 25, 1996, p. 49)

對於消費性電子產品來說，今年又是熱鬧滾滾的一年。東芝<u>推出</u>一款令人印象深刻的桌上型電腦，新力公司首度嘗試打入個人電腦市場，同時一大堆公司推出了手提型的設備。

註 crack (n.)（口語）嘗試；a swarm of 大群

□ 231 **render** [`rɛndɚ] (v.) 提供（援助、服務）

同 give

Teaming up with Jim Clark, then chairman of Silicon Graphics and now at Netscape, Lincoln devised a plan to stuff the graphics-<u>rendering</u> power of a $90,000 SGI Reality Engine park ... into a box that will be $250 in the U.S.

(TIME, May 20, 1996, p. 59)

林肯與當時的矽圖公司總裁，也就是今天網景公司的總裁克拉克合作，計劃將矽圖價值9萬美金的「實境引擎」中的圖形<u>生產</u>技術，塞到在美國售價250美元的電視遊樂器裡去。

註 to team with 與…合作；devise (v.) 設計，想出；stuff (v.) 將…塞進

☐ 232 **replace** [rɪ`ples] (v.) 取代

The White House is searching for a new World Bank president to <u>replace</u> Lewis Preston, who is stepping down because of illness.

(TIME, Feb. 13, 1995, p. 19)

白宮正在尋覓人選，<u>接替</u>因病離職的普雷斯頓出任世界銀行總裁。

☐ 233 **resemble** [rɪ`zɛmbl] (v.) 像

Ask Bill Gates about something he wants to talk about ... and he acts like the teenage boy that he still <u>resembles</u>. He grins. His voice breaks.

(TIME, June 5, 1995, p. 32)

當你問比爾‧蓋茲某些他感興趣的話題，外表還有點<u>像</u>年輕小伙子的他，表現得就<u>像</u>個小伙子似的，笑開了嘴，連聲音都變了。

註 grin (v.) 露齒而笑

☐ 234 **resent** [rɪ`zɛnt] (v.) 憤恨

While many of Clinton's closest advisers <u>resent</u> Morris' growing influence, he has his admirers in the White House .... (TIME, June 5, 1995, p. 22)

莫里斯愈來愈紅，令柯林頓身邊的心腹顧問大表<u>憤慨</u>，但在白宮，莫里斯還是有一些景仰者。

☐ 235 **reside** [rɪ`zaɪd] (v.) 居住

同 live

With Java, data and programs ... don't have to be stored on your computer anymore. They can <u>reside</u> anywhere on the Internet, called up by whoever needs them, whenever they need them.

(TIME, Jan. 22, 1996, p. 43)

有了「爪哇」之後，資料與程式就不需要再儲存在電腦裡面，可以<u>放在</u>網際網路上的任何地方，任何人需要，隨時可以叫下來。

☐ 236 **resort (to)** [rɪˋzɔrt] (v.) 訴諸，動用

> There is no right to <u>resort to</u> violence when you
> don't get your way. (TIME, May 15, 1995, p. 19)
> 無法愛怎樣就怎樣時，也無權<u>動用</u>武力。

☐ 237 **restore** [rɪˋstor] (v.) 恢復

> Mexican President Ernesto Zedillo's plan to
> <u>restore</u> stability to his country's wounded
> economy was rejected by investors for its lack of
> specific remedies, causing the peso to fall to a
> record low against the dollar by week's end.
> (TIME, Jan. 16, 1995, p. 13)
> 墨西哥總統塞迪約擬定計畫，企圖使該國殘破的經濟<u>恢復</u>穩
> 定，但因此計畫欠缺明確的改善措施，導致披索在本週末貶
> 值到有史以來最低點，投資客對此計畫也就敬謝不敏。

☐ 238 **resume** [rɪˋzjum] (v.) 在中斷之後重新開始

同 recommence

> A network of satellite-linked computer systems
> will guide the car safely to the exit, at which point
> the driver will <u>resume</u> control to the final
> destination. (TIME, Nov. 4, 1996, p. 52)
> 一套與衛星連線的電腦系統網路會將車安全引導到出口，此
> 時，再由駕駛者<u>重新</u>操控車輛前往目的地。

☐ 239 **revive** [rɪˋvaɪv] (v.) 復興

> To <u>revive</u> the ancient tradition, 129 members of
> the U.N. General Assembly co-sponsored a
> resolution calling for a worldwide cease-fire
> during the 17 days of the Altanta Olympics.
> (TIME, Jan. 8, 1996, p. 13)
> 為了<u>恢復</u>古代的傳統，聯合國大會有129個會員國共同推動
> 決議案，呼籲在亞特蘭大奧運進行的17天期間，全世界停
> 火。

240 **rush** [rʌʃ] (v.) 匆促行事

同 hurry

No wonder nation-states are <u>rushing</u> to get their levers[1014] of control into cyberspace while less than 1% of the world's population is online.

(TIME, Jan. 15, 1996, p. 51)

因為全球連線上網的人口還不到1%，怪不得各國都<u>迫不及待</u>想取得進入網路世界的控制權。

241 **sabotage** [ˈsæbəˌtɑʒ] (v.)（以間接的手段）破壞

Meanwhile, the U.S. and Israel regard Iran as a rogue state that seeks to export terror, build nuclear weapons and <u>sabotage</u> the Middle East peace process. (TIME, June 26, 1995, p. 92)

在這同時，美國與以色列視伊朗為流氓國家，致力於輸出恐怖活動，建立核武，<u>破壞</u>中東和平進程。

註 rogue (n.) 惡棍，流氓

242 **scatter** [ˈskætə] (v.) 散播，散布

Epstein ... notes that in recent years variants[1045] of the class of viruses that includes measles have killed seals in the North sea, lions in the Serengeti and horses in Australia—three very different animals widely <u>scattered</u> around the globe.

(TIME, July 8, 1996, p. 41)

艾普斯坦指出，最近幾年，幾種與麻疹同類型的濾過性病毒之變體已經害死了北海的海豹、塞倫加提的獅子及澳洲的馬——廣泛<u>分布</u>於世界不同地區、截然不同的3種動物。

243 **shed** [ʃɛd] (v.) 使瀉出，散發

Today the yellow arches of McDonald's <u>shed</u> their plastic gleam on Red Square, and gangsterism rules instead of socialist virtue. (TIME, Apr. 3, 1995, p. 64)

如今紅場上流瀉著麥當勞黃色的拱形標誌所<u>散發出</u>的虛幻光芒，統領一切的不是社會主義美德，而是逞凶鬥狠的幫派行徑。

☐ ²⁴⁴ **shrink** [ʃrɪŋk] (v.) 減少，變小

反 grow

Samsung Electronics, for example, which has seen its stock price <u>shrink</u> by half since the beginning of the year, has cut back 16-megabit chip production nearly 15%. (TIME, Aug. 5, 1996, p. 42)
舉例來說，韓國的三星電子公司眼見其股票價格自年初開始<u>下跌</u>到原來的一半，已經將其16百萬位元記憶體晶片的生產量減少近15%。

☐ ²⁴⁵ **slash** [slæʃ] (v.) 大幅削減（經費）

同 cut

Time and again, as La Mama's grants from government have been <u>slashed</u>, her theater has been on the verge of closing. (TIME, Jan. 13, 1997, p. 50)
隨著政府給拉瑪瑪的經費被<u>削減</u>，她的劇場多次瀕臨倒閉。
註 grant (n.)（機構給予的）補助金

☐ ²⁴⁶ **soar** [sor] (v.) 升高，（價格）暴漲

同 rocket

Relations with Japan could <u>soar</u>. Economic friction⁷⁰⁷ has eased. The trade deficit has dropped 30% in the past year. (TIME, Nov. 18, 1996, p. 32)
與日本的關係可能<u>大幅加強</u>，經濟磨擦已經緩和下來，貿易赤字在去年一年就下降了30%。

☐ ²⁴⁷ **spark** [spɑrk] (v.) 刺激，鼓舞

同 prompt
trigger

Chirac's task now is to heal the wounds of a bruising campaign²⁸⁵, restore²³⁷ public confidence and <u>spark</u> a job-creating burst of economic growth. (TIME, May 15, 1995, p. 44)
席哈克眼前的重責大任，就是撫平激烈的競選活動造成的創傷、重建人民的信心，以及<u>帶動</u>一陣足以創造就業機會的經濟成長。
註 bruising (a.) 激烈的；a burst of 一陣

☐ 248 **split** [splɪt] (v.) 分裂

Relations between the countries hit a high after World War II when they coalesced to lead the world communist movement. But they <u>split</u> in the 1960s over ideological differences.

(TIME, May 6, 1996, p. 21)

二次大戰結束後，兩國聯手領導世界的共產運動，當時兩國的關係達到最高點，但在1960年代因意識型態相左而<u>分道揚鑣</u>。

註 hit (v.) 達到；high (n.) 高水準；coalesce (v.) 聯合

☐ 249 **stage** [stedʒ] (v.) 推出，舉辦

同 hold

But then he felt compelled to <u>stage</u> an impromptu[830] press conference, at which he "revealed" that Russia's military possesses something called an "Elipton," a weapon of mass destruction more powerful than a nuclear weapon.

(TIME, Jan. 10, 1994, p. 34)

但他後來覺得應該<u>開</u>一場臨時記者會，會中他透露俄國軍方擁有一種叫做「埃利普頓」的大規模毀滅武器，其威力比核子武器還強。

註 to feel compelled to ... 覺得應該…，覺得…是為所當為

☐ 250 **stall** [stɔl] (v.) 使停止，阻擋

About 40,000 refugees were <u>stalled</u> Saturday just outside Tanzania after the country closed its borders. (TIME, Apr. 10, 1995, p. 50)

坦尚尼亞關閉國境後，星期六約有4萬名難民給<u>擋</u>在該國國境邊。

□ 251 **steer** [stɪr] (v.) 引導，帶領

同 guide

Firmly, I <u>steer</u> them away from cheap, ugly, weakling, mail-order clones and toward absurdly powerful machines that cost a fortune and make the room lights dim when they power up.

(TIME, Nov. 11, 1996, p. 16)

我毅然決然將他們<u>帶離</u>那些價錢便宜、外型醜陋、功能不齊全、可以郵購的仿製品，轉向那些功能強大得離譜，價錢高昂，而且開機時連房間的燈光都會暗下來的機種。

註 weakling (a.) 瘦弱的；clone (n.) 複製品

□ 252 **stem** [stɛm] (v.) 源自(from)；遏止

Zhu's tough measures to curb[154] growth clearly <u>stem</u> from his sense of how directly his own power is tied to the nation's balance sheet.

(TIME, Jan. 23, 1995, p. 50)

朱鎔基之所以採取強勢手段抑制經濟成長，<u>來自於</u>他了解到他的權位是否坐的安穩，與中國的負債高低密切相關。

註 balance sheet 資產負債表，決算表

□ 253 **stimulate** [ˈstɪmjə‚let] (v.) 刺激，激勵

During her campaign[285], she predicted that the tax cuts would help <u>stimulate</u> job growth of 450,000 over four years. (TIME, Feb. 6, 1995, p. 26)

她在競選時預言，減稅措施將有助於在未來4年<u>促成</u>45萬個工作機會的增加。

□ 254 **strain** [stren] (v.) 拉緊，過度使用

Then there is the eye-<u>straining</u> challenge of reading screenfuls of text from 2.4 m to 3.6 m away—the distance most people sit from their TV sets. (TIME, Aug. 12, 1996, p. 27)

再則從2.4公尺到3.6公尺遠的地方閱讀一整個螢幕的文字，是個極<u>耗費</u>眼力的挑戰——這是一般人坐離電視的距離。

255 stun [stʌn] (v.) 使…震驚

同 amaze
shock

The main charge by Onaruto and Hashimoto was that sumo is frequently rigged[948]. And they <u>stunned</u> readers by naming names and admitting that they themselves had helped fix bouts.

(TIME, Sept. 30, 1996, p. 30)

大鳴戶和橋本主要指控相撲比賽經常作弊，令讀者吃驚的是他們不但指名道姓，而且坦承曾參與作弊。

註 fix (v.) 用不正當手段操縱（選舉、比賽、陪審團等），買通（法官等）；bout (n.) 比賽

256 submit [səb`mɪt] (v.) 提出

Last week House Speaker Newt Gingrich sent Clinton a letter urging him to <u>submit</u> within a month a plan outlining the cuts he would make to balance the budget in seven years.

(TIME, Mar. 13, 1995, p. 52)

上星期眾議院議長金瑞契寄了一封信給柯林頓，促請他於一個月內<u>提出</u>計畫，勾勒出他為了在7年內平衡預算所削減的各項經費。

註 outline (v.) 概述

257 sue [su] (v.) 控告

Seeking to change the system, female spies <u>sue</u> the CIA for discrimination. (TIME, June 12, 1995, p. 46)

為了改變中情局體制，女情報人員<u>控告</u>該局有性別歧視。

258 suppress [sə`prɛs] (v.) 壓制，阻止…的生長、發展

同 restrain
restrict

I am not sure they will be successful in <u>suppressing</u> the flow of information.

(TIME, Feb. 17, 1997, p. 47)

他們是否能成功<u>阻止</u>這種型態的資訊流動，這我有點懷疑。

☐ 259 **surrender** [sə`rɛndə] (v.) 交出；放棄；投降

The World Wide Web, the interconnected computer universe that teems with affluent[2] consumers whose only means of spending money online is to <u>surrender</u> their credit card to insecure networks .... (TIME, Oct. 7, 1996, p. 40)
全球資訊網，這個由電腦所串連起來的世界裡，到處都是有錢的消費者。他們在網路上唯一的消費方式，就是將信用卡<u>交給</u>極不保險的網路系統。

註 to teem with 充滿，富於

☐ 260 **sustain** [sə`sten] (v.) 維持，養活

同 keep going

The government's $2 million annual fund for Taiwanese productions does help <u>sustain</u> specialty directors like Hou, but little effort is made to prod[608] the Taiwan commercial cinema back to health. (TIME, Jan. 29, 1996, p. 43)
政府每年200萬美元的基金的確有助於使像侯孝賢這樣的特殊導演<u>生存下去</u>，但是對商業電影的復興，則欠缺作為。

☐ 261 **tap** [tæp] (v.) 輕按（電腦鍵）

A motorist lost in the San Fernando Valley can <u>tap</u> into GPS and get an instant position on the digitized map.
(TIME, Spring 1995 Special Issue: Welcome to Cyberspace, p. 30)
汽車駕駛若在聖弗南度峽谷迷路，只要<u>按鍵</u>進入全球定位系統，就可立即在數位化地圖上找出自己的位置。

☐ 262 **testify** [`tɛstə,faɪ] (v.) 作證

I may sound clinical and unemotional when I <u>testify</u> about these operations, but it does not reflect my true feelings .... (TIME, Sept. 30, 1996, p. 9)
當我為這些行動<u>作證</u>時，人們可能覺得我客觀又冷靜，但那並非我內心真正的感受。

註 clinical (a.) 冷靜的，客觀的

263 **threaten** [ˋθrɛtṇ] (v.) 揚言，放話

Under the proposed reforms, ... anyone's neighbor could <u>threaten</u> to convert[148] his land into a toxic-waste dump and claim compensation from the government if he was not allowed to do it.

(TIME, Feb. 27, 1995, p. 58)

按照所提出的改革方案，任何人的鄰居都可能<u>放話</u>要將自己的土地變爲有毒廢物的棄置場，政府若不准他這麼做，就向政府索賠。

註 claim (v.) 要求，索討

264 **tolerate** [ˋtɑləˌret] (v.) 容忍

同 put up with

American capitalism likes entrepreneurs to have a gleam in their eye, and even <u>tolerates</u> some clawing and scratching as long as the playing field is level and the fight is fair. (TIME, June 5, 1995, p. 32)

美國資本主義喜歡企業家野心勃勃，甚至<u>容忍</u>彼此激烈競爭，只要一切競爭合乎公平原則。

註 a gleam in one's eye 尚未形成的想法；claw (v.)（用爪）抓；scratch (v.) 抓

265 **track** [træk] (v.) 追踪

Still other sensors (in smart cars) will <u>track</u> and record the wear on parts and systems, alerting[667] the driver to potential[343] trouble, and will even flash warning when pressure in the tires is too low. (TIME, Feb. 6, 1995, p. 60)

另外，（智慧車上的）其他感應器會<u>追踪</u>並紀錄零件與系統的磨損情形，藉此提醒駕駛人防備潛在的危機，胎壓過低時，這些感應器甚至會閃燈警示。

266 **transcend** [trænˋsɛnd] (v.) 超越

But because she is an African-American woman, her importance to and impact on her times <u>transcend</u> the literary. (TIME, June 17, 1996, p. 41)

但因爲她是非裔美人，又是女性，她在當時的重要性及影響力，<u>超越</u>了文學的範圍。

☐ [267] **transfer** [træn`sfɝ] (v.) 轉移，轉帳，轉變

The software acts like an ATM, allowing you to
<u>transfer</u> $20 to $100 from your bank into your
(electronic) wallet before heading off onto the
Web. (TIME, Oct. 7, 1996, p. 40)
這套軟體的功用類似自動提款機，讓你在上網採購之前先從
自己的銀行帳戶<u>轉帳</u>20至100美元到電子皮夾裡。

☐ [268] **transform** [træns`fɔrm] (v.) 改變

They would more radically[79] <u>transform</u> the system
by ending the income tax entirely and by shifting
to taxes on consumption. (TIME, Apr. 17, 1995, p. 26)
他們改革體制的作法更為激進，一方面整個廢除所得稅，一
方面將稅收來源轉至消費上。

☐ [269] **undergo** [ˌʌndɚ`go] (v.) 接受（檢查、手術等），經歷

同 go through

Foreigners who intend to spend more than three
months in Russia must now <u>undergo</u> mandatory
testing to prove they are not infected[196] with HIV
.... (TIME, Apr. 17, 1995, p. 13)
外國人凡欲在俄國境內居留超過3個月，都必須<u>接受</u>強制性
檢測，以確定是否染上HIV。
註 mandatory (a.) 強制的

☐ [270] **undermine** [ˌʌndɚ`maɪn] (v.) 損壞，破壞

Expectations among ordinary Chinese are rising
in a way that could rapidly <u>undermine</u> faith in the
party. (TIME, Jan. 23, 1995, p. 50)
中國老百姓心中的期望正在上升，而其上升的方式可能很快
就<u>動搖</u>了人民對共黨的信心。

271 **undertake** [ˌʌndɚˈtek] (v.) 採用，執行

同 take on

His army, he declared, had been ordered to <u>undertake</u> measures[329] to prevent any further strangulation of the city. (TIME, June 26, 1995, p. 38)

他宣稱他的軍隊係「受命去<u>採取</u>各種措施，以防止此城市受人宰制的情形更爲惡化。」

註 strangulation (n.)（成長、發展）受阻，窒息

272 **worship** [ˈwɝʃɪp] (v.) 崇拜，崇敬

同 adore
venerate

For most of this century, scientists have <u>worshipped</u> the hardware of the brain and the software of the mind; the messy powers of the heart were left to the poets. (TIME, Oct. 9, 1995, p. 26)

大半個世紀以來，科學家<u>崇拜</u>的是大腦這項硬體加上思想這項軟體，而情感這種捉摸不定的東西，一向留給詩人去歌頌。

註 messy (a.) 雜亂的

簡易字名詞(273～375)，共103字

■ access	（使用、看某物的）機會或權利	☐ expedition	遠征隊；探險
☐ agenda	議程，行動計畫	■ fantasy	幻想
☐ ally	盟邦	☐ feud	宿仇
☐ amateur	業餘愛好者	☐ flair	天賦的才能
☐ anarchy	無政府狀態	☐ foe	敵人，反對者
☐ anguish	苦楚，煩惱	☐ genre	（尤指藝術作品的）形式
☐ approach	方法，途徑	☐ glance	瞥見
☐ assault	攻擊	☐ glimpse	瞥一眼，瞄一眼
■ bailout	融資	☐ grandeur	偉大，富麗堂皇
☐ boom	繁榮	☐ grasp	掌握，了解
☐ boost	暴增	☐ greed	貪婪
☐ boycott	杯葛，抵制	■ impulse	衝動
■ campaign	競選活動	☐ incentive	誘因，動機
☐ chaos	混亂	☐ inclination	傾向
☐ character	角色，人物	☐ infrastructure	水、電等基礎設施
☐ clash	衝突，牴觸	☐ initiative	主動權，進取心
☐ clout	權力，影響力，威信	☐ insight	洞察，了解
☐ coalition	聯合，聯合政府	☐ integrity	廉潔，正直
☐ combat	戰鬥	■ legend	傳奇人物
☐ commonplace	尋常的事，老生常談	■ mandate	委託，授權
☐ compass	指南針	☐ measure	手段，措施
☐ compassion	同情	☐ menace	威脅
☐ conflict	衝突	☐ merchandise	商品
☐ consequence	後果	☐ mess	雜亂
☐ conspiracy	陰謀	☐ monopoly	專賣（機構），獨占事業；壟
☐ credibility	可信度		斷
■ debut	（法文）首演，初次上場表演	■ nomination	提名
☐ demonstration	抗議，示威	■ odds	可能性，機率
☐ disability	傷殘，無行為能力	☐ opponent	反對者，對手
☐ dispute	爭議	☐ ordeal	苦難，磨練
■ emergency	緊急事件	■ passion	激情，熱情
☐ encounter	邂逅，遭遇	☐ peril	危險
☐ epidemic	（傳染病等的）流行，盛行	☐ persecution	迫害
☐ equivalent	同等的東西	☐ phase	階段
☐ establishment	權勢集團，領導階層	☐ pledge	承諾，保證
☐ euphoria	幸福感	☐ potential	可能性，潛力

☐ priority 首要之務，優先	☐ sanctuary 避難所，庇護
☐ privilege 特權	☐ scenario 可能發生的情況
☐ proliferation 擴散，繁殖	☐ scheme 計畫，方案，陰謀
☐ propaganda 宣傳	☐ scorn 輕蔑，鄙視
☐ proponent 提議者，支持者	☐ scrutiny 仔細檢查，注目
☐ prospect 成功的機率，前景	☐ stretch 一段時間，距離
☐ prosperity 繁榮	☐ strife 鬥爭，衝突
▨ recession 蕭條，後退	▨ tactic 戰術，策略
☐ reign 統治，主宰	☐ torture 苦刑，折磨
☐ remains 遺跡，遺體	☐ transition 過渡（時期），轉移
☐ reputation 名聲	☐ turmoil 騷亂，動亂
☐ reservation 保留地	▨ verdict 判決
☐ retail 零售	☐ version 版本
☐ revolt 叛亂，暴動	☐ veteran 老兵，老手
☐ rival 競爭對手	▨ wrath 憤怒
▨ sanction 制裁，處罰	▨ yield 產量

□ 273 **access** [ˋæksɛs] (n.)（使用、看某物的）機會或權利

Theoretically at least, whole populations will have direct <u>access</u> to information without waiting for it to be filtered through a government, or a press. (TIME, Feb. 17, 1997, p. 46)
至少在理論上，全體人民都可以直接<u>取用</u>資訊，不必等候政府或媒體過濾。

□ 274 **agenda** [əˋdʒɛndə] (n.) 議程，行動計畫

He has a modest domestic <u>agenda</u> centered on improving education and strengthening families, and he believes most of those programs can run without much direct input from him.

(TIME, Nov. 18, 1996, p. 31)
他有一套保守的內政<u>方案</u>，主要是以改善教育和強化家庭為重點，而且他相信，這些政策大部分都不需要他太多的直接參與就可以運作。

□ 275 **ally** [əˋlaɪ] (n.) 盟邦

同 confederate
反 enemy

Just as Clinton's first official overseas trip, in 1993, was to Asia, ... his first post-election trip will take him back to the region for visits with three other major <u>allies</u>—Australia, the Philippines and Thailand. (TIME, Nov. 18, 1996, p. 31)
正如柯林頓上任後的首趟外交之旅是於1993年到亞洲，他連任後的第一次出訪也將再回到這個地區，訪問另外3個主要<u>盟邦</u>——澳洲、菲律賓和泰國。

□ 276 **amateur** [ˋæmə͵tʃʊr] (n.) 業餘愛好者

反 professional

In February their lovers' quarrel in Central Park was captured on an <u>amateur</u>'s videotape, which tabloid[1040] TV shows replayed over and over again. (TIME, Oct. 7, 1996, p. 42)
2月時，他們在中央公園爭吵的場面被一位<u>業餘</u>攝影師收入鏡頭之中，愛炒緋聞的小電視台就整日重播這一段。
註 tabloid (a.) 專報聳動、煽情新聞的

簡易字
名詞

□ ²⁷⁷ **anarchy** [ˋænəkɪ] (n.) 無政府狀態

同 chaos

Tirana is in total <u>anarchy</u>. (TIME, Mar. 24, 1997, p. 29)
地拉那完全陷入<u>無政府狀態</u>。

□ ²⁷⁸ **anguish** [ˋæŋgwɪʃ] (n.)（心理上的）苦楚，煩惱

同 agony

Not since 1932, when Franklin D. Roosevelt
promised a New Deal to ease the economic and
social <u>anguish</u> of the Great Depression, has a U.S.
presidential race been so focused on domestic
affairs. (TIME, Nov. 18, 1996, p. 31)
自從1932年羅斯福承諾以新政來減輕經濟大蕭條所帶來的經
濟與社會<u>苦痛</u>之後，歷來的美國總統選戰沒有一次像這次一
樣，如此關注內政事務。

□ ²⁷⁹ **approach** [əˋprotʃ] (n.) 方法，途徑

The <u>approach</u> favored by IDEC Pharmaceuticals
... is to target all active T cells with a custom-
made antibody that can temporarily knock the
immune cells out of commission.
(TIME, Oct. 28, 1996, p. 70)
IDEC製藥公司所偏愛的<u>方法</u>，是利用一種特製的抗體對付
所有活躍的T細胞，這種抗體能夠讓這些免疫細胞暫時失去
功能。

註 custom-made (a.) 訂製的，非現成的；
out of commission 損壞，無法運作

□ ²⁸⁰ **assault** [əˋsɔlt] (n.) 攻擊

同 attack

Such <u>assaults</u> are most likely to injure the large
service providers, sober institutions more
culturally attuned to their governmental attackers
than the info-guerrillas of cyberspace.
(TIME, Jan. 10, 1996, p. 51)
這些<u>攻擊手段</u>最可能打擊到的是那些大型的服務供應者，因
為它們是比較配合政府指示的正派機構，游走網路世界的反
叛者反而比較不受影響。

註 sober (a.) 嚴肅的，持重的；to be attuned to 適應於…，配合

□ 281 **bailout** [ˋbel͵aʊt] (n.) 融資

In Washington the Clinton Administration's proposed $40 billion <u>bailout</u> of the weakened peso met with stiff opposition from Democrats.

(TIME, Jan. 30, 1995, p. 15)

華盛頓的柯林頓政府提議以400億美元的<u>融資</u>援助幣值大貶的披索，遭到民主黨強硬反對。

□ 282 **boom** [bum] (n.v.) 繁榮，長紅

反 slump

The wealth comes from initial[428] public offerings of stock, or IPOs, which are experiencing an unprecedented[104] <u>boom</u> in the great American bull[12] market of the past two years.

(TIME, Feb. 26, 1996, p. 35)

他們的財富來自於股票上市。過去兩年，美國股市連續<u>長紅</u>，新股上市也創出前所未有的佳績。

□ 283 **boost** [bust] (n.) 暴增

Companies such as K Mart have performed brilliantly, slicing overhead and enjoying the resultant earnings <u>boost</u>, but have failed to grow once the cutting stopped. (TIME, Nov. 4, 1996, p. 49)

像K Mart百貨集團這樣的公司，原本表現奇佳，大砍固定支出，享受隨之而來的獲利<u>暴漲</u>，但一旦停止裁減，成長也隨之停滯。

註 slice（將麵包、肉等）切成薄片；overhead 經常開支，一般費用

□ 284 **boycott** [ˋbɔɪ͵kɑt] (n.) 杯葛，抵制

Harry Edwards, the American sociologist who attempted to organize a black <u>boycott</u> of the 1968 Games in Mexico City in a bid to call attention to the plight[756] of black athletes in America ....

(TIME, June 24, 1996, p. 52)

為了喚起世人注意到美國黑人運動員所處的困境，美國社會學家哈利・愛德華滋企圖發動黑人運動員<u>抵制</u>1968年墨西哥奧運。

註 bid (n.) 努力，試圖

☐ 285 **campaign** [kæm`pen] (n.)（社會、政治上的）運動，競選活動

(v.) 參加競選

Only once did Bill Clinton raise a significant[90] example of foreign policy. That came in the campaign's final fortnight, when he proposed that NATO begin admitting Central and East European nations to the Atlantic alliance by 1999.

(TIME, Nov. 18, 1996, p. 30)

在外交政策上，柯林頓只舉了一個較重大的事例。那是在選戰進入最後兩週時所提出的，當時他提議說，北大西洋公約組織應該在1999年之前，接受中歐和東歐國家加入這個大西洋聯盟。

☐ 286 **chaos** [`keɑs] (n.) 混亂

In the first few years there may be panic and chaos, but the people will learn to fit into the new system very fast. (TIME, Jan. 29, 1996, p. 42)

頭幾年他們也許會慌張與混亂，但很快就能適應新體制。

☐ 287 **character** [`kærɪktɚ] (n.) 角色，人物

The world's No. 1 toymaker, whose products range form Fisher-Price infant and preschool toys to Disney-licensed characters, gets more than one-third of its nearly $4 billion in sales from the 29.2-cm-tall mannequin. (TIME, Nov. 11, 1996, p. 36)

這家世界最大的玩具製造商，產品從費雪牌的嬰兒、學齡前兒童玩具到迪士尼授權的卡通人物玩具一應俱全；光是（芭比）這個高29.2公分的假人就佔了公司近40億美元營業額的三分之一。

註 mannequin (n.)（時裝店、藝術家使用的）人體模型

☐ 288 **clash** [klæʃ] (n.) 衝突，牴觸

Perhaps the greatest threat in the <u>clash</u> between science and politics is that researchers might allow potential controversy to deter[539] them from investigating sensitive[88] subjects.

(TIME, Nov. 7, 1994, p. 61)
科學與政治的衝突所引發的最大危險，可能就在於研發人員會因潛在的爭議而不再探索一些敏感的題材。

☐ 289 **clout** [klaut] (n.) 權力，影響力，威信

同 weight

His leadership abilities and attempt to bring some <u>clout</u> to the traditionally rubber-stamp Congress will be put to the test when it meets in March.

(TIME, Jan. 23, 1995, p. 50)
他的領導才能和試圖讓這個向來只是橡皮圖章的國會具有影響力的努力，將在3月國會開議時面臨考驗。

☐ 290 **coalition** [ˌkoəˋlɪʃən] (n.) 聯合，聯合政府

同 alliance

The Rev. Kang Shin Seok, a Presbyterian minister who witnessed the mayhem[743], now heads a <u>coalition</u> of victimized people's groups.

(TIME, Dec. 11, 1995, p. 21)
目擊了這場暴力事件的長老會牧師Kang Shin Seok，現在是幾個受難者團體組成的聯盟的領導人。

☐ 291 **combat** [ˋkɑmbæt] (n.) 戰鬥

Even now, despite Beijing's displeasure, Washington is selling Taiwan <u>combat</u> aircraft and other equipment. (TIME, Feb. 12, 1996, p. 18)
即使是現在，儘管中共不高興，華盛頓仍然出售戰鬥機及其他裝備給台灣。

□292 **commonplace** ［ˋkɑmənˏples］(n.) 尋常的事，老生常談
(a.) 尋常的，不稀奇的

It's become <u>commonplace</u> to note that voters treated Bill Clinton in 1992 the way Wall Street treats a stock. (TIME, July 8, 1996, p. 28)
現在<u>經常</u>可以聽到這番話：選民在1992年對柯林頓的態度就像今日華爾街對股票的態度一樣。

□293 **compass** ［ˋkʌmpəs］(n.) 指南針

A new Secretary of State will hold the <u>compass</u>. Warren Christopher will vacate his State Department office by January. (TIME, Nov. 18, 1996, p. 31)
國務卿克里斯多福於1月離開國務院之後，將會有新國務卿來<u>接掌</u>。
註 vacate (v.) 辭退（職位），讓出（位子）

□294 **compassion** ［kəmˋpæʃən］(n.) 同情，悲憫

At home, with the gap between rich and poor widening, the seemingly ingrained American notions of <u>compassion</u>, codified during the New Deal, are colliding with the fears of those who feel financially strapped[94] .... (TIME, Mar. 13, 1995, p. 66)
在國內，隨著貧富差距日益懸殊，似乎已深植美國人心中、且於「新政」期間化為具體條文的<u>同情心</u>，正與那些經濟拮据的美國人心中的恐懼相衝突。
註 ingrained (a.)（習慣、想法）根深蒂固的；codify (v.) 把…編成法典；collide (v.)（意見、目的）相衝突，牴觸，同clash

□295 **conflict** ［ˋkɑnflɪkt］(n.) 衝突

Even though Chechnya could not hope to win its secessionist war against Moscow, Dudayev warned that continued fighting might well draw neighboring republics into a wider regional <u>conflict</u>. (TIME, Jan. 23, 1995, p. 9)
儘管車臣共和國不敢奢望在脫離俄國的戰爭上打贏莫斯科，但杜達耶夫警告說，若戰爭持續下去，有可能把鄰近共和國也捲入，變成更大範圍的區域<u>衝突</u>。

□ 296 **consequence** [ˈkɑnsə,kwɛns] (n.) 後果

At home labor costs per unit of output are going down, a <u>consequence</u> of rising productivity, and falling oil prices are putting another damper on inflation. (TIME, Apr. 11, 1994, p. 24)

由於產能能提高，國內每單位產量耗費的勞動成本逐漸下降，而油價下跌也抑制了通貨膨脹。

註 to put a damper on 抑制，使掃興

□ 297 **conspiracy** [kənˈspɪrəsɪ] (n.) 陰謀

Hale became the target of a flood of hate E-mail, much of it accusing him of being part of a <u>conspiracy</u> to suppress the true nature of Hale-Bopp. (TIME, Mar. 17, 1997, p. 40)

海爾成爲眾矢之的，充滿恨意的電子郵件向他蜂湧而來，大部分都指控他是隱瞞海爾波普彗星眞相這項陰謀的一員。

註 suppress (v.) 隱瞞（姓名、證據、事實等）

□ 298 **credibility** [ˌkrɛdəˈbɪlətɪ] (n.) 可信度

Whatever the reasons, the fact remains that the organization (U.N.) desperately[25] needs a rapid-reaction capability if it is to maintain <u>credibility</u> in emergencies[303]. (TIME, Oct. 23, 1995, p. 30)

不管有什麼理由，至今仍毋庸置疑的事實是，聯合國若欲維持其在處理緊急事故上的<u>公信力</u>，就迫切需要快速應變能力。

□ 299 **debut** [deˈbju] (n.)（法文）首演，初次上場表演

That day Jordan made his <u>debut</u> against the Indiana Pacers, and though he shot only 7 of 28, he moved well considering he had been playing baseball for a year. (TIME, Apr. 3, 1995, p. 56)

那天喬丹在對印第安那溜馬隊的比賽中<u>首度上場</u>，儘管投28球中7球，但考慮到他先前打了一年棒球，這樣的成績已很出色。

☐300 **demonstration** [ˌdɛmənˈstreʃən] (n.) 抗議，示威

Just two weeks ago, 85,000 people, nearly 8% of Okinawa's population, joined the largest single <u>demonstration</u> in the island's history to call for the Americans' removal. (TIME, Nov. 6, 1995, p. 14)
僅在兩週前，幾占沖繩人口8%的8萬5千人參加了島上有史以來最大一次<u>示威</u>，要求美國人撤走。

☐301 **disability** [ˌdɪsəˈbɪlətɪ] (n.) 傷殘，無行為能力

同handicap

Most aid, including nearly all low-income programs, food stamps, Medicaid and <u>disability</u> assistance, will be denied during an immigrant's first five years in the U.S. (TIME, Aug. 12, 1996, p. 25)
移民美國後的前5年，大部分的救助金都不能領取，包括幾近全部的低收入戶援助、糧票、醫療補助與<u>傷殘</u>援助。

☐302 **dispute** [dɪˈspjut] (n.) 爭議

It has been a matter of <u>dispute</u> but now scholars of the subject agree that Bessette and Kennedy first met in 1992, when he chatted her up one day in Central Park as she was running. (TIME, Oct. 7, 1996, p. 42)
這個問題曾經<u>眾說紛紜</u>，但現在「專家」們都同意碧瑟與小甘迺迪初識應在1992年，該年某一天他在中央公園內向正在跑步的她搭訕。

☐303 **emergency** [ɪˈmɜdʒənsɪ] (n.) 緊急事件

同crisis

President Kim Young Sam was worried. The Korean economy, he gravely told a July 2 <u>emergency</u> ministerial meeting, "is in trouble."
(TIME, Aug. 5, 1996, p. 42)
韓國總統金泳三憂心忡忡。7月2日的內閣<u>緊急</u>會議中，他沈重地說道，韓國的經濟「正處於困境」。

□ 304 **encounter** [ɪn`kaʊntə] (n.) 邂逅，遭遇

In fact, the most unnerving <u>encounter</u> I've ever had took place in the CompuServe adult-chat area. (TIME, Spring 1995 Special Issue: Welcome to Cyberspace, p. 36)
事實上，最讓我心寒的<u>遭遇</u>發生在「電腦服務」網路上的成人聊天區。
註 unnerve (v.) 使沮喪，使膽怯

□ 305 **epidemic** [ˌɛpɪ`dɛmɪk] (n.)（傳染病等的）流行，盛行

The AIDS <u>epidemic</u> has been in full swing for more than a decade now. (TIME, Apr. 10, 1995, p. 62)
愛滋病已大肆<u>流行</u>了10年以上。
註 in full swing 表事物正如火如荼進行

□ 306 **equivalent** [ɪ`kwɪvələnt] (n.) 同等的東西

For the past 15 years, doctors have tried to treat the underlying disorder with the pharmaceutical <u>equivalent</u> of a sledgehammer, using anticancer drugs and steroids to beat down the body's hyperactive defense forces. (TIME, Oct. 28, 1996, p. 70)
15年來，醫師一直用抗癌藥和類固醇治療這個潛在性疾病，這些藥就<u>像</u>長柄大鎚<u>一樣</u>，用來打垮患者體內異常活躍的防禦系統。

□ 307 **establishment** [əs`tæblɪʃmənt] (n.) 權勢集團，領導階層，主流

He was the favorite of the girls whose screams dominated the early Beatles concerts, but he was not a guy's guy. No way could he satisfy the emerging <u>establishment</u> of rock critics, a male coterie. (TIME, Nov. 20, 1995, p. 52)
在早期披頭四的演唱會裡，他是最多小女生尖叫的對象，但男性聽眾並不這麼欣賞他。他不可能獲得正興起的搖滾樂評人<u>主流</u>的青睞，因爲這個領域是男人的天下。
註 coterie (n.) 排外的小圈子、集團，同circle

☐ **308 euphoria** [juˋforɪə] (n.) 幸福感

同 elation

So after a period of <u>euphoria</u>, the bond market tumbled. (TIME, Nov. 28, 1994, p. 38)
因此經過一段榮景後,債券市場垮了下來。

註 tumble (v.)(價格)暴跌

☐ **309 expedition** [ˌɛkspɪˋdɪʃən] (n.) 遠征隊,探險

So Mark Norell, a leader of the joint U.S. Mongolian <u>expedition</u>, gave him a consolation prize: digging out an unpromising specimen Norell had already found. (TIME, Jan. 8, 1996, p. 38)
所以,美國與蒙古聯合探險隊的一位領隊馬克‧諾瑞爾,給了他一個安慰獎:讓他去挖一個諾瑞爾已經找到但是看來沒什麼價值的標本。

註 unpromising (a.)(前景)不看好的,無望的

☐ **310 fantasy** [ˋfæntəsɪ] (n.) 幻想

同 dream

What we could take away from the grievous events is a grasp[318] not of the Unabomber's psychology but of our own which is full of <u>fantasies</u>. (TIME, Apr. 22, 1996, p. 32)
從這些悲慘事件中我們可以汲取的,並不是要了解郵包炸彈客的心理,而是了解我們自己的心理,裡面充滿不實際的<u>幻想</u>。

註 grievous (a.)(事故)悲慘的,嚴重的

☐ **311 feud** [fjud] (n.) 宿仇

同 vendetta

Still, in both communities there is a growing sense that the blood <u>feud</u>—and its cycle of violence—must be broken if anyone is to prosper.
(TIME, Sept. 5, 1994, p. 50)
但雙方也越來越清楚,如果要繁榮,彼此之間的血海深仇和暴力循環就必須打破。

□³¹² **flair** [flɛr] (n.) 天賦的才能

同 talent
gift

Phil Donahue invented the participatory approach to TV talk, but Winfrey brought a woman-to-woman empathy and a <u>flair</u> for self-revelation that he couldn't match. (TIME, June 17, 1996, p. 27)

唐納修發明了有觀眾參與的電視脫口秀節目，但（另一主持人）溫芙雷把女人間感同身受的同理心帶進節目，加上她善於自我表白，這是唐納修比不上的。

□³¹³ **foe** [fo] (n.) 敵人，反對者

同 enemy

Both speeches struck the same rhetorical chord: that Dole is no ditherer but a decisive, muscular leader who will stand up to foreign <u>foes</u>.

(TIME, July 8, 1996, p. 29)

這兩個演說採用同一種修辭語調：杜爾不是會慌亂的人，而是果決、強勢的領袖，敢於對抗外敵。

註 rhetorical (a.) 措詞的；ditherer (n.) 慌亂、不知所措的人

□³¹⁴ **genre** [ˋʒɑnrə] (n.)（尤指藝術作品的）形式

Lanier embodies[551] a whole new <u>genre</u> of music that uses computers to create and disseminate its own distinctive sounds.

(TIME, Spring 1995 Special Issue: Welcome to Cyberspace, p. 14)

拉尼爾運用電腦創造並發出獨特的聲音，體現了一種全新的音樂形式。

□³¹⁵ **glance** [glæns] (n.v.) 瞥見

At first <u>glance</u>, Jeanne Vertefeuille might have seemed an unlikely choice to hunt down the most damaging mole in the history of the Central Intelligence Agency. (TIME, May 22, 1995, p. 54)

乍看之下，揪出這個中情局有史以來危害最大的雙面間諜的工作，似乎不可能輪到韋特弗耶來做。

註 mole (n.) 長期潛伏的（雙面）間諜

☐ ³¹⁶ **glimpse** [glɪmps] (n.v.) 瞥一眼，瞄一眼

Mosaic (Web-browsing program) was the first glimpse of a multimedia future that giants such as Microsoft had been predicting but not delivering.

(TIME, Sept. 16, 1996, p. 38)

「馬賽克」（網路導覽軟體）讓人首度窺探到多媒體的未來世界，此前像微軟這樣的大公司已預料到這個未來世界，但未能實現。

註 deliver (v.) 實現，履行（諾言等）

☐ ³¹⁷ **grandeur** [ˋɡrændʒɚ] (n.) 偉大，富麗堂皇

We want to bring jazz to the people in all its grandeur and glory. And we don't believe the music is above people. (TIME, June 17, 1996, p. 22)

我們要把爵士樂的偉大與光榮帶給大家，我們不相信它會曲高和寡。

☐ ³¹⁸ **grasp** [græsp] (n.) 掌握，了解

同 understanding

Even after working for more than 20 years in the Russian area, I cannot hope to approach Yuri's knowledge and intuitive grasp of what is going on in his homeland. (TIME, Jan. 16, 1995, p. 10)

我在俄國工作已有20餘年，但尤里對其祖國俄國現狀的認識與直覺式的理解，卻是我不敢企及的。

☐ ³¹⁹ **greed** [grid] (n.) 貪婪

同 avarice

Hollywood must examine itself. Its greed is sickening. It must judge the social impact, not just the popularity impact, of what it does.

(TIME, June 12, 1995, p. 32)

好萊塢必須自我檢視，好萊塢的貪婪越來越令人厭惡。好萊塢必須就其所做所為對社會所造成的衝擊，而非是否受歡迎，做出判斷。

☐ 320 **impulse** [ˋɪmpʌls] (n.) 衝動

Online shopping centers are springing up everywhere, inviting customers to use their credit cards to buy on <u>impulse</u>, without even leaving their chairs.

(TIME, Spring 1995 Special Issue: Welcome to Cyberspace, p. 74)

網路購物中心正四處崛起，誘使顧客連起身離座都不必，就在一時<u>衝動</u>下刷信用卡購物。

註 to spring up 突然出現，突然產生

☐ 321 **incentive** [ɪnˋsɛntɪv] (n.) 誘因，動機

"China has every <u>incentive</u> to make the reversion[769] work," says a top presidential adviser, "but they could also be ham-handed enough to keep it from working." (TIME, Nov. 18, 1996, p. 31)

總統的一位高級顧問說，「中國有充足的<u>理由</u>做好回歸的工作，但也有可能笨手笨腳而搞砸。」

註 ham-handed (a.) 笨手笨腳的

☐ 322 **inclination** [ˌɪnkləˋneʃən] (n.) 傾向

But girls rarely seem to have either the chance or the <u>inclination</u> to get plugged in.

(TIME, Nov. 11, 1996, p. 37)

但女生似乎很少有機會或是<u>意願</u>玩電腦。

註 to plug in 插上插頭，喻開啓電腦

☐ 323 **infrastructure** [ˋɪnfrəˌstrʌktʃə] (n.) 水、電等基礎設施

The bill for this <u>infrastructure</u> binge has topped $60 billion, and some economists wonder whether Malaysia can afford it. (TIME, Dec. 4, 1995, p. 26)

這場<u>基礎建設</u>的搶建熱潮所需的經費高達600億美元，一些經濟學家懷疑馬來西亞政府是否承擔得起。

註 binge (n.)（飲食、花費等方面的）放縱，沒有節制

☐ 324 **initiative** [ɪˋnɪʃɪˏetɪv] (n.) 主動權，進取心

The North (Vietnam) kept the <u>initiative</u>, choosing when to attack and when to lie low and rebuild its strength. (TIME, Apr. 24, 1995, p. 44)
北越保有<u>主動權</u>，可以選擇何時出擊，何時潛藏，以恢復實力。

☐ 325 **insight** [ˋɪnˏsaɪt] (n.) 洞察，了解

If this discovery is confirmed, it will surely be one of the most stunning[255] <u>insights</u> into our universe that science has ever uncovered[655]. (TIME, Aug. 19, 1996, p. 40)
假如證明屬實，這毫無疑問將是科學史上對於<u>了解</u>宇宙最令人嘆爲觀止的一項發現。

☐ 326 **integrity** [ɪnˋtɛgrətɪ] (n.) 廉潔，正直

Both prosecutors eventually paid for their <u>integrity</u> and grit. In May 1992 Falcone and his wife ... were ambushed and mortally wounded by the Mafia's "men of honor" on a road near Palermo. (TIME, May 8, 1995, p. 91)
最後，兩名檢察官爲其<u>廉潔</u>與勇氣付出了代價。1992年5月，法可內及其妻子在快到帕勒摩的路上遭到黑手黨「替天行道者」的伏擊重傷。
註 grit (n.) （口語）勇氣，鬥志；ambush (v.) 埋伏突擊

☐ 327 **legend** [ˋlɛdʒənd] (n.) 傳奇人物

They are far too cool in Nashville to get excited about mere music <u>legends</u>. (TIME, July 22, 1996, p. 42)
美國田納西州首府納希維爾這批人很酷，光是幾個音樂界的<u>傳奇人物</u>是無法激起他們的熱情的。

☐ 328 **mandate** [ˋmændet] (n.) 委託，授權

> Prime Minister Ryutaro Hashimoto ... also has a new electoral <u>mandate</u> as head of an internationalist coalition no longer dominated by ambivalent[383] socialists. (TIME, Nov. 18, 1996, p. 32)
> 首相橋本龍太郎也再度贏得選民的<u>託付</u>，出掌具有國際派色彩、且不再由立場矛盾的社會主義者所把持的聯合內閣。
> 註 coalition (n.) 聯合政府

☐ 329 **measure** [ˋmɛʒɚ] (n.) 手段，措施

同 step

> There's no single <u>measure</u> that's fully adequate but a combination of measures taken together can make them relatively secure. (TIME, Oct. 7, 1996, p. 40)
> 單靠一種<u>方法</u>是不夠的，但是結合多種方法，可以使它們相較之下安全得多。

☐ 330 **menace** [ˋmɛnɪs] (n.) 威脅

同 threat

> Still worried about the pesticides' impact on the environment, government scientists think they may have a better answer to the fire-ant <u>menace</u>.
> (TIME, June 5, 1995, p. 57)
> 官方科學家仍擔心殺蟲劑會破壞環境，認為或許還有更好的方法來對付這火蟻的<u>威脅</u>。

☐ 331 **merchandise** [ˋmɝtʃənˌdaɪz] (n.) 商品

同 goods

> That's one reason why each restaurant is designed with a <u>merchandise</u> shop to tempt[648] customers to buy such must-have souvenirs as jogging suits, $20 T shirts or baby baseball togs.
> (TIME, July 22, 1996, p. 44)
> 為什麼每一家餐廳都設計了一間<u>商品</u>店，以引誘消費者買一些非有不可的紀念品，如慢跑衣、20美元的T恤或是小孩的棒球衣，這是原因之一。

☐ 332 **mess** [mɛs] (n.) 雜亂

Army Captain Stuart Herrington ... remembers
that the scene inside the embassy also was a
"monstrous <u>mess</u>." (TIME, Apr. 24, 1995, p. 24)
陸軍上尉赫林頓想起那時大使館內也是「一片<u>混亂</u>，慘不忍
睹。」
🈑 monstrous (a.)（用以加強語氣）極度的，強烈的

☐ 333 **monopoly** [mə`nɑplɪ] (n.) 專賣（機構），獨占事業；壟斷

Although they welcomed the news that Mexico
will sell off many of the state's power plants, they
had also hoped Zedillo would privatize parts of
the country's lucrative[435] oil <u>monopoly</u>.
(TIME, Jan. 16, 1995, P. 53)
墨西哥將以廉價售出許多國營電廠，他們對此大表歡迎，但
他們也盼望總統塞迪約能將該國會賺錢的<u>獨占性</u>石油公司予
以部分民營化。

☐ 334 **nomination** [ˌnɑmə`neʃən] (n.) 提名

The President (Lee) is apparently unwilling to
risk a <u>nomination</u> battle over a new candidate.
(TIME, June 17, 1996, p. 54)
很明顯地，李總統不願意因重新<u>提名</u>而冒著產生閣揆攻防戰
的危險。

☐ 335 **odds** [ɑdz] (n.) 可能性，機率

同 chances

<u>Odds</u> are better than ever that high tech will get
their jobs. (TIME, Apr. 15, 1996, p. 22)
比起以往任何時期，高科技都更<u>可能</u>搶走他們的飯碗。

□ 336 **opponent** [ə`ponənt] (n.) 反對者，對手

反 supporter

Among the most extreme <u>opponents</u>, there were even paranoiac suggestions that once gone, the art might be hijacked and never returned.

(TIME, Apr. 1, 1996, p. 47)

某些<u>反對</u>最烈<u>的人</u>甚至神經質地暗示，這些寶物一旦出國可能會被（中共）劫持，再也回不了家鄉。

註 paranoiac (a.) 偏執狂的；
hijack (v.) 劫持（飛機），劫奪（運輸中的貨物）

□ 337 **ordeal** [ɔr`diəl] (n.) 苦難，磨練

Laura B did not tell anyone about the assault[280] because, she claims[508], she repressed all memory of the <u>ordeal</u>. (TIME, Apr. 17, 1995, p. 54)

B小姐沒有把所遭受的攻擊告訴別人，因為她聲稱她已把這椿<u>慘痛的經歷</u>完全壓抑在腦海深處。

註 repress (v.) 壓抑（感情、慾望等）

□ 338 **passion** [`pæʃən] (n.) 激情，熱情

同 feeling

Paleontology is much like politics: <u>passions</u> run high, and it's easy to draw very different conclusions from the same set of facts.

(TIME, Jan. 8, 1996, p. 38)

古生物學和政治很像：<u>情緒</u>很激昂，而且從同一組事實中可以推出數個截然不同的結論。

□ 339 **peril** [`pɛrəl] (n.) 危險

Climate change threatens[263] more than megastorms, floods and droughts. The real <u>peril</u> may be disease. (TIME, July 8, 1996, p. 40)

氣候改變帶來的威脅還不只是巨大風暴、洪水和乾旱，真正的<u>危險</u>可能是疾病。

□ 340 **persecution** [ˌpɝsɪˋkjuʃən] (n.) 迫害

They must disappear by the change in sovereignty or face <u>persecution</u>. (TIME, Feb. 10, 1997, p. 26)
他們必須在主權轉移之前消失，否則就得面對<u>迫害</u>。

□ 341 **phase** [fez] (n.) 階段

同 period

More significant[90] is Clinton's plan to take an enhanced[172] role in transatlantic affairs in the next four years, a transitional moment in European history when the postwar structures are being tidied up and the next historic <u>phase</u> has yet to begin. (TIME, Nov. 18, 1996, p. 32)
更重要的是，柯林頓計劃往後4年在大西洋兩岸的事務中，扮演更積極的角色，因爲這4年正是歐洲歷史上的一個過渡期：正值歐洲戰後結構的重整，而下個歷史<u>階段</u>尚未來臨。
註 to tidy up 整頓，弄整齊

□ 342 **pledge** [plɛdʒ] (n.) 承諾，保證

同 promise

Israeli Prime Minister Yitzhak Rabin deemed the comment a violation of the (PLO) Chairman's <u>pledge</u> to forgo[567] violence and threatened[263] to stop the peace process. (TIME, May 30, 1994, p. 47)
以色列總理拉賓認爲，這段話違反了巴解主席放棄暴力的<u>承諾</u>，因而揚言中止和平進程。

□ 343 **potential** [pəˋtɛnʃəl] (n.) 可能性，潛力 (a.) 潛在的，可能的

同 (n.) possibility

Netscape's Navigator had the <u>potential</u> to be the next Windows: a method for launching programs and calling up information not only from the Internet but also from corporate networks and even from the user's own PC. (TIME, Sept. 16, 1996, p. 40)
網景的「領航員」有<u>潛力</u>成爲下一個「視窗」：透過它，可以啓動程式，可以自網際網路、公司的網路，甚至個人電腦中叫出資訊。

☐ [344] **priority** [praɪˋɑrətɪ] (n.) 首要之務，優先

China is a big second-term <u>priority</u> for Clinton because it cuts across security and economic issues .... (TIME, Nov. 18, 1996, p. 31)
對柯林頓而言，中國是他第二任內的一個<u>重點國家</u>，因爲它跨越安全議題與經濟事務。

☐ [345] **privilege** [ˋprɪvlɪdʒ] (n.) 特權

But Djilas' criticism of the power and <u>privilege</u> granted to party leaders eventually led to years of imprisonment .... (TIME, May 1, 1995, p. 33)
吉拉斯批評該黨領導人所擁有的權力和<u>特權</u>，最終卻惹來數年牢獄生活。
註 grant (v.) 給予，授予

☐ [346] **proliferation** [proˌlɪfəˋreʃən] (n.) 擴散，繁殖

同 spread

I'd explicitly[37] couple Pakistan with Taiwan. If China behaves on Taiwan, I'd let them off the hook on Pakistan and deal with the <u>proliferation</u> questions later. (TIME, Feb. 12, 1996, p. 36)
〔柯林頓說〕我會明確地把巴基斯坦問題和台灣問題連在一起，假如中國規規矩矩地對待台灣，我就不追究巴基斯坦這檔事，而把核武<u>擴散</u>問題擺在以後再處理。
註 to let ... off the hook （對某人犯的錯）不予懲罰

☐ [347] **propaganda** [ˌprɑpəˋgændə] (n.)（偏頗、不正確的官方）宣傳

Today, a handful of business groups, each with political alliances, control Russia's media, and news has once again become <u>propaganda</u>.
(TIME, Feb. 17, 1997, p. 47)
現在少數幾家擁有政壇盟友的企業集團控制了俄國的媒體，新聞再次淪爲<u>傳聲筒</u>。

348 **proponent** [prə`ponənt] (n.) 提議者，支持者

同 advocate
反 critic

<u>Proponents</u> imagine a morning someday in the next century when a smart car will pull out of the garage, drive down local roads in the conventional[19] manner and head for the "smartway." (TIME, Nov. 4, 1996, p. 52)
<u>倡議者</u>想像在下個世紀的某天早上，你將智慧車從車庫裡開出來，以傳統的方式行駛在地方道路上，朝著「智慧道路」駛去。

349 **prospect** [`prɑspɛkt] (n.) 成功的機率，前景

But an eager start-up looks at risk differently, and so might consumers intrigued[588] by the <u>prospect</u> of shopping in cyberspace. (TIME, Oct. 7, 1996, p. 40)
但是迫不及待的新興公司對「風險」有不同的看法，而被網際空間購物的<u>前景</u>所吸引的消費者也可能是如此看待。
註 start-up (n.) 剛成立的小公司

350 **prosperity** [prɑs`pɛrətɪ] (n.) 繁榮

同 affluence

The peace and <u>prosperity</u> of the world in the next century depend in many ways on what Beijing does. (TIME, Mar. 25, 1996, p. 13)
下一世紀的世界和平與<u>繁榮</u>，在許多方面都取決於北京的所作所為。

351 **recession** [rɪ`sɛʃən] (n.) 蕭條，後退

同 slump

A more outrageous example is the Ministry of Finance, which in the wake of five years of <u>recession</u> is widely considered too powerful for Japan's own good. (TIME, Sept. 30, 1996, p. 28)
更離譜的例子是大藏省。在連續5年<u>經濟不景氣</u>之後，人民普遍認為大藏省權力過大，對日本整體利益有害。
註 outrageous (a.) 令人無法接受的，駭人聽聞的；
    in the wake of 隨著…之後

☐ 352 **reign** [ren] (n.v.) 統治，主宰

同 rule

The (anti-apartheid) movement publicly condemned[140] her in 1989 for inflicting[584] a "<u>reign</u> of terror" on Soweto with her gang of bodyguards. (TIME, Feb. 27, 1995, p. 28)
這個（反種族隔離）運動團體，於1989年公開譴責她與她那幫貼身侍衛在索威托施行「恐怖<u>統治</u>」。

☐ 353 **remains** [rɪˋmenz] (n.) 遺跡，遺體

Tucked deep within the rock are what appear to be the chemical and fossil <u>remains</u> of microscopic organisms that lived on Mars 3.6 billion years ago. (TIME, Aug. 19, 1996, p. 40)
深深埋在石塊中間的，看起來像是36億年前曾生存在火星上的微生物的化學殘留和化石<u>遺跡</u>。
註 tuck (v.) 將…擠進、塞進

☐ 354 **reputation** [ˌrɛpjəˋteʃən] (n.) 名聲

That approach[279] will likely prove particularly profitable in Asia and Europe, where IBM has built a 50-year <u>reputation</u> as a systems integrator.
(TIME, Nov. 4, 1996, p. 50)
這著棋在亞、歐兩洲可能會帶來特別的利潤，IBM在這些地區已經以系統整合者的身分<u>享譽</u>50年。

☐ 355 **reservation** [ˌrɛzəˋveʃən] (n.) 保留地

The disease, which first appeared on a Navajo <u>reservation</u>, has since spread to 20 U.S. states and killed 45 people, nearly half of those infected[196].
(TIME, July 8, 1996, p. 40)
這種疾病首先出現在某納瓦霍印第安人保留區，後來擴散到美國20個州，導致45人喪生，死亡人數幾乎占受感染人數的一半。

☐ ³⁵⁶ **retail** [`ritel] (n.) 零售

Some estimates place the overall movie tie-in business at $10 billion annually in <u>retail</u> sales worldwide. (TIME, Dec. 2, 1996, p. 70)
有人估算電影相關商品全球<u>零售</u>的收入每年約100億美元。
註 tie-in (n.) 搭配銷售的商品

☐ ³⁵⁷ **revolt** [rɪ`volt] (n.) 叛亂，暴動

同 insurrection
rebellion

Although much of the imperial collection amassed by China's rulers has been lost, it is miraculous that so many landmark works have survived a thousand years of violent dynastic changes, <u>revolts</u> and theft. (TIME, Apr. 1, 1996, p. 48)
中國歷代帝王的珍藏中，有很多已經遺失，但仍有許多劃時代的重要作品，歷經一千年來改朝換代的戰爭、<u>叛亂</u>以及偷盜，還能留存至今，真是奇蹟。
註 amass (v.) 積聚；landmark (n.) 里程碑，劃時代的重要事件

☐ ³⁵⁸ **rival** [`raɪvl̩] (n.) 競爭對手　(v.) 與…匹敵

Nonetheless, Malaysia is in some ways more insular than its Asian <u>rivals</u>. (TIME, Dec. 4, 1995, p. 26)
儘管如此，馬來西亞在某些方面要比其他亞洲<u>競爭對手</u>更具有島國根性。
註 insular (a.) 島國根性的，心胸狹隘的

☐ ³⁵⁹ **sanction** [`sæŋkʃən] (n.) 制裁，處罰

The bill would hold expression on the Net to the same standards of purity, using far harsher criminal <u>sanctions</u>—including jail terms—to enforce them. (TIME, Jan. 15, 1996, p. 51)
這個法案將對網路言論設定同樣的淨化標準，並採用更嚴厲的<u>刑罰</u>（包括坐牢）來執行此項法律。

☐ 360 **sanctuary** [ˈsæŋktʃʊˌɛrɪ] (n.) 避難所，庇護

同 haven

Still on China's list of wanted criminals, given only temporary <u>sanctuary</u> in the British colony, she was forced to change her name and keeps mostly in hiding. (TIME, Feb. 10, 1997, p. 26)

她的名字還在中國的通緝犯名單上，這個英國殖民地只能提供她暫時性的<u>庇護</u>，所以她被迫改名換姓，而且大部分時間是躲躲藏藏。

☐ 361 **scenario** [sɪˈnɛrɪˌo] (n.) 可能發生的情況

Nunn said, a handful of fanatics[410] could crash a radio-controlled drone aircraft into the building, "engulfing it with chemical weapons and causing tremendous[101] death and destruction." This <u>scenario</u>, said Nunn, "is not far-fetched," and the technology is all readily available[7].

(TIME, Apr. 3, 1995, p. 38)

努恩說，有一小撮狂熱份子可能操縱無線搖控飛機衝進這棟大樓，「使大樓完全為化學武器所吞沒，造成極大的人員死亡與財物破壞。」努恩說，這種<u>假想情況</u>「並非完全不可能發生」，而這種科技很容易就可取得。

註 to crash (a plane or car) into ... 使（飛機或汽車）猛撞上；
drone (n.) 無線遙控的飛機或汽車；engulf (v.) 吞沒，使陷入；
far-fetched (a.)（故事、想法）牽強的，靠不住的

☐ 362 **scheme** [skim] (n.) 計畫，方案，陰謀

同 plan

There are, however, as many variations on this latest get-rich-on-the-Internet <u>scheme</u> as there are firms that want to cash in on it. (TIME, Aug. 12, 1996, p. 26)

然而，最近這「上網際網路賺一票」的<u>方案</u>有許多不同的作法，就如同想利用它來賺錢的廠商一樣多。

註 to cash in on ... 用…來賺錢

□363 **scorn** [skɔrn] (n.) 輕蔑，鄙視

同contempt
disrespect

He heaps[575] <u>scorn</u> on federal judges who have used the bench to enforce and expand[177] civil rights, accusing them of a paternalistic belief in black inferiority. (TIME, June 26, 1995, p. 36)

他對那些利用法官職務去執行並擴大黑人民權的聯邦法官非常<u>鄙視</u>，指控他們有一種家長式的自以為是觀念，認定黑人就是弱勢（需要特別保護）。

註 bench (n.) 法官（職位）；paternalistic (a.) 家長式統治或管理的，把員工或子民都當小孩一樣看待而為他們做好一切安排的

□364 **scrutiny** [ˈskrutənɪ] (n.) 仔細檢查，注目

If that evidence stands up to the intense scientific <u>scrutiny</u> that is certain to follow, it will confirm for the first time that life is not unique to Earth. (TIME, Aug. 19, 1996, p. 40)

如果這個證據能通過隨後必定得面對的密集科學<u>檢測</u>，將首度確認生命並非地球所獨有。

註 to stand up to （理論、東西）耐用，經得起…

□365 **stretch** [strɛtʃ] (n.) 一段時間，距離

同spell

But one of the effects of the unusual <u>stretch</u> of weather over the past 15 years has been to alert[667] researchers to a new and perhaps even more immediate threat of the warming trend: the rapid spread of disease-bearing bugs and pests. (TIME, July 8, 1996, p. 40)

但過去15<u>年</u>間氣候異常所產生的結果之一，是使研究人員警覺到氣溫上升趨勢所帶來的一個新的、也許是更立即的威脅，那就是帶病原的昆蟲和小動物快速蔓延。

□ 366 **strife** [straɪf] (n.) 鬥爭，衝突

同 conflict

From <u>strife</u>-torn Georgia comes Giya Kancheli, who may be the most important Soviet composer since Shostakovich. (TIME, Apr. 10, 1995, p. 89)
從飽受<u>戰火</u>折磨的喬治亞共和國，出現了坎且利這號人物，他可能是蕭斯塔哥維契之後蘇聯最重要的作曲家。

□ 367 **tactic** [ˋtæktɪk] (n.) 戰術，策略

Turning to the well-tested <u>tactic</u> of seeking a scapegoat, he (Yeltsin) fired Moscow police chief Vladimir Pankratov and city chief prosecutor Gennadi Ponomaryov for failing to "provide proper organization" to deal with "grave crimes."
(TIME, Mar. 20, 1995, p. 54)
棄俥保帥是屢試不爽的<u>策略</u>，葉爾欽改採這項策略，以未能「設立適當組織」對付「嚴重犯罪」之名，免掉莫斯科警察局長潘克拉托夫與該市檢察長波諾馬尤夫的職務。

註 scapegoat (n.) 代罪羔羊；grave (a.)（事態、疾病）嚴重的

□ 368 **torture** [ˋtɔrtʃə] (n.) 苦刑，折磨

同 torment

Twenty minutes of relaxation and 20 minutes of <u>torture</u>. You never knew what was next.
(TIME, Jan. 9, 1995, p. 54)
20分鐘的舒緩之後，是20分鐘的<u>苦刑</u>，你根本搞不清楚下一分鐘會有什麼遭遇。

□ 369 **transition** [trænˋzɪʃən] (n.) 過渡（時期），轉移

Making the <u>transition</u> to true no-hands smart roads ... is an engineering challenge that will probably take another 20 years to complete.
(TIME, Nov. 4, 1996, p. 53)
要<u>過渡</u>到真正無人駕駛的智慧型道路，是工程上的一大挑戰，可能要再花上20年才能完成。

370 **turmoil** [ˈtɜmɔɪl] (n.) 騷亂，動亂

No one in authority in Washington or Tokyo will say publicly that current <u>turmoil</u> is likely to unhinge the 35-year-old U. S.-Japan security alliance, but week by week a sense of alarm is growing. (TIME, Nov. 6, 1995, p. 15)

華盛頓和東京的權威人士無人願意公開表示，目前的<u>騷亂</u>可能會使已有35年歷史的美日安全同盟毀於一旦，但是惶恐之情與日俱增。

註 unhinge (v.) 使分離，拆卸

371 **verdict** [ˈvɜdɪkt] (n.) 判決

Hollywood madam Heidi Fleiss was convicted of running a call-girl ring and faces up to six years in prison. Fleiss reacted to the <u>verdict</u> by throwing her head on the defense table. (TIME, Dec. 12, 1994, p. 101)

好萊塢媽媽桑弗利絲因經營應召站被判有罪，將面對6年牢獄生活。聆聽<u>判決</u>後，弗利絲將頭猛然貼上被告席的桌上作為回應。

註 convict (v.) 判決（某人）有罪

372 **version** [ˈvɜʒən] (n.) 版本

Indonesia's government, which vigorously[107] suppressed[258] the newsmagazine *Tempo*, does not seem at all concerned that a digital <u>version</u> has appeared on the Net. (TIME, Aug. 19, 1996, p. 52)

印尼政府曾經以鐵腕鎮壓新聞性雜誌《節拍》，可是該雜誌的電子<u>版</u>已經在網路上露面，印尼政府卻好像全不在意。

373 **veteran** [ˈvɛtərən] (n.) 老兵，老手

Consequently, Cuba's national team is made up largely of hardened <u>veterans</u>, some of whom have played together for a decade. (TIME, Feb. 5, 1996, p. 13)

所以，古巴國家代表隊成員大多是身經百戰的<u>老手</u>，其中有些人更是並肩打了10年的隊友。

註 hardened (a.)（歷經各種不幸或逆境淬鍊而變得）堅毅的，冷酷無情的

□ 374 **wrath** [ræθ] (n.) 憤怒

After U.S. soldiers prevented the mob from venting its <u>wrath</u> on several men suspected of throwing the bomb, the crowd turned on the warehouse itself. (TIME, Oct. 10, 1994, p. 42)
暴民欲將滿腔的<u>怒火</u>發洩在數名丟擲炸彈的嫌犯上，但遭到美軍阻止，於是將發洩對象轉到倉庫上面。

註 vent (v.) 發洩

□ 375 **yield** [jild] (n.) 產量

The federal government has built a maze of greenhouses, labs and research facilities dedicated[24] to spawning[953] new high-<u>yield</u> varieties of bug-resistant wheat, potatoes, sunflowers and sugar beets. (TIME, Mar. 6, 1995, p. 60)
聯邦政府蓋了一堆溫室、實驗室與研究設施，錯落如迷宮一般；這些機構是爲了大量生產高<u>產量</u>且防蟲咬的小麥、馬鈴薯、向日葵、甜菜的新變種而設立的。

普通字

TIME
Key Words 1000

- acute 強烈的，嚴重的
- affable 和藹可親的
- affiliated 有緊密關係的，附屬的
- aggressive 富侵略性的，挑釁的
- allegedly 據稱，據說
- aloft 在高處，在空中
- alternate 交替的，替代的
- ambivalent 感覺矛盾的
- assorted 各式各樣的
- audacious 大膽的
- austere 嚴肅的，樸實的
- avant-garde 前衛的
- benevolent 仁慈的
- bewildered 迷惑的，張惶失措的
- bizarre 怪異的
- blatant 大剌剌的，極明顯的，公然的
- blue-chip 最獲利的，最賺錢的
- capricious 善變的，反覆無常的
- chronic 慢性的
- compatible 相容的
- compelling 極吸引人的，令人無法抗拒的
- complacent 自滿的
- confidential 機密的
- congenial 意氣相投的
- consistent 前後一致的
- conspicuous 顯著的
- consummate 造詣極高的，技藝精湛的
- daunting 令人畏懼的
- eclectic 兼容並蓄的
- eligible 合格的
- enigmatic 謎一般難解的
- epic 雄渾的，大規模的
- exuberant 興奮難抑的
- exultant 雀躍的，欣喜若狂的
- fanatic 狂熱的
- feasible 可行的，行得通的
- feeble 性格軟弱的，不敢採取強勢作為的
- fervent 熱烈的，強烈的
- forthcoming 即將來到的
- fractious 倔強的，難駕馭的
- frantical 十萬火急的，著急的
- full-fledged 經過充分訓練的，發展成熟的
- furious 激烈的，用力的
- genetic 遺傳上的
- giddy 令人頭昏眼花的
- gorgeous 很美的
- heady 令人興奮的，飄飄然的
- illiterate 不識字的
- incessant 不停的，不斷的
- incumbent 現職的
- indignant 憤憤不平的
- inherent 固有的，天生的
- initial 首度的，最初的
- integral 必需的，不可或缺的
- intricate 複雜的
- invalid 無效的，作廢的
- invariably 必定地，不變地
- lavish 鋪張的，奢華的
- lethal 致命的
- lucrative 可獲利的，賺錢的
- ludicrous 可笑的，滑稽的
- malicious 懷惡意的，居心不良的
- mock 煞有其事的，假裝的；模擬的
- mundane 世俗的，平凡的
- optional 可選擇的，非強制的
- perennial 長期間持續的
- placid 平靜的
- poised 準備好做…
- precarious 岌岌可危的
- predominant 主要的
- prestigious 有名望的
- presumably 據推測，大概

- [ ] prone 傾向於，易於
- ■ quaint 因樣式古老、罕見而吸引人的
- ■ rampant 猖獗的
- [ ] rash 鹵莽的
- [ ] requisite 必需的，不可或缺的
- [ ] resurgent 復活的，復甦的
- [ ] robust 健康的，強健的
- ■ sentimental 多愁善感的
- [ ] sheer 完全的
- [ ] simmering 即將爆發的
- [ ] simplistic 過分單純化的
- [ ] simultaneously 同時地
- [ ] snap 倉促的，突然的
- [ ] speculative 投機的，熱衷於投機買賣的
- [ ] sporadic 零星的，時有時無的
- [ ] sprawling 蔓延的，廣大的
- [ ] stationary 靜止的，固定的

- [ ] stringent 嚴格的
- [ ] sublime 卓越的，出色的
- [ ] subsequent 後來的
- ■ tantalizing 令人迫不急待的，吊胃口的
- [ ] tedious 冗長而乏味的
- [ ] tentative 初步的，未完全定案的
- [ ] thrilling 令人興奮的，刺激的
- [ ] trivial 微不足道的
- [ ] tumultuous 騷亂的
- [ ] turbulent 動盪不安的
- ■ untapped 未被開發的
- ■ vaunted 炫耀的，自誇的
- [ ] versatile 多才多藝的
- [ ] viable 可行的
- [ ] vocal 大聲說出主張的
- ■ with a vengeance 徹底地，完全地

□ 376 **acute** [ə`kjut] (a.) 1. (感覺) 強烈的, (事態) 嚴重的;
2. (視覺、嗅覺等) 敏銳的

同 1. severe
2. keen

In the past, the (Mexican) ruling classes emphasized our <u>acute</u> differences with the Anglo-Saxons in order to affirm our separate identity.

(TIME, Mar. 6, 1995, p. 40)

過去 (墨西哥) 統治階級刻意突顯我們與盎格魯撒克遜人之間<u>強烈</u>不同之處,以確立本身與眾不同的民族認同。

□ 377 **affable** [`æfəbl] (a.) 和藹可親的

同 amicable

Indeed, Clinton was more than conciliatory[17] when he met with Gingrich on Thursday and the new Speaker was <u>affable</u> in return.

(TIME, Jan. 16, 1995, p. 24)

的確,星期四柯林頓與金瑞契會面時顯露十足和解之意,而金瑞契這位新出爐的眾院議長,也投桃報李,<u>友善</u>相待。

□ 378 **affiliated** [ə`fɪlɪ,etɪd] (a.) (與某較大組織) 有緊密關係的,附屬 (某較大組織) 的

Games' sponsor Visa International and three <u>affiliated</u> banks are using Atlanta as a beachhead for the introduction to the U.S. of "smart cards," an electronic substitute for cash.

(TIME, Jan. 8, 1996, p. 13)

奧運贊助廠商威世卡國際機構與3家<u>合作</u>銀行,正利用亞特蘭大做爲在美國發行IC卡的立足點。

註 beachhead (n.) 灘頭陣地,立足點

□ 379 **aggressive** [ə`grɛsɪv] (a.) 富侵略性的,挑釁的

同 belligerent

Says former Secretary of Defense Caspar Weinberger: "Their whole foreign policy has turned suddenly much more <u>aggressive</u>, and that bodes[500] no good for the nature of any people."

(TIME, Mar. 25, 1996, p. 13)

前國防部長溫柏格說:「他們的外交政策突然整個變得更<u>富侵略性</u>,這對任何民族天性來說都不會有好結果。」

□ 380 **allegedly** [əˋlɛdʒɪdlɪ] (adv.) 據稱，據說，
（證據不足的情況下）遭指控地

Hard Rock creator Peter Morton sued[257] Earl for
<u>allegedly</u> purloining Hard Rock's business plans.
The issue was settled without a trial.

(TIME, July 22, 1996, p. 44)

硬石的創辦人彼得·摩頓控告厄爾，<u>稱其</u>偷取硬石的營業計
畫。這件案子已在庭外和解。

註 purloin (v.) 偷

□ 381 **aloft** [əˋlɔft] (adv.) 在高處，在空中

The bronze sculpture depicts a man holding a pipe
<u>aloft</u> as an offering to the Great Spirit.

(TIME, Sept. 5, 1994, p. 21)

這件銅雕表現一個將煙斗<u>高高舉起</u>，以供奉「大神」〔北美
某些印第安部落崇拜的神祇〕的男子。

□ 382 **alternate** [ˋɔltənɪt] (a.) 交替的，替代的

The opposition says the government should
concentrate on <u>alternate</u> energy sources and
restrict the growth of industries like petro-
chemicals that consume a lot of energy.

(TIME, June 17, 1996, p. 54)

反對黨說政府應專注在開發<u>替代</u>能源上，並且應該限制消耗
大量能源的工業如石化業之成長。

□ 383 **ambivalent** [æmˋbɪvələnt] (a.) 感覺矛盾的

同 unsure

Gates is <u>ambivalent</u> about his celebrity[680].

(TIME, Jan. 13, 1997, p. 38)

對於自己聲名大噪，蓋茲是<u>又愛又恨</u>。

□384 **assorted** [əˋsɔrtɪd] (a.) 各式各樣的

同 various

His personal arsenal, including a Czech machine gun and <u>assorted</u> pistols, shotguns and rifles, was stashed in the trunk of his car. (TIME, May 8, 1995, p. 50)

他個人的武器，包括一支捷克製機槍、<u>各式各樣</u>的手槍、獵槍、步槍，全藏在車子的行李廂。

註 arsenal (n.) 儲藏的武器；stash (v.) 藏放

□385 **audacious** [ɔˋdeʃəs] (a.) 大膽的

同 daring

Last year, after months of deliberation, Collins left his faculty post at the University of Michigan Medical School to lead the Human Genome Project, an <u>audacious</u> effort to decipher the complete genetic script contained in human cells. (TIME, Jan. 17, 1994, p. 54)

去年，柯林斯經數月的考慮，決定辭掉在密西根醫學院的職務，前往主持人類基因組工程，這是一項<u>大膽的</u>工程，宗旨在解讀出人類細胞中的全部遺傳訊息。

註 decipher (v.) 譯解（密碼）

□386 **austere** [ɔˋstɪr] (a.)（人）嚴肅的，（東西、生活）樸實的

The Puppetmaster (1993) and last year's *Good Men Good Women*, with their <u>austere</u> poignancies, played all the best festivals, though they remain a coterie taste. (TIME, Jan. 29, 1996, p. 43)

《戲夢人生》(1993)與去年的《好男好女》，以<u>樸素</u>而尖銳的風格打遍各大影展，然而這些戲仍只有少數內行人能欣賞。

註 poignancy (n.) 尖銳，深刻；coterie (n.)（具排他性的）小圈圈，集團

□387 **avant-garde** [ˌævɑŋˋgɑrd] (a.) 前衛的

Kosuke Tsumura, another Miyake student, launched[203] his K-Zelle line in 1992 and two years later debuted[299] in Paris with <u>avant-garde</u> *Mad Max* costume. (TIME, Oct. 9, 1995, p. 47)

三宅一生另一個徒弟津村小介於1992年推出了K-Zelle系列，兩年後首次在巴黎推出<u>前衛的</u>《衝鋒飛車隊》服裝展。

☐ 388 **benevolent** [bəˋnɛvələnt] (a.) 仁慈的

Ruthless company-downsizing[988] drives and continued layoffs, coupled with rising pay for top managers, have made their bosses look a good deal less <u>benevolent</u>. (TIME, June 13, 1994, p. 56)
無情的公司縮編行動、不斷的解僱員工，加上付給高階經理人員的薪資節節上漲，使得他們的老闆看來不再那麼<u>慈祥</u>。

註 layoff (n.) 解僱；a good deal 非常，極其

☐ 389 **bewildered** [bɪˋwɪldəd] (a.) 迷惑的，張惶失措的

同 perplexed

One thing that has observers <u>bewildered</u> is how the White House could have put forward Foster's nomination[334] without getting the abortion issue squared away in advance. (TIME, Feb. 20, 1995, p. 32)
令觀察家<u>莫名所以的</u>一點是，白宮敢提名佛斯特，卻不事先擺平墮胎議題。

註 to square away 把（難題）處理掉、擺平（以放手進行其他事）

☐ 390 **bizarre** [bɪˋzɑr] (a.) 怪異的

同 weird

Floods. Droughts. Hurricanes. Twisters. Are all the <u>bizarre</u> weather extremes we've been having lately normal fluctuations in the planet's atmospheric systems? (TIME, July 8, 1996, p. 40)
洪水，乾旱，颶風，龍捲風。究竟這些近來我們看到的<u>怪異</u>氣候極端現象是不是地球大氣系統的正常變化？

註 extremes (n.) （行為、情勢上的）極端；
fluctuation (n.) （氣候、市價等的）變動

☐ 391 **blatant** [ˋbletn̩t] (a.) 大剌剌的，極明顯的，公然的

What the network didn't know—and didn't bother to find out—was that Jammal was a hoaxer and that large segments of its program were based on <u>blatant</u> and ludicrous[436] pseudo-science.
(TIME, July 5, 1993, p. 51)
該電視台所不知道的、也未曾特意去探究的，就是詹瑪爾是個騙子，而且該電視台的節目大部分都是<u>公然</u>利用可笑的偽科學來製作。

□ 392 **blue-chip** [`blu`tʃɪp] (a.)（在同行業中）最獲利的，最賺錢的

Such entreaties (to safeguard the patents of manufacturers) have become essential for America's <u>blue-chip</u> companies as they charge into the vast markets of China and its East Asian neighbors. (TIME, Oct. 10, 1994, p. 61)

懇求保護產品專利權，已經成為美國績優公司挺進中國大陸和其鄰國廣大市場時，必然要做的事。

註 entreaty (n.) 懇求，乞求；charge (v.) 衝鋒，向前衝

□ 393 **capricious** [kə`prɪʃəs] (a.) 1.（性情）善變的，反覆無常的；
                                      2.（事物）變化無常的

同 1. impulsive
    mercurial
同 2. unpredictable
反 2. dependable

Earthquakes ... are <u>capricious</u> beasts ruled by what physicists refer to as nonlinear dynamics, which means precise forecasting of when and where they will occur is impossible.

(TIME, Jan. 30, 1995, p. 34)

地震是<u>變化莫測</u>的動物，受物理學家所謂的非線性力學的支配，這表示要精確預測地震將於何時何地發生是不可能的事。

註 nonlinear (a.) 非線性的

□ 394 **chronic** [`krɑnɪk] (a.) 1.（疾病）慢性的；
                                  2.（行為、惡習）習以為常的，積習成癖的

同 1. persistent
    2. habitual
       inveterate

Psychiatrists stress, however, that a few injections of medication and some sessions with a psychotherapist are just the beginning. Pedophilia is a <u>chronic</u> disorder. (TIME, Sept. 2, 1996, p. 41)

然而心理學家強調，藥物注射及與心理治療師諮商協談不過是個開始，因為戀童癖是種<u>慢性</u>病。

註 pedophilia (n.) 戀童癖

普通字
形容詞/副詞

□ 395 **compatible** [kəm`pætəbl] (a.) 相容的

反 incompatible

No one except Microsoft executives disputes the fact that Microsoft is, in fact, a monopoly[333] at least in IBM-<u>compatible</u> computer-operating systems. Some 8 out of 10 desktop computers run the Microsoft software. (TIME, Feb. 27, 1995, p. 31)

事實上，微軟公司至少壟斷了與IBM<u>相容的</u>電腦操作系統，這一點除了微軟的各主管，沒人會有異議。10台桌上型電腦中約有8台是用微軟的軟體在操作。

註 dispute (v.) (對事實等) 懷疑，持異議

□ 396 **compelling** [kəm`pɛlɪŋ] (a.) 極吸引人的，令人無法抗拒的

Winfrey, 42, had a troubled childhood, but her genius was to realize that those troubles—and similar ones experienced by ordinary people all over America—could make for <u>compelling</u> television. (TIME, June 17, 1996, p. 27)

42歲的溫芙雷童年並不愉快，但是她的天分在於能了解到她的問題，以及全美一般百姓面臨的類似問題，這將可以成為<u>精采感人的</u>電視題材。

□ 397 **complacent** [kəm`plesənt] (a.) 自滿的

That does not mean that the people of Kwangju are growing <u>complacent</u> or law-enforcement agencies less vigilant. (TIME, Dec. 11, 1995, p. 21)

這並不代表光州人民已<u>志得意滿</u>，也不代表執法當局放鬆了警戒心。

註 vigilant (a.) 提防的，帶戒心的

□398 **confidential** [ˌkɑnfəˈdɛnʃəl] (a.) 機密的

反 public

Although labeled "privileged and <u>confidential</u>," copies of the telephone survey are mysteriously ending up in the hands of reporters and environmentalists in both Alabama and Missouri. (TIME, May 22, 1995, p. 48)

這份電話問卷的影本雖已註明「僅供特定人士觀看，<u>機密</u>」，但神不知鬼不覺，最後仍落入阿拉巴馬與密蘇里兩州的記者與環保人士手中。

註 privileged (a.) 僅供少數人知道的，機密的；to end up 最後變成…

□399 **congenial** [kənˈdʒinjəl] (a.)（人）意氣相投的；（環境）令人愉快的

同 agreeable

If we really mean to lead, and to bring about a world more or less <u>congenial</u> to us, we should stop pretending that we can do the job on the cheap and by remote control. (TIME, June 26, 1995, p. 82)

如果我們〔美國〕真有意領導世界，並使世界變的多少<u>看得順眼一些</u>，那就不要再欺騙自己說這件工作不必花大錢、遠遠的發號施令就可以做到。

□400 **consistent** [kənˈsɪstənt] (a.) 前後一致的

TIME-CNN polls have shown a <u>consistent</u> majority of voters—56% vs. 34% in last week's survey favoring creation of a full-fledged[417] new party. (TIME, Mar. 13, 1995, p. 91)

對於成立另一個正式政黨，TIME與CNN合作的多項民意調查<u>一致</u>顯示有過半數選民同意，如上週的調查即是56%贊成34%反對。

□401 **conspicuous** [kənˈspɪkjuəs] (a.) 顯著的

反 inconspicuous

But the White House sees any <u>conspicuous</u> effort to placate Jackson as dangerous to its efforts to win back disaffected white moderates. (TIME, Mar. 13, 1995, p. 91)

但白宮認為任何<u>大張旗鼓</u>安撫傑克遜的動作，都不利於白宮挽回那些對政府不滿的溫和派白人的心。

註 placate (v.) 安撫；disaffected (a.)（對政府等）不滿的

402 **consummate** [kən`sʌmɪt] (a.) 造詣極高的，技藝精湛的

But he did have a <u>consummate</u> technical command of his instrument, which ... gives his performances an irresistible strut and swagger.

(TIME, Jan. 31, 1994, p. 113)

但他的彈奏技巧的確非常<u>高明</u>，使他的演出顯得神氣活現，盛氣凌人，令人無法抗拒。

註 strut (n.) 神氣活現，昂首闊步；swagger (v.) 大搖大擺地走

403 **daunting** [`dɔntɪŋ] (a.) 令人畏懼的

同 intimidating

The Rosens instead plan to blow away the field in part because Harold and his team of engineers have solved a set of <u>daunting</u> technological issues just in the past year. (TIME, Sept. 23, 1996, p. 41)

但羅森氏打算掃平群雄，獨占鰲頭，部分原因是哈洛和他的工程小組在過去一年裡，已解決了許多<u>棘手的</u>科技問題。

註 to blow away （尤指運動場上）徹底打敗（敵人）；
the field 指某一比賽中所有的競爭對手

404 **eclectic** [ɛk`lɛktɪk] (a.) 兼容並蓄的，兼採各種不同觀點或方法的

同 diverse

Adams' <u>eclectic</u>, pop-oriented music ... is a radical[79] departure from the expansive minimalism[1015] that marked his earlier stage works. (TIME, May 29, 1995, p. 70)

先前亞當的舞臺音樂，以全面的簡約主義為特色，如今他的作品博採<u>各種風格</u>，走流行音樂取向，代表對先前風格的徹底揚棄。

405 **eligible** [`ɛlɪdʒəbl] (a.) 合格的

He may not be <u>eligible</u> because of a failure to make himself available[7] for Davis Cup play in recent years. (TIME, Feb. 5, 1996, p. 13)

他的<u>資格</u>可能會有問題，因為他近來一直不參加台維斯杯。

□ 406 **enigmatic** [ˌɛnɪɡˋmætɪk] (a.) 謎一般難解的

The last Stalinist's (Kim Il Sung) sudden demise[692] leaves his realm more <u>enigmatic</u> than ever.

(TIME, July 18, 1994, p. 26)

最後一位史達林信徒金日成的猝逝，使他的國家變得更<u>難以捉摸</u>。

□ 407 **epic** [ˋɛpɪk] (a.) 雄渾的，大規模的

After an infernal global odyssey and an <u>epic</u> chase by U.S. intelligence agencies, the mastermind of the Trade Center bombing is captured in Pakistan.

(TIME, Feb. 20, 1995, p. 24)

美國情治人員歷經又氣又惱的全球奔波和<u>大規模</u>追緝後，終於在巴基斯坦逮到世貿中心爆炸案的主謀。

註 infernal (a.) 令人惱怒的；odyssey (n.) 長期的冒險旅行

□ 408 **exuberant** [ɪɡˋzjubərənt] (a.) 興奮難抑的

同 lively

"We think," says an <u>exuberant</u> Larry Gilbert, CyberCash's vice president and general manager, "it's going to be the core of electronic commerce on the Internet." (TIME, Oct. 7, 1996, p. 40)

網路現金公司的副總裁兼總經理賴瑞‧吉爾伯特<u>興奮難抑</u>說：「我們認為，這將成為網際網路電子交易的核心。」

□ 409 **exultant** [ɪɡˋzʌltn̩t] (a.) 雀躍的，欣喜若狂的

同 delighted

For the men and women who fought and won the war in Europe, V-E day meant the <u>exultant</u>, resounding vindication of good against evil.

(TIME, May 15, 1995, p. 52)

對第二次世界大戰期間參加歐戰並戰勝的男男女女而言，德國投降日是對邪不勝正的一項<u>令人雀躍的</u>偉大證明。

註 resounding (a.) 轟動的，極大的（成功）；vindication (n.) 證明

☐ 410 **fanatic** [fə`nætɪk] (a.) 狂熱的　(n.) 狂熱份子

同 (a.) fanatical
(n.) extremist

The two <u>fanatic</u> Puerto Rican nationalists who tried to assassinate[492] Harry Truman in 1950 attacked him when he was living across the street in Blair House while the White House was being renovated. (TIME, Nov. 14, 1994, p. 66)
這兩名<u>狂熱的</u>波多黎各民族主義份子，於1950年試圖暗殺杜魯門，當他們攻擊杜魯門時，白宮因正在翻修，杜魯門住在白宮對面的布萊爾館。

☐ 411 **feasible** [`fizəbl̩] (a.) 可行的，行得通的

同 practicable

Reading to children is easy, affordable and <u>feasible</u> for parents no matter what their level of education or economic station in life.
(TIME, Feb. 24, 1997, p. 37)
不管父母的教育水準、經濟地位是高是低，唸書給孩子聽都是容易、負擔得起且<u>可行的</u>事。

☐ 412 **feeble** [`fibl̩] (a.) 1.性格軟弱的，不敢採取強勢作為的；2.虛弱的，脆弱的

同 1. ineffectual

Soldiers will vote in the next presidential election for a leader who will protest more vigorously[107] the <u>feeble</u> overall reforms of the present government .... (TIME, Jan. 23, 1995, p. 48)
下次總統選舉軍人會支持的候選人，將是敢更大聲反對現行政府<u>軟弱的</u>整體政策改革的領導者。

☐ 413 **fervent** [`fɜvənt] (a.) 熱烈的，強烈的

同 ardent

The Sony Playstation has acquired[115] a <u>fervent</u> following. (TIME, May 20, 1996, p. 60)
新力公司的「遊戲站」遊戲機推出後獲得<u>熱烈的</u>支持。

☐ 414 **forthcoming** [forθ`kʌmɪŋ] (a.) 即將來到的

Whether more money will be <u>forthcoming</u> is an open question. (TIME, Aug. 19, 1996, p. 44)
是否<u>會有</u>更多經費尚在未定之天。

☐ 415 **fractious** [ˈfrækʃəs] (a.) 倔強的，難駕馭的

Italy's embattled Prime Minister Silvio
Berlusconi resigned on Dec. 22 after serving just
seven <u>fractious</u> months. (TIME, Jan. 9, 1995, p. 13)
坐困愁城的義大利總理貝魯斯孔尼，上任才7個月，卻一直
<u>無法順利推行政策</u>，因而在12月22日辭職。
註 embattled (a.) 陷入困境的

☐ 416 **frantic** [ˈfræntɪk] (a.) 十萬火急的，著急的

At a time when American businesses are <u>frantic</u> to
set up shop on the computer networks, those
networks and the telecommunications systems
that carry their traffic are turning out to be
terminally insecure. (TIME, Feb. 27, 1995, p. 34)
當美國商界<u>拼命</u>在電腦網路上設立店面之際，賴以傳送他們
產品訊息的網路和電傳系統的命運卻日益顯得凶多吉少。
註 terminally (adv.) 末期

☐ 417 **full-fledged** [ˌfʊlˈflɛdʒd] (v.) 經過充分訓練的，發展成熟的；
正式的，完全合格的

Brown dwarfs are not quite big and hot enough to
ignite[577] the nuclear-fusion reaction that would
make them shine as <u>full-fledged</u> stars.
(TIME, June 26, 1995, p. 23)
棕矮星的體積還不夠大，熱度也不夠高，還不足以引發核融
合反應；棕矮星必須經過此一反應才會發光，成為<u>成熟的星
星</u>。

☐ 418 **furious** [ˋfjʊrɪəs] (a.)（速度、活動）激烈的，用力的；憤怒的

There was Australian sculler Henry R. Pearce, who rested his oars during an Olympic heat in Amsterdam in 1928 to let a family of ducks paddle across his path, then picked up the stroke at a <u>furious</u> pace, and won by 20 lengths ....

(TIME, June 24, 1996, p. 52)

澳洲的輕艇選手伯爾斯在1928年阿姆斯特丹奧運的一場預賽中停下了槳，讓一家子的鴨子游過他的航道，然後拾起槳拚命划，最後以20個船身長的差距贏得比賽。

☐ 419 **genetic** [dʒəˋnɛtɪk] (a.) 遺傳上的

In fact, the diversity among individuals is so enormous that the whole concept of race becomes meaningless at the <u>genetic</u> level.

(TIME, Jan. 16, 1995, p. 54)

事實上人與人間差異極大，就<u>遺傳</u>的層面來講，種族這一概括性的意涵也就變得毫無意義。

☐ 420 **giddy** [ˋgɪdɪ] (a.)（速度、高度）令人頭昏眼花的；非常快樂的，異常興奮的

Clark and Andreessen find themselves riding the decade's <u>giddiest</u> economic bubble, counting their stock options and cutting deals with everyone from telephone companies to Hollywood.

(TIME, May 27, 1996, p. 67)

克拉克與安德里森發現自己正享著90年代<u>最快速</u>的經濟成長，一面算著自己的優先認股權，一面談著生意，從電話公司到好萊塢，都是生意對象。

註 stock option　優先認股權，通常指企業給予內部高級主管的一項特別權利，讓他們可以在特定期間內用特別優惠的價格購買該公司的股票或債券。

☐ 421 **gorgeous** [`gɔrdʒəs] (a.) 很美的

同 beautiful

The decline in estrogen often coincides[886] with many life changes. Your children grow up and move away. You don't look as <u>gorgeous</u> as you used to, and your husband leaves you for a younger woman. (TIME, June 26, 1995, p. 46)

雌激素的減少，往往伴隨著許多生活上的改變：孩子長大，搬出去了；你不再年輕<u>貌美</u>；丈夫棄你而去，投向年輕女子的懷抱。

☐ 422 **heady** [`hɛdɪ] (a.) 令人興奮的，飄飄然的，心花怒放的

In the <u>heady</u> days after Netscape's ballistic[805] initial[428] public offering in August last year—the stock shot from \$27 to \$71 during its first day of trading—Barksdale preached humility in the company's cramped halls. (TIME, Sept. 16, 1996, p. 41)

去年8月網景股票公開上市後，股票迅速增值，在第一個交易日就從27美元跳升至71美元，在那段<u>飄飄然的</u>日子裡，巴斯迪爾在公司狹窄的大廳裡諄諄教導公司員工要謙虛一點。

註 public offering（證券）公開發行；shoot (v.)（價格）暴漲；preach (v.) 倡導，鼓吹（理念、善行）；cramped (a.)（空間）狹小的

☐ 423 **illiterate** [ɪ`lɪtərɪt] (a.) 不識字的

The Chinese in Singapore were the descendants of <u>illiterate</u>, landless peasants from Guangdong and Fujian. (TIME, Mar. 3, 1997, p. 39)

新加坡的中國人都是來自廣東福建那<u>些目不識丁</u>、無田無地的貧苦農夫的後裔。

☐ 424 **incessant** [ɪn`sɛsənt] (a.) 不停的，不斷的

同 constant
反 intermittent

Offscreen, the couple's marriage was marred by Amaz's drinking, gambling and <u>incessant</u> philandering. (TIME, Nov. 21, 1994, p. 117)

在實際的生活裡，這對明星夫妻的婚姻卻毀在阿瑪茲酗酒、賭博與風流韻事<u>不斷</u>上。

註 offscreen (adv.)（影視明星）實際生活上；mar (v.) 破壞，糟蹋；philandering (n.) 玩弄女人，拈花惹草

☐ 425 **incumbent** [ɪn`kʌmbənt] (a.) 現職的

Ronald Reagan crushed Jimmy Carter in 1980 in part because the <u>incumbent</u> Carter had been flummoxed by the taking of American hostages in Iran. (TIME, Sept. 2, 1996, p. 23)
雷根之所以能在1980年擊敗卡特當選總統，部分是因為美國人被伊朗挾持為人質的事件，讓<u>在職的</u>卡特總統不知所措。
註 flummox (v.) 使驚慌失措

☐ 426 **indignant** [ɪn`dɪgnənt] (a.) 憤憤不平的

It drew nearly 800 letters from readers (many predictably <u>indignant</u>), the fourth largest mail response to any story this year. (TIME, Oct. 31, 1994, p. 4)
這篇報導引來近800封讀者來函（其中有許多可想而知是<u>非常憤慨</u>），是本雜誌今年激起第四多讀者來函的一項報導。

☐ 427 **inherent** [ɪn`hɪrənt] (a.) 固有的，天生的

同 intrinsic

Says Cardinal Edward Clancy, head of the Roman Catholic Church in Australia: "With the introduction of the principle <u>inherent</u> in euthanasia, our society as we know it begins immediately to unravel[963]." (TIME, Oct. 7, 1996, p. 34)
澳洲天主教領袖、樞機主教克蘭西說：「隨著安樂死這個行為裡<u>固有</u>原則的引進，我們所熟悉的社會立即開始崩解。」

☐ 428 **initial** [ɪ`nɪʃəl] (a.) 首度的，最初的，開始的

Clouds and dust from the (comet's) <u>initial</u> impact and gases from subsequent volcanoes could have spread around the globe, blocking sunlight and altering the climate, killing off the dinosaurs.
(TIME, Jan. 9, 1995, p. 59)
（彗星的）<u>第一擊</u>所產生的煙、塵，以及隨後火山噴出的氣體，可能布滿整個地球，遮天蔽日，改變氣候，使恐龍死亡。
註 block (v.) 阻礙

☐ 429 **integral** [ˋɪntəɡrəl] (a.) 必需的，不可或缺的

同 basic
fundamental

When people understand that being gay or lesbian is an <u>integral</u> characteristic, they are more open-minded about equality for gay Americans.

(TIME, June 12, 1995, p. 60)

當人們知道男同性戀或女同性戀傾向是人類<u>不可或缺的</u>心理特質後，對於美國同性戀者的平等權就更能坦然面對。

☐ 430 **intricate** [ˋɪntrəkɪt] (a.) 複雜的

反 simple

A touch of paranoia is not a bad thing to bring to the computer-software business, where shifting alliances, rapid technological changes and <u>intricate</u> co-dependencies make plotting long-term strategies hazardous. (TIME, June 5, 1995, p. 46)

踏入電腦軟體這個行業，帶點偏執狂並不是件壞事，因為在這個行業裡，業者間分分合合，科技日新月異，互依的關係<u>錯綜複雜</u>，制定長程發展策略反倒危險。

註 a touch of 些許，微量；hazardous (a.) 危險的，同 dangerous

☐ 431 **invalid** [ɪnˋvælɪd] (a.) 無效的，作廢的

If it is proved that the President-elect's campaign[285] received drug-trafficking money, he should resign because his mandate[328] would be <u>invalid</u>. (TIME, July 4, 1994, p. 49)

如果總統競選活動證實曾收受毒品走私所獲得的金錢，那他就該辭職下台，因為選舉授予他的權力將屬<u>無效</u>。

☐ 432 **invariably** [ɪnˋværɪəblɪ] (adv.) 必定地，不變地

Known as one of the best golfers in Taiwan's officialdom, Lee Teng-hui can break 80 on a good day. His drives off the tee are almost <u>invariably</u> long and true. (TIME, Jan. 1, 1996, p. 54)

李登輝被認為是台灣政壇最高桿的高爾夫球手之一，狀況好時能打出低於80桿的成績。他從球座上揮出的長打幾乎<u>都是</u>既遠又準。

□ 433 **lavish** [ˋlævɪʃ] (a.) 鋪張的，奢華的

同 extravagant

The <u>lavish</u> dinner that chef John Folse prepared for a private party of Procter & Gamble executives tasted rich enough to make a cardiologist apoplectic. (TIME, Jan. 8, 1996, p. 30)
大廚師福爾斯替寶鹼公司高級主管的私人晚宴所準備的<u>奢華</u>晚餐，豐盛的程度足以讓心臟血管學家腦中風。

註 apoplectic (a.) 中風的

□ 434 **lethal** [ˋliθəl] (a.) 致命的

Too often, they have found, the one-drug approach allows a few malignant cells to survive and blossom[499] into an even more <u>lethal</u> tumor. (TIME, Jan. 6, 1997, p. 30)
他們發現單一藥物的治療方式往往會使一些癌細胞存活下來，並且演變成更<u>要命的</u>腫瘤。

註 malignant (a.) 惡性的，癌的

□ 435 **lucrative** [ˋlukrətɪv] (a.) 可獲利的，賺錢的

With concert fees reportedly in the $40,000-plus range, the show seems a <u>lucrative</u> proposition. (TIME, Mar. 18, 1996, p. 56)
據說每場音樂會的酬勞超過4萬美金，所以這表演看來是筆<u>賺錢</u>生意。

註 proposition (n.)（擬議中或正在興辦的）事業，生意

□ 436 **ludicrous** [ˋludɪkrəs] (a.) 可笑的，滑稽的

同 ridiculous

The surgeon denounces[534] that allegation as <u>ludicrous</u>. (TIME, May 15, 1995, p. 60)
這名外科醫生痛斥那項指控，指其為<u>荒誕不稽</u>。

註 allegation (n.) 法律用語，（尤指有待證實的）指控

□ 437 **malicious** [məˈlɪʃəs] (a.) 懷惡意的，居心不良的

Earlier in the week Nichols was charged with "malicious damage" to the Alfred P. Murray Federal Building .... (TIME, May 22, 1995, p. 43)
本週稍早尼古拉遭人指控，罪名是「蓄意破壞」穆拉聯邦大樓。

□ 438 **mock** [mɑk] (a.) 煞有其事的，假裝的

Clinton, he reported with a tone of mock confidence, was at a prayer breakfast across town with religious leaders. (TIME, Feb. 14, 1994, p. 20)
他裝出很肯定的語氣報導說，柯林頓就在對面城鎮與宗教領袖舉行祈禱早餐會。

(a.) 模擬的，演習的

The Pentagon revealed that three weeks ago Army Rangers and Navy Seals had conducted[141] practice runs for an invasion of Haiti: staging[249] a mock attack on an isolated[589] airfield at Eglin Air Force Base in Florida. (TIME, July 18, 1994, p. 20)
美國國防部透露，3週前陸軍突擊部隊和海軍「海豹」特種部隊已針對入侵海地進行了數場演習，也就是在佛羅里達的埃格林空軍基地對一孤立無援的機場進行模擬攻擊。

□ 439 **mundane** [mʌndeɪn] (a.) 世俗的，平凡的

(Film critic) Libby's columns serve as a continuing account of her amusingly mundane life and the peripheral role that movies play in it.
(TIME, Dec. 5, 1994, p. 102)
影評家李比寫專欄文章，等於是在不斷描寫自己那平凡而快意的生活，以及電影在她生活中所扮演的次要角色。
註 peripheral (a.) 周邊的，次要的

普通字
形容詞／副詞

□ 440 **optional** [ˋɑpʃən!] (a.) 可選擇的，非強制的

反 mandatory
compulsory

China is not Haiti or Bosnia, places where America's involvement may be desirable but is ultimately <u>optional</u>. China is not optional.

(TIME, Mar. 25, 1996, p. 13)

中國不是海地，也不是波士尼亞。美國介入那兩個國家，或許不是賠本生意，但要不要介入終究可自主決定；要不要介入中國事務，則不是美國能<u>選擇的</u>。

□ 441 **perennial** [pəˋrɛnɪəl] (a.) 長期間持續的

同 constant
continual

As she did in her <u>perennial</u> best seller, ... Tannen argues that the sexes baffle and bewilder each other, not because they have vastly different psychological makeups, but because they have distinct[29] conversational styles. (TIME, Oct. 3, 1994, p. 60)

正如譚內在其<u>歷久不衰的</u>暢銷書中所述，她堅稱男女兩性會對對方感到迷惘，捉摸不透，並非因為雙方在心理特質上有極大的差異，而是因為截然不同的對談風格。

註 baffle (v.) 使困惑，使張惶失措；make-up (n.) 特質，性格

□ 442 **placid** [ˋplæsɪd] (a.) 平靜的

同 tranquil

The view from Quemoy's Horse Hill military observation station across the 2.4 km of sea that separates the island from China seems too <u>placid</u> to be true. (TIME, Feb. 19, 1996, p. 21)

從金門馬丘軍事瞭望台放眼望過這片分隔金門與中國大陸的2.4公里海域，景象似乎太平靜了，<u>平靜</u>得讓人以為不是真的。

□ 443 **poised** [pɔɪzd] (a.) 準備好做⋯

同 all set

China, its treasury bursting with foreign reserves and its stock markets surging[643], is <u>poised</u> for stable growth. (TIME, Feb. 24, 1997, p. 50)

中國大陸的國庫塞滿了外匯，股市暢旺，已經<u>具備</u>穩定成長的<u>條件</u>。

註 to burst with 充滿

| optional | perennial | placid | poised | **135** |

☐ 444 **precarious** [prɪˋkɛrɪəs] (a.) 岌岌可危的

同 uncertain
　　unstable
反 stable
　　secure

We are in a very <u>precarious</u> position because investors' confidence is disconnected from any hard-hitting analysis of what is underlying the economy. (TIME, Feb. 24, 1997, p. 44)

我們正處於<u>非常危險的</u>狀態中，因為投資人的信心已與對經濟深層因素的坦率分析脫節。

註 hard-hitting (a.)（對難題或爭議）大膽直言的

☐ 445 **predominant** [prɪˋdɑmənənt] (a.) 主要的

In the two small Central African nations of Rwanda and Burundi, where politics is still dominated by the ancient rivalry between the <u>predominant</u> Hutu and minority Tutsi tribes, pure tribal enmity was behind the bloodshed.

(TIME, Apr. 18, 1994, p. 44)

中非兩小國盧安達、蒲隆地，其政治仍為<u>居優勢的</u>胡圖族和居少數的圖西族間的世仇對立所左右，這次的流血事件其背後純粹是種族仇恨在作崇。

註 enmity (n.) 敵意，對立

☐ 446 **prestigious** [prɛsˋtɪdʒɪəs] (a.) 有名望的

Privileged and smart, he had been accepted by the <u>prestigious</u> All-India School of Medical Sciences at 17. (TIME, June 24, 1996, p. 47)

出生在優渥環境再加上聰明，他17歲就得到<u>極負盛名的</u>全印度醫科大學入學許可。

註 privileged (a.)（因有錢或居上流階層而）比別人占優勢的

☐ [447] **presumably** [prɪˋzuməblɪ] (adv.) 據推測，大概

The government also unveiled[658] an emergency plan to lower the yen by, among other things, spending more on public works, which would presumably stimulate[253] the economy and thus perk up demand for imports. (TIME, Apr. 24, 1995, p. 58)

政府當局也宣布了一項緊急應變計劃，以讓日圓貶值，其中最重要的措施就是提高公共支出，此舉大概可刺激經濟，進而提振內需市場。

註 to perk up 使…振作

☐ [448] **prone** [pron] (a.) 傾向於，易於

The tactic[367] is only moderately effective and has side effects that can be as bad as the disease itself, leaving patients drained[547] of energy and prone to sores and other infections. (TIME, Oct. 28, 1996, p. 70)

這種方法療效平平，所產生的副作用可能和疾病本身一樣嚴重，耗盡病患的精力，讓病患容易產生痠痛，受到其他感染。

☐ [449] **quaint** [kwɛnt] (a.) 因樣式古老、罕見而吸引人的

When a trend went out of style, we used to be forgiving of it and think it was quaint ....

(TIME, Aug. 8, 1994, p. 48)

當流行不再流行，我們總是寬大爲懷，認爲它還饒富古趣。

☐ [450] **rampant** [ˋræmpənt] (a.) 猖獗的

They said that tax evasion is rampant; that the *yakuza*, Japan's mafia, has its hooks in the sport; and most stingingly, that many of the matches are fixed. (TIME, Sept. 30, 1996, p. 28)

他們指出逃漏稅相當猖獗，日本的黑社會也插上一腳; 最尖銳的指控是許多比賽勝負都早已定好。

註 stingingly (adv.) （言詞）刺傷人的，尖刻的;
　　fix (v.) 以不正當手段操縱（比賽、選舉等）

☐ 451 **rash** [ræʃ] (a.) 鹵莽的

同 hasty
impulsive
反 careful

Says a China specialist at the U.S. State Department: "The folks in Taiwan who might do something <u>rash</u> should not assume[493] we would come to their aid, and the folks in Beijing who might do something militarily should not assume[493] we won't." (TIME, Feb. 12, 1996, p. 18)
美國國務院某中國專家說：「台灣那些想採取<u>激進</u>舉動的人別認爲我們會去幫忙；而北京那些想動武的人也別認爲我們不會去幫台灣。」

☐ 452 **requisite** [ˈrɛkwəzɪt] (a.) 必需的，不可或缺的

同 required

TIME has picked 50 with the <u>requisite</u> ambition, vision and community spirit to help guide us in the new millennium. (TIME, Dec. 5, 1994, p. 48)
時代雜誌挑出了50人，作爲我們在下一個一千年處事的明燈，他們都具備了<u>不可或缺的</u>雄心、遠見和關懷社會的精神。

☐ 453 **resurgent** [rɪˈsɜdʒənt] (a.) 復活的，復甦的

The President's Russia policy, he charged, was based not on recognition of Moscow's threatening[263], <u>resurgent</u> nationalism but on misguided romanticism. (TIME, July 8, 1996, p. 29)
他指責總統的俄國政策不是建立在對莫斯科<u>已復活</u>而具威脅性的民族主義的了解之上，而是建立在錯誤的浪漫主義上。

☐ 454 **robust** [roˈbʌst] (a.) 健康的，強健的

Communist China, contrasted by Taiwan's <u>robust</u> economy and the blooming[677] of individual liberty, is threatening[263] to punish any country that even considers a two-China policy. (TIME, Jan. 29, 1996, p. 38)
台灣享有<u>強大的</u>經濟與充分的個人自由，與之形成強烈對比的共產中國則威脅將懲罰任何考慮「兩個中國」政策的國家。

☐ 455 **sentimental** [ˌsɛntəˋmɛntl̩] (a.) 多愁善感的

Americans have sometimes sought a kind of moral cleansing in children's adventures. It is part of an American theology of redemption by kids— a <u>sentimental</u> reassertion of the nation's conception of its own innocence.

(TIME, Apr. 22, 1996, p. 39)

美國人有時想藉著孩童的冒險旅程，來尋求道德的滌清，這個習慣植於美國人深信兒童可以帶來救贖——這是一種<u>溫情主義式</u>的重申，強調美國人純真一如孩童。

註 theology (n.)（某一種）神學理論；redemption (n.)（宗教）救贖；
reassertion (n.)（意見、觀念）再次被提出，重申

☐ 456 **sheer** [ʃɪr] (a.) 完全的

It's true that farmers there will suffer as protective trade barriers fall. But a deeper source of their discontent is <u>sheer</u>, longstanding poverty.

(TIME, Jan. 9, 1995, p. 46)

的確，一旦保護性的貿易壁壘廢掉，那裡的農民日子將會難過，但農民心中更深的不滿，來自長久以來未曾改善的<u>赤貧</u>處境。

☐ 457 **simmering** [ˋsɪmərɪŋ] (a.)（爭吵、暴力）即將爆發的

A major pact was signed by the two leaders (of China and Russia) and the Presidents of Kazakhstan, Kyrgyzstan and Tajikistan to quell[613] long <u>simmering</u> disputes[302] along Russia's southern border. (TIME, May 6, 1996, p. 21)

中、俄領袖和哈薩克、吉爾吉斯與塔吉克三共和國總統簽署了一項主要協定，以消弭俄羅斯南疆長久以來一直<u>蠢蠢欲動</u>的邊界爭端。

□ 458 **simplistic** [sɪmˋplɪstɪk] (a.) 過分單純化的

His lack of leadership allowed the reform forces to fragment and be swamped by such <u>simplistic</u> nationalists as Vladimir Zhirinovsky.

(TIME, Jan. 31, 1994, p. 88)

由於他領導無方，導致改革陣營分崩離析，並被季里諾夫斯基這種總把事情看得<u>太簡單的</u>民族主義分子搞得暈頭轉向。

註 fragment (v.) 分裂，破碎；
to be swamped by... (麻煩、物件等) 大量湧至，應付不來的

□ 459 **simultaneously** [͵saɪməlˋtenɪəslɪ] (adv.) 同時地

A couple of mathematical models ... suggested that HIV would have a hard time <u>simultaneously</u> undergoing[269] the minimum three mutations necessary to resist combination therapy.

(TIME, Dec. 30, 1996/Jan. 6, 1997, p. 30)

根據幾組數學模型，HIV病毒要<u>同時</u>進行最少三種突變才能對抗混合治療法，但要做這樣的突變並不容易。

□ 460 **snap** [snæp] (a.) 倉促的，突然的

<u>Snap decision</u> making ... is a survival skill if you are a hunter. (TIME, July 18, 1994, p. 48)

<u>當機立斷</u>是獵人的一項求生技能。

□ 461 **speculative** [ˋspɛkjə͵letɪv] (a.) 投機的，熱衷於投機買賣的

American investors pour <u>speculative</u> money into Mexico, then snatch it back when times grow hard and Mexico needs it most. (TIME, Mar. 6, 1995, p. 40)

美國投資者抱著<u>投機的</u>心態投資墨西哥，一旦時局變壞，墨國亟需資金時，就突然撤回。

註 snatch (v.) 攫取，搶走

□ 462 **sporadic** [spo`rædɪk] (a.) 零星的，時有時無的

反 continuous

Once inside Grozny, Zarakhovich was struck by the large number of armed citizens, many of whom were making <u>sporadic</u> checks of entering cars. (TIME, Jan. 16, 1995, p. 10)
一進格洛茲尼市，札拉克維奇就被大批的武裝市民給嚇了一跳，其中許多市民正在攔檢進城車輛，但攔檢動作<u>時有時無</u>。

□ 463 **sprawling** [`sprɔlɪŋ] (a.) 蔓延的，廣大的

Chen and Zhang have both said they can not imagine shooting films outside their <u>sprawling</u> homeland. (TIME, Jan. 29, 1996, p. 44)
陳凱歌與張藝謀都說無法想像在自己土生土長的<u>廣大</u>家園來拍戲。

□ 464 **stationary** [`steʃə,nɛrɪ] (a.) 靜止的，固定的

Agriculture boasts its kudzu, the miracle vine promoted[222] as a soil protector in the American Southeast and now despised[895] as an unstoppable weed, able, as Tenner reports, to overwhelm[215] almost any <u>stationary</u> object ....
(TIME, May 27, 1996, p. 67)
「葛」素有「魔藤」之稱，在美國東南部曾被奉爲土壤保護者而大肆推廣，現卻被貶爲除不掉的雜草；農業人士誇稱，他們所引進的葛，依照田納的說法，幾乎可以爬滿所有<u>靜止的</u>物體。

□ 465 **stringent** [`strɪndʒənt] (a.) 嚴格的

同 rigorous

The House approved and sent to the Senate for its expected approval a <u>stringent</u> ban[128] on gifts from lobbyists. (TIME, Oct. 10, 1994, p. 19)
衆議院通過了一項針對遊說者的贈禮所制定的<u>嚴格</u>禁令，並已送往參院審議，可望也會通過。

□ [466] **sublime** [sə`blaɪm] (a.) 卓越的，出色的

同 heavenly

By the final shot, of a <u>sublime</u> Beauty and her transformed[268] Beast borne magically aloft[381] and soaring[246] through the clouds, the audience is as enchanted as the characters[287]. (TIME, Dec. 19, 1994, p. 72)

在這影片的最後一段，一名<u>出色的</u>美女和她那位由人變成的野獸，神奇地被高高舉起，向上高飛，衝破雲霄，這時觀眾就像劇中的角色一樣也著了迷。

註 enchanted (a.) 陶醉的，著迷的

□ [467] **subsequent** [`sʌbsɪ͵kwɛnt] (a.) 後來的

反 prior

She spent her first eight years in what is now Slovakia, and after her parents' divorce and her mother Melanie's <u>subsequent</u> marriage to a Swiss computer executive, she moved to Trubbach, Switzerland. (TIME, Sept. 16, 1996, p. 49)

8歲以前她都待在現在的斯洛伐克共和國，在父母仳離及母親米蘭妮<u>再嫁</u>給一名瑞士電腦公司主管之後，她搬到瑞士杜魯巴赫。

□ [468] **tantalizing** [`tænt͵laɪzɪŋ] (a.) 令人迫不急待的，吊胃口的

It is a <u>tantalizing</u> but daunting[403] target. (TIME, Feb. 27, 1995, p. 21)

這個目標讓人<u>既期待</u>又害怕。

□ [469] **tedious** [`tidɪəs] (a.) 冗長而乏味的

同 boring

To do this, the scientists will have to track[265] the locations of hundreds of aftershocks, a lengthy and <u>tedious</u> process. (TIME, Jan. 31, 1994, p. 45)

要這麼做，就表示科學家必須查出數百次餘震的發生位置，而這過程將是<u>冗長而乏味的</u>。

☐ 470 **tentative** [`tɛntətɪv] (a.) 初步的，未完全定案的

同 uncertain
反 firm

Still, it's easy to understand the <u>tentative</u> sense of hope and excitement that has spread across the AIDS community in the months since the Vancouver conference. Ho's speech provided the first concrete evidence that HIV is not insurmountable. (TIME, Dec. 30, 1996/Jan. 6, 1997, p. 26)
儘管如此，溫哥華會議之後幾個月裡，愛滋病圈<u>一時間</u>瀰漫著希望與激動，這種感覺是不難理解的。因爲何大一的演講首次提供了明確的證據，證明愛滋病並非不治之症。

註 insurmountable (n.)（障礙）不能克服的

☐ 471 **thrilling** [`θrɪlɪŋ] (a.) 令人興奮的，刺激的

同 exciting

Susan McCray ... struggles daily to convince[150] her students that learning can be <u>thrilling</u> for its own sake as well as a ticket to a better life. (TIME, Jan. 30 1995, p. 52)
麥克瑞每天都在努力讓學生相信，學習不僅是獲得更美滿生活的手段，爲學習而學習也足以令人<u>感動莫名</u>。

☐ 472 **trivial** [`trɪvɪəl] (a.) 微不足道的

同 insignificant

There is no evidence of criminality in Whitewater --but that doesn't mean it's <u>trivial</u>. (TIME, Mar. 21, 1994, p. 39)
白水案並未發現任何犯罪證據，但這不表示此案<u>無關緊要</u>。

☐ 473 **tumultuous** [tjuˋmʌltʃuəs] (a.) 騷亂的

Later the Kennedys visited France, and the welcome was <u>tumultuous</u>. (TIME, May 30, 1994, p. 28)
接著甘迺迪一家人訪問了法國，歡迎場面人群<u>騷動</u>。

☐ 474 **turbulent** [ˋtɝbjələnt] (a.) 動盪不安的

In a <u>turbulent</u> world, peace, law and some degree of order will have to be established before the human race can begin seriously to tackle the great problems and opportunities of the next century.
(TIME, Oct. 23, 1995, p. 30)

在<u>亂世</u>，人類必須先建立和平、法律和某種程度的秩序，才能眞正開始處理下一世紀的重大問題和機會。

註 tackle (v.) 解決，處理

☐ 475 **untapped** [ʌnˋtæpt] (a.) 未被開發的

反 exploited

On the contrary, this is an age of uncommonly universal productivity, in which the spread of education, affluence and the means to communicate has released <u>untapped</u> mental powers in every corner of the planet.
(TIME, Sept. 11, 1995, p. 60)

相反的，這是個生產力全面爆發的不尋常時代，因爲敎育、財富與傳播工具的普及，讓全球每個角落<u>潛藏的</u>心智才能都得以釋放出來。

註 affluence (n.) 富裕

☐ 476 **vaunted** [ˋvɔntɪd] (a.) 炫耀的，自誇的

His most <u>vaunted</u> exploits were exposed as largely fictitious. (TIME, Aug. 29, 1994, p. 53)

他最<u>自豪</u>的功績，攤開一看大抵都是虛構的。

註 exploit (n.) 偉業，功績；fictitious (a.) 虛構的，想像的

☐ 477 **versatile** [ˋvɝsətl̩] (a.) 多才多藝的

He was the Beatles' most <u>versatile</u> singer, and not just as a balladeer. (TIME, Nov. 20, 1995, p. 50)

他是披頭四中最<u>多才多藝的</u>歌手，不只是個民謠歌手。

☐ 478 **viable** [ˋvaɪəbl] (a.) 可行的

Barksdale knows that long-term success lies in turning Navigator into a <u>viable</u> alternative to Windows. (TIME, Sept. 16, 1996, p. 43)

巴斯迪爾知道，長遠的成功端賴把「領航員」轉型成<u>可以取代</u>「視窗」的代用品。

☐ 479 **vocal** [ˋvokl] (a.) 大聲說出主張的

In a blistering op-ed article in the Los Angeles *Times*, Ross Perot, NAFTA's most <u>vocal</u> adversary[665], declared the devaluation would cost the U.S. thousands more jobs and as much as $20 billion in lost investment capital.

(TIME, June 5, 1995, p. 22)

培洛是反對設立北美自由貿易區<u>最有力</u>的大將，他在《洛杉磯時報》寫了一篇充滿火藥味的專欄文章，指出貶值將使美國喪失數千個工作機會，並流失高達200億美元的投資額。

註 blistering (a.) (言詞) 充滿怒氣的，尖酸的；
op-ed (n.) (報紙的) 專欄文章

☐ 480 **with a vengeance** 徹底地，完全地

The communist northern tier of a peninsula once known as the Hermit Kingdom has lived up to that name <u>with a vengeance</u> .... (TIME, July 18, 1994, p. 26)

這座半島一度稱爲「隱士王國」，如今這個半島北部的共產國度就眞的成爲<u>不折不扣</u>的隱士王國。

註 tier (n.) 層，段

普通字動詞(481~663)，共183字

- [ ] abhor 痛恨，厭惡
- [ ] accelerate 加速
- [ ] accommodate 包容，適應，容納
- [ ] accumulate 累積
- [ ] administer 給藥，施行
- [ ] adore 熱愛
- [ ] afflict 折磨，使苦惱
- [ ] alleviate 減輕
- [ ] annihilate 毀滅
- [ ] appease 平息，安撫
- [ ] articulate 清楚說明
- [ ] assassinate 刺殺
- [ ] assume 假定，以為
- [ ] backfire 招致反效果
- [ ] banish 排除
- [ ] bar 禁止
- [ ] bill 宣傳
- [ ] blast 引爆，炸開
- [ ] blossom 開花，出現成果
- [ ] bode 預示
- [ ] bounce 彈起，反彈
- [ ] bully 威嚇，欺侮
- [ ] bust 逮捕；搜查
- [ ] bypass 避開，繞過
- [ ] capitalize (on) 利用
- [ ] circumvent 規避
- [ ] cite 提到，舉出
- [ ] claim 奪走（性命）
- [ ] collaborate 合作
- [ ] commit 使承諾，使作出保證
- [ ] complement 補足
- [ ] compliment 讚美，恭維
- [ ] comprehend 理解
- [ ] comprise 擁有，由…構成
- [ ] conceal 掩飾
- [ ] confiscate 沒收，充公
- [ ] conjure (up) 使浮現腦際，想起
- [ ] consult 諮詢
- [ ] contain 圍堵
- [ ] contract 收縮
- [ ] contradict 與…矛盾，牴觸
- [ ] convene 召開會議
- [ ] coordinate 協調，整合
- [ ] covet 垂涎，覬覦
- [ ] crash 電腦當機
- [ ] crave 渴求
- [ ] cripple 使不良於行

- [ ] cruise 汽車定速行駛，（船，飛機）巡航
- [ ] crumble 崩潰，消失
- [ ] crunch 咬嚼，引申為電腦高速處理
- [ ] cultivate 培養，磨練
- [ ] defect 變節
- [ ] defy 反抗
- [ ] denounce 公開指責
- [ ] deploy 部署
- [ ] depreciate 貶值，折舊
- [ ] derail 使出軌，破壞
- [ ] derive 源自，獲得
- [ ] deter 制止，妨礙
- [ ] dictate 指揮
- [ ] diminish 減少，衰退
- [ ] discipline 懲罰
- [ ] disclose 揭發
- [ ] disdain 厭惡
- [ ] dissolve 解體
- [ ] distract 使分神
- [ ] drain 排乾，流掉，逐漸耗竭
- [ ] dwarf 令相形見絀
- [ ] elaborate 詳述
- [ ] embed 植入，深植於
- [ ] embody 體現
- [ ] emulate 仿效
- [ ] engineer 策劃，創造，設計
- [ ] enlist 召募
- [ ] envision 預見，想像
- [ ] eradicate 根除，拔除
- [ ] erupt 爆發
- [ ] escalate 升高
- [ ] escort 護送，伴隨
- [ ] evaluate 評估
- [ ] evoke 喚起，引起
- [ ] expire 到期
- [ ] fake 假裝，佯做
- [ ] feature (in) 以…為號召，特別介紹
- [ ] foresee 預料
- [ ] foreshadow 預示，先兆
- [ ] for(e)go 放棄
- [ ] foster 促進，助長
- [ ] fret 煩惱，煩躁
- [ ] hamper 阻礙
- [ ] harass 騷擾
- [ ] harbor 抱持（情感）
- [ ] harness 駕馭，利用
- [ ] haunt （如幽靈般）縈繞於…之腦海中

☐ heap (on)	對（某人）一再加以（稱讚或侮辱）	☐ renounce	宣誓放棄
☐ hobble	妨礙，使難以運作	☐ repent	悔改
☐ ignite	點燃，激發	☐ restrain	抑制，遏止
☐ illustrate	闡明	☐ retrieve	取回
☐ immerse (oneself)	熱衷於，專心於	☐ savor	品味
☐ imply	暗指，含…之意，意謂	☐ scramble	爭相搶奪
☐ incorporate	使合併，併入，納入	☐ scrape	刮除
☐ induce	引發	☐ seduce	誘惑
☐ indulge	隨心所欲地享受	☐ shatter	使粉碎
☐ inflict	施加	☐ shell	砲擊
☐ instill	逐漸灌輸，注入	☐ shun	規避
☐ intervene	介入	☐ shuttle	往返，穿梭
☐ intimidate	威脅，恐嚇	☐ snap	毫不留情面地說
☐ intrigue	激起（某人）好奇心	☐ snap up	爭相搶購
☐ isolate	孤立，隔離	☐ spell	意味，招致
☐ jeopardize	危及	☐ spur	刺激，激勵
☐ lapse	陷入（某種狀態）	☐ strand	使進退兩難，使束手無策
☐ lobby	遊說	☐ strangle	（把人）勒死，抑制
☐ locate	尋找	☐ stride	大跨步
☐ loom	（危險）迫近	☐ stuff	充塞，裝滿
☐ loot	掠奪，搜括	☐ stumble	摔倒，喻失敗
☐ manifest	表明，顯露	☐ subsidize	給與補助金
☐ marvel	表示驚異，讚嘆	☐ surf	衝浪，喻上網遨遊
☐ monitor	監視	☐ surge	急速上升，暴漲
☐ moonlight	兼差	☐ surpass	超越，凌駕
☐ mourn	哀悼	☐ swarm	蜂擁
☐ multiply	大量增加	☐ tamper	篡改
☐ nurture	培育，養成	☐ tap	開發，利用
☐ outfit	配備，供給	☐ tempt	誘惑
☐ penetrate	看透他人心思，識破	☐ tip	使傾斜
☐ phase (in/out)	逐漸引進或逐步廢除	☐ topple	推翻，傾倒
☐ plunge	衝進，跳進	☐ torment	折磨
☐ proclaim	宣稱	☐ trail	尾隨，追蹤
☐ prod	刺激，激勵	☐ trigger	觸發
☐ prompt	促使	☐ tug	用力拉
☐ prosecute	起訴，告發	☐ uncover	揭發，發現
☐ provoke	引起，激發	☐ underline	強調
☐ prowl	潛行（尋找竊取機會）	☐ unravel	弄清楚，解開（謎題、祕密等）
☐ quell	壓制	☐ unveil	首次發表（新產品、計畫）
☐ rebound	止跌回升，反彈	☐ vanish	消失
☐ reclaim	索回	☐ verify	證實
☐ reconcile	調解	☐ warrant	視…為正當，認可
☐ recruit	召募，吸收	☐ whip	擊敗
☐ relate	敘述	☐ wreck	破壞
☐ relinquish	放棄		

☐ 481 **abhor** [əb`hɔr] (v.) 痛恨，厭惡

同 detest

In a culture that traditionally <u>abhors</u> confrontation, the first native Taiwanese head of state prefers to stand on principle and say what's on his mind. (TIME, Jan. 1, 1996, p. 54)

中國文化的傳統是<u>厭惡</u>衝突，這位首位的台灣人領袖卻喜歡堅持原則並敢於說出心中的想法。

☐ 482 **accelerate** [æk`sɛlə,ret] (v.) 加速

There are some who want to <u>accelerate</u> the pace on reform and those who want it to slow down.

(TIME, May 1, 1995, p. 79)

有人想<u>加快</u>改革的腳步，有人則想放慢。

☐ 483 **accommodate** [ə`kɑmə,det] (v.) 包容，適應，容納

Netscape perpetually updates its browser to <u>accommodate</u> new Web applications.

(TIME, June 17, 1996, p. 16)

網景不斷在更新它的導覽器，以求與新的全球資訊網應用軟體<u>相容</u>。

☐ 484 **accumulate** [ə`kjumjə,let] (v.) 累積

同 build up

In sumo's complicated, multitiered ranking system, there are contests in which a win is crucial[21] for one wrestler to gain promotion but is meaningless to his opponent, who may already have <u>accumulated</u> enough victories.

(TIME, Sept. 30, 1996, p. 29)

相撲的體制複雜、層級眾多，有時一場比賽的輸贏對其中一人能否升級事關重大，但對於也許已<u>累積</u>足夠勝場的對手卻無所謂。

註 multitier (a.) 多層的

☐ 485 **administer** [əd`mɪnəstə] (v.) 給藥，施行

同 give

That settled, he <u>administered</u> a stimulant called atropine to strengthen her heartbeat.

(TIME, Sept. 23, 1996, p. 43)

確定了這點之後，他<u>使用</u>一劑叫阿托品的興奮劑來增強她的心跳。

註 stimulant (n.) 興奮劑

☐ 486 **adore** [ə`dor] (v.) 熱愛

For sumo to maintain its special place in the Japanese heart, it will have to deliver the naked displays of girth, strength and purity that the people <u>adore</u>—not the more recent images of greed[319] and dishonesty. (TIME, Sept. 30, 1996, p. 31)

相撲若想保持在日本人心中特別的地位，就得將人們<u>熱愛</u>的嘲位、力量與純潔真正表現出來，而不是最近貪婪、欺瞞的形象。

註 deliver (v.) 履行（所承諾的事物）；girth (n.) 腰圍

☐ 487 **afflict** [ə`flɪkt] (v.) 折磨，使苦惱

同 affect

"The message I take home," he says, "is that diseases <u>afflicting</u> plants and animals can send ripples through economies and societies no less disastrous[28] than those affecting[118] humans."

(TIME, July 8, 1996, p. 41)

他說：「我所得到的重要訊息是：<u>加害</u>於植物和動物的疾病，可能會在經濟與社會領域間接造成多方面的影響，其所帶來的災害不下於那些影響人類的疾病。」

註 ripple (n.) 水面漣漪，喻間接而多方面的影響

□ 488 **alleviate** [ə`livɪ,et] (v.) 減輕

同 ease
反 aggravate

The club's 12,000 members include AIDS patients who say marijuana stimulates[253] their appetite and cancer sufferers who say it <u>alleviates</u> nausea[1016] caused by chemotherapy.

(TIME, Aug. 19, 1996, p. 8)

這個俱樂部有1萬2千名會員，其中包括聲稱大麻可刺激食欲的愛滋病患者以及聲稱大麻可減輕化學治療所引發的作嘔症狀的癌症患者。

註 chemotherapy (n.) 化學治療

□ 489 **annihilate** [ə`naɪə,let] (v.) 毀滅

The Kurds are threatening to <u>annihilate</u> themselves because two rival[358] leaders each hope to establish and control an independent Kurdistan overlapping the borders of Iraq, Turkey, Syria and Iran. (TIME, Mar. 27, 1995, p. 36)

庫德族人正面臨自我毀滅的危險，因為兩支敵對派系的領袖，都想在伊拉克、土耳其、叙利亞、伊朗4國邊界交疊處建立獨立的庫德斯坦國，並將其納入自己控制。

註 overlap (v.) 與…重疊

□ 490 **appease** [ə`piz] (v.) 平息，安撫

同 placate

To salvage the exhibition and <u>appease</u> angry Taiwanese protesters, National Palace Museum director Chin Hsiao-yi and officials from the Metropolitan Museum began a series of delicate diplomatic maneuvers[740]. (TIME, Apr. 1, 1996, p. 47)

為了挽救這次展覽且安撫憤怒的台灣示威者，故宮館長秦孝儀及大都會博物館的官員展開一連串如履薄冰的外交周旋。

註 salvage (v.) 搶救

☐ 491 **articulate** [ɑr`tɪkjə,let] (v.) 清楚說明

The world has had a week to conjure[517] up
nightmare scenarios[361], yet no one has <u>articulated</u>
the most frightening peril[339] posed[219] by human
cloning: rampant[450] self-satisfaction.
(TIME, Mar. 10, 1997, p. 41)

世人已經有一個星期的時間來幻想出各種夢魘式的景象，但
是還沒有人<u>清楚說明</u>複製人類所帶來最駭人的危險：狂妄的
自滿。

☐ 492 **assassinate** [ə`sæsn̩,et] (v.) 刺殺

While Vice President, Nixon allegedly[380]
organized an ill-fated covert plan to <u>assassinate</u>
Fidel Castro. (TIME, Mar. 20, 1995, p. 13)

據說尼克森擔任副總統時，曾策劃了一樁注定失敗的<u>刺殺</u>卡
斯楚秘密計畫。

註 covert (a.) 秘密的，偷偷摸摸的

☐ 493 **assume** [ə`sum] (v.) 假定，以為

同 presume

This occasion may have been the most important
of Kennedy's adult life so far, publicly as well as
privately, and he carried it off with an imagination
and delicacy that not everyone <u>assumed</u> he
possessed. (TIME, Oct. 7, 1996, p. 42)

這次婚禮該算是小甘迺迪成人後至目前，於公於私都最重要
的一樁大事，而且他用想像力與細膩——並非每個人都<u>認為</u>
他具有這些特質——達成任務。

☐ 494 **backfire** [`bæk,faɪr] (v.) 招致反效果

According to Tenner, every technological
endeavor is riddled with "solutions" that <u>backfire</u>.
(TIME, May 27, 1996, p. 67)

就田納的看法，每一項科技的努力，都深受<u>弄巧成拙</u>的「解
決方案」之困擾。

註 to be riddled with 充滿…

☐ 495 **banish** ［ˋbænɪʃ] (v.) 排除

同 expel

We rewrote our legal and regulatory system in the past few decades essentially to <u>banish</u> human judgment from government decisions.

(TIME, Apr. 10, 1995, p. 40)

過去幾十年我們重寫了法律體系與管制規定，基本上就是爲了使政府做決定時<u>不會有人</u>爲判斷攙雜其中。

☐ 496 **bar** [bɑr] (v.) 禁止

同 ban

Pretoria was <u>barred</u> from every Olympic competition for 32 years. (TIME, Aug. 19, 1996, p. 51)

南非被<u>阻</u>於奧運門外達32年。

☐ 497 **bill** [bɪl] (v.) 宣傳

In fact, computers become outdated so fast, you're crazy to buy anything that's <u>billed</u> as "state of the art." (TIME, Nov. 11, 1996, p. 16)

事實上，電腦汰舊換新的速度非常快，要是去買<u>號稱</u>「最新技術」的產品，那就太想不開了。

☐ 498 **blast** [blæst] (v.) 引爆，炸開

With one informal visit to his alma mater in rural upstate New York, Lee managed to <u>blast</u> out of Taiwan's prolonged diplomatic isolation.

(TIME, Dec. 25, 1995/Jan. 1, 1996, p. 54)

李登輝藉著這次非官方訪問其位於紐約州北部郊區的母校，<u>突破</u>了台灣長期以來的外交孤立。

註 alma mater (n.) 母校

☐ 499 **blossom** ［ˋblɑsəm] (v.) 開花，出現成果

同 bloom

Not only has their theory been confirmed, but it has <u>blossomed</u> into a thriving[100] branch of research. (TIME, Oct. 21, 1996, p. 42)

他們的理論不僅獲得證實，而且還<u>蔚爲顯學</u>。

□ 500 **bode** [bod] (v.) 預示

同 augur

Nor do the ironies he culls from the history of medicine <u>bode</u> well for the disease-free future imagined by some prophets[763] of biotech.

(TIME, May 27, 1996, p. 67)

他從醫學史上挑出來的一些頗富諷刺性的事件，也同樣並不<u>預示</u>生物科技所想像出來的「無病痛的未來」。

註 cull (v.) 挑選

□ 501 **bounce** [bauns] (v.) 彈起，反彈

As we chat, the Jeep changes lanes from smooth asphalt to rough cobblestone, which sets us <u>bouncing</u> around in the backseat.

(TIME, Nov. 4, 1996, p. 52)

我們聊著天，這時吉普車從平順的柏油路車道變換到顛簸的鵝卵石路上，使我們在後座被<u>彈</u>上彈下。

註 asphalt (n.) 瀝青，柏油

□ 502 **bully** [ˋbulɪ] (v.) 威嚇，欺侮

同 push around

Beijing was delighted to hear him say "China cannot be <u>bullied</u> by an American President."

(TIME, July 8, 1996, p. 29)

北京對於他所說的「中國不可能受美國總統<u>威嚇</u>」感到相當高興。

□ 503 **bust** [bʌst] (v.) 逮捕；搜查

Anyone would agree that a club openly selling an illegal drug to thousands of people deserves to get <u>busted</u>, right? (TIME, Aug. 19, 1996, p. 8)

俱樂部裡公開販售非法毒品給數千人使用，就應該予以<u>搜查</u>，這一點大家都會同意吧！

□ 504 **bypass** [ˈbaɪˌpæs] (v.) 避開，繞過

同 sidestep

Lee wants to <u>bypass</u> the nomination[334] process, noting that just last February Lien had been approved as Premier by the legislature.

(TIME, June 17, 1996, p. 54)

李登輝想<u>規避</u>提名的程序，表示連戰已於去年2月經立法院同意成爲閣揆。

□ 505 **capitalize (on)** [ˈkæpətlˌaɪz] (v.) 利用

同 take advantage of

The question now is how effectively Arafat will <u>capitalize on</u> these assets[672]. (TIME, May 16, 1994, p. 66)

現在的問題是，阿拉法特將如何有效地<u>利用</u>這些資產。

註 effectively (adv.) 有效地

□ 506 **circumvent** [ˌsɜkəmˈvɛnt] (v.) 規避

同 get around

Last month American customs agents arrested a pair of Jordanian nationals ... on charges of using a home-based front company in Midlothian, Virginia, to <u>circumvent</u> the Iraqi embargo.

(TIME, May 23, 1994, p. 30)

上個月美國海關人員逮捕了兩名約旦籍人士 ，罪名是以維吉尼亞州米洛息安一家家庭式公司作幌子，<u>規避</u>對伊拉克的禁運措施。

註 front (n.) 掩護非法活動的人或機構，掛羊頭賣狗肉者；
embargo (n.) 貿易禁運

□ 507 **cite** [saɪt] (v.)（爲了例證或確認而）提到，舉出

Richard Ellis, a professor of politics at Oregon's Willamette University who is skeptical of the whole EQ theory, <u>cites</u> two 19th-century Presidents who did not fit the mold.

(TIME, Oct. 9, 1995, p. 30)

奧勒岡州的威勒梅特大學政治學敎授艾利斯，對整個EQ理論抱持質疑的態度，他<u>舉出</u>19世紀兩位不符合這個理論的總統。

☐ 508 **claim** [klem] (v.) 奪走（性命）

同 take

A routine ascent turns into a desperate ordeal[337] as a storm rakes Mount Everest, <u>claiming</u> at least eight lives in the ultracold "Death Zone."
(TIME, May 27, 1996, p. 13)

一場暴風掃過聖母峰，在超冷的「死亡區」<u>奪走</u>了至少8條人命，一場例行的登山行動隨之變成艱險的煎熬。

註 desperate (a.) 危急的；rake (v.)（暴風雨等）掠過

☐ 509 **collaborate** [kə`læbə,ret] (v.) 合作

Earlier in the year, two veterans[373] of the sport <u>collaborated</u> on *Yaocho* (Match Rigging), a book stuffed with explosive revelations.
(TIME, Sept. 30, 1996, p. 26)

今年稍早，兩名已退休的相撲選手<u>合寫</u>了一本叫《八百長》（即放水的比賽）的書，充滿爆炸性的內幕。

註 to be stuffed with 塞滿

☐ 510 **commit** [kə`mɪt] (v.) 使承諾，使作出保證

In Australia he (Clinton) will stress that politics, security and economics guarantee the U.S. determination to stay <u>committed</u> to a region that by the year 2000 will have a combined gross national product of $13 trillion, twice that of Europe. (TIME, Nov. 18, 1996, p. 31)

到澳洲時，柯林頓將強調政治、安全和經濟3項因素會確保美國絕對信守對亞洲地區所做的<u>承諾</u>，這個地區在公元2000年時國民生產毛額總計將高達美金13兆，是歐洲的兩倍。

☐ 511 **complement** [`kɑmplə,mɛnt] (v.) 補足

So, undaunted, she hired a new director, designer, conductor and soprano to <u>complement</u> her original cast. (TIME, Feb. 7, 1994, p. 65)

所以她毫不氣餒，在原有的陣容之外<u>加聘</u>了導演、設計師、指揮、女高音各一名。

□ 512 **compliment** [ˋkɑmpləˏmɛnt] (v.) 讚美，恭維

He paid me a <u>compliment</u>, then reached over and put his right hand on my left butt cheek. Fortunately, the elevator had reached our floor, so I just stepped aside and walked him to the (building's) exit. (TIME, Apr. 17, 1995, p. 51)
他恭維了我一番，然後靠過來，把右手放在我左臀上。所幸電梯門開，於是我把身體往旁一側，陪著他一起走到大樓出口。
註 walk (v.)（陪著走一段路）送走（某人）

□ 513 **comprehend** [ˏkɑmprɪˋhɛnd] (v.) 理解

同 understand　To <u>comprehend</u> the distrust between the two sides in this dispute[302], look to Northern Ireland for guidance. (TIME, Feb. 20, 1995, p. 48)
要<u>了解</u>此爭議中雙方的不信任，可以拿北愛爾蘭當例子。

□ 514 **comprise** [kəmˋpraɪz] (v.) 擁有，由…構成

The U.S. Pacific Command <u>comprises</u> 200 ships, 2,000 aircraft and 300,000 soldiers, sailors, airmen and marines, of whom 100,000 are forward deployed[535] in South Korea, Japan and at sea. (TIME, Mar. 25, 1996, p. 16)
美國太平洋指揮部<u>轄有</u>200艘船艦、2千架飛機與30萬名陸、海、空軍及陸戰隊，其中有10萬名就在前部署於南韓、日本及海上。

□ 515 **conceal** [kənˋsil] (v.) 掩飾

反 reveal　In a 1986 air strike at Libya, he (Ronald Reagan) showed no qualms[1029] about ordering F-111 bombers to blast[498] Gaddafi's living quarters as well as his command post, and could scarcely <u>conceal</u> his disappointment when the colonel escaped. (TIME, Sept. 23, 1996, p. 35)
1986年空襲利比亞的行動，雷根泰然自若地命令F-111轟炸機不僅要轟炸格達費的指揮部，還要炸掉他的住家。格達費上校逃過一劫，雷根則難<u>掩</u>失望之情。

516 **confiscate** [kɑnfɪs,ket] (v.) 沒收，充公

同 seize

The influential criminologist cited[507] trials in Indianapolis and Kansas City that suggested that violent crime can be cut drastically[32] through campaigns[285] to locate and <u>confiscate</u> illegal guns. (TIME, Mar. 27, 1995, p. 29)

這位具影響力的犯罪學家舉了印第安那波里、堪薩斯市的一些審判，藉此表示透過搜尋並<u>沒收</u>非法槍枝的活動，可使暴力犯罪銳減。

517 **conjure (up)** [kʌndʒɚ] (v.) 使浮現腦際，想起

He remains one of the handful of players—and just about the only American—who can <u>conjure up</u> the world of Josef Lhevinne, Rachmaninoff and Horowitz. (TIME, July 25, 1994, p. 71)

當今鋼琴家中，能令人<u>想起</u>Lhevinne、拉赫曼尼諾夫、赫洛維茨3位大師風格的並不多，而他依舊是其中的一位，也稱得上是其中唯一的一位美國人。

518 **consult** [kən`sʌlt] (v.) 諮詢

Gorton told the New York *Times* that he did not <u>consult</u> environmentalists about the bill because "I already know what their views are." (TIME, Apr. 24, 1995, p. 75)

高登告訴《紐約時報》說，關於這項法案他未<u>徵詢</u>過環保人士的看法，因爲「我已知道他們的觀點。」

519 **contain** [kən`ten] (v.) 圍堵

同 control

For the Chinese, a closer bond with Russia is a way of countering[152] pressure from the U.S., which they accuse of trying to <u>contain</u> their economic and military growth. (TIME, May 6, 1996, p. 21)

對中國來說，加強與俄羅斯的關係是反制美國壓力的一項方法，中國指控美國想要<u>圍堵</u>其經濟與軍事力量的成長。

☐ 520 **contract** [kən`trækt] (v.) 收縮

The cuts are irrational, Christopher said two weeks ago, when "our global presence should be expanding[177], not <u>contracting</u>." (TIME, Nov. 18, 1996, p. 33)
兩星期前克里斯多福說，這些刪減是毫無道理的，因爲這時候「我們對國際事務的參與應該是愈來愈積極，而非愈來愈萎縮。」

☐ 521 **contradict** [͵kɑntrə͵dɪkt] (v.) 與…矛盾，牴觸

A survey found that those who had given up cigarettes two decades ago had a higher risk of stroke than people who had never smoked. The results <u>contradict</u> two other studies that show that after five years of abstinence a former smoker's stroke risk is essentially the same as that of someone who never lit up. (TIME, May 22, 1995, p. 23)
有份調查發現，戒煙20年的人比從未抽過煙的人，中風的機率更高。另有兩項研究顯示，吸煙者戒煙5年後，其中風機率基本上與從未抽過煙的人相同。前項調查結果與後兩項研究的結果正好<u>相牴觸</u>。

📖 abstinence (n.) 禁戒（菸、酒等）

☐ 522 **convene** [kən`vin] (v.) 召開會議

He wants a specific timetable to expand[177] NATO eastward, and pledged[342] to <u>convene</u> a 1998 summit in Prague at which the Czech Republic, Hungary and Poland would join the alliance.
(TIME, July 8, 1996, p. 29)
他主張訂出北大西洋公約組織向東擴展的明確日期表，並且承諾將於1998年在布拉格<u>召開</u>高峰會議，在會議中捷克、匈牙利和波蘭都將加入北約聯盟。

□ 523 **coordinate** [ko`ɔrdə,net] (v.) 協調，整合

London said it would establish an elected 90-seat Northern Ireland Assembly. Members of the new Assembly would join with parliamentarians from the Irish Republic in a new cross-border body to <u>coordinate</u> issues that affect[118] both ....

(TIME, Mar. 6, 1995, p. 63)

倫敦當局表示將建立北愛爾蘭議會，由90名民選議員組成，這個新議會的議員將與愛爾蘭共和國的國會議員合組一跨國組織，以<u>協調</u>與雙方相關的議題。

□ 524 **covet** [`kʌvɪt] (v.) 垂涎，覬覦

同 desire

The man represents the Internet industry's most <u>coveted</u> market: the estimated 85% to 90% of American homes that aren't yet connected.

(TIME, Aug. 12, 1996, p. 26)

這名男子代表了網際網路業者最<u>渴望</u>掌握的市場：就是那些尚未連線的美國家庭，據估計這樣的家庭約占美國家庭的85%到90% 。

□ 525 **crash** [kræʃ] (v.) 電腦當機

Every computer I've got has <u>crashed</u>.

(TIME, Apr. 7, 1997, p. 44)

我的電腦全<u>當掉</u>了。

□ 526 **crave** [krev] (v.) 渴求

People were <u>craving</u> the simple pleasures of the sea and the sun. (TIME, July 1, 1996, p. 54)

人們<u>渴望</u>著海洋和陽光所帶來那種單純的樂趣。

□ 527 **cripple** [ˋkrɪpl̩] (v.) 使不良於行

It was her own immune system, attacking the joints in her body and <u>crippling</u> her so badly that she often had to use a wheelchair.
(TIME, Oct. 28, 1996, p. 70)
就是她自己的免疫系統，攻擊她體內的關節，嚴重<u>削弱</u>她的<u>行動能力</u>，使她必須經常借助輪椅。

□ 528 **cruise** [kruz] (v.) 汽車定速行駛，（船，飛機）巡航

The Grand Cherokee wends its lazy way along the gently curving road, <u>cruising</u> at 40 km/h through rural Michigan's autumnal landscape of gold-and-orange-dappled trees. (TIME, Nov. 4, 1996, p. 52)
大柴拉基型吉普車沿著彎度不大的路緩緩前進，以時速40公里的速度在密西根鄉間的秋色中<u>定速巡行</u>，沿途可見金、橙色斑駁的樹木。

註 lazy (a.) 慢吞吞的；dappled (a.) 有斑點的，花斑的

□ 529 **crumble** [ˋkrʌmbl̩] (v.) 崩潰，消失

同 fall apart

But the deal may not go through, and with its demise[692] the three-decade-old edifice of affirmative action may begin to <u>crumble</u>.
(TIME, Mar. 20, 1995, p. 36)
但這筆交易可能談不成，隨之造成的後果是，鼓勵僱用少數民族、婦女這個實行已30年的贊助性制度，可能因此而步上<u>崩潰</u>之途。

註 edifice (n.) 體系

□ 530 **crunch** [krʌntʃ] (v.) 咬嚼，引申為電腦高速處理

The number of bits a chip can <u>crunch</u> is a rough measure of its power. The old Atari games ran on 8-bit machines; Sega Genesis and Super Nintendo are 16-bit systems. (TIME, May 20, 1996, p. 59)
一個晶片所能夠<u>處理</u>的位元數，大致與其功能成正比。老式的Atari遊戲是在8位元的機器上執行；世嘉的「創世紀」和超級任天堂是16位元的系統。

☐ 531 **cultivate** [ˈkʌltə͵vet] (v.) 培養，磨練

> Nurmi, who had never gone beyond elementary schooling, <u>cultivated</u> his mind in adulthood and became a devoted[160] fan of classical music, often attending concerts—but always alone.
> (TIME, June 24, 1996, p. 66)
> 努爾米的學歷只有小學，在成年之後，他自我陶冶心靈，成爲古典音樂的樂迷，經常參加音樂會，但都是孤單一人。

☐ 532 **defect** [dɪˈfɛkt] (v.) 變節

> He preferred to <u>defect</u> to the South (Korea) while on a U.S. trip during the summer and asked Mr. A if he would arrange an invitation from former President Jimmy Carter. (TIME, Feb. 24, 1997, p. 18)
> 他比較傾向於趁夏天赴美訪問時<u>變節</u>投奔南韓，並且問了A先生是否可居中安排由前總統卡特邀他訪美。

☐ 533 **defy** [dɪˈfaɪ] (v.) 反抗

> Policymakers in Washington note that if he is re-elected, Lee will have to make a clear choice between soothing or <u>defying</u> Beijing.
> (TIME, Feb. 12, 1996, p. 18)
> 華府決策人士指出李登輝如果連任，就必須作出清楚的抉擇，是要安撫中共還是和它<u>唱反調</u>。
> 註 soothe (v.) 安撫

☐ 534 **denounce** [dɪˈnaʊns] (v.) 公開指責

> During the Cultural Revolution, hundreds of thousands of Chinese fled across the border, some of whom founded publications to <u>denounce</u> the regime in Beijing. (TIME, Feb. 24, 1997, p. 37)
> 文化大革命期間，數十萬中國人逃過邊界，其中有些人辦刊物<u>抨擊</u>北京政權。

☐ 535 **deploy** [dɪˋplɔɪ] (v.) 部署

He would deploy—in Europe, Asia and the U.S.—an antiballistic-missile defense system of the Star Wars sort first proposed during the Reagan Administration. (TIME, July 8, 1996, p. 29)
他將在歐洲、亞洲和美國部署類似雷根當政時首先提出的「星際大戰」反彈道飛彈防禦系統。

☐ 536 **depreciate** [dɪˋpriʃɪ͵et] (v.) 貶值，折舊

反 appreciate

Recent studies have shown that by the time you've driven home your new 2.3-gigabyte hard drive, 32 megs of RAM, 180-megahertz StreamLined, tangerine-flake baby, it has depreciated 76%. (TIME, Nov. 11, 1996, p. 16)
根據最近的研究顯示，當你把你那台新買的，配備著2.3 gigabyte的硬碟，32megabyte的記憶體，掃描頻率180 megahertz的流線型、且帶著橘色斑點花紋的寶貝電腦載回家時，它已經貶值了76%。

註 tangerine (n.) 深橙色，紅橙色；flake (n.) 雪片，點狀花紋。tangerine flaked一詞出自 *The Kandy-Kolored Tangerine Flake Streamline Baby* 一書，書名代表一輛車特別的顏色和車身的風格，整本書是介紹六〇年代的文化改變。tangerine flaked因而成為「很酷」的代名詞。

☐ 537 **derail** [dɪˋrel] (v.) 使出軌，破壞

同 wreck

And in the days leading up to the balloting, there are even concerns that China may provoke[611] violence to derail the electoral process.
(TIME, Dec. 4, 1995, p. 24)
隨著選舉腳步的接近，有人甚至擔心中共會挑起暴力來破壞選舉的進行。

☐ 538 **derive** [dəˋraɪv] (v.) 源自，獲得

同 stem

Some scientists are beginning to look seriously at just what benefits patients may derive from spirituality. (TIME, June 24, 1996, p. 40)
有些科學家開始認真研究病人由心靈學上能獲得哪些益處。

□ 539 **deter** [dɪ`tɜ] (v.) 制止，妨礙

同 discourage

A mini-Louvre Website exists on the Net, allowing visitors to call up a grainy version of works such as Monet's *Pont Neuf*. Some in the real (as opposed to virtual) art world are concerned that on-screen viewing will <u>deter</u> actual museumgoing.

(TIME, Spring 1995 Special Issue: Welcome to Cyberspace, p. 14)

網路上有一處叫「迷你羅浮宮」的網站，讓上網者可以叫出顆粒狀質感的作品，呈現在螢幕上，如莫內的《新橋》。在真實的藝術世界裡（相對於虛擬世界），有人擔心螢幕瀏覽將<u>阻礙</u>實存的博物館的營運。

註 grainy (a.)（照片等）粒子粗以致上面的線條或形狀模糊不清的

□ 540 **dictate** [`dɪk,tet] (v.) 指揮

Indeed, the very shape and nature of working lives are being <u>dictated</u> by technology.

(TIME, Apr. 15, 1996, p. 22)

事實上，人類職業生活的外貌及本質都正受到科技的<u>支配與控制</u>。

□ 541 **diminish** [də`mɪnɪʃ] (v.) 減少，衰退

反 increase

She has talked of ending her program in the next year or two and moving on to other projects, but her charismatic appeal is unlikely to <u>diminish</u>.

(TIME, June 17, 1996, p. 27)

她曾提到在明年或後年收掉現在的節目，進行別的計畫，但她的群眾魅力將不會<u>稍減</u>。

註 charismatic (a.) 富群眾魅力的

542 **discipline** [ˈdɪsəplɪn] (v.) 懲罰

同 punish

Angered by what they interpret as Beijing's uncompromising, uncooperative behavior, the containment forces are convinced China is a bully that needs to be <u>disciplined</u>, not indulged.

(TIME, Mar. 25, 1996, p. 13)

圍堵政策陣營把中國的作爲解釋爲不妥協、不合作，因而忿忿不平。他們相信中國就是愛以大欺小，應該加以<u>懲戒</u>而不能放任。

註 bully (n.) 欺侮弱小的惡霸；indulge (v.) 縱容

543 **disclose** [dɪsˈkloz] (v.) 揭發

同 reveal

Tax authorities <u>disclosed</u> in July that they had conducted[141] their first ever investigation of a sumo stable. (TIME, Sept. 30, 1996, p. 28)

稅捐機關在7月<u>宣布</u>，已經對某相撲道館進行首次查稅工作。

544 **disdain** [dɪsˈden] (v.) 厭惡

同 contempt
scorn

By his own account, he does not simply <u>disdain</u> coffee; he rages against it, preaches of its evils, overturns coffee urns in restaurants.

(TIME, Apr. 24, 1995, p. 74)

套用他的說辭，他不只<u>厭惡</u>咖啡，還大罵咖啡，四處宣揚咖啡的不好，在餐廳裡打翻咖啡壺。

註 preach (v.) 宣揚，提倡

545 **dissolve** [dɪˈzɑlv] (v.) 解體

When the Soviet Union <u>dissolved</u> and Russian-style communism expired[562] in the late 1980s, many thought the bear and the dragon would become even more fundamentally antagonistic[800].

(TIME, May 6, 1996, p. 21)

1980年代末期，蘇聯<u>瓦解</u>，俄國式的共產主義壽終正寢，很多人以爲俄羅斯和中國將在基本觀念上更加不和。

164   discipline   disclose   disdain   dissolve

☐ 546 **distract** [dɪ`strækt] (v.) 使分神

同 sidetrack

He played in Little League while growing up in Delaware, partly to <u>distract</u> himself from a "horrible childhood" marked by his mother's dying of cancer. (TIME, Sept. 12, 1994, p. 76)

他在德拉瓦長大，當時他在少棒聯盟打球，這麼做部分是為了讓自己<u>遠離</u>因母親死於癌症而烙下的「悲慘童年」。

☐ 547 **drain** [dren] (v.) 排乾，流掉，逐漸耗竭

If the conflict[295] descends into guerrilla warfare, it may move off the world's front pages, but it will continue to <u>drain</u> Moscow's resources and weaken Yeltsin. (TIME, Jan. 23, 1995, p. 46)

如果戰爭轉為零星的游擊戰，這場戰爭或許就會失去世人的關注，但仍將繼續<u>耗去</u>莫斯科的資源，削弱葉爾欽的氣勢。

☐ 548 **dwarf** [dwɔrf] (v.) 令相形見絀

The social and economic changes that are taking place there (China) are so sweeping[98] as to <u>dwarf</u> all others I see elsewhere in this dynamic part of the world. (TIME, Dec. 19, 1994, p. 4)

中國大陸正進行的社會、經濟改變非常廣泛，<u>相較之下</u>，在這個充滿活力的〔亞洲〕地區，其他國家的改變反而顯得<u>微不足道</u>。

☐ 549 **elaborate** [ɪ`læbə,ret] (v.) 詳述 [ɪ`læbərɪt] (a.) 精心製作的，精巧的

<u>Elaborates</u> Time Zagat, publisher of the Zagat restaurant guides, ... "The food doesn't have to be all that good, as long as it doesn't poison you. You go because you are interested."
(TIME, July 22, 1996, p. 43)

「札加特」餐廳指南發行人札加特<u>解釋</u>說：「食物不需要那麼好，只要不會毒死你就可以了。你到那裡去是因為你有興趣。」

☐ 550 **embed** [ɪmˋbɛd] (v.) 植入，深植於

Already familiar in Western Europe and parts of
Asia, smart cards resemble[233] credit cards but
contain an embedded microchip that keeps track
of values stored on the silicon. (TIME, Jan. 18, 1996, p. 13)
IC卡在西歐以及亞洲某些地區已行之有年，外型類似信用
卡，但卡中嵌入一塊微晶片，會記錄該卡的剩餘價值。

註 to keep track of 隨時注意（某人或情況的發展）

☐ 551 **embody** [ɪmˋbɑdɪ] (v.) 體現

同 represent

Just as the 1889 Paris Exposition gave rise to the
Eiffel Tower, this (Internet) world's fair will leave
behind a structure that embodies its vision of the
future: a transoceanic railroad of high-speed fiber-
optic links. (TIME, Mar. 11, 1996, p. 35)
就如同1889年的巴黎博覽會中搭起的艾菲爾鐵塔一樣，這次
的網路博覽會也將留下一項能體現未來憧憬的實體建設：就
是一條以高速光纖線路所連結而成的越洋「鐵路」。

☐ 552 **emulate** [ˋɛmjə͵let] (v.) 仿效

同 imitate

Warner and Paramount, the two newest entrants in
the network derby, see Fox not as a nemesis but
as a network to emulate. (TIME, Jan. 16, 1995, p. 68)
華納和派拉蒙公司是新近加入電視台經營戰的兩位角逐者，
在他們眼中，福克斯公司不只是強敵，還是效法的對象。

註 entrant (n.) 參賽者；derby (n.) 競賽；nemesis (n.) 強敵

☐ 553 **engineer** [͵ɛndʒəˋnɪr] (v.) 策劃，創造，設計

Gerstner and Thoman, however, have engineered
a corporate future that takes more from their
corporate customers' body language than their
own. (TIME, Nov. 4, 1996, p. 48)
不過葛斯納與托曼所要創造的公司(IBM)遠景，卻得視客戶
而非他們自己的身體語言而定。

554 **enlist** [ɪn`lɪst] (v.) 召募

The U.S. should be hard-nosed on nuclear proliferation[346] and intellectual-property rights, and may find it advantageous to <u>enlist</u> friends and allies[275] support in that endeavor instead of going it alone. (TIME, Mar. 25, 1996, p. 15)

美國對核武擴散以及智慧財產權這兩個問題應該採取強硬的態度；而爲了達成此一目標，美國如能<u>網羅</u>友人與盟邦的支持，而不要單打獨鬥，可能是最有利的。

註 hard-nosed（美俚）堅毅的，執拗的，精明而務實的

555 **envision** [ɪn`vɪʒən] (v.) 預見，想像

同 imagine

Andreessen, Barksdale and Clark <u>envision</u> a future Netscape product that will assume many of the computer's operating-system functions, browsing local files as seamlessly[851] as it browses today's Web. (TIME, Sept. 16, 1996, p. 43)

安德里森、巴斯代爾和克拉克<u>想像</u>網景未來的產品，將具備許多電腦作業系統的功能，能像現在瀏覽全球資訊網一樣，毫無窒礙地瀏覽個人檔案。

註 assume (v.) 擔任，擔負；browse (v.) 瀏覽

556 **eradicate** [ɪ`rædɪ,ket] (v.) 根除，拔除

同 eliminate

Several days later, however, Clinton reversed himself again, saying it was more important to safeguard vital social programs than to <u>eradicate</u> the deficit in the relatively near future.
(TIME, June 5, 1995, p. 22)

數天後，柯林頓的態度又有了180度的轉變，說保住重大的社會計畫比在更短的時間內<u>消除</u>赤字更爲重要。

註 reverse (v.) 使倒轉，徹底改變

□ [557] **erupt** [ɪˋrʌpt] (v.) 爆發

Then a controversy <u>erupted</u> over an unnamed woman's decision to abort one of two healthy fetuses because she felt unable to care for twins. (TIME, Aug. 26, 1996, p. 8)

接著<u>爆發</u>一場爭議,爭執點在於一名不知名的婦女,因為自覺無力撫養雙胞胎,而決定拿掉腹中兩個健康胎兒的其中一個。

註 abort (v.) 墮胎;fetus (n.) 胎兒

□ [558] **escalate** [ˋɛskə‚let] (v.) 升高

His Zucca line does well at home, but the <u>escalating</u> yen has kept it out of the export market. (TIME, Oct. 9, 1995, p. 47)

他所設計的「祖卡」系列在國內賣得很好,但<u>持續升值的</u>日圓使它無法打開外銷市場。

註 line (n.) 系列產品

□ [559] **escort** [ɪˋskɔrt] (v.) 護送,伴隨

At some Spanish resorts tourists who flouted[907] the law would be sternly <u>escorted</u> back to their hotels by the Civil Guard. (TIME, July 1, 1996, p. 55)

在西班牙某些觀光區,遊客若違反這條法律,就會被民兵隊毫不客氣地<u>護送</u>回旅館。

註 resort (n.) 度假勝地

□ [560] **evaluate** [ɪˋvæljʊ‚et] (v.) 評估

同 assess

We must investigate, <u>evaluate</u> and validate this discovery, and it is certain to create lively scientific controversy. (TIME, Aug. 19, 1996, p. 41)

我們必須調查、<u>評估</u>並確認這項發現,而它肯定會在科學上引起熱烈的爭議。

註 validate (v.) 證實

□ 561 **evoke** [ɪˋvok] (v.) 喚起，引起

Public polls record strong support for voluntary euthanasia—a recent Morgan poll found that 70% of Australians were in favor—but Dent's death also <u>evoked</u> sorrow and anger. (TIME, Oct. 7, 1996, p. 39)
民意調查顯示，人們強力支持志願安樂死——最近的一次摩根民意調查發現，70%的澳洲人支持安樂死——可是鄧特的死，仍然<u>引發</u>了悲嘆和憤怒。
註 euthanasia (n.) 安樂死

□ 562 **expire** [ɪkˋspaɪr] (v.) 到期，期滿

同 run out

His work visa <u>expires</u> in August.
(TIME, Feb. 10, 1997, p. 26)
他的工作證8月<u>到期</u>。

□ 563 **fake** [fek] (v.) 假裝，佯做

Johnson <u>faked</u> a pass, and defender Latrell Sprewell was so fooled that Magic simply sashayed past him and laid the ball in.
(TIME, Feb. 12, 1996, p. 42)
魔術強森做個傳球的<u>假動作</u>，騙過防守的史培威爾，把球放進籃框。
註 sashay (v.)（美口語）大搖大擺地走

□ 564 **feature (in)** [ˋfitʃə] (v.) 以…為號召，特別介紹

Scientists and patients will be celebrating the promising[78] new HIV treatments to be <u>featured in</u> Vancouver next week, but animal-rights activists almost certainly won't be cheering them on.
(TIME, July 8, 1996, p. 39)
下週在溫哥華將要<u>推出</u>愛滋病的幾種新療法，療效似乎頗看好。科學家與病人屆時都會大肆慶祝，但是提倡動物權利的人士幾乎可以肯定不會為他們喝采。

□ [565] **foresee** [for`si] (v.) 預料

同 predict

The company expects to have a working prototype[764] of this power train next year and even <u>foresees</u> limited sales to gotta-have car fanatics[410] in 1998. (TIME, Sept. 23, 1996, p. 41)

該公司期望動力組的原型機明年能製造出來，甚至<u>預估</u>在1998年就可以限量賣給汽車狂。

註 gotta-have 等於got to have，表示非買不可的

□ [566] **foreshadow** [for`ʃædo] (v.) 預示，先兆

同 forebode

The fall of Danang late in the month produced scenes of horror that appeared to <u>foreshadow</u> what might happen later in Saigon ....

(TIME, Apr. 24, 1995, p. 24)

本月底峴港陷落，一幕幕恐怖的場景隨之出現，好似<u>預示</u>了此後在西貢可能上演的同樣場面。

□ [567] **for(e)go** [for`go] (v.) 放棄

同 do without

But, saying he wanted to appear above reproach and quell[613] any controversy, he announced he would <u>forgo</u> a $4.5 million advance for two books on politics. (TIME, Jan. 9, 1995, p. 13)

但他說不想形象受損，也想讓爭議平息，於是他宣布<u>放棄</u>兩本政治學著作的450萬美元預付金。

註 reproach (n.) 責備；advance (n.) 預付版稅

□ [568] **foster** [`fɔstə] (v.) 促進，助長

In *Rishi* he suggests that by purveying short-term cures but ignoring long-term prevention, the typical Western physician "was <u>fostering</u> a diseased system and beyond that, a diseased world .... " (TIME, June 24, 1996, p. 47)

在《哲人歸來》一書中，他認為一般的西方醫生大量供應短期的治療，卻忽略長期的預防，等於是「<u>助長</u>一個病態的系統，甚至於病態的世界。」

註 purvey (v.) 供應

☐ 569 **fret** [frɛt] (v.) 煩惱，煩躁

In his 1994 book *The Agenda*, Bob Woodward recounts an Oval Office meeting at which Clinton was <u>fretting</u> about how he could get his legislation passed. (TIME, June 17, 1996, p. 30)

伍德沃德在他1994年出版的《議程》一書中寫到，在總統辦公室的一次會議上，柯林頓為了如何讓法案過關而<u>大傷腦筋</u>。

註 recount (v.) 詳述

☐ 570 **hamper** [ˋhæmpɚ] (v.) 阻礙

Hong Kong's cultural and intellectual development has been <u>hampered</u>, no doubt, by its lack of political development. (TIME, Mar. 17, 1997, p. 22)

香港文化及知識的發展，無疑地因政治上缺乏發展而受到<u>阻礙</u>。

☐ 571 **harass** [həˋræs] (v.) 騷擾

Getty claims[133] that animal-rights activists made <u>harassing</u> phone calls to his hospital bedside while he was recovering. (TIME, July 8, 1996, p. 39)

蓋提說，他在醫院復健時，有保護動物人士打電話到他的病房<u>騷擾</u>他。

☐ 572 **harbor** [ˋhɑrbɚ] (v.) 抱持（情感）

And he still <u>harbors</u> a grudge against Bolduc, who attempted to bring the semi-independent medical services under his control. (TIME, Apr. 17, 1995, p. 51)

而他對波爾杜奇仍<u>心懷</u>怨恨，因為波爾杜奇想把這些半獨立性的醫學服務部門納入他的管轄。

註 grudge (n.) 怨恨，不滿

□ 573 **harness** [ˈhɑrnɪs] (v.) 駕馭，利用

The CIA and Defense Department are about to harness some of their most sensitive[88] technologies against a new enemy: cancer.
(TIME, Oct. 17, 1994, p. 17)
中央情報局和國防部正打算運用他們手中某些最靈敏的科技器材對付癌症這個新敵人。

□ 574 **haunt** [hɔnt] (v.)（如幽靈般）縈繞於…之腦海中

同 plague

Until the I.R.A. and the Protestant paramilitaries give up their vicious beatings, the legacy[732] of the years of violence will continue to haunt Northern Ireland, and the faces of the children of war will continue to show fear. (TIME, June 12, 1995, p. 58)
在愛爾蘭共和軍和基督教準軍事部隊成員停止殘暴的攻擊行動前，多年暴力活動所留下的影響，仍將繼續籠罩著北愛爾蘭，而戰爭下兒童的臉龐仍將露出驚懼的神情。
註 paramilitary (n.) 準軍事部隊成員；vicious (a.) 兇殘的

□ 575 **heap (on)** [hip] (v.) 對（某人）一再加以（稱讚或侮辱）

同 pile on

For survivors of the massacre, the most gnawing injustice is the blame heaped on the victims by military officers who accused them of being agents of communist North Korea, yet refused to say who gave the orders to shoot and how many died. (TIME, Dec. 11, 1995, p. 20)
對〔光州〕大屠殺的倖存者來說，最令他們感到痛苦的是軍方對死難者一再加諸的罪名，指他們是北韓間諜，卻又不願透露到底是誰下令軍隊開火與確切的死亡人數。
註 gnawing (a.) 令人苦惱的，令人痛苦的

☐ 576 **hobble** [ˋhɑbl] (v.) 妨礙，使難以運作

同 hinder

Low points out, Thailand's poor education system—only about 30% of teenagers go on to secondary school, half the rate in Malaysia—will hobble its ability to move up the value-added chain. (TIME, Aug. 5, 1996, p. 42)

羅指出，泰國的教育體制不良——就讀中學的青少年大約只有30%，是馬來西亞的一半——將會<u>妨礙</u>它的高附加價值產業的升級。

☐ 577 **ignite** [ɪgˋnaɪt] (v.) 點燃，激發

He (Clinton) is pleased to have frozen the North Korea nuclear program, but wants North and South speaking to each other to stabilize the Korean peninsula, where he still fears World War III could ignite. (TIME, Nov. 18, 1996, p. 31)

凍結了北韓的核子計畫，令柯林頓覺得很滿意，但是他希望南、北韓展開對話以穩定朝鮮半島局勢，因為他仍然害怕第三次世界大戰的戰火會在此地<u>點燃</u>。

☐ 578 **illustrate** [ˋɪləstret] (v.) 闡明

同 demonstrate
　 exemplify

The Ebola affair and the emergence of AIDS illustrate how modern travel and global commerce can quickly spread disease. (TIME, Sept. 12, 1994, p. 62)

伊波拉病毒事件和愛滋病的出現，<u>說明</u>了現代人的旅遊和全球化商業活動足以使疾病快速散播。

☐ 579 **immerse (oneself)** [ɪˋmɝs] (v.) 熱衷於，專心於

同 engross

A President need not <u>immerse himself</u> in the details of foreign policy to conduct[141] it successfully. (TIME, May 2, 1994, p. 52)

總統要把外交做好，並不需要<u>自己下海去</u>管外交政策上的枝微末節。

580 **imply** [ɪm`plaɪ] (v.) 暗指，含…之意，意謂

同 suggest

Homicide may <u>imply</u> abuse[113], but abuse[113] does not <u>imply</u> homicide. (TIME, Jan. 23, 1995, p. 41)
殺人或許<u>意謂</u>著虐待，但虐待不<u>意謂</u>著殺人。

581 **incorporate** [ɪn`kɔrpə,ret] (v.) 使合併，併入，納入

同 include

Early on, sumo was <u>incorporated</u> into Shinto purification rituals, after which it became court entertainment. (TIME, Sept. 30, 1996, p. 28)
相撲很早就<u>融入</u>神道教的淨化儀式之中，後來才成為宮廷娛樂。

582 **induce** [ɪn`djus] (v.) 引發

In one classic 1950 study, ... pregnant women suffering from severe morning sickness were given syrup of ipecac, which <u>induces</u> vomiting, and told it was a powerful new cure for nausea[1016]. Amazingly, the women ceased vomiting.
(TIME, June 24, 1996, p. 41)
在1950年一項有名的研究中，實驗者把催吐樹的糖漿給一組在早晨患有嚴重妊娠嘔吐現象的婦女，告訴她們這是新的強效止吐劑，奇妙的是她們停止了嘔吐。
註 syrup (n.) 含藥糖漿

583 **indulge (in)** [ɪn`dʌldʒ] (v.) 隨心所欲地享受，恣意而為

They <u>indulge in</u> a manic idealization of their young; it is the obverse of child battering but sometimes has equally fatal effects.
(TIME, Apr. 22, 1990, p. 39)
他們狂熱地把自己的孩子理想化，並且<u>樂此不疲</u>。這與打小孩是相對的兩極，但有時具有相同的毀滅性。
註 obverse (n.)（如表裡的）相對物；fatal (a.) 致命的，具毀滅性的

□584 **inflict** [ɪn`flɪkt] (v.) 施加

The biggest impact of the U.S. economic restrictions is the damage they <u>inflict</u> on American businesses. (TIME, Feb. 20, 1995, p. 50)
美國經濟制裁所導致的最大衝擊，就是美國商界因此制裁所蒙受的傷害。

□585 **instill** [ɪn`stɪl] (v.) 逐漸灌輸，注入

同 implant

Both writers were emerging from a Victorian tradition that saw children's literature as a didactic form whose function ... was to <u>instill</u> a respect for adult values and behavior.
(TIME, May 6, 1996, p. 69)
這兩位作家都掙脫了維多利亞時代的傳統，在那個時代兒童文學具有「文以載道」的功能，要<u>教導</u>兒童尊敬成人的價值觀和行為模式。
註 to emerge from 脫離，終結（某困境）；didactic (a.) 說教的

□586 **intervene** [ˌɪntɚ`vin] (v.) 介入

The U.S. would not <u>intervene</u>, the official said, because it would not risk losing Los Angeles—presumably[447] to nuclear missile attack—in order to protect Taiwan. (TIME, Feb. 12, 1996, p. 16)
這位官員說美國不會<u>介入</u>，因為它不會為了保護台灣而冒著丟掉洛杉磯的危險，言下之意是中共會對洛杉磯發射核彈。

□587 **intimidate** [ɪn`tɪməˌdet] (v.) 威脅，恐嚇

同 browbeat

I heard a top Clinton aide trying to <u>intimidate</u> Jay by yelling at him, and I heard Jay, without losing his cool, raising his voice right back and demanding that his questions get answered.
(TIME, Aug. 1, 1994, p. 2)
我聽到柯林頓一名高級助理向傑嘶吼恫嚇，也聽到傑不慍不火地立即提高音量反擊回去，並要求對方回答他的問題。
註 yell (v.) 大叫，大吼

☐ 588 **intrigue** [ɪnˋtrig] (v.) 激起（某人）好奇心

同 fascinate

Senators Daniel Inouye and Robert Byrd, <u>intrigued</u> by stories of psychic successes, pushed hard during many years to keep Star Gate going. (TIME, Dec. 11, 1995, p. 29)
亦努葉參議員及畢德參議員，被靈媒成功的故事所<u>吸引</u>，多年來一直大力推動「星際之門計畫」，使其不致中斷。
註 psychic (n.) 通靈的人，靈媒

☐ 589 **isolate** [ˋaɪsḷˏet] (v.) 孤立，隔離

同 cut off

Those who were both religious and socially involved had a 14-fold advantage over those who were <u>isolated</u> or lacked faith. (TIME, June 24, 1996, p. 40)
有宗教信仰又參與社交活動的人，其健康要比<u>孤獨</u>或無信仰的人強上14倍。

☐ 590 **jeopardize** [ˋdʒɛpɚˏdaɪz] (v.) 危及

同 threaten
endanger

Her doctor advocates[666] aborting all but two of the (eight) fetuses, warning that continuing the full pregnancy will <u>jeopardize</u> the health of both mother and babies. (TIME, Aug. 26, 1996, p. 8)
她的醫生主張她腹中的8個胎兒只留兩個，其餘都拿掉，並警告說如果繼續讓8個胎兒留在肚子裡，將<u>危及</u>母子健康。
註 abort (v.) 墮胎；fetus (n.) 胎兒

☐ 591 **lapse** [læps] (v.) 陷入（某種狀態）

同 slip

The risk ... was that without immediate surgery, Bradley would quickly <u>lapse</u> into a coma and die. (TIME, May 1, 1995, p. 56)
風險在於如果不立即動手術，布萊德雷會立即<u>陷入</u>昏迷，然後死掉。
註 coma (n.) 昏迷

☐ 592 **lobby** [ˋlɑbɪ] (v.) 遊說

Malamud, 36, spent the past year shuttling[631] among 30 countries, <u>lobbying</u> companies that initially[428] dismissed[162] the project as unwieldy and unworkable. (TIME, Mar. 11, 1996, p. 35)

36歲的馬拉末，過去一年裡奔走於30個國家，並向那些打從一開始就認定這個計畫內容過於龐大而不可行的公司進行<u>遊說</u>工作。

註 unwieldy (a.)（組織、體系）過於龐雜而運作不良的

☐ 593 **locate** [ˋloket] (v.) 尋找

同 find

According to CIA documents that TIME has obtained, two agency officers went to Alexandria, Virginia, in May 1981 and asked a psychic to <u>locate</u> a group of POWs on a map of Laos.

(TIME, Dec. 11, 1995, p. 29)

據《時代雜誌》所得到的中情局文件顯示，在1981年5月，兩名情報員前往維吉尼亞州的亞歷山卓，請靈媒在寮國地圖上<u>指出</u>一群戰俘的所在位置。

註 psychic (n.) 靈媒；POW prison of war的縮寫，戰俘之意

☐ 594 **loom** [lum] (v.)（危險）迫近

While the political stakes[779] of the devaluation (of the Peso) are enormous for Zedillo, they <u>loom</u> large as well for Bill Clinton. (TIME, Jan. 16, 1995, p. 53)

（披索的）貶值對塞迪約的政治前途關係重大，對柯林頓而言，也是日益<u>逼近</u>的問題。

☐ 595 **loot** [lut] (v.) 掠奪，搜括

同 plunder

Hundreds of Vietnamese had swarmed[645] over the walls and were <u>looting</u> the warehouse, the office, the snack bar. (TIME, Apr. 24, 1995, p. 24)

越過圍牆的數百名越南人，在倉庫、辦公室、小吃店<u>搜括</u>了起來。

☐ 596 **manifest** [ˋmænəˏfɛst] (v.) 表明，顯露

同 show

As Francis Fukuyama predicted, the West, triumphant, faces the sheer[456] ennui of normal life, ennui that <u>manifests</u> itself in an eccentric[33] taste in heroes. (TIME, Feb. 17, 1997, p. 64)

如同福山所預言，西方在戰勝後面對著正常生活十足的百無聊賴，這種百無聊就<u>表現</u>在對英雄的奇特胃口上。

註 ennui (n.)（法文）無聊

☐ 597 **marvel** [ˋmɑrvl̩] (v.) 表示驚異，讚嘆

"Just three hours after receiving the medication, I was able to talk again." Bisla <u>marvels</u>.

(TIME, Sept. 16, 1996, p. 48)

「服藥3小時後，我又能說話了。」俾斯拉<u>嘖嘖稱奇</u>。

☐ 598 **monitor** [ˋmɑnətə] (v.) 監視

The presence of 47,000 U.S. troops in Japan reassures[224] not only Tokyo, which is carefully <u>monitoring</u> its great neighbor's rise to power, but even China, which along with other Asian countries is worried about Japan's rearming.

(TIME, Mar. 25, 1996, p. 16)

美國駐紮在日本的4萬7千名士兵，一方面讓東京安心（東京正<u>密切注意</u>強鄰中國的興起），另一方面也讓中國吃了定心丸，因為中國和其他亞洲國家一樣，都在擔心日本重整軍備。

☐ 599 **moonlight** [ˋmunˏlaɪt] (v.) 兼差

He sometimes <u>moonlights</u> as a chef at Rover's, a French restaurant in Seattle. (TIME, Jan. 13, 1997, p. 37)

他有時去西雅圖一家法國餐廳「羅浮」<u>兼差</u>當主廚。

☐ 600 **mourn** [morn] (v.) 哀悼

同 grieve for

At François Mitterrand's graveside not long ago, the mistress <u>mourned</u> alongside the widow.
(TIME, Sept. 23, 1996, p. 60)
不久前，在密特朗的新墳邊，他的情婦與寡婦並肩<u>致哀</u>。

☐ 601 **multiply** [ˋmʌltəˏplaɪ] (v.) 大量增加

Most industrial pollution comes from small factories, which have <u>multiplied</u> from 15,000 in 1950 to nearly 2 million today. (TIME, Mar. 25, 1996, p. 46)
工業污染大多來自小工廠，1950年小工廠有1萬5千家，現在已<u>暴增</u>到近兩百萬家。

☐ 602 **nurture** [ˋnɝtʃə] (v.) 培育，養成

同 cultivate

The organizers hope that the infrastructure[323]— and awareness—<u>nurtured</u> by this exposition will launch[203] a boom[282] in Net use. (TIME, Mar. 11, 1996, p. 35)
這次博覽會的創辦人希望藉由博覽會所<u>促成</u>的基礎建設和所喚起的網路意識，讓網際網路的使用蓬勃發展。

☐ 603 **outfit** [ˋaʊtˏfɪt] (v.) 配備，供給

同 fit out

General Motors is <u>outfitting</u> a convoy of 10 Buick LeSabres that are scheduled to make a test run next year on a modified stretch of I-15 outside San Diego. (TIME, Nov. 4, 1996, p. 53)
通用汽車公司正著手裝備一支由10部別克LeSabre汽車所組成的車隊，預計明年在聖地牙哥郊外一段經過修改的15號州際公路進行測試。

註 convey (n.) 車隊，船隊；stretch (n.) 範圍

604 **penetrate** [ˈpɛnəˌtret] (v.) 看透他人心思，識破

同 grasp
fathom

Little Women gently but firmly asks us to penetrate its 19th century disguises[694] and discover something of ourselves hiding in the dim past.
(TIME, Dec. 19, 1994, p. 74)

《小婦人》以委婉但堅定的語氣要求我們，識破其中19世紀的偽裝，發掘隱藏於幽微過去的我們的真面目。

605 **phase (in/out)** [fez] (v.) 逐漸引進或逐步廢除

Called Integrion, the partnership will phase in such activities as bill paying, electronic lending and stock and bond trading beginning next year.
(TIME, Sept. 23, 1996, p. 42)

名叫Integrion的這家合資公司預計明年開始陸續提供各種費用的代收、電子借貸和股票、債券買賣等服務。

606 **plunge** [plʌndʒ] (v.) 衝進，跳進

After drifting through interplanetary space for millions of years, one of these Martian rocks ventured[794] close to Earth 13,000 years ago ... and plunged into the atmosphere, blazing a meteoric path across the sky. (TIME, Aug. 19, 1996, p. 38)

在星際漂流數百萬年後，其中一塊火星岩石在1萬3千年前逼近地球，並一頭栽進大氣層，在空中燃燒，劃出一道流星的光芒。

註 drift (v.) 漂流，游蕩；meteoric (a.) 流星的

607 **proclaim** [prəˈklem] (v.) 宣稱

同 declare
announce

Whatever PETA says, he proclaims, is all lies and nonsense. (TIME, July 8, 1996, p. 39)

他表示，反虐待動物組織再怎麼說，都是騙人的，胡說八道！

□ [608] **prod** [prɑd] (v.) 刺激，激勵

同 stimulate

Ho last year staged[249] the exhibition *Being China (Being Hong Kong)* to help prod people to ponder the territory's identity. (TIME, Mar. 17, 1997, p. 22)

何先生去年推出了名爲《是中國（是香港）》的美展，以刺激港人思考香港這片土地的定位問題。

□ [609] **prompt** [prɑmpt] (v.) 促使

同 encourage

Kim's warning was prompted by a slump in exports and a rise in imports that forced the government to double its estimate of the country's 1996 current account deficit to as high as $12 billion. (TIME, Aug. 5, 1996, p. 42)

金泳三之所以會提出警告，是因爲出口急速下滑以及進口增加，迫使韓國政府把1996年經常帳赤字的預估提高一倍，高達120億美元。

註 slump (n.) 暴跌

□ [610] **prosecute** [ˈprɑsɪˌkjut] (v.) 起訴，告發

We've tried to prosecute him, but it's hopeless because he controls the court system and the judges ... He's also protected under parliamentary immunity. (TIME, Apr. 18, 1994, p. 48)

告發他我們也試過，但他控制了司法體系和法官，終究是徒勞無功；而且他還受到國會議員免責權的保護。

註 immunity (n.)（責任、義務等的）豁免

□ [611] **provoke** [prəˈvok] (v.) 引起，激發

A first reading of this book provokes a mix of outrage[212] and hilarity. (TIME, Oct. 21, 1996, p. 57)

初次讀這本書，令人感到半是氣憤，半是好笑。

註 hilarity (n.) 高興，歡樂

☐ ⁶¹² **prowl** [praʊl] (v.n.) 潛行（尋找竊取機會）

> Reporters now regularly stroll[785] the Internet for stories in the same way they used to <u>prowl</u> the corridors of City Hall. The tradecraft is a little different, but journalists are learning fast.
> (TIME, Spring 1995 Special Issue: Welcome to Cyberspace, p. 60)
> 記者現在定期上網路逛逛尋找報導題材，其方式就和他們過去常到市政廳走廊<u>悄悄尋覓</u>新聞如出一轍，打探消息的方式有所改變，但記者學得倒挺快。
> 註 tradecraft (n.) 諜報術

☐ ⁶¹³ **quell** [kwɛl] (v.) 壓制

> Prime Minister Benazir Bhutto resorts[236] to force to <u>quell</u> her own family's challenge to her power.
> (TIME, Jan. 17, 1994, p. 39)
> 總理班娜姬・布托最後動用武力，以<u>壓制</u>其家人的奪權挑戰。

☐ ⁶¹⁴ **rebound** [rɪ`baʊnd] (v.) 止跌回升，反彈

> Among the good omens: U.S. and Japanese economies are strengthening, and the Japanese yen is expected to <u>rebound</u>. (TIME, Aug. 5, 1996, p. 42)
> 好兆頭包括：美國及日本的經濟正在轉強，而日圓預期會<u>止跌回升</u>。
> 註 omen (n.) 前兆，預兆

☐ ⁶¹⁵ **reclaim** [rɪ`klem] (v.) 索回

> Foreign Ministry spokesman Chen Jian even suggested a timetable of sorts, saying that after China <u>reclaims</u> Hong Kong in 1997 and Macao in 1999, then Taiwan will be high on the agenda[274] of the Chinese people. (TIME, Feb. 12, 1996, p. 17)
> 外交部發言人陳健甚至暗示一份時間表，說在中共於1997年<u>收回</u>香港，1999年<u>收回</u>澳門以後，台灣問題將成為中國人民優先處理的議題。

□ [616] **reconcile** [ˋrɛkənˏsaɪl] (v.) 調解

Washington has blocked China's membership in the World Trade Organization, which Beijing wants as a venue[1046] for <u>reconciling</u> trade disputes[302] and obtaining more favorable tariff treatment. (TIME, Mar. 25, 1996, p. 15)

華盛頓一直阻撓中國加入世界貿易組織，中國本想藉此組織來<u>調解</u>貿易糾紛並獲得更有利的關稅待遇。

註 tariff (n.) 關稅

□ [617] **recruit** [rɪˋkrut] (v.) 召募，吸收

To find out, Ho and one of his team, Dr. Martin Markowitz, <u>recruited</u> two dozen men in the earlist stages of infection and placed them on combination therapy. (TIME, Dec. 30, 1996/Jan. 6, 1997, p. 31)

為了找出答案，何大一與他研究小組的一員馬可維茲博士<u>找來</u>24位處於初期感染的男性，對他們施以混合式治療。

註 therapy (n.) 療法

□ [618] **relate** [rɪˋlet] (v.) 敘述

同 tell

She would love to <u>relate</u> what happened that night, Thomasson told Congress, but felt she should talk first only to special counsel Robert Fiske. (TIME, Apr. 4, 1994, p. 26)

托馬森告訴國會，她很想<u>說明</u>當天晚上發生的事，但又覺得應該先跟特別顧問費斯克單獨談談。

□ [619] **relinquish** [rɪˋlɪŋkwɪʃ] (v.) 放棄

同 give up

Nearly one-third of those who <u>relinquished</u> triad ties were already in custody. (TIME, Mar. 17, 1997, p. 19)

這些<u>脫離</u>幫派的人，有近三分之一是在牢中。

註 triad (n.) 幫派；tie (n.) 關係，瓜葛；custody (n.) 羈押，拘禁

普通字 動詞

☐ 620 **renounce** [rɪ`naʊns] (v.) 宣誓放棄

One in seven Taiwanese mobsters turned themselves in to police and <u>renounced</u> their lives of crime. (TIME, Mar. 17, 1997, p. 19)
有七分之一的臺灣幫派份子向警方自首並<u>宣誓告別</u>道上生活。

註 mobster (n.)（俚）犯罪集團成員；
to turn oneself in （向警方）自首

☐ 621 **repent** [rɪ`pɛnt] (v.) 悔改

Specifically, he (the Pope) suggested that the church needs to <u>repent</u> for its sometimes intolerant treatment of other faiths. That notion shocked some bishops .... (TIME, Dec. 26, 1994, p. 60)
換句話說，教皇話中隱然指出教會必須對其偶有不寬容其他信仰的作為<u>懺悔</u>，這想法令某些主教大感震驚。

☐ 622 **restrain** [rɪ`stren] (v.) 抑制，遏止

同 check

But Templeton reminds us that not all Mexican companies will be hurt if the government fails in its attempt to <u>restrain</u> prices. (TIME, Jan. 9, 1995, p. 48)
但騰普頓提醒我們，如果墨國政府<u>抑制</u>物價的努力失敗，也只是傷害到該國的部分公司，而非全部。

☐ 623 **retrieve** [rɪ`triv] (v.) 取回

同 recover
get back

He lost his heart to her almost at once. Never did he <u>retrieve</u> it. (TIME, Jan. 23, 1995, p. 63)
他幾乎在當下就被她完全迷住，從此不想<u>抽身</u>。

☐ 624 **savor** [`sevə] (v.) 品味

Fully <u>savoring</u> Tsai Ming-liang's *He Liu* (The River) requires patience. (TIME, Apr. 14, 1997, p. 48)
要完全<u>品味</u>蔡明亮的《河流》需要耐心。

□ 625 **scramble** [ˋskræmbl] (v.) 爭相搶奪

Rebecca Runkle, a Morgan Stanley analyst who has watched toymakers <u>scramble</u> in the digital age, calls the new CD-ROMs a strategic coup[984].

(TIME, Nov. 11, 1996, p. 37)

摩根史坦利的分析師朗柯目睹了玩具廠商在數位時代的<u>爭奪戰</u>，稱美泰兒公司的這片新光碟是策略出擊成功。

□ 626 **scrape** [skrep] (v.) 刮除

No useful devices exist yet, but the prophets[763] of nanotechnology insist that it may be only a few years before cell-size robots swirl through the body <u>scraping</u> fatty deposits off the walls of blood vessels .... (TIME, July 17, 1995 , p. 44)

目前微細科技還沒有可運作的裝置，但微細科技的預言者堅稱，在短短數年之內，或許就會有像細胞大小的機器，在身體中旋轉移動，<u>括除</u>血管壁的脂肪沉積。

註 nanotechnology (n.) 微細科技，即製造分子或原子大小的材料或機器的技術；swirl (v.) 旋轉移動；deposit (n.) 沉澱物，淤積物

□ 627 **seduce** [sɪˋdjus] (v.) 誘惑

同 tempt

Over the past three months, Microsoft programmers have released[230] a stream of new products designed to <u>seduce</u> Net users away from Netscape. (TIME, Sept. 16, 1996, p. 40)

過去3個月以來，微軟的程式設計師推出一大堆新產品，以<u>吸引</u>網路使用者遠離網景。

□ 628 **shatter** [ˋʃætɚ] (v.) 使粉碎

同 destroy

The Nintendo 64 <u>shatters</u> the convention of two-dimensional horizontal scrolling video games.

(TIME, May 20, 1996, p. 60)

「任天堂64」<u>打破</u>了傳統的電視遊樂器那種兩度空間的水平捲動模式。

☐ 629 **shell** [ʃɛl] (v.) 砲擊

They <u>shelled</u> and blockaded Visoko, where Canadians (peacekeepers) were posted.

(TIME, June 26, 1995, p. 38)

他們<u>砲轟</u>並封鎖加拿大和平維持部隊駐紮的維索科鎮。

註 blockade (v.) 封鎖

☐ 630 **shun** [ʃʌn] (v.) 規避

同 avoid

In an era in which management gurus[713] strive to push decision making down the chain, E-mail has made it easier for middle managers to <u>shun</u> responsibility by bucking decisions up the ladder.

(TIME, Apr. 21, 1997, p. 50)

這個時代，管理大師大力推動將決策權責下放，電子郵件卻使中階主管更輕易就能將決策往上推而<u>逃避</u>責任。

註 strive (v.) 努力去做；buck (v.) (口語) 推卸 (責任等)

☐ 631 **shuttle** [ˈʃʌtl] (v.) 往返，穿梭

For three years, the West has sought a diplomatic solution to the conflict[295] in Bosnia while sending in U.N. peacekeepers to <u>shuttle</u> around a war zone and provide humanitarian aid. (TIME, June 12, 1995, p. 50)

3年來，西方各國一方面透過外交途徑尋找波士尼亞戰爭的解決之道，一方面派遣聯合國和平維持部隊<u>穿梭</u>於交戰區內提供人道援助。

☐ 632 **snap** [snæp] (v.) 毫不留情面地說

During rehearsals[767], Love and guitarist Eric Erlandson <u>snap</u> at each other. (TIME, Mar. 27, 1995, p. 70)

在彩排時，羅芙和吉他手艾蘭森互相<u>數落</u>對方，<u>措辭非常尖銳</u>。

□ 633 **snap up** [snæp ʌp] 爭相搶購

They (moviegoers) <u>snap up</u> copies of Winston Groom's 1986 novel, on which the film (*Gump*) was based .... (TIME, Aug. 1, 1994, p. 52)
《阿甘正傳》的影迷<u>爭相搶購</u>該電影的原著——葛倫1986年的小說。

□ 634 **spell** [spɛl] (v.) 意味，招致

同 signal

It has become commonplace[292], in this digital era, that electronic communication will <u>spell</u> doom[698] for authoritarian regimes. (TIME, Aug. 19, 1996, p. 52)
在這個數位化的時代，電子通訊將為專制政權<u>敲響喪鐘</u>，已是老生常談的說法。

□ 635 **spur** [spɜ] (v.) 刺激，激勵

PC sales are likely to pick up too, <u>spurring</u> demand for Asian-made components like disk drives and monitors. (TIME, Aug. 5, 1996, p. 42)
個人電腦的銷售也可能會好轉，因而<u>刺激</u>對亞洲製的元件如磁碟機和顯示器的需求。
註 to pick up（情勢、健康、成績等）好轉

□ 636 **strand** [strænd] (v.) 使進退兩難，使束手無策

The role is oddly similar to Schwarzenegger's persona in *Last Action Hero*: someone who plays a superman at work but in the real world is <u>stranded</u> without a script. (TIME, July 18, 1994, p. 55)
這個角色與阿諾史瓦辛格在《最後魔鬼英雄》中所扮演的角色出奇地相似，在銀幕上扮演超人，在真實世界裡卻<u>一籌莫展，不知所適</u>。
註 persona (n.)（戲劇、小說裡的）角色，人物；
script (n.)（戲劇、電影等的）腳本

□ 637 **strangle** [ˈstræŋgl̩] (v.)（把人）勒死，抑制，阻撓

The members of the larger patriot movement are usually family men and women who feel <u>strangled</u> by the economy, abandoned[111] by the government .... (TIME, Dec. 19, 1994, p. 48)

這個較大的愛國組織，其成員通常是來自家庭、覺得被生計<u>壓得喘不過氣</u>，且有被政府遺棄之感的男女。

□ 638 **stride** [straɪd] (v.) 大跨步

But Chiappe's foot had been so badly burned he could barely hobble[576], let alone <u>stride</u> around looking for ancient dinosaur bones.

(TIME, Jan. 8, 1996, p. 38)

可是〔古生物學家〕賈普的腳嚴重灼傷，連跛著走都很吃力，更別說是<u>跑來跑去</u>尋找古代的恐龍骨頭了。

□ 639 **stuff** [stʌf] (v.) 充塞，裝滿

同 cram

Browsers brought order to the chaos[286] of the World Wide Web, a corner of the Net <u>stuffed</u> with text, sounds and pictures. (TIME, Sept. 16, 1996, p. 40)

導覽器使處在網際網路一角<u>充塞</u>著文字、聲音與圖片的「全球資訊網」這個混亂的世界，變得井然有序。

□ 640 **stumble** [ˈstʌmbl̩] (v.) 摔倒，喻失敗

In January she <u>stumbled</u> in her men's fall collection, showing loose garments in prison stripes; Jewish groups protested that they looked like concentration-camp garb. (TIME, Oct. 9, 1995, p. 47)

1月時，她〔川久保玲〕<u>栽</u>在秋季男裝系列上。當時展示的是有囚服條紋的寬鬆衣服，猶太團體抗議這些服裝看起來像是集中營的衣服。

641 **subsidize** [ˈsʌbsəˌdaɪz] (v.) 給與補助金

Fel-Pro also <u>subsidizes</u> tutoring for children having trouble at school and helps with college counseling. (TIME, May 6, 1996, p. 52)
Fel-Pro公司也<u>補助</u>學業有困難的員工子女家敎費用，並在申請大學方面提供諮詢。

642 **surf** [sɝf] (v.) 衝浪，喩上網遨遊

But it's not hard to imagine millions of people a few years from now <u>surfing</u> the World Wide Web through their video-game players with Sonic and Mario at their side. (TIME, May 20, 1996, p. 60)
但是我們不難想像數年之後，會有數百萬人利用他們的電視遊樂器，在音速小子與瑪俐歐的陪伴下，<u>暢遊</u>全球資訊網。

643 **surge** [sɝdʒ] (v.) 急速上升，暴漲

同 increase

Sales of Japanese cars equipped with CD-ROMs and satellite navigation systems are already <u>surging</u>—from 306,000 in 1994 to a projected 750,000 this year. (TIME, Nov. 4, 1996, p. 54)
配備有唯讀光碟磁以及衛星導航系統的日本車，銷售量正<u>大幅上升</u>，從1994年的30萬6千輛增加到今年預估的75萬輛。
註 project (v.) 預估

644 **surpass** [səˈpæs] (v.) 超越，凌駕

Star Wars demonstrated[155] that revenues from film-related action figures, magnets and whatnot could rival[358] a movie's ticket sales—and in at least two cases, *Batman* and *Jurassic Park*, even <u>surpass</u> box-office revenues. (TIME, Dec. 2, 1996, p. 70)
《星際大戰》顯示與電影相關的動感小玩偶、冰箱吸鐵與雜七雜八小玩意的收入足可與票房收入匹敵，至少在《蝙蝠俠》和《侏儸紀公園》這兩個例子中，商品的收入甚至<u>超過</u>票房收入。
註 revenue (n.) 收入；whatnot (n.) 種種東西，等等；
　　box-office (a.) 票房的，叫座的

□ ⁶⁴⁵ **swarm** [swɔrm] (v.) 蜂擁

The beggars who <u>swarm</u> through other Indian cities are almost nowhere to be seen, making Surat, by many standards, a picture of India's prosperous future. (TIME, Mar. 25, 1996, p. 46)
在印度秀拉市，沒有像其他城市一樣乞丐蜂擁而入，就許多標準來看，秀拉市呈現的是印度一片美好的前景。

□ ⁶⁴⁶ **tamper** [ˋtæmpɚ] (v.) 篡改

Before Java allows any line of code to be executed, it determines whether the command is a legal one, using powerful encryption to ensure[173] that the program hasn't been <u>tampered</u> with.
(TIME, Jan. 22, 1996, p. 44)
在「爪哇」執行任何一行程式碼之前，它會先判斷這個指令是否合法，在這過程裡它會利用有效的編碼方式來確定這個程式沒有遭到篡改。
註 encryption (n.) 譯成密碼，密碼化

□ ⁶⁴⁷ **tap** [tæp] (v.) 開發，利用

Eager to <u>tap</u> international aid before the P.L.O. gets it all, Hussein hinted that he might agree to terms of a full peace treaty even if Syria is still haggling. (TIME, Aug. 1, 1994, p. 39)
〔約旦國王〕胡笙急著想覺得國際援助，以免國際援助被巴解組織獨占，因此他暗示，即使敘利亞對於簽訂全面和平條約仍爭論不休，他還是可能同意該條約的條件。
註 haggle (v.) 與人討價還價，爭論

☐ [648] **tempt** [tɛmpt] (v.) 誘惑

Even with the price cutting that started last week and is likely to continue through the holiday season, the (32-bit) systems are still far too expensive to <u>tempt</u> consumers used to paying $100 or less for a game machine with plenty of good software. (TIME, May 22, 1995, p. 66)
32位元系統的遊戲機上週開始降價並可能在此長假期間維持此價不變,儘管如此,對於那些慣於用百元或更低的價錢,就可買到一部配備許多好軟體的消費者而言,還是貴得買不下手。

☐ [649] **tip** [tɪp] (v.) 使傾斜

The new finding <u>tips</u> the balance steeply toward the bird-as-dinosaur camp. (TIME, Jan. 8, 1996, p. 38)
這次的新發現為「鳥類是恐龍」這一派帶來壓倒性的優勢。

☐ [650] **topple** [ˈtɑpl] (v.) 推翻,傾倒

同 overthrow

Then <u>toppling</u> him would have meant U.S. occupation of Iraq, which was untenable for America, its allies[275] and the Arab world.
(TIME, Sept. 23, 1996, p. 35)
當時,若推翻了海珊,美國就得占領伊拉克,這是美國、盟國與阿拉伯國家都不樂見的。
註 untenable (a.)(理論、立場)難獲支持的

☐ [651] **torment** [tɔrˈmɛnt] (v.) 折磨

同 torture

The Bosnian Serbs <u>torment</u> them, humiliate them, take them hostage. (TIME, June 12, 1995, p. 52)
波士尼亞的塞爾維亞人折磨他們,侮辱他們,把他們當作人質。
註 hostage (n.) 人質

☐ ⁶⁵² **trail** [trel] (v.) 尾隨，追踪

同 follow

He got three speeding tickets—two from the same cop who was <u>trailing</u> him .... (TIME, Jan. 13, 1997, p. 35)
他拿了3張超速罰單，其中兩張是<u>尾隨</u>他的同一警察開的。

☐ ⁶⁵³ **trigger** [ˋtrɪgɚ] (v.) 觸發

American policymakers assume⁴⁹³ a declaration of Taiwan's independence would <u>trigger</u> an attack from the mainland. (TIME, Feb. 12, 1996, p. 18)
美國決策者認爲，台灣宣布獨立將<u>引發</u>中共攻台。

☐ ⁶⁵⁴ **tug** [tʌg] (v.) 用力拉

同 yank

With his fractious⁴¹⁵ party <u>tugging</u> in different directions and the opposition united against him, stability is unlikely to be a characteristic of the new culture Lee promised so loftily at his inauguration. (TIME, June 17, 1996, p. 54)
面對黨員不聽使喚且對黨的發展方向意見分歧，而反對陣營卻聯合起來對付他，李登輝在就職時所高舉的「新文化」很可能不會以穩定爲特色。

註 loftily (adv.)（目的、主義）崇高地

☐ ⁶⁵⁵ **uncover** [ʌnˋkʌvɚ] (v.) 揭發，發現

同 discover

The specialists did not <u>uncover</u> any noticeable deviations from the norm. (TIME, May 8, 1995, p. 74)
專科醫師並未<u>發現</u>任何值得注意的異狀。

☐ ⁶⁵⁶ **underline** [ˋʌndɚ͵laɪn] (v.) 強調

同 underscore

The veto has been used only three times in the legislature's 49 years, which <u>underlines</u> how hard pressed Lee feels at the moment.
(TIME, June 17, 1996, p. 54)
立法院49年來只用過3次否決權，這也<u>凸顯</u>了李登輝此刻眞的是被逼急了。

註 hard pressed 處於強大壓力下的，窘迫的

☐ 657 **unravel** [ʌnˋrævl] (v.) 弄清楚，解開（謎題、祕密等）

It was an extraordinarily productive year for the genetic engineers racing to <u>unravel</u> the secrets of human DNA. (TIME, Jan. 3, 1994, p. 75)

對於急著想要<u>解開</u>人類DNA之謎的基因工程學家而言，這是個格外豐收的一年。

☐ 658 **unveil** [ʌnˋvel] (v.) 首次發表（新產品、計畫）

同 reveal

Last week IBM and a group of 15 U.S. and Canadian banking behemoths[972] <u>unveiled</u> a venture[794] that aims to provide a full range of financial services to the banks' 60 million customers at the touch of a telephone button or the click[884] of a mouse. (TIME, Sept. 23, 1996, p. 42)

上週IBM與美加地區15家重量級銀行<u>宣布成立</u>一家合夥公司，其目標是為這些銀行的6千萬客戶提供全方位的金融服務，客戶只需按按電話按鍵或滑鼠，一切就可以辦妥。

☐ 659 **vanish** [ˋvænɪʃ] (v.) 消失

同 disappear

It's a bad idea to let Cruise <u>vanish</u> for almost an hour in the middle of his picture.

(TIME, Nov. 21, 1994, p. 112)

他在影片中讓克魯斯<u>消失</u>將近一個小時，實在不智。

☐ 660 **verify** [ˋvɛrə͵faɪ] (v.) 證實

同 confirm

If the results are <u>verified</u>, it is a turning point in human history, suggesting that life exists not just on two planets in one paltry[843] solar system but throughout this magnificent universe.

(TIME, Aug. 19, 1996, p. 38)

假如結果<u>證實</u>無誤，這可以說是人類史上的一個轉捩點，表示生命不只存在於一個小小的太陽系裡的兩顆行星，而是遍布整個浩瀚的宇宙。

661 **warrant** [ˋwɔrənt] (v.) 視…爲正當，認可

同merit

Though Targ has not yet published her results, she describes them as sufficiently "encouraging" to <u>warrant</u> a larger follow-up study with 100 AIDS patients. (TIME, June 24, 1996, p. 39)

塔格醫生尚未發表她的實驗結果，但她形容這結果令人精神爲之一振，<u>使她可名正言順</u>再做一個較大的、有100名愛滋病人受試的後續實驗。

註 follow-up (a.) 後續的，補充的（調查、報導）

662 **whip** [hwɪp] (v.) 擊敗

同defeat

Newly ascendant to the No. 1 world ranking after last week's Australian Open, Agassi is likely to be surrounded by fellow stars (at Atlanta), but Michael Chang, who <u>whipped</u> Agassi in straight sets in the semifinals at Melbourne, is less certain to appear. (TIME, Feb. 5, 1996, p. 13)

上週打完澳洲公開賽後新登上世界第一寶座的阿格西，在亞特蘭大奧運也不乏明星級對手，可是在澳洲公開賽的準決賽中以直落三<u>痛宰</u>阿格西的張德培，卻不是那麼確定會參加奧運。

註 ascendant (a.) 上升的；straight (a.) 連續的，不間斷的

663 **wreck** [rɛk] (v.) 破壞

Tull, feeling only jealousy and hatred, attempts to <u>wreck</u> Barry's career and his posh life.
(TIME, May 1, 1995, p. 90)

心中只有嫉妒與恨意的杜爾，想著要去<u>破壞</u>巴利的事業與其優渥的生活。

註 posh (a.) 奢侈的，豪華的

- addict 上癮者
- adversary 對手
- advocate 提倡者
- alert 戒備
- anecdote 軼聞，小故事
- antidote 解毒劑，（解決問題的）對策
- arbitration 仲裁
- arrogance 傲慢
- assets 資產
- autonomy 自治（權），自主性
- beneficiary 受益人
- bid 努力，嘗試
- blockbuster 大受歡迎的人事物
- bloom 盛開，繁盛
- capacity 職位
- casualty 傷亡
- celebrity 聲譽，名流
- censorship 審查制度
- chunk 大塊
- clamor 喧嚷
- cliche 陳腔濫調
- consolation 安慰
- context 背景，大環境
- conviction 信念
- counterpart 相當的人（物）
- cult 教派，引申為崇拜
- curfew 宵禁
- delinquency （債務、稅款的）拖欠
- demise 逝世
- dilemma 兩難的困境
- disguise 偽裝
- dismay 喪膽，驚慌
- disruption 中斷，混亂，運行失常
- dissident 異議份子
- doom 滅亡的命運，劫數
- edge 優勢，有利地位
- expertise 專門技術
- fiasco 徹底失敗
- flaw 缺陷，缺點
- foul 犯規，不合法
- franchise 製造商授予的某特定地區的經銷權
- fraud 詐欺
- frenzy 狂亂，發狂，狂熱
- friction 摩擦
- gear （供某種用途的）工具，裝備，服裝
- glamo(u)r 魅力，魔力
- gratification 滿足
- gross 總收入，毛利
- guise 外表，偽裝
- guru 大師，專家，權威
- gut(s) （口語）膽量，毅力
- handicap 殘障，障礙
- haul 一段時間，距離
- havoc 大肆蹂躪，混亂
- hedge 預防措施
- heed 注意，留意
- hegemony 霸權
- heyday 全盛時期
- hub 中心
- hurdle 困難，挑戰
- hybrid 混合，雜種
- hypocrisy 偽善
- infidelity 不忠，偷情
- instinct 本能
- intuition 直覺
- knack 竅門，高明的本領
- lag 落後
- landscape 景色，地貌
- legacy 傳承，遺產，影響
- legitimacy 合法性，認可
- lieutenant 助手
- limelight 公眾矚目的焦點，光采

- [ ] literacy 讀寫的能力
- [ ] loophole （法律）漏洞
- [ ] lure 吸引力，誘餌
- [ ] lyrics 歌詞
- [ ] maneuver 技巧，手法
- [ ] mania 狂熱，熱中
- [ ] manipulation 不正當手法
- [ ] mayhem 失控，脫序，暴力橫行
- [ ] melodrama 通俗劇
- [ ] memoir 回憶錄
- [ ] moderation 適度，節制
- [ ] namesake 同名的人或物
- [ ] newsletter （機關的）內部刊物
- [ ] obsession 偏執，迷戀，耽溺
- [ ] onset 發作
- [ ] outfit 一套服裝
- [ ] parallel 可相比擬的事物，比較
- [ ] peer 同輩，同儕
- [ ] perspective 看法，觀點
- [ ] pinnacle 頂點，高峰
- [ ] plight 苦境
- [ ] poise 平衡，姿態
- [ ] portfolio （投資者持有的）投資組合
- [ ] precedent 先例
- [ ] predator 獵捕者，掠奪者
- [ ] predicament 困境
- [ ] prohibition 禁令
- [ ] prophet 預言者
- [ ] prototype 原型
- [ ] psyche 心靈
- [ ] rally 群眾大會，聚會
- [ ] rehearsal 排演

- [ ] retaliation 報復
- [ ] reversion 復歸
- [ ] rhetoric 辭令，浮誇不實的話
- [ ] sensation 轟動的人、事、物
- [ ] setback 挫折，失敗
- [ ] siege 圍城，包圍
- [ ] skirmish 小戰鬥
- [ ] smash 轟動，熱門人物
- [ ] spell 一段時間
- [ ] spoiler 選舉中無望選上但可拉低他人得票數的攪局者
- [ ] stagnation 不景氣，停滯
- [ ] stake 賭注，投資，利害關係
- [ ] staple 主要成分，經常出現的內容
- [ ] stereotype 刻板印象
- [ ] stewardship 管理
- [ ] stigma 污名，恥辱
- [ ] stroke 中風
- [ ] stroll 溜達，散步
- [ ] suspense 懸疑
- [ ] symptom 徵候，前兆
- [ ] threshold （事物的）開端
- [ ] transaction 交易，買賣
- [ ] transmission 傳遞
- [ ] treason 叛國（罪）
- [ ] upheaval 大變動，動亂
- [ ] velocity 速度
- [ ] venture 冒險的活動，有風險的事業
- [ ] visionary 有遠見的人
- [ ] watershed 轉捩點，開啟新發展的關鍵
- [ ] windfall 意外之財

☐ 664 **addict** [ə`dɪkt] (n.) 上癮者　(v.) 使…上癮

Oprah, who once confronted[142] her own childhood sexual abuse[113] on her show, last week broke down during a program featuring[564] female drug users and revealed that she had smoked cocaine in the mid-1970s and become an <u>addict</u>.

(TIME, Jan. 23, 1995, p. 63)

奧普拉曾經在自己的節目中挺身面對自己童年遭到性虐待的事實，上週在一個以女吸毒者現身說法爲號召的節目中，她的心防再度崩潰，並透露她在1970年代中期吸古柯鹼成<u>癮</u>。

註 to break down （情感、精神）崩潰

☐ 665 **adversary** [`ædvə,sɛrɪ] (n.) 對手

同 opponent
　　enemy
反 ally

Diplomacy without force against an <u>adversary</u> without scruples is useless. (TIME, May 15, 1995, p. 48)

要與一個肆無忌憚的<u>對手</u>進行外交，沒有實力作後盾是不行的。

註 scruple (n.) 道德上的顧忌

☐ 666 **advocate** [`ædvəkɪt] (n.) 提倡者　[`ædvə,ket] (v.) 提倡，主張

同 (n.) proponent
　　(v.) recommend

That's because much of AIDS research would be impossible without experiments that animal <u>advocates</u> consider unethical. (TIME, July 8, 1996, p. 39)

因爲，愛滋病研究有一大部分非依賴動物實驗不行，而<u>保護動物人士</u>認爲這種實驗有違道德。

☐ 667 **alert** [ə`lɜt] (n.) 戒備　(v.) 警告，提醒

Hundreds of thousands of Chinese troops move to embarkation ports in the provinces of Zhejiang, Fujian and Guangdong. In response, Lee puts Taiwan's armed forces on the highest level of <u>alert</u> and mobilizes all reserves. (TIME, Aug. 28, 1995, p. 14)

數十萬中國軍隊集結在浙江、福建、廣東的登船碼頭。李登輝下令三軍進入最高<u>警戒</u>狀態，並全員動員後備軍人作爲因應。

註 embarkation (n.) 搭乘

☐ 668 **anecdote** [ˈænɪkˌdot] (n.) 軼聞，小故事

Princeton astrophysicist David Spergel offered a telling historical <u>anecdote</u> in an address to colleagues at the American Astronomical Society's January meeting .... (TIME, Mar. 6, 1995, p. 76)
1月份美國天文學會上，普林斯敦大學的天體物理學家史柏格對其同僚做了一場演講，演講中他說了一則很有代表性的歷史<u>小故事</u>。
註 telling (a.) 有力的

☐ 669 **antidote** [ˈæntɪˌdot] (n.) 解毒劑，（解決問題的）對策，手段

同 cure
remedy

Jessica Dubroff's adventure ... might have worked as a cute, uplifting <u>antidote</u> to the shaming mess of the O.J. Simpson trial. (TIME, Apr. 22, 1996, p. 39)
杜布若夫的冒險故事，也許可以成為在丟人現眼的辛普森案醜聞過後，一劑既俏皮又振奮人心的清涼劑。
註 mess (n.) 麻煩，困境

☐ 670 **arbitration** [ˌɑrbəˈtreʃən] (n.) 仲裁

A clause added to athletes' entry forms stipulates that competitors' disputes[302] be resolved by the Court of <u>Arbitration</u> for Sport, a 12-member body set up by the International Olympic Committee in 1994. (TIME, June 3, 1996, p. 17)
在運動員的報名表上，多了一條規則，規定參賽者間的爭議應由12人組成的「運動<u>仲裁</u>法庭」來解決。這個法庭是國際奧會在1994年設置的。
註 stipulate (v.)（合約等）規定，載明

☐ 671 **arrogance** [ˈærəgəns] (n.) 傲慢

But Fidelity, the biggest fund company of all, known for its <u>arrogance</u> and aggressiveness, is under unprecedented[104] strain. (TIME, Sept. 30, 1996, p. 44)
但是，全球最大，並以<u>托大</u>的態度和積極的手段著稱的富達基金公司，卻面臨空前的吃緊狀態。
註 strain (n.)（面臨困境產生的身心）壓力，緊張

□ 672 **assets** [ˈæsɛts] (n.) 資產

Mutual funds have topped $3.145 trillion in <u>assets</u> .... (TIME, Sept. 30, 1996, p. 44)
共同基金的<u>資產</u>已經超過3兆1,450億美元。

□ 673 **autonomy** [ɔˈtɑnəmɪ] (n.) 自治（權），自主性

同 independence

But China's dismissal of the elected legislature and warning of a crackdown on the press have Washington very nervous that Beijing may not give Hong Kong the <u>autonomy</u> called for in its 1984 transfer[267] agreement with Britain.

(TIME, Nov. 18, 1996, p. 31)
但是中國要解散民選立法局的動作和要整飭新聞界的警告都使華盛頓相當緊張，害怕北京不會給予香港<u>自治權</u>，這是中國於1984年與英國達成的轉移協定中所允諾的。

註 crackdown (n.) 大力整飭，鎮壓；to call for 要求

□ 674 **beneficiary** [ˌbɛnəˈfɪʃərɪ] (n.) 受益人

同 recipient

The new law will turn welfare over to the 50 states, where <u>beneficiaries</u> will be required to find work within two years, be limited to five years of benefits during their lifetime and face stringent[465] restrictions aimed at limiting out-of-wedlock births. (TIME, Aug. 25, 1996, p. 25)
新的法律規定把福利政策下放給50個州政府來主管，<u>接受福利金救助者</u>必須在兩年內找到工作，一輩子最多領取5年的福利金，同時受到嚴格的限制，以期控制非婚生子女的人數。

註 to turn over 將（工作、責任等）移交；wedlock (n.) 婚姻；out-of-wedlock 指庶出的，私生的

□ 675 **bid** [bɪd] (n.v.) 努力，嘗試

同 attempt

Because of pressure from the U.S., Beijing believes, it lost its <u>bid</u> to host[190] the 2000 Olympics, which went instead to Sydney, Australia. (TIME, Mar. 25, 1996, p. 14)

北京相信是美國施壓才使中國無法獲得公元2000年奧運主辦權，而輸給澳洲雪梨。

□ 676 **blockbuster** [blɑk,bʌstə] (n.) 非常暢銷的、大受歡迎的人事物

The Soul of Chant, in any event, has risen to No. 10 on the classical charts, not a <u>blockbuster</u> like *Chant*, but enough to make Milan (Records) Chairman Emmanuel Chamboredon rejoice.

(TIME, May 22, 1995, p. 72)

不管怎樣，《聖詠之魂》這張專輯已升上古典音樂排行榜第10名，雖沒有《聖詠》那張專輯那樣大賣，但成績還是足以讓米蘭唱片公司的董事長錢伯敦感到高興。

註 rejoice (v.) 感到高興

□ 677 **bloom** [blum] (n.v.) 盛開，繁盛

同 (v.) blossom

Along with the wastewater came a strain of cholera that found a home in huge algal <u>blooms</u> stimulated[253] by unusually warm ocean waters and abundant pollution. (TIME, July 8, 1996, p. 40)

這種廢水夾帶了一種霍亂病毒，這些病毒在因異常溫暖的海水及大量污染的刺激而滋長的大群海藻中，找到溫床。

註 strain (n.)（動植物）品種；algal (a.) 海藻的

□ 678 **capacity** [kə`pæsətɪ] (n.) 職位

"My job is to help our clients expand[177] their perceived range of possibilities," Saffo says. Of course, in that <u>capacity</u>, he acknowledges[114], "you can affect[118] outcomes." (TIME, July 15, 1996, p. 40)

「我的工作是幫助客戶擴展視野，了解有更多的可能性。」薩佛說。他承認以這種角色，當然「可以影響到結果。」

註 perceive (v.) 察覺，看見

☐ 679 **casualty** [ˋkæʒʊəltɪ] (n.) 傷亡

同 victim

U.S. military experts estimate that Beijing would have to deploy[535] half a million men for a victorious assault[280] and that casualties would be in the range of 50% . (TIME, Mar. 25, 1996, p. 16)
美國軍事專家估計北京得動用50萬大軍才有勝算，而且傷亡估計會在50%之譜。

☐ 680 **celebrity** [səˋlɛbrətɪ] (n.) 聲譽，名流

同 star

A master at elevating his own celebrity, Calvin Klein may be one of the most recognizable names anywhere in the world. (TIME, June 17, 1996, p. 19)
卡文‧克萊是打知名度的高手，可能是世界上最廣爲人知的名字之一。

☐ 681 **censorship** [ˋsɛnsɚˏʃɪp] (n.) 審查制度

As Internet pioneer John Gilmor once said, "The Net interprets censorship as damage and routes around it." (TIME, Jan. 15, 1996, p. 51)
如同網際網路的先驅約翰‧吉爾摩爾說過的：「網際網路將言論檢查視爲一種傷害，會想法子避開它。」
註 route (v.) 安排路線

☐ 682 **chunk** [tʃʌŋk] (n.) 大塊

Magellan underperformed because Vinik put an enormous chunk of the fund in bonds, believing that stocks were overvalued. (TIME, Sept. 30, 1996, p. 44)
麥哲倫基金之所以表現差勁，是因爲維尼克相信股票指數已經被高估，而把大筆的資金投注於債券。

□ 683 **clamor** [ˈklæmɚ] (n.) 喧嚷　(v.) 吵著要…

同 (n.) uproar

As Okinawans' <u>clamor</u> for the expulsion of U.S. bases grows, Tokyo and Washington are listening. (TIME, Nov. 6, 1995, p. 14)

隨著將美軍基地掃出沖繩的<u>聲浪</u>與日俱增，美日政府也開始正視此一問題。

□ 684 **cliche** [kliˈʃe] (n.) 陳腔濫調

She challenges the <u>cliche</u> that women are more indirect than men and that tentativeness reflects a lack of confidence. (TIME, Oct. 3, 1994, p. 60)

人們常說女人言行不如男人直接，猶豫不決表示缺乏信心，她就是要挑戰這種<u>陳腔濫調</u>。

註 tentativeness (n.) 猶豫

□ 685 **consolation** [ˌkɑnsəˈleʃən] (n.) 安慰

It seemed odd when the Dick Morris story broke open that the President, First Lady and Vice President placed calls of <u>consolation</u> to Dick Morris. (TIME, Sept. 23, 1996, p. 60)

摩理斯的事情曝光時，總統、第一夫人與副總統都打電話去<u>安慰</u>他，這不是有點奇怪嗎？

□ 686 **context** [ˈkɑntɛkst] (n.) 背景，大環境

"We are concerned about what kind of China will emerge," says Singapore's Lee. "The problem is of such gigantic size that it is not solvable in the Asian <u>context</u> alone." (TIME, Mar. 25, 1996, p. 16)

「我們關切的是將來會出現怎樣的一個新中國，」新加坡的李光耀說，「這個問題太龐大了，不是在亞洲<u>之內</u>解決得了的。」

☐ 687 **conviction** [kən`vɪkʃən] (n.) 信念

It (the discovery) would ... strongly support the growing <u>conviction</u> that life, possibly even intelligent life, is commonplace[292] throughout the cosmos. (TIME, Aug. 19, 1996, p. 40)

這項發現將大力支持一個日漸盛行的<u>信念</u>，那就是生命，甚至可能包括有智慧的生命，其遍及宇宙乃是不稀奇的事。

☐ 688 **counterpart** [`kaʊntə͏,pɑrt] (n.) 相當的人（物）

同 equivalent

Last month Wu King-chan, the official whom Taiwan has appointed "governor" of Fujian province moved his office from Taipei to Quemoy for the first time ... Significantly, his Beijing-appointed <u>counterpart</u> across the strait did not utter a single word of protest. (TIME, Feb. 19, 1996, p. 21)

上個月台灣當局所任命的福建省省長吳金讚，首度把辦公室從台北遷至金門。值得注意的是，海峽對岸由北京所任命的<u>福建省長</u>並沒有發出任何抗議。

☐ 689 **cult** [kʌlt] (n.) 教派，引申為崇拜

Following the trail trod recently by (Jackie) Chan, Chow (Yun-fat) is already a <u>cult</u> idol in the U.S.

(TIME, May 6, 1996, p. 63)

依循成龍最近走出來的路線，周潤發已經是美國人<u>崇拜</u>的偶像。

註 trod 行走，踩踏，是tread的過去式

☐ 690 **curfew** [`kɝfju] (n.) 宵禁

Officials ordered a <u>curfew</u>, to no avail.

(TIME, Nov. 28, 1994, p. 46)

官員下令<u>宵禁</u>，但無效。

註 to no avail 完全沒用

☐ 691 **delinquency** [dɪˋlɪŋkwənsɪ] (n.)（債務、稅款的）拖欠

He made the $6,000 payment covering seven years of <u>delinquency</u> after being offered the Cabinet post. (TIME, Jan. 3, 1994, p. 17)

他被提名入閣後，償還了7年間<u>未付</u>的稅款6千美元。

☐ 692 **demise** [dɪˋmaɪz] (n.) 逝世

Yet no matter how hard the current leadership tries to forestall political challenge, Deng's <u>demise</u> will throw open the question of how to fill the space he leaves behind. (TIME, Jan. 23, 1995, p. 50)

不管目前的領導班子如何努力去防範未來的政治挑戰，鄧的<u>死亡</u>將打開一道問題，那就是如何填補他留下的權力真空。

註 forestall (v.)（以先發制人的手段去）阻止

☐ 693 **dilemma** [dəˋlɛmə] (n.) 兩難的困境

A panel finds that corporate and public policies in the U.S. do not ease the work-family <u>dilemma</u>.

(TIME, May 6, 1996, p. 52)

一專題討論小組發覺美國企業內部政策和政府公共政策，皆不能紓解工作與家庭<u>無法兼顧的困境</u>。

☐ 694 **disguise** [dɪsˋgaɪz] (n.v.) 偽裝

Clinton feels so physically isolated[589] at the White House that he slipped out of the compound ... five or six times last year. (Hillary Clinton does the same, but more often and usually in <u>disguise</u>.)

(TIME, Feb. 7, 1994, p. 24)

柯林頓覺得待在白宮憋得讓人受不了，因此去年就溜出去白宮五、六次。（希拉蕊也一樣，只是溜得更頻繁，而且通常是<u>喬裝</u>出去。）

註 compound (n.) 有圍牆的房子或大院

☐ 695 **dismay** [dɪs`me] (n.) 喪膽，驚慌

For its part, Mexico will have to abide by an austerity plan that, to the <u>dismay</u> of most Mexicans, will give the U.S. unprecedented[104] say over the country's economic policies.

(TIME, Mar. 6, 1995, p. 25)

對墨西哥而言，將不得不遵行這個緊縮國家支出的計畫，賦予美國對墨國經濟政策前所未有的發言權，儘管墨國人民大多對此感到驚愕。

註 to abide by 遵行，奉行；austerity (n.)（國家開支上）緊縮

☐ 696 **disruption** [dɪs`rʌpʃən] (n.) 中斷，混亂，運行失常

Similarly, climate <u>disruptions</u> may be giving new life to such ancient scourges[1036] as yellow fever, meningitis and cholera, while fostering[568] the spread of emerging diseases like hantavirus.

(TIME, July 8, 1996, p. 40)

同樣地，<u>不正常的氣候變化</u>也可能於助長新興疾病如漢他病毒的擴散之際，使那些古老的災禍如黃熱病、腦膜炎及霍亂再度爆發。

☐ 697 **dissident** [`dɪsədənt] (n.) 異議份子

The imposition of an 11-year prison sentence on <u>dissident</u> Wang Dan last month will complicate the talks (between China and the U.S.) but will not wreck[663] economic interests. (TIME, Nov. 18, 1996, p. 31)

上個月對<u>異議份子</u>王丹的11年牢獄判決，將會增加中美會談的複雜性，但還不至於破壞經濟利益。

☐ 698 **doom** [dum] (n.) 滅亡的命運，劫數

同 fate

After the comet hit, a second jolt[922] from volcanoes may have helped send the dinosaurs to their <u>doom</u>. (TIME, Jan. 9, 1995, p. 59)

彗星撞擊後，火山爆發引起的第二次劇烈震動，可能加速恐龍<u>劫數</u>的到來。

☐ 699 **edge** [ɛdʒ] (n.) 優勢，有利地位

> With a new 41-to-39 <u>edge</u> over Democrats, Republicans in the California state assembly should have been able to oust veteran[373] Democratic speaker Willie Brown and install[198] one of their own. (TIME, Feb. 6, 1995, p. 15)
> 加州議會改選後，對民主黨議員占有41比39<u>優勢</u>的共和黨議員，應能把資深的民主黨籍議長布朗拉下台，改由共和黨籍的出任。
> 註 oust (v.) 逐出，趕走

☐ 700 **expertise** [ˌɛkspɚˈtiz] (n.) 專門技術

> And across Asia the company (IBM) is deploying[535] a new generation of salespeople who plan to offer IBM's hardware and software and also Big Blue's <u>expertise</u> in setting up business networks in underdeveloped areas.
> (TIME, Nov. 4, 1996, p. 50)
> IBM正在整個亞洲部署新一代的業務員，將提供IBM硬、軟體以及「藍色巨人」的<u>專長</u>，以協助低度開發地區建立商用網路。

☐ 701 **fiasco** [fɪˈæsko] (n.)（因準備或計畫不周詳，而很沒面子地）徹底失敗

同 debacle

> Rusk was second only to Lyndon Johnson as an architect of America's greatest foreign policy <u>fiasco</u>: the divisive, ultimately fruitless war in Vietnam. (TIME, Jan. 9, 1995, p. 19)
> 這場引發國內分裂、徒然無功的越戰，是美國有史以來最大的外交<u>挫敗</u>，而這場挫敗的主其事者，首推詹森（總統），再來就是魯斯克。
> 註 divisive (a.) 引發不和的，造成對立的

□ 702 **flaw** [flɔ] (n.) 缺陷，缺點

同 defect

The researchers found that these executives failed most often because of "an interpersonal <u>flaw</u>" rather than a technical inability. (TIME, Oct. 9, 1995, p. 30)

研究人員發現，這些主管之所以失敗，往往是因為「人際關係<u>不好</u>」，而非技術上有問題。

□ 703 **foul** [faʊl] (n.) 犯規，不合法

China, with seven top women banned[128] from Atlanta on drug charges, cried <u>foul</u> when an American and an Australian who had flunked drug tests were allowed to enter their countries' trials. (TIME, May 13, 1996, p. 13)

大陸有7名頂尖女將因被控使用禁藥而被禁止參加亞特蘭大奧運，而當美國與澳洲各有一位未通過禁藥檢驗的選手得以參加她們國內的資格賽時，大陸立刻嚷嚷，指稱<u>犯規</u>。

註 flunk (v.) 沒通過（測驗）

□ 704 **franchise** [ˈfræntʃaɪz] (n.) 製造商授予的某特定地區的經銷權
(v.) 給…特許經銷權

The 8-megabyte behemoth[972] matched Netscape's <u>franchise</u> browser, Navigator, feature for feature, and at a much better price—free.

(TIME, Sept. 16, 1996, p. 40)

這套占8MB空間的巨大軟體，與網景授權的「領航員」導覽器，在每一項功能上都能相匹敵，而且價錢更誘人——免費。

□ 705 **fraud** [frɔd] (n.) 詐欺

And according to the Los Angeles *Times*,
Gerchas, a jewelry-store owner, has been sued[257]
at least 34 times in recent years for complaints
including allegations of <u>fraud</u> and failure to pay
creditors. (TIME, Feb. 6, 1995, p. 56)
而根據《洛杉磯時報》的報導,珠寶店老闆格恰斯最近幾年
至少就被指控了34次,訴由包括<u>詐欺</u>、欠債不還。

註 complaint (n.)(法律)控告;
allegation (n.)(尤指未經證實的)指控

□ 706 **frenzy** [ˋfrɛnzɪ] (n.) 狂亂,發狂,狂熱

As the stars step from their limos and navigate the
red carpet, the crowds erupt[557] in full <u>frenzy</u>.
(TIME, July 22, 1996, p. 42)
當明星們步下豪華禮車,走過紅地毯,群眾瞬間陷入一片<u>瘋
狂</u>。

註 navigate (v.)(口語)行進於,走過

□ 707 **friction** [ˋfrɪkʃən] (n.) 摩擦

同 conflict

The Administration wants to fight for the U.S.
computer-chip industry, but it does not want trade
<u>friction</u> to topple[650] Japan's fragile[46] reform
coalition government. (TIME, Jan. 10, 1994, p. 9)
美國政府當局想為其國內的電腦晶體業爭些權益,但可不想
因貿易<u>摩擦</u>,而動搖了日本矢志改革、但體質脆弱的聯合政
府。

註 coalition (n.) 聯合政府

□ 708 **gear** [gɪr] (n.)（供某種用途的）工具，裝備，服裝

The state of Louisiana spent $79,000 in 1968 for riot-control equipment. This included such useful civilian <u>gear</u> as machine guns and an armored personnel carrier. (TIME, Feb. 27, 1995, p. 11)

1968年路易斯安那州花了7萬9千美元購置鎮暴裝備，包括機關槍與裝甲運兵車等有用的民用<u>配備</u>。

(n.) 齒輪，（汽車）檔位；
into gear 搭上齒輪，開動運轉，喻進入運作狀態；
into high gear（汽車、自行車）開高速齒輪，喻事物正如火如荼進行

Campaign '96 is roaring <u>into high gear</u>.

(TIME, Mar. 13, 1995, p. 66)

1996年的競選活動鬧哄哄地<u>進入了白熱化</u>。

註 roar (v.)（火車等）轟響著快速前進

□ 709 **glamo(u)r** [ˋglæmə] (n.) 魅力，魔力

同 glitter

The scene would be repeated the following week in Seattle, with cyberczar Bill Gates adding his virtual <u>glamour</u>, and soon in the most touristed spots in the U.S. and a score of other countries.

(TIME, July 22, 1996, p. 42)

下個禮拜，同樣的戲碼將在西雅圖再上演一遍，而且還會加上網路大帝比爾·蓋茲逼真的<u>魅力</u>，不久之後，在美國的幾個熱門觀光勝地以及大約20個國家都會重現這一幕。

□ 710 **gratification** [ˌgrætəfəˋkeʃən] (n.) 滿足

同 satisfaction

Notes Worrble's Sprechial, "We're taking a principle of instant <u>gratification</u> and applying it to a game." (TIME, Oct. 7, 1996, p. 40)

華波公司的斯派若基亞說：「我們採行立即<u>滿足</u>的原則，並將其應用到電腦遊戲上。」

☐ **711 gross** [gros] (n.) 總收入，毛利

Its restaurant at Disney World in Orlando, Florida, claims the world's highest <u>gross</u>, at $45 million in 1995, its first year. (TIME, July 22, 1996, p. 43)

該餐廳在佛羅里達州奧蘭多迪士尼世界的分店，在1995年，也就是其開幕的第一年，總收入是4,500萬美元，創下全球最高<u>總收入</u>的紀錄。

註 claim (v.) 獲得，贏得

☐ **712 guise** [gaɪz] (n.) 外表，偽裝

For the boys, Mattel's new offering is a computer mouse in the <u>guise</u> of a Hot Wheels car, complete with flashing lights and revving engine.

(TIME, Nov. 11, 1996, p. 36)

美泰兒公司給男生的新產品是Hot Wheels玩具車<u>造型</u>的電腦滑鼠，有會閃的燈光和隆隆作響的引擎音效。

註 to be complete with 有，具有；rev (v.) 加快（引擎）轉速

☐ **713 guru** [ˈguru] (n.) 大師，專家，權威

Ide is now Sony's <u>guru</u>, instructing engineers ... in the art of merging[207] home electronics with information technology. (TIME, Feb. 24, 1997, p. 42)

現在井出是新力的<u>宗師</u>，指導他的工程師致力於融合家用電器與資訊科技。

☐ **714 gut(s)** [gʌt(s)] (n.) （口語）膽量，毅力

Yet Haiti's military ... believe that the U.S. lacks the <u>guts</u> for a sustained occupation. "It'd be just like Somalia," says a senior Haitian officer. "Clinton will run away when the first U.S. soldier is returned in a body bag." (TIME, May 16, 1994, p. 47)

但海地軍方認為，美國是孬種，不敢在此長期駐軍。海地一名高階軍官表示：「局勢演變將如索馬利亞一樣，當第一具美軍屍體裝進運屍袋送回美國，柯林頓就會逃之夭夭。」

☐ 715 **handicap** [ˈhændɪˌkæp] (n.) 殘障；障礙

"Enjoy life," he (Magic Johnson) says. "Live. I'm not just talking about people with HIV or AIDS, but about people with problems or <u>handicaps</u> or whatever." (TIME, Feb. 12, 1996, p. 38)

「享受生命的樂趣，」魔術・強森說：「努力活下去。我不只是說那些感染了HIV或愛滋病的人，也是說那些生活遭遇困難、殘障或其他任何問題的人。」

☐ 716 **haul** [hɔl] (n.) 一段時間，距離

As portfolio[758] managers know, the value of diversity may not be obvious in the short run, but it is the wisest policy <u>over the long haul</u>.

(TIME, July 15, 1996, p. 41)

就如有價證券經營者所知，走多樣化路線，其價值短期內可能無法明顯看出，但<u>長遠來看</u>，這是最聰明的策略。

☐ 717 **havoc** [ˈhævək] (n.) 大肆蹂躪，混亂

同 chaos

The real threat for people ... may not be a single disease, but armies of emergent microbes raising <u>havoc</u> among a host of creatures.

(TIME, July 8, 1996, p. 41)

對人類真正的威脅，可能不是單一的疾病，而是大群新興的微生物對許多生物的<u>肆虐</u>。

註 an army of 大群；a host of 許多

☐ 718 **hedge** [hɛdʒ] (n.) 預防措施 (v.) 預防

Tokyo's joint security treaty with Washington allows its defense budget to remain low, and it abhors[481] even thinking about developing a nuclear <u>hedge</u> against North Korea's (nuclear) capabilities. (TIME, Feb. 28, 1994, p. 45)

美日安條約讓日本的國防支出得以一直保持很低，而日本甚至不願意去思考是否發展核子武力，以<u>預防</u>北韓的核武。

☐ 719 **heed** [hid] (n.v.) 注意，留意

As she heads to court this week to contest her estranged husband's petition for custody of the couple's two young boys, Clark should take <u>heed</u> of a similar case decided last fall in Washington.

(TIME, Mar. 20, 1995, p. 40)

本週克拉克前往法庭就其分居的先生所提出兩個小兒子的監護權的訴狀而抗辯時，應該<u>留意</u>去年秋天在華盛頓判定的一個類似案例。

註 estranged (a.)（夫妻）分居的；
petition (n.)（向法院提出的）請求、訴狀；custody (n.) 監護

☐ 720 **hegemony** [`hɛdʒə,monɪ] (n.) 霸權

Judaism, the first faith to crack Christian <u>hegemony</u>, is today deeply rooted in the U.S., although it is being eroded by secularization, low birthrates and high levels of intermarriage.

(TIME, Jan. 30, 1995, p. 52)

猶太教是史上第一個欲打破基督教<u>獨尊地位</u>的宗教，如今雖然受到世俗化、低生育率、高通婚率的衝擊而日漸式微，但在美國依舊根深蒂固。

註 erode (v.) 逐步毀壞

☐ 721 **heyday** [`he,de] (n.) 全盛時期

Apple makes 3.3% profit on every dollar of sales. Compared with nearly 25% for Microsoft. In some respects, the power Microsoft wields over the computer industry may exceed IBM's in its <u>heyday</u>. (TIME, June 5, 1995, p. 32)

蘋果電腦每銷售1元有3.3%的利潤，相形之下，微軟有近乎25%的利潤。從某些方面來看，微軟在電腦業的影響力恐怕要勝過IBM<u>全盛時期</u>。

註 wield (v.) 運用，操縱

☐ 722 **hub** [hʌb] (n.) 中心

同 center

Their view is that, given Singapore's position as a hub, they've got to have the best information tools. (TIME, Feb. 17, 1997, p. 46)
他們的看法是，由於新加坡居於營運中心的地位，必須擁有最佳的資訊工具。

☐ 723 **hurdle** [ˋhɝdl̩] (n.) 困難，挑戰

同 challenge

The biggest hurdle for Chevron will be getting the crude to market as production increases from 30,000 bbl. to 700,000 bbl. a day by 2010. (TIME, July 4, 1994, p. 54)
隨著原油日產量由3萬桶增加到2010年的70萬桶，雪芙隆公司面臨的最大困難將是如何把原油送到市場。
註 crude (n.) 原油；bbl. 桶，是barrel(s)的縮寫

☐ 724 **hybrid** [ˋhaɪbrɪd] (n.) 混合，雜種

The TV-PC hybrid idea is attractive to computer makers, although most would prefer to add TV reception to their PC lines than get into the TV business. (TIME, Aug. 12, 1996, p. 26)
大部分的電腦製造商比較傾向將電視的接收功能加到他們的電腦產品上，而比較不願涉足電視機這一行，但對他們來說，將電視與個人電腦結合的想法，還是很有吸引力。
註 line (n.) 系列產品

☐ 725 **hypocrisy** [hɪˋpɑkrəsɪ] (n.) 偽善

反 sincerity

Hypocrisy and selfishness seem to be the prevailing[221] rules, complained Beijing's official *China Daily*. (TIME, May 13, 1996, p. 13)
北京官方的《中國日報》抱怨說：「偽善與自私似乎成了普遍接受的規則」。

☐ 726 **infidelity** [ˌɪnfəˈdɛlətɪ] (n.) (婚姻上) 不忠，偷情

If you rinse away its deliciously corrupt excitement, <u>infidelity</u> means the infliction of pain upon one's spouse for the sake of fresher pleasure. (TIME, Sept. 23, 1996, p. 60)
如果除去那層墮落得令人覺得很爽的刺激感，<u>偷情</u>代表的是為了追求更新鮮的愉悅，而讓另一半承受痛苦。

註 rinse (v.) 用清水沖洗掉；infliction (n.) 施加；spouse (n.) 配偶

☐ 727 **instinct** [ˈɪnstɪŋkt] (n.) 1. 本能；2. 直覺

同 2. intuition

Now a dramatic discovery announced in the current *Science* suggests that the carnivores (dinosaurs) had a nesting <u>instinct</u> as well.
(TIME, Nov. 14, 1994, p. 78)
現在有一項震撼性的發現，發表在當期《科學》雜誌上，這項發現指稱肉食性（恐龍）也有築巢的<u>本能</u>。

☐ 728 **intuition** [ˌɪntjuˈɪʃən] (n.) 直覺

同 instinct

Sequels, like blind dates, inspire a certain terror. We fear they will be losers; we suspect they will never measure up to past loves—and often <u>intuition</u> proves true. (TIME, Nov. 14, 1994, p. 83)
電影續集，就像是一場別人代為安排、但卻從未見過對方的男女約會一樣，總讓人感到些許忐忑不安。我們擔心它們賣座差，懷疑它們無法達到前集引起的熱潮，而結果證明<u>直覺</u>往往是對的。

註 sequel (n.) （小說、電影等的）續篇，續集；
to measure up to 符合，達到

☐ 729 **knack** [næk] (n.) 竅門，高明的本領

Conner also posseses a <u>knack</u> for compromise[138].
(TIME, May 15, 1995, p. 67)
康納還擁有一項<u>高明的本事</u>——懂得何時妥協。

☐ 730 **lag** [læg] (n.v.) 落後

Japan is now determined to make up for its lag on the info highway and give the U.S. some competition. (TIME, Mar. 6, 1995, p. 66)
如今在發展資訊高速公路上落後的日本下定決心迎頭趕上，並與美國一較長短。
註 to make up for 彌補，補回

☐ 731 **landscape** [ˋlænd͵skep] (n.) 景色，地貌

Wallerstein took an ever growing readership through a dispiriting landscape of anger and grief, of children unable to fit in with peers[753], and young adults crippled[527] in their own attempts at love. (TIME, Feb. 27, 1995, p. 53)
華勒斯坦筆下，有憤怒與悲傷，有跟不上同儕的小孩，還有在愛情道路上跌倒的青年男女，營造出令人心情慘淡的世界，從而獲得愈來愈多讀者的肯定。
註 dispiriting (a.) 令人沮喪的，令人意志消沉的

☐ 732 **legacy** [ˋlɛgəsɪ] (n.) 傳承，遺產，影響

"He's much more comfortable with it," says a top aide, "and he's come to the view that foreign policy will be an important part of his legacy."
(TIME, Nov. 18, 1996, p. 30)
〔柯林頓的〕一位高級助理說：「他現在在外交方面比較得心應手，而且逐漸認為外交政策將會是他的功績中重要的一部分。」

☐ 733 **legitimacy** [lɪˋdʒɪtəməsɪ] (n.) 合法性，認可

And royal legitimacy was conveyed[149] by Princess Diana in the Caribbean surf[642]. (TIME, July 1, 1996, p. 56)
黛安娜王妃在加勒比海的海浪中展現比基尼泳裝，比基尼自此受到皇室認可。

☐ 734 **lieutenant** [lu`tɛnənt] (n.) 助手

同 second-in-command | Gates had been warning his top <u>lieutenants</u> that the Net could change everything about the way people used computers, perhaps even the fact that they needed an $89 copy of Windows to make their machines work. (TIME, Sept. 16, 1996, p. 38)
蓋茲一直警告他的重要<u>幹部</u>：網路可能讓使用電腦的方式完全改觀，甚至人們可能不再需要89美元一套的視窗軟體來運作硬體。

☐ 735 **limelight** [`laɪm,laɪt] (n.) 公眾矚目的焦點，光采

From the gossip columns to the Oscar preshow promenade, they (supermodels) are stealing the <u>limelight</u> from Hollywood's film goddesses.
(TIME, Apr. 17, 1995, p. 66)
從報刊的漫談欄到奧斯卡頒獎典禮開幕前名人悠閒走進會場，超級模特兒都搶盡了好萊塢衆女星的<u>光采</u>。

註 promenade (n.)（悠閒地）散步，這裡指在兩旁衆人注目下悠閒走過

☐ 736 **literacy** [`lɪtərəsɪ] (n.) 讀寫的能力

In addition, <u>literacy</u> among Malaysia's 20 million people is a relatively high 80% , English is widely spoken, and a greater percentage of Malaysians study abroad than do residents of any other Asian country. (TIME, Dec. 4, 1995, p. 26)
除此之外，馬來西亞兩千萬人口中的<u>識字率</u>相對較高，達到80%，國民廣泛使用英語，而與亞洲其他國家相比，出國留學的比例也最高。

☐ 737 **loophole** [`lup,hol] (n.)（法律）漏洞

There may be consumer-price shifts once tax shelters and <u>loopholes</u> vanish[659]. (TIME, Apr. 17, 1995, p. 26)
一旦合法避稅手段和<u>法律漏洞</u>消失，消費者物價就可能變動。

註 tax shelter 合法的減冤所得稅手段，如設立慈善事業基金

☐738 **lure** [lur] (n.) 吸引力，誘餌

Some people wonder what <u>lure</u> the words Chow Yun-fat could have on a movie marquee in Dallas or Denver. (TIME, May 6, 1996, p. 63)

有些人懷疑，「周潤發」這三個字若擺在達拉斯或丹佛市的電影院看板上，能有多少吸引力？

註 marquee (n.)（戲院門口的）頂蓬，放廣告看板處

☐739 **lyrics** [`lırıks] (n.) 歌詞

At one point in the meeting, Tucker rose from the audience and delivered a 17-minute attack on violent and misogynistic <u>lyrics</u> in songs recorded by Time-Warner performers. (TIME, June 12, 1995, p. 37)

會議中，塔克從觀眾席中站起，針對時代華納公司旗下的歌手錄製的歌曲中，涉及暴力與厭惡女人的歌詞，發表了17分鐘長的抨擊。

註 misogynistic (a.) 厭惡女人的

☐740 **maneuver** [mə`nuvə] (n.)（用以度過難關、解決問題的）技巧，手法

同 ploy

Many feel Kennedy's commitment was a desperate political <u>maneuver</u> to lift himself out of the calamity of the Bay of Pigs ....

(TIME, July 25, 1994, p. 58)

許多人覺得甘迺迪之所以做出承諾，是一種狗急跳牆的政治手法，爲的就是讓他脫離豬邏灣慘劇的陰影。

註 commitment (n.) 承諾，保證；
desperate (a.) 孤注一擲的，拼死一搏的；calamity (n.) 災難，不幸

☐741 **mania** [`menıə] (n.) 狂熱，熱中

Gates confessed that the Internet <u>mania</u> ... had taken him by surprise. Millions of people were communicating via computers using software standards and application programs that Microsoft had no hand in developing. (TIME, June 5, 1995, p. 46)

蓋茲坦承，網際網路激起的熱潮確曾令他大吃一驚，數百萬人正以微軟公司未著力發展的軟體標準和應用程式，透過電腦互通訊息。

註 hand (n.) 插手，參與

□ **742 manipulation** [məˌnɪpjuˋleʃən] (n.)（用以操縱比賽的）不正當手法

Onaruto acknowledged[114] that a series of such <u>manipulations</u> allowed him to propel a wrestler named Kitanofuji to the title of grand champion in 1970. (TIME, Sept. 30, 1996, p. 30)

大鳴戶承認透過一連串這樣的<u>不正當手法</u>，他得以在1970年將一名叫北富士的選手送上了「橫綱」的寶座。

□ **743 mayhem** [ˋmehɛm] (n.) 失控，脫序，暴力橫行

同 chaos

Natural Born Killers isn't an attempt to profit from murder and <u>mayhem</u>, says Oliver Stone. (TIME, June 12, 1995, p. 32)

《閃靈殺手》這部戲並無意利用謀殺、<u>暴力的情節</u>來賺錢，奧立佛‧史東這麼說。

□ **744 melodrama** [ˋmɛləˌdrɑmə] (n.) 通俗劇

Half his other movies show him chain-smoking; he keeps three cigarettes going at once in his most recent <u>melodrama</u>, *Peace Hotel*. (TIME, May 6, 1996, p. 62)

有一半的電影裡他都是菸不離手，甚至在他最近的<u>娛樂電影</u>《和平飯店》中，還一次同時抽3根煙。

註 chain-smoke (v.) 一根接一根抽煙

□ **745 memoir** [ˋmɛmwɑr] (n.) 回憶錄

Warren Zimmermann, the last U.S. ambassador to Yugoslavia, who published his <u>memoirs</u>, *Origins of a Catastrophe*, last week, wrote that the Serb leader was "responsible for the deaths of tens of thousands of Bosnians ...." (TIME, Sept. 23, 1996, p. 35)

美國前任駐南斯拉夫大使辛默曼上週出版了<u>回憶錄</u>《災難的源起》，裡面寫到這位塞爾維亞領袖「造成數以萬計的波士尼亞人喪生。」

註 catastrophe (n.) 慘劇，不幸

☐ 746 **moderation** [ˌmɑdəˈreʃən] (n.) 適度，節制

同 restraint

But as Clinton has soared[246] in the polls by emphasizing <u>moderation</u>, Gore's standing with the President, says a senior presidential adviser, "is unparalleled." (TIME, June 17, 1996, p. 30)

但當柯林頓強調<u>溫和政策</u>而使得民意支持升高後，根據一位柯林頓資深顧問的說法，高爾在總統心目中的地位是「無人能比的」。

☐ 747 **namesake** [ˈnemˌsek] (n.) 同名的人或物

Martina Hingis charms the fans and reminds them of her <u>namesake</u>. (TIME, Sept. 16, 1996, p. 49)

辛吉絲迷倒球迷，並使他們想起與她<u>同名</u>的網壇前輩。

☐ 748 **newsletter** [ˈnjuzˌlɛtə] (n.)（機關的）內部刊物

同 bulletin

"Not all the fund companies are that competitive," says Eric Kobren, the publisher of the <u>newsletter</u> *Fidelity Insight*. (TIME, Sept. 30, 1996, p. 48)

〔富達基金〕<u>內部刊物</u>《富達觀察》的發行人克布倫說：「並非每家基金公司都如此競爭。」

☐ 749 **obsession** [əbˈsɛʃən] (n.) 偏執，迷戀，耽溺

同 fixation

Carl Lewis has always had an <u>obsession</u> with image that made would-be fans a little uneasy.

(TIME, June 24, 1996, p. 66)

卡爾・劉易士一向<u>太在意</u>形象，這一點使那些想成為他的運動迷的人有些不自在。

註 would-be (a.) 想要成為…的，未來的

☐ 750 **onset** [ˋɑn,sɛt] (n.) 發作

Then the physicians must ensure[173] that less than three hours have elapsed since the stroke's <u>onset</u>. Otherwise the risk of bleeding into the brain is too great. (TIME, Sept. 16, 1996, p. 48)
然後,醫生必須確定中風<u>發作</u>的時間沒有超過3小時,否則,腦溢血的風險會非常高。

註 elapse (v.)(時間)消逝,過去

☐ 751 **outfit** [ˋaʊt,fɪt] (n.) 一套服裝

It is a picture of his two-year-old son Matthew, dressed in a red plaid <u>outfit</u> and sitting in front of a Christmas tree .... (TIME, Nov. 21, 1994, p. 92)
那是一張他兩歲大兒子馬修的照片,穿著有褶邊的紅色<u>套裝</u>,坐在一棵聖誕樹前。

同 organization

(n.) 公司,機構

Today, and tomorrow, any ambitious entertainment <u>outfit</u> must be an all-purpose, universal, joint conglomerate[980] for two big reasons. (TIME, Mar. 27, 1995, p. 54)
基於兩大理由,任何雄心遠大的娛樂<u>事業機構</u>,不管在今天或明天,都必須是滿足各種需求、全球性的大型綜合企業。

☐ 752 **parallel** [ˋpærə,lɛl] (n.) 可相比擬的事物,比較

同 equivalent

If there is an explanation for Zhirinovsky's unique appeal[120], perhaps it is to be found in the <u>parallel</u> between the young boy who grew up feeling rejected, humiliated and despised[895] and a nation that has just emerged from seven decades of dictatorship feeling abused[113], deprived[156] and defeated. (TIME, July 11, 1994, p. 38)
季里諾夫斯基這小伙子,成長過程中飽嘗被排斥、羞辱、瞧不起的感受,而這個剛脫離70年獨裁統治的國家,也正感到受虐、受剝奪與潰敗,如果要解釋季里諾夫斯基為何擁有如此獨特的魅力,或許可從他和這個國家之間的<u>相似性</u>尋得。

註 to merge from ... 擺脫(困境)

□ 753 **peer** [pɪr] (n.) 同輩，同儕

Johnson had to quit basketball then, supposedly for the sake of his own health and definitely for the peace of mind of his <u>peers</u>. (TIME, Feb. 12, 1996, p. 39)
當時強森必須退出籃壇，部分原因可能是為了自己的健康，但是為了讓球場上的<u>球員</u>安心則是毫無疑問的。

□ 754 **perspective** [pə`spɛktɪv] (n.) 看法，觀點

同 view

Even more interesting, from a business <u>perspective</u>, is the so-called intranet—the collection of networks that connect computers within corporations—that both Sun and Microsoft have targeted as a rich area for growth.
(TIME, Jan. 22, 1996, p. 44)
就商業的<u>觀點</u>來看，更引人興趣的是所謂的「內部網路」，即連接公司內部電腦的網路系統，目前昇陽與微軟都把焦點對準了這個會有豐富成長機會的領域。

□ 755 **pinnacle** [`pɪnəkl̩] (n.) 頂點，高峰

We asked each to select his or her choice of the five greatest Olympians and to tell us precisely the qualities that place them at the very <u>pinnacle</u>.
(TIME, June 24, 1996, p. 52)
我們要求他們挑選出自己所認為的5位最偉大的奧運選手，並且明確告訴我們這些運動員所以能登上<u>巔峰</u>的特質。

□ 756 **plight** [plaɪt] (n.) 苦境

Gorbachev seemed fully aware of the military's <u>plight</u> only two months ago when he warned the Russian parliament that "no army in the world is in such a poor state as ours." (TIME, Jan. 16, 1995, p. 50)
戈巴契夫似乎在兩個月前才全盤瞭解軍方的<u>困境</u>，當時他向俄國國會提出警告：「世上沒有哪個國家的軍隊比我國的還慘。」

☐ 757 **poise** [pɔɪz] (n.) 平衡，姿態

At that point, Lee's most prudent course might have been soft-pedaling his differences with the People's Republic, allowing his prosperous society to regain its poise.

(TIME, Dec. 25, 1995/Jan. 1, 1996, p. 54)

發展至此，李登輝最審慎的步驟可能就是低調處理他與中國大陸的差異，好讓台灣這個繁榮的社會能重新取得平衡。

註 soft-pedal (v.) 低調處理，使（事情）不惹人注目

☐ 758 **portfolio** [portˋfolɪˏo] (n.) （投資者持有的）投資組合，（銀行等投資單位持有的）有價證券財產目錄

Johnson, along with other Fidelity executives, insists that the company's homegrown style of managing portfolios doesn't need much fixing.

(TIME, Sept. 30, 1996, p. 46)

強森與其他富達公司的高級主管都堅持，公司自創的有價證券操作風格並不需要太多的修正。

☐ 759 **precedent** [ˋprɛsədənt] (n.) 先例

One problem is that if the U.S. tries to kill leaders it doesn't like, chances are someone will try to do the same to the American President. There is precedent for such concern. (TIME, Sept. 23, 1996, p. 35)

有一個問題就是，如果美國設法刺殺它不喜歡的外國領袖，別人也可能對美國總統如法炮製。這層顧慮是有先例可循的。

註 (The) chances are ... 有可能，也許

☐ 760 **predator** [ˋprɛdətə] (n.) 獵捕者，掠奪者

It turns out the pesticides had all along been doing less damage to the invader than to its predators.

(TIME, May 27, 1996, p. 67)

結果顯示，殺蟲劑對入侵者的天敵造成的傷害，反而一直高於對入侵者本身。

761 **predicament** [prɪˋdɪkəmənt] (n.) 困境

同 dilemma

This sort of <u>predicament</u> is what the Founders designed representative democracy to solve.

(TIME, Jan. 23, 1995, p. 14)

這種<u>困境</u>正是當初建國者設計的代議民主制度所要解決的。

762 **prohibition** [ˌproəˋbɪʃən] (n.) 禁令

The tyrannicide game changed in 1976 when President Gerald Ford issued an Executive Order banning[128] political assassinations. All Presidents since have extended the <u>prohibition</u>, though Ronald Reagan must have had his fingers crossed when he went along. (TIME, Sept. 23, 1996, p. 35)

1976年，福特總統頒布行政命令禁止政治刺殺的行動，刺殺暴君的遊戲從此改變。此後每一位總統都延長<u>禁令</u>的時效，不過雷根在決定蕭規曹隨之際，可能不是由衷的。

註 to have one's fingers crossed 言不由衷的

763 **prophet** [ˋprɑfɪt] (n.) 預言者

The <u>prophets</u> of this healing offensive are photogenic and media-friendly, but here their common traits end. They speak in different tongues to reach different audiences.

(TIME, June 24, 1996, p. 44)

領導這一波新療法攻勢的<u>眾先知</u>，個個都很上相而且和媒體保持良好關係，但他們的相似之處僅止於此。他們各說各派的話，給不同的觀眾聽。

註 offensive (n.) 進攻，攻勢；
photogenic (a.) 上鏡頭的，適於拍照的；trait (n.) 特點，特性

☐ 764 **prototype** [ˋprotəˌtaɪp] (n.) 原型

Someday, say the futurists, our streets will be filled with computer-controlled cars so "smart" they will make the <u>prototype</u> I'm riding in look like a brain-damaged Model T. (TIME, Nov. 4, 1996, p. 52)
根據未來學家的說法，將來有一天，我們的道路上會布滿由電腦控制的車輛，這些車輛非常聰明，相形之下使我現在乘坐的這輛<u>原型</u>車像是輛頭殼壞去的T型車。

☐ 765 **psyche** [ˋsaɪkɪ] (n.) 心靈

The grisly slashing of throats—the method of murder favored by Islamist militants—has instilled[585] terror in the country's collective <u>psyche</u>. (TIME, Mar. 6, 1995, p. 64)
回教民兵偏愛的殺人方式——令人毛骨悚然的割喉，已在該國全體人民的<u>心靈</u>蒙上恐怖的陰影。
註 grisly (a.) 恐怖的；slashing (n.) 砍擊

☐ 766 **rally** [ˋrælɪ] (n.) 群眾大會，聚會 (v.) 召集，團結

Last month, with a group of nine other AIDS patients, Getty sat down in the middle of a driveway and blocked traffic outside an animal-rights <u>rally</u> in Washington. (TIME, July 8, 1996, p. 39)
上個月華盛頓市有一項聲援動物權益的<u>群眾大會</u>，蓋提和另9名愛滋病患聚在一起，在會場外圍的一條馬路中央坐下來，擋住車流。

☐ 767 **rehearsal** [rɪˋhɝsl] (n.) 排演

The performance, however, suffered from an obvious lack of <u>rehearsal</u>, with the pianist and the conductor ... unable to agree on basic matters of tempo. (TIME, July 25, 1994, p. 71)
這場演出明顯因為沒有<u>彩排</u>而進行得不順利，在拍子這個基本的問題上，鋼琴師和指揮家都不能步調一致。

☐ 768 **retaliation** [rɪ,tælɪˋeʃən] (n.) 報復

Questions still linger about whether <u>retaliation</u> could have been a factor in Kennedy's death.

(TIME, Sept. 23, 1996, p. 35)

甘迺迪之死是否有<u>報復</u>的因素在內，到今天還無法斷定。

註 linger (v.) 徘徊，流連不去

☐ 769 **reversion** [rɪˋvɝʒən] (n.) 復歸

Hong Kong's <u>reversion</u> may have the biggest effect on bilateral[9] relations. (TIME, Nov. 18, 1996, p. 31)

香港<u>回歸</u>中國大陸可能對〔中美〕雙方關係有最大的影響。

☐ 770 **rhetoric** [ˋrɛtərɪk] (n.) 辭令，浮誇不實的話

Such high-level contacts could do much to soften Chinese <u>rhetoric</u> against the U.S., as did the historic Beijing visits of Henry Kissinger and Richard Nixon in 1971 and 1972.

(TIME, July 22, 1996, p. 37)

這樣的高層接觸可以大幅緩和中國對美國的<u>嚴詞抨擊</u>，一如1971、1972年季辛吉、尼克森訪問北京的歷史之旅所達到的效果。

☐ 771 **sensation** [sɛnˋseʃən] (n.) 轟動的人、事、物

The game's eye-popping graphics were an instant <u>sensation</u>: DKC not only became the best-selling game of 1994 but also ratcheted up pressure on the teams designing games for the new machine.

(TIME, May 20, 1996, p. 58)

這個遊戲裡令人驚奇的圖形效果馬上就造成<u>大轟動</u>：DKC不只成為1994年最暢銷的遊戲，同時也逐漸加重了為新機器設計遊戲的工作小組的壓力。

註 eye-popping (a.)（口語）令人驚奇的；
ratchet 名詞義是「棘齒輪」，動詞義是像棘齒輪一樣一步步推動

☐ 772 **setback** [`sɛt,bæk] (n.) 挫折，失敗

His (Lee's) government's latest <u>setback</u> means he
will have a difficult time pushing bold initiatives
through the Legislative Yuan, especially on
contentious issues like Taiwan's policy toward
China. (TIME, June 17, 1996, p. 54)
李登輝政府最近的<u>挫折</u>，意味著今後他在立法院推動有開創
性的法案將不會很順利，尤其是像台灣對大陸的政策這樣有
爭議性的議題。

註 initiative (n.) 動議，首倡；
contentious (a.)（問題等）引起爭議的

☐ 773 **siege** [sidʒ] (n.) 圍城，包圍

Though seahorses are under <u>siege</u>, "they are not
yet on the verge of extinction," so any ban[128] on
their fishing now would harm traditional
livelihoods. (TIME, Jan. 13, 1997, p. 43)
海馬雖然<u>四面楚歌</u>，但「目前還不至於瀕臨絕種。」所以嚴
禁捕撈將會影響傳統漁民的生計。

☐ 774 **skirmish** [`sk3mɪʃ] (n.) 小戰鬥

One of the fiercest <u>skirmishes</u> in recent months
has been over the market for so-called Web
browsers, in which Microsoft, Netscape and Sun
all compete. (TIME, Jan. 22, 1996, p. 43)
最近幾個月有幾場最激烈的<u>混戰</u>，其中之一就是對所謂的
「全球資訊網導覽器」的市場爭奪戰，微軟、網景及昇陽等
公司都投入這場競爭。

☐ 775 **smash** [smæʃ] (n.) 轟動，熱門人物

In the 1989 box-office <u>smash</u> *God of Gamblers*,
he (Chow Yun-fat) munched on chocolates.
(TIME, May 6, 1996, p. 62)
在1989年<u>大賣座</u>的《賭神》中，周潤發口中嚼著巧克力。

註 box-office (a.) 票房的，賣座的；munch (v.) 用力咀嚼

□ 776 **spell** [spɛl] (n.) 一段時間

同 period

Unusual weather such as dry <u>spells</u> in wet areas or torrential[857] rains in normally dry spots tends to favor so-called opportunistic pests ... while making life more difficult for the predators[760] that usually control them. (TIME, July 8, 1996, p. 40)

異常的氣候，例如多雨的地區出現數次<u>乾旱</u>，平常乾燥的地方下了傾盆大雨，都有利於所謂投機性的有害生物的生存，同時使得一向控制這些生物數目的掠食者愈來愈難生存。

註 favor (v.)（天氣、事情等）對⋯有利

□ 777 **spoiler** [ˋspɔɪlɚ] (n.) 選舉中無望選上但可拉低他人得票數的攪局者

Though radically[79] different in ideology, (the presidential candidates) Perot and Jackson both yearn to advance an ambitious agenda[274], even if that means playing the <u>spoiler</u>. (TIME, Mar. 13, 1995, p. 91)

培洛和賈克遜兩名總統候選人儘管在意識形態上南轅北轍，但都想提出一份志在必得的競選計畫，即使<u>明知這麼做也是當選無望</u>。

註 yearn (v.) 渴望

□ 778 **stagnation** [stægˋneʃən] (n.) 不景氣，停滯

Economists say the nation's anemic savings rate of 4%, in contrast to Germany's 12% and Japan's 17%, is a key reason behind the <u>stagnation</u> in many workers' wages since 1973.

(TIME, May 22, 1995, p. 35)

經濟學家表示，該國的儲蓄率很低，只有4%，相對的德、日分別有12%和17%；該國許多工人的薪資之所以自1973年之後就<u>停滯不漲</u>，這是一大原因。

註 anemic (a.) 貧血的，疲軟無力的，衰弱的

☐ [779] **stake** [stek] (n.) 賭注，投資，利害關係

> The financial <u>stakes</u> are enormous as well. P&G has already invested $200 million in developing, studying and testing olestra. (TIME, Jan. 8, 1996, p. 31)
> 金錢上的<u>投注</u>也相當驚人。寶鹼已經投資了2億美金在脫脂油的研究發展和測試上。

☐ [780] **staple** [ˋstepl] (n.) 主要成分，經常出現的內容

> Both Miles Davis and Quincy Jones experimented with rap-jazz fusion in the '80s, but a decade later it is becoming a <u>staple</u>. (TIME, Nov. 21, 1994, p. 108)
> 1980年代戴維斯和昆西‧瓊斯嘗試融合饒舌和爵士風格，實驗新的音樂形式，10年後這種音樂形式卻成爲<u>司空見慣的東西</u>。

☐ [781] **stereotype** [ˋstɛrɪoˏtaɪp] (n.) 刻板印象

> Those who are urgently trying to reach females end up reinforcing sexist <u>stereotypes</u>, such as "Girls like cooperative games,'not action."
>
> (TIME, Nov. 11, 1996, p. 36)
> 急於想打進女性市場的人，結果強化了性別歧視的<u>刻板印象</u>，像是「女生喜歡合作的遊戲，不喜歡動作的遊戲」這類說法。
>
> 註 to end up 結果變成

☐ [782] **stewardship** [ˋstjuwəd͵ʃɪp] (n.) 管理

> In the next few weeks parliament must still consider the fate of (the central bank chairman Victor) Gerashenko and vote on the economic <u>stewardship</u> of Prime Minister Victor Chernomyrdin. (TIME, Oct. 24, 1994, p. 43)
> 未來數星期，國會仍需思索（央行總裁）傑拉申柯的去留問題，並對總理車諾米丁是否<u>有權主導</u>經濟投票表決。

□783 **stigma** [ˋstɪɡmə] (n.) 污名，恥辱

As long as the <u>stigma</u> and discrimination exist around AIDS out there, we're going to have to treat it differently from other diseases.
(TIME, July 4, 1994, p. 60)
只要人們繼續以<u>不恥</u>、歧視的心態看待愛滋病，我們就必須把此病與其他病區隔開來，特別看待。

□784 **stroke** [strok] (n.) 中風

Of all the medical catastrophes that can befall a person, suffering a <u>stroke</u> is one of the most terrifying. (TIME, Sept. 16, 1996, p. 48)
在人類可能罹患的各種重大疾病之中，<u>中風</u>是最可怕的之一。

註 catastrophe (n.) 慘事，不幸；
befall (v.)（不幸、災禍等）降臨在

□785 **stroll** [strol] (n.v.) 溜達，散步

同 (v.) wander

A <u>stroll</u> through the center of the city reveals the transformation nearly everywhere.
(TIME, July 4, 1994, p. 50)
到市中心<u>走一趟</u>，就可看出這改變幾乎遍及各地。

□786 **suspense** [səˋspɛns] (n.) 懸疑

In Savannah these days, when people talk about "the Book," they are referring not to the Bible but to *Midnight in the Garden of Good and Evil*, the best-selling <u>suspense</u> yarn by journalist John Berendt. (TIME, Apr. 3, 1995, p. 79)
最近在薩瓦納市當有人談起「聖經」，並不是指真正的《聖經》，而是指《午夜的善惡花園》這本由新聞記者貝蘭特所寫的暢銷<u>懸疑</u>小說。

註 yarn (n.) 故事，奇談

☐ [787] **symptom** [ˋsɪmptəm] (n.) 徵候，前兆

All this activity, many scientists speculate, may be a <u>symptom</u> that overall tectonic pressure in the region is increasing. (TIME, Jan. 31, 1994, p. 45)
許多科學家推測，這一切活動可能是加諸此地區地殼整體壓力逐漸增強的徵兆。

註 speculate (v.) 推測；tectonic (a.) 地殼構造上的

☐ [788] **threshold** [ˋθrɛʃold] (n.)（事物的）開端

Those who will really pay for the fiasco[701] are Mexico's emerging middle class, who had come to believe they were finally on the <u>threshold</u> of prosperity. (TIME, Mar. 6, 1995, p. 34)
真正得為這場經濟挫敗付出代價的是墨西哥正崛起的中產階級，這批人先前一直以為他們終於要富<u>起來了</u>。

(n.) 門檻限制，稅的起徵點

Through a long chain of intermediary companies, Murdoch's Australia-based News Corp. would own the remaining 24% of the voting stock, just under the federal <u>threshold</u>. (TIME, Apr. 17, 1995, p. 45)
透過一系列中介公司，梅鐸以澳洲為大本營的新聞公司，將取得剩下的24%有投票權的股權，此一比例剛好貼近聯邦對此的<u>門檻限制</u>(25%)。

☐ [789] **transaction** [trænˋsækʃən] (n.) 交易，買賣

The company's CyberCoin system will allow online "micro-<u>transactions</u>" of as little as a quarter. (TIME, Oct. 7, 1996, p. 40)
這家公司的「網路銅板」系統能讓網路進行少至25分錢的「微量<u>交易</u>」。

☐ 790 **transmission** [trænsˋmɪʃən] (n.) 傳遞

After doctors determined that AZT could block the <u>transmission</u> of HIV to the fetus in some pregnant women, researchers wondered if they could make the therapy more effective.

(TIME, July 8, 1996, p. 39)

醫生確定AZT用於某些孕婦身上，可以隔絕愛滋病毒不至於傳染給胎兒；於是研究人員就想法子看能不能加強這種療法的效果。

註 block (v.) 圍堵，阻擋；fetus (n.) 胎兒

☐ 791 **treason** [ˋtrizn̩] (n.) 叛國（罪）

He was sentenced to 15 years for high <u>treason</u>.

(TIME, May 22, 1995, p. 56)

他因嚴重<u>叛國罪</u>判刑15年。

☐ 792 **upheaval** [ʌpˋhivl̩] (n.)（社會等的）大變動，動亂

Or are they a precursor[1026] of the kind of climactic <u>upheavals</u> that can be expected from the global warming caused by the continued buildup of CO_2 and the other so-called greenhouse gases?

(TIME, July 8, 1996, p. 40)

或者說那是某種氣候遽變的前兆，而這種遽變可預見係源自不斷增加的二氧化碳及其他所謂的溫室氣體所引起的全球性溫度上升。

註 buildup (n.) 逐漸增加

☐ 793 **velocity** [vəˋlɑsətɪ] (n.) 速度

The Heisenberg Uncertainty Principle states that you cannot know a subatomic particle's exact position and its exact direction and <u>velocity</u> at the same time. (TIME, Nov. 28, 1994, p. 78)

根據海森堡不確定原則，你無法同時知道亞原子粒子的確切位置與其確切方向、<u>速度</u>。

☐ 794 **venture** [ˋvɛntʃə] (n.) 冒險的活動，有風險的事業 (v.) 冒險前去

No fan of the United Nations, Dole opposes U.S. participation in U.N. peacekeeping <u>ventures</u> and in nation-building exercises in third-tier countries like Haiti and Somalia. (TIME, July 8, 1996, p. 29)
杜爾對聯合國沒好感，反對美國參與聯合國維持和平的冒險行動，或第三世界國家如海地和索馬利亞的建國活動。
註 tier (n.) 層

☐ 795 **visionary** [ˋvɪʒə͵nɛrɪ] (n.) 有遠見的人

The steadfast[856] <u>visionary</u> who began his career by bringing land reform to his island had started to win more equal ground for Taiwan in the world's eyes. (TIME, Dec. 25, 1995/Jan. 1, 1996, p. 54)
這位以實行土地改革開始其政治生涯的堅定<u>理想家</u>，已經開始在世人的目光下為台灣贏得更公平的地位。

☐ 796 **watershed** [ˋwɑtə͵ʃɛd] (n.) 轉捩點，開啟新發展的關鍵

同 turning point

In a <u>watershed</u> decision, the U.S. Supreme Court sharply restricted the ability of the Federal Government to fashion affirmative-action programs. (TIME, June 26, 1995, p. 23)
美國最高法院做出一項<u>劃時代</u>的判決，清楚限制聯邦政府在制定鼓勵雇用少數民族、婦女的贊助性措施之上的權力。
註 fashion (v.) 製造；
affirmative-action 鼓勵雇用少數民族、婦女的贊助性措施

☐ 797 **windfall** [ˋwɪnd͵fɔl] (n.) 意外之財

Kazakhstan President Nursultan Nazarbayev visited Washington last week and came away with a <u>windfall</u> of $311 million .... (TIME, Feb. 28, 1994, p. 13)
哈薩克總統納札巴耶夫上週訪問華盛頓，並帶著3億1,100萬美金的<u>意外收穫</u>離開。

進階字

TIME
Key Words 1000

- abysmal 無底的，極差勁的
- all-out 盡全力的，徹底的
- antagonistic 敵對的，不相容的
- apace 急速地
- appalling 可怕的，糟透的
- astute 精明的
- awry 背離正確方向的，異常的
- ballistic 勃然大怒的
- benign 無害的，有利的
- breezy 輕快的，無憂無慮的
- bulky 笨重的
- cameo 短暫而精彩的
- canny 精明的
- chagrined 悔恨的，懊惱的
- comely 漂亮的
- consecutive 連續的
- cutthroat （競爭）激烈的
- cynical 憤世嫉俗的
- deadpan 撲克臉孔的，不帶個人感情的
- demure 矜持的
- dubious 存疑的，不確定的
- edgily 焦急地，焦躁地
- eerily 怪異地
- engaging 吸引人的，有趣的
- engrossing 使全神貫注的，有趣的
- feisty 精力充沛的，強硬的
- fickle （人）多變的
- formidable 優秀的，傑出的
- graphic （敘述）生動的，栩栩如生的
- grass-roots 一般民眾的，草根性的
- hilarious 喧鬧的，極可笑的
- hip 內行的，時髦的
- impromptu 即興的，臨時起意的
- invincible 無敵的
- lackluster 乏善可陳的，平凡的
- malign （影響）有害的，惡意的
- maverick 不合流俗的（人）
- mercurial 善變的
- microscopic 非常微小的
- nascent 初期的，剛開始的
- nimble 動作敏捷的
- no-holds-barred 為達目的無所不用其極的
- oblivious 渾然不覺的
- ostensible 表面上的
- palatable 美味的；愉快的
- paltry 微不足道的
- provisional 臨時的，暫時的
- replete 充滿的
- resilient 韌性十足的
- riveting 有趣的，引人入勝的
- runaway 成長快速的，勢不可遏的
- saturated 飽和的
- savvy 精通的
- seamless 無接縫的，組合完美的
- sinister 邪惡的
- sleek （人）時髦闊氣的
- stark （對比）分明的
- staunch 堅定的
- steadfast 堅定不移的
- torrential 猛烈的，洶湧的
- trailblazing 開路先鋒的，創新大膽的
- ubiquitous 無所不在的
- unfathomable 深不可測的
- unfettered 不受拘束的
- unscrupulous 無道德原則的，不擇手段的
- virtuoso 大師級的，精湛的
- voracious 貪婪的
- wayward 不聽話的，任性的
- whizzy 快速的，出色的
- wistful 渴望的，企盼的

□ 798 **abysmal** [əˋbɪzml] (a.) 無底的，極差勁的

同 dismal

Because he believes that economic liberalization will eventually yield political pluralism, Forbes has long abhorred[481] linking trade issues to an improvement in China's <u>abysmal</u> human-rights record. (TIME, Feb. 19, 1996, p. 36)

富比士認為經濟的自由化終究會導致政治的多元化，所以他一直不願意把貿易問題與中國大陸<u>低到谷底的</u>人權紀錄牽扯在一起。

註 yield (v.) 產生

□ 799 **all-out** [ˋɔlˋaut] (a.) 盡全力的，徹底的

Digital change has evolved from an amusing walk toward the future to an <u>all-out</u> sprint.

(TIME, Nov. 4, 1996, p. 49)

數位科技的進展已經從迎向未來的愉悅漫步，變成<u>拼命向前</u>衝刺。

註 sprint (n.)（長距離賽跑中的）衝刺

□ 800 **antagonistic** [æn͵tægəˋnɪstɪk] (a.) 敵對的，不相容的

The <u>antagonistic</u> ants have been harassing[571] (the U.S.) people, mostly in the South, for decades.

(TIME, June 5, 1995, p. 57)

美國人，特別是美國的南方人，已被這與之<u>處處作對</u>的螞蟻騷擾了數十年。

□ 801 **apace** [əˋpes] (adv.) 急速地

同 speedily
swiftly

Despite ... two rounds of Chinese missile exercises directed at Taiwan last year, preparations for eventual direct transport links between Quemoy and the nearby Chinese island of Xiamen continue <u>apace</u>. (TIME, Feb. 19. 1996, p. 21)

去年中共對台灣舉行了兩次飛彈演習，但是雙方為金門與鄰近的中國大陸廈門之間的直航所作的準備，仍在<u>快速地</u>進行。

☐ 802 **appalling** [ə`pɔlɪŋ] (a.) 可怕的，糟透的

同 dreadful

Both (Senators) Kennedy and Helms are in a pro-Taiwan mode, ... the former because of China's <u>appalling</u> human-rights record, the latter because Taiwan is the last anticommunist country in the world. (TIME, Mar. 25, 1996, p. 13)
甘迺迪議員和赫姆斯議員都站在支持台灣的<u>立場</u>，前者支持台灣是因為中共人權紀錄<u>太惡劣</u>，後者則是因為台灣是碩果僅存的反共國家。

☐ 803 **astute** [ə`stjut] (a.) 精明的

同 shrewd

Lawrence Korb, an Assistant Secretary of Defense in the Reagan Administration, calls Powell "as <u>astute</u> a politician as I've met."
(TIME, Mar. 13, 1995, p. 88)
雷根政府的國防部助理部長科爾布稱包威爾是「我所見過最<u>精明的</u>政治人物。」

☐ 804 **awry** [ə`raɪ] (a.) 背離正確方向的，異常的

Scientists are studying how genetic abnormalities that make hormone levels go <u>awry</u> may play a role in sexual orientation. (TIME, Sept. 2, 1996, p. 41)
科學家正在研究，會導致荷爾蒙分泌<u>異常的</u>基因變異，對人的性傾向有多大影響。
註 abnormality (n.) 異常，反常

☐ 805 **(go) ballistic** [bə`lɪstɪk] (a.) 勃然大怒的

In short, do household pets really have a mental and emotional life? Their owners think so, but until recently, animal-behavior experts would have <u>gone ballistic</u> on hearing such a question.
(TIME, Mar. 22, 1993, p. 60)
簡言之，寵物是否真有心智活動與情緒反應？飼主對此都持肯定態度，但直到最近，動物行為專家聽到這個問題，大概都還會<u>勃然大怒</u>。

□ 806 **benign** [bɪˋnaɪn] (a.) 無害的，有利的

Private cars will virtually be banned[128]—Mahathir envisions[555] an environmentally benign metropolis—and replaced by a public transport system combining buses, metros, trams and ferries. (TIME, Dec. 4, 1995, p. 26)
馬哈迪擬想出一個「環保」大都會，幾乎所有的私家轎車都不准駛入城內，取而代之的是一套結合公車、地下鐵、電車及渡輪的公共運輸系統。

□ 807 **breezy** [ˋbrizɪ] (a.) 輕快的，無憂無慮的

Invented at a time when optimism was in the air and hedonistic pleasures were beginning to be celebrated, the breezy little bikini shows no sign of growing up or growing old. (TIME, July 1, 1996, p. 56)
在樂觀主義瀰漫、享樂主義開始盛行時，輕薄短小的比基尼問世，時至今日，比基尼完全沒有長大或是過時的跡象。
註 hedonistic (a.) 享樂主義的

□ 808 **bulky** [ˋbʌlkɪ] (a.) 笨重的

They include the most bulky medalist—U.S. super-heavyweight freestyle wrestler Chris Taylor, ... and the most petite—among them mothlike Chinese gymnast Li Lu.
(TIME, June 24, 1996, p. 51)
這當中包括塊頭最大的奧運獎牌得主——美國的超重量級自由式摔角選手克利斯·泰勒，還有體型最嬌小的——其中中國體操選手李露像隻小蛾似的。
註 petite (a.) （女人）身材嬌小的

□ 809 **cameo** [ˋkæmɪ‚o] (a.) 短暫而精采的

He (Magic Johnson) made cameo appearances, first at the 1992 N.B.A. All-Star Game and then as a member of the USA's Dream Team in the Barcelona Olympics. (TIME, Feb. 12, 1996, p. 39)
魔術強森曾兩度短暫出現在球場上，一次是1992年的NBA明星賽，另一次則是入選巴賽隆納奧運的美國夢幻籃球隊。

☐ 810 **canny** [ˋkænɪ] (a.) 精明的

同 shrewd

The next step after getting a job was to find a woman to marry, and Kennedy has settled this matter as well, finding someone chic[979], canny and appealing. (TIME, Oct. 7, 1996, p. 42)
有了事業之後，下一步就是討個老婆，而甘迺迪也搞定了，找了一位時髦、精明、迷人的妻子。

☐ 811 **chagrined** [ʃəˋgrɪnd] (a.) 悔恨的，懊惱的

When Bush lost the 1992 election, Milt was chagrined. (TIME, Jan. 9, 1995, p. 43)
布希輸掉1992年總統選舉時，米爾特很懊惱。

☐ 812 **comely** [ˋkʌmlɪ] (a.) 漂亮的

Jacqueline Joyner came into the world in 1962 in godforsaken poverty in the town of East St. Louis, Illinois, and was named after the then President's comely wife. (TIME, June 24, 1996, p. 61)
賈桂琳・喬依娜在1962年誕生於伊利諾州東聖路易市，家中一貧如洗，她的名字取自當時漂亮的總統夫人之名。
註 godforsaken (a.) 被上帝遺棄的，悲慘的

☐ 813 **consecutive** [kənˋsɛkjutɪv] (a.) 連續的

同 successive

Employees work 10-hour days, four days a week, with rotating day and night shifts. At the end of each three-week cycle, they get five consecutive days off. (TIME, May 6, 1996, p. 52)
員工每天工作10小時，一星期4天，並有白天班及夜間班輪流。每3禮拜一循環之後，他們有5天的連假。
註 shift (n.) 輪班（制）

☐ 814 **cutthroat** [`kʌt,θrot] (a.)（競爭）激烈的

同 ruthless

It's <u>cutthroat</u>, but not enough to concern game guru[713] Eno, who predicts a booming[282] future—in online games. (TIME, Apr. 14, 1997, p. 35)
〔電腦遊戲軟體的〕競爭是很<u>激烈</u>，但還不足以讓遊戲軟體大師Eno擔憂，因為他預測網路遊戲未來會很蓬勃。

☐ 815 **cynical** [`sɪnɪk]] (a.) 憤世嫉俗的，覺得世間人都是自私自利的

反 idealistic

<u>Cynical</u>, cool, Lennon was the eye of sanity in the Beatlemania hurricane. (TIME, Nov. 20, 1995, p. 52)
藍儂是<u>憤世嫉俗</u>又很酷的那種人，在披頭熱的颶風中，他是平靜的颶風眼。
註 sanity (n.) 神智清醒

☐ 816 **deadpan** [`dɛd,pæn] (a.) 撲克臉孔的，不帶個人感情的

Cook was a Cambridge undergraduate preparing for a career in foreign service when he joined the comic quartet known as *Beyond the Fringe*, wowing West End and Broadway stages in the 1960s with his <u>deadpan</u> surrealism.
(TIME, Jan. 23, 1995, p. 13)
1960年代庫克加入了名叫「非主流之外」的4人喜劇團，以<u>不帶個人情感的</u>超寫實主義風格，贏得倫敦西區劇院及美國百老匯的熱烈喝采，當時他還是個劍橋大學生，正打算從事外交工作。
註 quartet (n.) 四人一組；
fringe (n.) 邊緣位置，理念怪異或極端而不為一般人所接受的少數人；wow (v.) 使（觀眾）高聲叫好

☐ 817 **demure** [dɪ`mjʊr] (a.) 矜持的

同 reserved

<u>Demure</u> and sexy at the same time, Brigitte Bardot at 21 stunned[255] in a gingham bikini in the movie *And God Created Woman*.
(TIME, July 1, 1996, p. 56)
<u>矜持</u>又性感的碧姬‧芭杜在21歲時，於《上帝創造女人》一片中穿了一件格子布的小比基尼，迷倒眾生。

□ 818 **dubious** [`djubɪəs] (a.) 存疑的，不確定的

同 questionable
uncertain

Wallerstein insists that "I have never told people to stay together at all costs," and opposes tougher divorce laws for being of <u>dubious</u> value for the children. (TIME, Feb. 27, 1995, p. 53)
華勒斯坦堅稱：「我從未告訴人們無論如何都要廝守終身」，並反對制定更嚴苛的離婚法，因為對孩子而言，這麼做其得失之間仍<u>難斷定</u>。

□ 819 **edgily** [`ɛdʒɪlɪ] (adv.) 焦急地，焦躁地

同 tensely

Some Hong Kongers look <u>edgily</u> toward July 1, 1997, when the British government will hand its crown colony over to the People's Republic, and back to June 4, 1989, when Chinese soldiers crushed the Tiananmen Square revolt[357].
(TIME, Jan. 29, 1996, p. 38)
香港人往前看，對1997年7月1日英國將此直轄殖民地交還中共感到<u>不安</u>，而往回看呢，1989年6月4日的天安門軍事鎮壓，也讓他們<u>焦慮</u>。
註 crown colony 英王直轄的殖民地

□ 820 **eerily** [`ɪrɪlɪ] (adv.) 怪異地

Your clone might be <u>eerily</u> like you, or perhaps <u>eerily</u> like someone else. (TIME, Mar. 10, 1997, p. 41)
你的複製體可能會跟你<u>出奇</u>得像，也可能和別人像得<u>出奇</u>。
註 clone (n.) 無性繁殖系的個體，複製（人）

□ 821 **engaging** [ɪn`gedʒɪŋ] (a.) 吸引人的，有趣的

In a series of <u>engaging</u> dramas, Ryder grew up on film and matured in her skills. (TIME, Jan. 9, 1995, p. 64)
萊德演過一部部<u>動人的</u>電影，成長過程在演電影中度過，演技也變得成熟洗鍊。

☐ 822 **engrossing** [ɪnˋgrosɪŋ] (a.) 使全神貫注的，有趣的

Our discussion of sexual fantasies[310], adultery and homosexuality was so <u>engrossing</u> that more than four hours had passed before we noticed the time.
(TIME, Oct. 17, 1994, p. 4)
對於性幻想、通姦、同性戀的討論實在太<u>有趣</u>，以致於已過了4個多小時我們還沒察覺。

☐ 823 **feisty** [ˋfaɪstɪ] (a.)（雖然年老或有病在身，但仍）精力充沛的，強硬的

同 spunky

Clinton has not named a replacement, but one possibility is Madeleine Albright, the <u>feisty</u> ambassador to the U.N., who would be the first woman in the post. (TIME, Nov. 18, 1996, p. 31)
柯林頓目前尚未提出新的人事案，但可能的人選是歐布萊特，即是那位<u>強悍又有幹勁的</u>駐聯合國大使，如果沒錯，她將是第一位出任此職務的女性。

☐ 824 **fickle** [ˋfɪkl] (a.) 1.（人）多變的；2.（物）善變的

同 1. capricious
反 2. dependable

Fashion is <u>fickle</u>; fads[993] are fundamental; careers are often brief. Except in Japan. There not only do quality and creativity reign[352], but stability rules.
(TIME, Oct. 9, 1995, p. 47)
流行瞬息萬變；短暫是時尚的根本特性；這一行的壽命經常很短，但日本例外。在那裡，主導流行的不只是品質和創意，還有穩定性。

☐ 825 **formidable** [ˋfɔrmɪdəbl] (a.) 優秀的，傑出的

The small central African republic (Burundi) didn't have a national Olympic Committee until 1993, but it has had <u>formidable</u> runners for several years .... (TIME, Jan. 8, 1996, p. 13)
蒲隆地這個中非小國一直到1993年才成立國家奧會，但多年來它一直擁有一批<u>非常優秀的</u>賽跑選手。

826 **graphic** [ˋgræfɪk] (a.) （敘述）生動的，栩栩如生的

同 explicit

Theater in the U.S. is filled these days with graphic homosexual stories. (TIME, Sept. 23, 1996, p. 60)

最近美國戲劇充斥著鮮活的同性戀故事。

827 **grass-roots** [ˋgræsˌruts] (a.) 一般民眾的，草根性的

His message ... has helped make the Christian Coalition one of the most powerful grass-roots organizations in American politics.

(TIME, May 15, 1995, p. 28)

他的主張有助於使基督教聯盟成為美國政壇最有力的草根性組織。

828 **hilarious** [həˋlɛrɪəs] (a.) 喧鬧的，極可笑的

The North Korea myths exalting (Kim) Jong Il are so elaborate[549] as to be hilarious.

(TIME, July 18, 1994, p. 26)

北韓頌揚金正日的神話，其體大思精的程度，到了令人發噱的地步。

註 exalt (v.) 頌揚

829 **hip** [hɪp] (a.) 內行的，時髦的

同 trendy

Friends quoted in the press say Bessette is hip and determined[26], a natural socializer who knows how to get what she wants. (TIME, Oct. 7, 1996, p. 42)

媒體引用碧瑟的朋友的話說，碧瑟時髦且意志堅定，是天生的社交高手，知道如何得到她想要的。

830 **impromptu** [ɪmˋprɑmptu] (a.) 即興的，臨時起意的

同 spontaneous

The following day Coetsee paid an impromptu, unannounced visit to the world's most famous political prisoner. (TIME, Mar. 6, 1995, p. 98)

翌日，科特西在毫無預先聲明的情況下，興起走訪了這位世上最著名的政治犯。

☐ 831 **invincible** [ɪn`vɪnsəbl] (a.) 1. 無敵的；2. (精神、理念等) 不屈的，頑強的

同 1. unbeatable

Some analysts were saying Netscape had an <u>invincible</u> lead in the browser business, even against Microsoft. (TIME, Sept. 16, 1996, p. 40)

有些分析家說，網景在導覽器市場擁有<u>所向無敵的</u>領先優勢，甚至微軟也不是它的對手。

☐ 832 **lackluster** [`læk,lʌstə] (a.) 乏善可陳的，平凡的

Sasser triumphed in their first debate, but Frist turned his <u>lackluster</u> performance into another sign that he wasn't a smoothie from the big city. (TIME, Nov. 21, 1994, p. 54)

在第一場演講中，薩瑟獲勝，而弗利斯特的表現雖然<u>乏善可陳</u>，卻讓人了解到他的另一面，那就是他不是來自大城市的滑頭小子。

註 smoothie (n.) 油嘴滑舌的人

☐ 833 **malign** [mə`laɪn] (a.) (影響) 有害的，惡意的

同 harmful
反 benign

Presenting four-year-old information and focusing on just one of China's hundreds of orphanages, it boldly concludes that "the pattern of cruelty, abuse[113] and <u>malign</u> neglect ... now constitutes[144] one of the country's gravest human-rights problems." (TIME, Jan. 22, 1996, p. 21)

這份報告提供的是4年前的舊資料，而且焦點只放在中國數百家孤兒院中的一家，報告中大膽總結「對於孤兒的殘忍、虐待和<u>惡意</u>忽視是中國最嚴重的人權問題之一。」

註 grave (a.) 嚴重的

□834 **maverick** [ˋmævərɪk] (a.n.) 不合流俗的（人），特立獨行的（人）

同 outsider

<u>Maverick</u> director Ann Hui should feel flush now: her sweet, minor-key family drama *Summer Snow* just won four of Taiwan's Golden Horse awards, including Best Picture and Best Actress.

(TIME, Jan. 29, 1996, p. 42)

<u>特立獨行的</u>導演許鞍華現在應該很有錢，因爲她的溫馨小品《女人四十》剛贏得4項金馬獎，包括最佳影片與最佳女主角。

註 flush (a.)（口語）很有錢的；minor-key 較小規模的

□835 **mercurial** [mɝˋkjʊrɪəl] (a.) 善變的

同 volatile

<u>Mercurial</u> and erratic, Kim Jong Il rarely meets foreign dignitaries. (TIME, July 18, 1994, p. 29)

金正日性格<u>善變</u>、難以捉摸，幾乎不見外國要人。

註 erratic (a.) 反覆無常的，不按牌理出牌的；
dignitary (n.) 要人，名流

□836 **microscopic** [ˌmaɪkrəˋskɑpɪk] (a.) 非常微小的

Now candidates openly in favor of political independence are standing up as they never could before, and their campaign[285] speeches are setting <u>microscopic</u> attention on the mainland.

(TIME, Dec. 4, 1995, p. 22)

公然支持台獨的候選人，在這次選舉終於可以史無前例地侃侃而談他們的政見，政見裡只有<u>極少的</u>部分提到中共。

□837 **nascent** [ˋnæsənt] (a.) 初期的，剛開始的

同 budding

The country's <u>nascent</u> green lobby has found an ally[275] in the 25-member Supreme Court, which has ordered several polluting factories to close.

(TIME, Mar. 25, 1996, p. 46)

該國<u>新組成的</u>綠色遊說團體找到了並肩作戰的盟友：25人的最高法院，該法院已下令幾家造成污染的工廠關門。

838 **nimble** [`nɪmbl] (a.) ¹·動作敏捷的；²·聰明伶俐的，機警的

同 ¹· sprightly
　²· alert

"I don't think you'd be interviewing me on this topic if we were any less <u>nimble</u>," Gates told TIME. "You'd be writing our epitaph."

(TIME, Sept. 16, 1996, p. 41)

蓋茲對《時代雜誌》說：「假如我們動作稍慢一點，你們也不用就此問題訪問我了，現在應該正在寫我們的墓誌銘才對。」

註 epitaph (n.) 墓誌銘

839 **no-holds-barred** [no holdz bɑrd] (a.) 為達目的無所不用其極的，無限制的

Cramer is a hedge-fund manager who for years has written a <u>no-holds-barred</u> financial column for a succession of magazines, most recently the two-year-old *Smart Money*. (TIME, Mar. 6, 1995, p. 73)

克拉莫是一家投機性投資集團的經理，數年來陸續為多家雜誌的金融專欄撰寫文章，<u>筆下據理直陳，毫無隱諱</u>，最近的一家雜誌是創刊兩年的《智慧錢》。

840 **oblivious** [ə`blɪvɪəs] (a.) 渾然不覺的

反 conscious

Chinese citizens have greater freedom today than they have had in 50 years. To be <u>oblivious</u> to that is foolish. (TIME, Mar. 25, 1996, p. 15)

中國人民今天享有的自由遠比過去50年來得多，如連這個<u>都沒看到</u>就太愚蠢了。

841 **ostensible** [ɑs`tɛnsəbl] (a.) 表面上的

同 alleged

Some of the funds were not doing as well as they ought to have been, and many were wandering far from their <u>ostensible</u> mandates[328].

(TIME, Sept. 30, 1996, p. 48)

有些基金表現比預期差，而且很多已偏離投資人<u>表面上</u>交付的任務相當遠。

註 to wander from ... 偏離（正途、本題）

☐ [842] **palatable** [`pælətəbl] (a.) [1] 美味的；[2] 愉快的，可接受的

同 [1] tasty
　 [2] acceptable
反 unpalatable

The Clinton Administration has no intention of withdrawing, but it will reduce[225] U.S. intrusiveness and do everything it can to make the situation more palatable. (TIME, Nov. 18, 1996, p. 32)

柯林頓政府並無意撤回駐軍，但會減少對民眾的干擾，並竭盡一切力量來使整個情況比較爲當地人所接受。

註 intrusiveness (n.) 入侵，干擾

☐ [843] **paltry** [`pɔltrɪ] (a.) 微不足道的

In 1993, 84% of its diversified U.S. equity funds outperformed the market; in 1994 about 51% did; last year the figure dropped to a paltry 21%.

(TIME, Sept. 30, 1996, p. 48)

1993年，它有84%的不限類股股票基金獲利率超過市場成長率；1994年這個比例是51%；去年卻滑落至微不足道的21%。

註 outperform (v.) （表現）比…更出色

☐ [844] **provisional** [prə`vɪʒənl] (a.) 臨時的，暫時的

Iraq was in provisional compliance with that significant[90] U.N. requirement.

(TIME, Oct. 24, 1994, p. 34)

伊拉克暫時遵守聯合國那項重大要求。

註 in compliance with 順從，遵守

☐ [845] **replete** [rɪ`plit] (a.) 充滿的

It was clear that the concept of Hong Kong is replete with ambiguity. (TIME, Mar. 17, 1997, p. 22)

很明顯的，「香港」這個概念相當晦澀不明。

註 ambiguity (n.) 充滿歧義，含意模糊

☐ 846 **resilient** [rɪˋzɪlɪənt] (a.) 韌性十足的，很快就能自創傷中恢復的

But the Japanese economy is so big and <u>resilient</u> that while it might stagger, it could absorb the quake's blow. (TIME, Feb. 6, 1995, p. 45)

但日本經濟非常強大，而且<u>韌性十足</u>，因此這次地震後日本經濟或許呈現不穩，但終會挺過這次地震的打擊。

🈟 stagger (v.) 搖搖晃晃，蹣跚

☐ 847 **riveting** [ˋrɪvətɪŋ] (a.) 有趣的，引人入勝的

The words were powerful, but not as <u>riveting</u> as the three Polaroid photos that Edwards later took at the West Los Angeles station house.

(TIME, Feb. 13, 1995, p. 44)

這些文字的敘述非常有力，但說起<u>引人入勝</u>，還不如愛德華後來在西洛杉磯車站所拍的3張拍立得照片。

☐ 848 **runaway** [ˋrʌnəˌwe] (a.) 成長快速的，勢不可遏的

Since the <u>runaway</u> success of his book *Ageless Body, Timeless Mind* in 1993, he has written one best seller after another, selling an astonishing 6 million copies. (TIME, June 24, 1996, p. 46)

自從1993年以《超時空身心》一書<u>一夕</u>成名，他接連寫了好多本暢銷書，賣了驚人的6百萬本之多。

☐ 849 **saturated** [ˋsætʃəˌretɪd] (a.) 飽和的

Its new Microsoft Home division, for example, is an attempt to leverage[924] its position in the market for business desktops, which is becoming <u>saturated</u> and move into the so-called SOHO (small office, home office) market.

(TIME, June 5, 1995, p. 32)

例如，Microsoft Home這個新部門的成立，就是企圖利用微軟在市場上的地位，在逐漸<u>飽和的</u>商用桌上型電腦市場上攻城掠地，並轉進所謂蘇活（小辦公室、家庭辦公室）市場。

進階字
形容詞／副詞

□ [850] **savvy** [ˈsævɪ] (a.) 精通的

> In Moscow and St. Petersburg, ... we can find
> only 100 people here and there who are Internet-
> savvy. (TIME, Feb. 17, 1997, p. 47)
> 在莫斯科和聖彼得堡，我們東找西找，大概只能找到100人
> 熟悉網際網路。

□ [851] **seamless** [ˈsimlɪs] (a.) 無接縫的，組合完美的，渾然一體的

> By creating a seamless global-economic zone,
> borderless and unregulatable, the Internet calls
> into question the very idea of a nation-state.
> (TIME, Jan. 15, 1996, p. 51)
> 網際網路創造出一個綿密無縫的全球經濟區域，這個區域廣
> 闊無邊，無從管制，從而使民族國家這個字的定義有待釐
> 清。

□ [852] **sinister** [ˈsɪnɪstɚ] (a.) 邪惡的

> The Chinese say they want to use them (the U.S.
> military hardware and technology) for jets, but
> some nuclear nonproliferation experts insist that
> Beijing has more sinister plans.
> (TIME, Apr. 25, 1994, p. 39)
> 中共說他們要把美國的軍事裝備與技術用來製造飛機，但一
> 些研究核子非擴散問題的專家堅稱北京當局別有更惡毒的居
> 心。

□ [853] **sleek** [slik] (a.)（人）時髦闊氣的；（汽車、房子等）造形優美豪華的

> More than half a million people will reside[235] in
> Putrajaya and surrounding suburbs, and sleek
> commercial buildings will accommodate[483]
> 135,000 workers. (TIME, Dec. 4, 1995, p. 26)
> 超過50萬人將會居住在〔馬來西亞〕普特拉吉亞及其郊區，
> 優美豪華的商業大樓將容納13萬5千名工作人員。

248 | savvy | seamless | sinister | sleek

☐ 854 **stark** [stɑrk] (a.) （對比）分明的

That courthouse seriousness, however, is in <u>stark</u> contrast to the playful tone that Barksdale has set inside Netscape. (TIME, Sept. 16, 1996, p. 44)
但是法院裡的嚴肅氣氛與巴斯迪爾在網景公司內部營造的輕鬆氣氛，形成<u>鮮明</u>對比。

☐ 855 **staunch** [stɔntʃ] (a.) 堅定的

同 steadfast

A <u>staunch</u> conservative on monetary policy, Tietmeyer nonetheless has supported European integration. (TIME, Feb. 24, 1997, p. 41)
提特邁爾在貨幣政策上是<u>堅定的</u>保守派，卻支持歐洲統合。

☐ 856 **steadfast** [ˋstɛd͵fæst] (a.) 堅定不移的

同 firm

An innocent person ... will remain <u>steadfast</u> in denying guilt. (TIME, May 22, 1995, p. 51)
無辜者必然<u>死</u>不肯承認有罪。

☐ 857 **torrential** [tɔˋrɛnʃəl] (a.) 猛烈的，洶湧的

The flow of money into mutual funds this year is <u>torrential</u>, and has already set an annual record.
(TIME, Sept. 30, 1996, p. 44)
今年流入共同基金的錢潮稱得上是<u>波濤洶湧</u>，而且已經創下年度紀錄。

☐ 858 **trailblazing** [ˋtrel͵blezɪŋ] (a.) 開路先鋒的，創新大膽的

Thanks to Morrison's <u>trailblazing</u> success, black women are not only writing more; their books are being bought and read in droves.
(TIME, June 17, 1996, p. 41)
由於莫里森成功的<u>開疆拓土</u>，黑人女性不僅更辛勤寫作，她們的書籍銷售量與讀者群也大幅成長。

註 in droves 成群結隊地，大量地

859 **ubiquitous** [ju`bɪkwətəs] (a.) 無所不在的

The city's seemingly <u>ubiquitous</u> statues of communist-era heroes ... have been disdainfully torn down. Gone too are the metronomic boot clicks[884] of the goose-stepping guard outside Lenin's tomb .... (TIME, July 4, 1994, p. 50)

市內原本似乎<u>隨處可見的</u>共產時代英雄雕像，已在人們的唾棄聲中拆掉，列寧墓外踢正步衛兵所發出的呆板皮靴撞擊聲，也已消失。

註 disdainfully (adv.) 輕蔑地；
metronomic (a.) 有節奏的，機械呆板的

860 **unfathomable** [ʌn`fæðəməbl] (a.) 深不可測的，難以理解的

同 incomprehensible

For most adults, the very idea of considering children as sexual objects is an <u>unfathomable</u> deviancy. (TIME, Sept. 2, 1996, p. 41)

對多數的成年人而言，將兒童視爲性的對象是<u>匪夷所思的</u>反常行爲。

861 **unfettered** [ʌn`fɛtəd] (a.) 不受拘束的

同 unconstrained

We don't live under free, <u>unfettered</u> capitalism. Isn't that why we have antitrust laws?
(TIME, June 5, 1995, p. 52)

我們並非生活在自由、<u>不受束縛的</u>資本主義體制下，我們制定反托辣斯法，不就是基於這個緣故？

862 **unscrupulous** [ʌn`skrupjələs] (a.) 無道德原則的，不擇手段的

同 unprincipled

Arguing that Gregorian chants cannot be arranged, EMI called the former monks "shameless and <u>unscrupulous</u>," and refuses to pay (royalties). (TIME, July 25, 1994, p. 73)

EMI公司堅稱格列高里聖詠不可改編，指改編這些聖詠的已還俗的僧侶「無恥、無格」，並拒絕付給他們版稅。

註 arrange (v.) 改編（樂曲、小說、劇本）

☐ 863 **virtuoso** [ˌvɝtʃʊˋoso] (a.) 大師級的，精湛的 (n.) 名家，巨匠

> Yamamoto calls himself a nomad in the fashion world, but he brings a visionary Eastern quality to whatever he touches. Last year he rang <u>virtuoso</u> changes on the ancient art of kimono design.
> (TIME, Oct. 9, 1995, p. 47)
> 山本〔耀司〕自稱是時裝界的遊牧民族，但他能將夢幻的東方特質帶進每個設計裡。去年，他把「和服設計」這門古老的藝術，做了<u>大師級的</u>精湛改革。

☐ 864 **voracious** [voˋreʃəs] (a.) 貪婪的

同 insatiable

> If we (banks) are dinosaurs, then we're putting competitors on notice that a new breed has evolved with a <u>voracious</u> appetite for expanded[177] market share. (TIME, Sept. 23, 1996, p. 42)
> 如果我們銀行是行將滅絕的恐龍，那麼我們正在昭告競爭者，一種新品種的恐龍已經演化出來，牠們的<u>胃口很大</u>，想占有更大的市場。
> 註 breed (n.)（動植物的）品種

☐ 865 **wayward** [ˋwewəd] (a.) 不聽話的，任性的

同 unruly
unmanageable

> Four times out of five, the cause of a stroke is a <u>wayward</u> clot that blocks an artery and robs the brain of oxygen-rich blood. (TIME, Sept. 16, 1996, p. 48)
> 中風的發生，有五分之四肇因於一個<u>不安分的</u>血塊堵塞動脈，使腦部無法獲得富含氧分的血液。

☐ 866 **whizzy** [ˋhwɪzɪ] (a.) 快速的，出色的

> Netscape and Microsoft, whose Web-browsing software dominates the market, are currently engaged[171] in a life-or-death struggle to be the first to introduce the newest and <u>whizziest</u> Internet embellishments. (TIME, Aug. 12, 1996, p. 27)
> 網景和微軟這兩家主控網路導覽軟體市場的公司正在進行一場殊死戰，搶先推出最新、<u>最出色的</u>網際網路改良產品。
> 註 embellishment (n.)（使更有趣、更迷人的）裝飾物

□ 867 **wistful** [ˈwɪstfəl] (a.) 渴望的，企盼的

When Michael Jordan successfully returned to the game last year, the original M.J. felt somewhat wistful. (TIME, Feb. 12, 1996, p. 41)
當飛人喬丹去年成功地回到了職籃場上，老招牌的魔術強森也忍不住<u>躍躍欲試</u>。

進階字動詞(868〜967)，共**100**字

- abide 忍受
- abscond （帶著錢等）潛逃
- adapt 改編，改寫
- annex 併吞
- apprehend 逮捕
- arrest 使停止，抑制
- assail 攻擊
- beef up 加強
- bolster 增強
- brandish （得意地）揮舞
- breach 突破，攻破
- bristle 林立，豎立
- brush aside 漠視，不理會（問題等）
- chasten 懲罰，使變乖
- chide 責備
- churn out 大量生產
- click 發出「喀嗒」之聲
- clobber 猛擊，痛擊
- coincide 同時發生
- confine 限定
- consolidate 合併
- contravene 觸犯
- culminate 到達（極點）
- dabble 涉獵，淺嘗
- debilitate 使（人）衰弱
- decry 非難，貶抑
- deluge 使…大量湧至
- despise 鄙視
- dissemble 隱瞞，掩飾
- diverge 分歧
- diversify 使多樣化
- don 穿上，戴上
- dub 命名
- elude 逃避
- entertain 抱持（信念、感情）
- entitle 使有資格，使有權利

- epitomize 作為典範，代表
- evaporate 蒸發，消失
- extol(l) 宣揚
- flout 抗拒，違反
- flush (out) 將…趕出隱藏處
- foil 阻撓，使受挫折
- garner 獲得，收穫
- gobble (up) 大口猛吃，狼吞虎嚥
- grab 急匆匆，胡亂地做某事
- gridlock 交通堵塞
- grill 在長時間內問許多問題，盤問
- huddle 擠成一團
- hurtle 飛速前進
- impede 阻止
- indict 起訴
- infringe 侵犯（法律）
- inhibit 阻止，抑制
- invoke 引用，求助於
- jolt 劇烈搖晃，衝擊
- languish （在長久的困境中）受苦
- leverage 使（事情）變容易
- mimic 酷似，呈現…的形象
- molest 騷擾，調戲
- mushroom 快速增長，快速蔓延
- negotiate 順利通過，成功越過
- nibble （小口）咬
- nudge 輕推
- override 使無效，推翻（決定）
- peg 斷定
- perch 使坐在…
- precipitate 加速（壞事的來臨）
- prescribe 開藥方，規定
- pursue 走（路）
- rankle 使憤慨，使痛苦
- ravage 破壞，蹂躪
- recede 後退

- [ ] rehabilitate 平反，恢復
- [ ] reiterate 重述，重申
- [ ] relish 特別喜歡（做…）
- [ ] rendezvous 會面，約會
- [ ] repeal 廢除（法律）
- [ ] replenish 補充，補滿
- [ ] revile 謾罵，痛斥
- [ ] revitalize 再給予…活力，使復甦
- [ ] rig 以不正當手法操縱（比賽、選舉等）
- [x] scurry 急匆匆地走
- [ ] shell out 付款
- [ ] simulate 模仿，模擬
- [ ] solicit 請求，徵求
- [ ] spawn （大量）生產，引起

- [ ] spearhead 作…先鋒
- [ ] stifle 壓制，遏制
- [ ] synchronize 使…同步，使…一致
- [x] torpedo 破壞
- [ ] tout 吹捧，吹噓
- [ ] traverse 橫越
- [ ] trudge 步履艱難地走
- [ ] trumpet 大力宣傳
- [x] underscore 強調
- [ ] unravel 散開，瓦解
- [ ] usher in 預告，宣告…的到來
- [x] vilify 污衊，詆毀
- [ ] vindicate 證明…為正確、合理
- [x] wink 眨眼，使眼色

□ 868 **abide** [ə`baɪd] (v.) 忍受

同 endure

In fact, interviews with Travers suggest little more than that she couldn't <u>abide</u> journalists and had little patience with people who yearned to elicit trivial[472], simplistic[458] or self-evident answers from her. (TIME, May 6, 1996, p. 69)
實際上，特拉維斯的受訪中所透露的不過是，她不能忍受報社記者，也受不了一些人專問一些很瑣碎、簡單或不問自明的問題。
註 yearn (v.) 渴望；elicit (v.)（從…）誘出（回答、笑聲等）

□ 869 **abscond** [æb`skɑnd] (v.)（帶著錢等）潛逃

The owner of a Kobe sporting-goods store was arrested after allegedly[380] <u>absconding</u> with $64,000 in advance payments for Air Maxes (athletic shoes). (TIME, Oct. 7, 1996, p. 12)
神戶一家運動用品公司老闆因涉嫌捲款潛逃而被捕，款項是Air Maxes運動鞋的預付金6萬4千美元。

□ 870 **adapt** [ə`dæpt] (v.) 改編，改寫

It should be a snap to <u>adapt</u> a John Grisham thriller. (TIME, Jan. 3, 1994, p. 70)
把格利森的驚悚小說改編成電影，應該是件很容易的事。
註 snap (n.) 容易的事

□ 871 **annex** [ə`nɛks] (v.) 併吞（土地）

He has threatened[263] to restore[237] Russia's imperial borders, <u>annex</u> Alaska, invade[200] Turkey, repartition Poland, give Germany "another Chernobyl," turn Kazakhstan into a "scorched desert." (TIME, July 11, 1994, p. 38)
他揚言要恢復帝俄時期的疆界，併吞阿拉斯加，入侵土耳其，再次瓜分波蘭，讓德國人嘗嘗「車諾比」核電廠事件，讓哈薩克成為「荒涼的焦土」。
註 scorch (v.) 燒焦，使成焦土

□ 872 **apprehend** [͵æprɪˋhɛnd] (v.) 逮捕

同 catch

After the U.S. embassy receives a tip, American agents and local police <u>apprehend</u> Yousef in Room 16 at the Su Casa Guest House.

(TIME, Feb. 20, 1995, p. 24)

美國大使館收到線報後，美國情治人員和當地警方在Su Casa賓館16室<u>逮捕</u>了尤瑟夫。

□ 873 **arrest** [əˋrɛst] (v.) 使停止，抑制

同 stop

If the flowering of Taiwanese democracy has been chilled by a wind from the mainland, it has hardly been <u>arrested</u>. (TIME, Dec. 4, 1995, p. 24)

台灣民主的花朵雖已感受到大陸吹來的寒風，但並沒有因此<u>停止</u>生長。

註 chill (v.) 使感覺冷

□ 874 **assail** [əˋsel] (v.) 攻擊

同 attack

Tensions between the two groups exploded last December, when People for the Ethical Treatment of Animals <u>assailed</u> an AIDS treatment that involved taking immune cells from a baboon and then killing it for autopsy. (TIME, July 8, 1996, p. 39)

這兩個團體的緊張關係在去年12月終於爆發。當時「反虐待動物組織」(PETA)<u>攻擊</u>一種愛滋病療法，這種療法要從狒狒身上取出免疫細胞，然後殺死狒狒來解剖。

註 baboon (n.) 狒狒；autopsy (n.) 屍體解剖

□ 875 **beef up** [bif ʌp] 加強

同 strengthen

The Vietnamese defense budget has recently increased nearly 50%, largely to <u>beef up</u> its air force with an eye toward protecting the reserves.

(TIME, May 30, 1994, p. 15)

越南國防預算近來增加了近50%，大抵是用於<u>增強</u>其空軍武力，而目的則是保護〔南海〕礦藏。

進階字
動詞

□876 **bolster** [ˋbolstɚ] (v.) 增強

同strengthen

The danger is that otherwise healthy men will take sildenafil to <u>bolster</u> their sexual performance and then become psychologically addicted[664], unable to achieve an erection without it.

(TIME, May 20, 1996, p. 60)
危機是：本來健康的人也服用sildenafil來<u>增加</u>自己的雄風，養成依賴的心理，若不服用就無法勃起。

□877 **brandish** [ˋbrændɪʃ] (v.)（得意地）揮舞

AmEx clients could <u>brandish</u> their cards in 3.7 million upscale establishments[307] worldwide; Visa cards open 11 million doors, MasterCard 12.3 million. (TIME, Sept. 12, 1994, p. 60)
美國運通卡的使用者可以在全球370萬家高消費的店家，<u>得意地揮舞</u>手中的卡片，刷卡付費，威士卡則可在1,100萬家商店使用，萬事達卡則是1,230萬商店。

註 upscale (a.) 高消費階層的

□878 **breach** [britʃ] (v.) 突破，攻破

同violate

But in 1995 rising temperatures allowed *Aedes aegypti* mosquitoes to <u>breach</u> the coastal barrier and invade[200] the rest of the country.

(TIME, July 8, 1996, p. 41)
但1995年氣溫上升，使埃及斑蚊突破沿海的屏障，<u>侵入</u>這個國家其他地區。

□879 **bristle** [ˋbrɪsl̩] (v.) 林立，豎立

同stand on end

A mountain range <u>bristling</u> with antennas harbors a maze of bombproof underground arsenals and shelters served by a tunnel 4 km long.

(TIME, Feb. 19, 1996, p. 21)
天線<u>林立</u>的山脈中，隱藏著如迷宮般不怕砲擊的地下軍火庫，以及有4公里長的隧道與外界連接的防空洞。

註 harbor (v.) 隱藏；maze (n.) 迷宮；arsenal (n.) 軍火庫

進階字
動詞

☐ 880 **brush aside** [brʌʃ ə`saɪd] 漠視，不理會（問題等）

同 ignore

I saw him (Kennedy) <u>brush aside</u> the doubts and point this nation toward great adventure.
(TIME, July 25, 1994, p. 58)
我看著甘迺迪<u>不顧</u>這些質疑，把國家帶往險境。

☐ 881 **chasten** [`tʃesn̩] (v.) （為矯正行為而）懲罰（人），使變乖

同 discipline

These <u>chastening</u> experiences have caused governments to be more reluctant to provide the military contingents upon which the U.N. entirely depends. (TIME, Oct. 23, 1995, p. 30)
嘗過這些苦頭，各國政府更不願提供部隊給聯合國，而聯合國完全仰賴這些部隊才能執行和平任務。
註 contingent (n.) 代表團，派遣團

☐ 882 **chide** [tʃaɪd] (v.) 責備

同 scold

In his last public appearance, during the 1972 World Series, he <u>chided</u> major league baseball for not having a black manager. (TIME, Apr. 28, 1997, p. 100)
他最後一次公開露面是在1972年總冠軍賽時，當時他<u>抨擊</u>大聯盟連一個黑人經理都沒有。

☐ 883 **churn out** [tʃɝn aʊt] 大量生產

同 turn out

In one bedroom police found eight (software-) copying machines that could <u>churn out</u> 130 floppy disks an hour. (TIME, June 5, 1995, p. 56)
在一間臥房裡，警方查獲8部軟體仿冒機器，這些機器每小時可<u>大量生產</u>130片軟碟。

☐ 884 **click** [klɪk] (v.) 發出「喀嗒」之聲 (n.) 喀嗒聲

Its (Netscape's) killer application was a program
that made navigating the Net as simple as
pointing at what you wanted to see and <u>clicking</u>
on it. (TIME, Sept. 16, 1996, p. 40)
網景公司最厲害的應用軟體，讓遨遊網路簡便到只要<u>按一下</u>滑鼠，就可以想到哪兒，就到哪兒。

☐ 885 **clobber** [ˋklɑbɚ] (v.) 猛擊，痛擊

同 hit

What researchers now realize is that to treat the
joint disease they don't have to <u>clobber</u> the whole
immune system, just certain portions of it.
(TIME, Oct. 28, 1996, p. 70)
現在研究人員了解到，要治療這種關節疾病並不需要<u>打垮</u>整個免疫系統，只需對某部分進行即可。

☐ 886 **coincide** [͵koɪnˋsaɪd] (v.) 同時發生

Disney's *Toy Story* is being given an especially
big push to <u>coincide</u> with its video release[230],
because Disney felt it had underestimated the
marketing possibilities when the film was
released[230] in theaters last fall.
(TIME, Dec. 2, 1996, p. 70)
迪士尼的電影《玩具總動員》，在錄影帶發行的同時發動超強促銷攻勢，因為迪士尼覺得去年秋天該片在電影院上映時，公司低估了它的市場潛力。

☐ 887 **confine** [kənˋfaɪn] (v.) 限定

同 restrict

The coastal mountain ranges of Costa Rica had
long <u>confined</u> dengue fever, a mosquito-borne
disease accompanied by incapacitating bone pain,
to the country's Pacific shore. (TIME, July 8, 1996, p. 40)
長久以來哥斯大黎加的登革熱（一種由蚊子傳播的疾病，伴隨使人軟弱無力的骨骼疼痛症），一直被沿海山脈給<u>限制</u>在該國太平洋沿岸地區。
註 incapacitate (v.) 使虛弱，使無能為力

☐ 888 **consolidate** [kən`sɑlə,det] (v.) 合併

Murayama is pressing a more substantive gambit[999]: to get the U.S. to <u>consolidate</u> some bases on Okinawa. (TIME, Nov. 6, 1995, p. 15)
〔日本首相〕村山正在推動一個比較實際的策略，那就是要求美國將沖繩島上的<u>一些基地</u><u>合併</u>。
註 substantive (a.) 實在的，實質的

☐ 889 **contravene** [,kɑntrə`vin] (v.) 觸犯

同 break

Legally, I have not <u>contravened</u> any laws by helping Chinese dissidents[697] obtain asylum, but politically I may have intruded into a very sensitive area. (TIME, Feb. 10, 1997, p. 26)
就法律層面而言，我幫助中國異議人士取得庇護的舉動並未<u>違反</u>任何法律，但是從政治觀點來看，我可能已經闖入一個非常敏感的地帶。
註 to intrude into 闖入，侵入

☐ 890 **culminate** [`kʌlmə,net] (v.) 到達（極點，指某件事情的結束）

There it (the Olympic torch) began an 84-day, 24,000-km odyssey that will <u>culminate</u> in Atlanta's Olympic Stadium at the climactic moment of the July 19 opening ceremony.
(TIME, May 13, 1996, p. 13)
奧運聖火自該地展開84天、長達2萬4千公里的旅程，<u>全程的高潮</u>是7月19日在亞特蘭大奧林匹克運動場的開幕典禮。
註 odyssey (n.) 長期旅程；climactic (a.) 最高潮的，頂點的

☐ 891 **dabble** [`dæbl] (v.) 涉獵，淺嘗

But Bonnie Lu Nettles, who <u>dabbled</u> in astrology, believed it (their relationship) was fated in stars.
(TIME, Apr. 7, 1997, p. 36)
但對占星術有所<u>涉獵</u>的內托斯深信，他們的關係在星象中早已註定。

☐ 892 **debilitate** [dɪ`bɪlə,tet] (v.) 使（人）衰弱

同 weaken

More than half the 122 patients in one study showed significant[90] improvement without <u>debilitating</u> side effects. (TIME, Oct. 28, 1996, p. 70)
在一項針對122名病患的研究中，超過半數的人病情有了顯著的改善，而且沒有出現<u>使身體衰弱的</u>副作用。

☐ 893 **decry** [dɪ`kraɪ] (v.) 非難，貶抑

同 condemn

Abuse[113] experts also <u>decry</u> the argument that a man's obsessive love can drive him beyond all control. (TIME, July 4, 1994, p. 18)
男人愛得太深，會失去理性，鑽研虐待問題的專家，也<u>譴責</u>這種論點。

註 obsessive (a.) 沈溺的，無法自拔的

☐ 894 **deluge** [`dɛljudʒ] (v.) 使…大量湧至

同 flood

Disney Interactive has been <u>deluged</u> with calls from unhappy parents who purchased the Lion King Animated Storybook CD-ROM and were unable to get it to roar. (TIME, Jan. 9, 1995, p. 61)
迪士尼互動公司<u>接到許多</u>父母的抱怨電話，因為他們買了獅子王動畫光碟故事書，卻沒辦法使光碟運作。

☐ 895 **despise** [dɪ`spaɪz] (v.) 鄙視

We don't <u>despise</u> the veterans[373] of America's 90's war, the Gulf War, we merely pity them.
(TIME, Feb. 17, 1997, p. 64)
我們不<u>鄙視</u>90年代美國波斯灣戰爭的老兵，只是可憐他們。

☐ 896 **dissemble** [dɪˋsɛmbl] (v.) 隱瞞（真正的意圖），掩飾（內心的感受）

They discounted his (Clinton's) womanizing and his dissembling about the draft because they like his energy and intelligence and the fact that he wasn't George Bush. (TIME, July 8, 1996, p. 28)
他們對柯林頓的緋聞與他對兵役問題的遮遮掩掩並不在意，因為他們喜歡柯林頓的幹勁與才智，而且因為他不是布希。

註 discount (v.) 不予重視，同 disregard；
womanize (v.)（口語）玩女人；draft (n.) 服役，徵兵

☐ 897 **diverge** [daɪˋvɜdʒ] (v.) 分歧

同 part

Their paths diverged when Ben went East to get a master's degree in business and Harold started building satellites on the West Coast.
(TIME, Sept. 23, 1996, p. 42)
後來，班去東部唸商學碩士，哈洛則去西岸製造衛星，兩人分道揚鑣。

☐ 898 **diversify** [daɪˋvɜsəˌfaɪ] (v.) 使多樣化

同 branch out

Says ... a Nissan dealer who now also sells Fords: "We'll never sell Toyotas, but there is definitely a move to diversify. Consumers want variety."
(TIME, Oct. 17, 1994, p. 36)
一名兼售福特汽車的日產汽車經銷商表示，「我們絕不賣豐田汽車，但確實有股力量要我們的產品多元化；顧客總希望產品五花八門，琳瑯滿目。」

☐ 899 **don** [dɑn] (v.) 穿上，戴上

同 put on

Today's bikini offers more support, and the body-conscious woman is able to don a bikini in confidence. (TIME, July 1, 1996, p. 56)
今天的比基尼給人體多一些支撐，讓在意身材的女士敢穿上它。

900 **dub** [dʌb] (v.) 命名

同 name

Lee Teng-hui abandoned[111] the (One China) policy in 1991, calling for unification only when the two economic and political systems are compatible[395]. Some have <u>dubbed</u> this "One China, But Not Now." (TIME, Aug. 7, 1995, p. 13)

1991年李登輝放棄了一個中國政策，要求唯有在這兩種經濟及政治體制能相容的狀況下才能統一。有人將此<u>戲稱</u>為：「一個中國，但不是現在」。

901 **elude** [ɪˋlud] (v.) 逃避

同 escape

But when Clinton imposed[195] sanctions[359] on firms doing business with Cuba, he infuriated allies[275] like Canada but <u>eluded</u> a certain Republican trap. (TIME, Sept. 2, 1996, p. 23)

但柯林頓對於與古巴有生意往來的公司施加制裁，一方面激怒了像加拿大這樣的盟國，一方面也<u>避開</u>了共和黨的某種圈套。

902 **entertain** [ˏɛntɚˋten] (v.) 抱持（信念、感情）

同 harbor

Many progressive, westernized Albanians had continued to <u>entertain</u> hopes for a rational settlement of the crisis. (TIME, Mar. 24, 1997, p. 29)

許多前進、西化的阿爾巴尼亞人原本一直<u>抱持</u>危機有理性化解的希望。

903 **entitle** [ɪnˋtaɪtl̩] (v.) 使有資格，使有權利

Ever since Franklin Roosevelt sat in the White House six decades ago ... one U.S. tenet has never changed: if you are poor and eligible[405], you are <u>entitled</u> to cash paid by the Federal Government to improve your life. (TIME, Aug. 12, 1996, p. 25)

60年前小羅斯福總統入主白宮以來，美國有一項信條就始終維持不變：只要你是窮人，而且符合資格，你就<u>有權</u>領取聯邦政府支付的現金來改善生活。

☐ 904 **epitomize** [ɪ`pɪtə,maɪz] (v.) 作為典範，代表

There are hardly any major designers who have not been influenced by the kind of American style Calvin epitomizes .... (TIME, June 17, 1996, p. 14)
設計師裡面鮮有不受到卡文所代表的那種美國風格的影響。

☐ 905 **evaporate** [ɪ`væpə,ret] (v.) 蒸發，消失

同 disappear

When Bill Clinton ran for president four years ago, he missed no opportunity to distance himself from incumbent[425] George Bush's foreign policy. Once he triumphed, though, Clinton's differences evaporated like dew in July. (TIME, July 8, 1996, p. 29)
4年前，柯林頓選總統時，從不錯過任何一個機會來顯示他與在任總統布希外交政策不同的地方；一旦選上，柯林頓與布希的不同就像7月的露珠一樣消失了。

☐ 906 **extol(l)** [ɪk`stol] (v.) 宣揚

A brochure promoting[222] investment opportunities in Kwangju touts[958] its reputation as "the Vanguard of Democracy" and extols those citizens "who sacrificed so much against the past unjust regime in order to recover its freedom."
(TIME, Dec. 11, 1995, p. 21)
為提升光州投資機會而製作的小冊子中，以「民主先鋒」之名來宣揚光州，也誇耀光州人民「為了恢復光州的自由，對抗不公正的舊政權，做過重大的犧牲」。

☐ 907 **flout** [flaʊt] (v.) 抗拒，違反

同 defy

Last July 4, Nye County commissioner Richard Carver, flouting federal law, used a bulldozer to break open a road in a national forest and then filed[180] a criminal complaint against forest-service workers who tried to stop him. (TIME, Mar. 20, 1995, p. 46)
去年7月4日，奈郡首長卡弗踐踏了聯邦法律，用推土機在國有土地開出一條道路，並對試圖阻撓他的林管局人員提出刑事訴訟。

☐ 908 **flush (out)** [flʌʃ] (v.) 將…趕出隱藏處

Only a week after ordering the Mexican army to
<u>flush out</u> the Chiapas rebels[80] from their mountain
hideouts, Mexican President Ernesto Zedillo
abruptly changed course and called off the troops.
(TIME, Feb. 27, 1995, p. 11)
墨西哥總統塞迪約下令軍隊將奇阿帕斯叛軍<u>掃出</u>其山區根據
地後才一星期，突然改弦易轍，召回軍隊。

☐ 909 **foil** [fɔɪl] (v.) 阻撓，使受挫折

同 thwart

It's been a long time since the U.S. was on the
right side of a good coup. Take this latest <u>foiled</u>
attempt on the part of the Kurds and the CIA to
knock Saddam Hussein out of power in Iraq.
(TIME, Sept. 23, 1996, p. 35)
很久以來美國都沒能在外國成功的政變中押對寶。就以最近
這次來說吧！庫德族和美國中情局合作，想推翻伊拉克總統
海珊的政權，就<u>受挫</u>了。

☐ 910 **garner** [ˈɡɑrnɚ] (v.) 獲得，收穫

同 gather
　　acquire

That was also the day the initial[428] public stock
offering for Netscape Communications, a
company that had yet to turn a profit, instantly
<u>garnered</u> $2 billion on the strength of one idea
(World Wide Web). (TIME, June 17, 1996, p. 14)
也就在這一天，「網景通訊公司」的股票首次公開上市，網
景還沒開始賺錢，就靠著全球資訊網這個觀念<u>匯集</u>了20億美
元的資金。

☐ 911 **gobble (up)** [ˈɡɑbl] (v.) 大口猛吃，狼吞虎嚥

After watching everyone from Microsoft to Meca
Software <u>gobble up</u> online-banking customers,
banks have become eager to prove that they're not
headed for extinction. (TIME, Sept. 23, 1996, p. 42)
眼看從微軟到麥加軟體等公司都<u>大舉搶奪</u>上網銀行的顧客，
銀行也開始急於向世人證明他們並非一意等著被市場淘汰。
註 to head ... for ... 使…朝（某方向）前進

□ 912 **grab** [græb] (v.) 急匆匆、胡亂地做某事（如吃飯、喝飲料等）

Barksdale slipped into a suit, <u>grabbed</u> a quick breakfast and pointed his Mercedes toward Netscape's Mountain View headquarters.

(TIME, Sept. 16, 1996, p. 40)

巴斯戴爾穿上西裝，<u>草草用完</u>早餐，然後開著他的賓士車直奔山景城的網景公司總部。

□ 913 **gridlock** [ˋgrɪd͵lɑk] (v.) 交通堵塞

Japan's Intelligent Transportation System master plan calls for fully-automated cars to be plying the island nation's dreadfully <u>gridlocked</u> roadways by the year 2010. (TIME, Nov. 4, 1996, p. 53)

日本的智慧運輸系統主計畫要求在公元2010年之前，全自動車輛可以在這個島國<u>塞得動彈不得</u>的道路中穿梭往返。

註 ply (v.) 定期往返於…之間

□ 914 **grill** [grɪl] (v.) 在長時間內問許多問題，盤問

同 interrogate

Detectives who <u>grill</u> suspects in *Homicide* (TV series) do it with verbal cunning[22], not strong-arm bullying[502]. (TIME, Feb. 1, 1993, p. 66)

在《殺人》這齣電視連續劇裡，警察是以精明的言詞<u>盤問</u>嫌犯，而非動粗威脅。

□ 915 **huddle** [ˋhʌdl̩] (v.) 擠成一團

同 cluster

At 10 a.m. a U.S. Coast Guard plane appears. Hoping not to be seen, passengers <u>huddle</u> on the floor of the boat, which is slimy with vomit and seawater. (TIME, Apr. 10, 1995, p. 56)

早上10點，美國海岸防衛隊的飛機出現，船上的乘客為了不被發現，<u>全擠</u>在船底肋板上，那裡布滿了嘔吐物和海水，黏糊一片。

註 slimy (a.) 黏糊糊的

☐ 916 **hurtle** [ˋhɝtl] (v.) 飛速前進

同 plunge

He was about to send a company with $6 billion in sales and 19,641 workers—all $70 billion worth—<u>hurtling</u> in that direction.

(TIME, Sept. 16, 1996, p. 40)

他將領著這銷售額達60億美元，擁有1萬9,641名員工，總價值700億美元的公司，循此方向<u>全速前進</u>。

☐ 917 **impede** [ɪmˋpid] (v.) 阻止

同 hinder
　　hamper

In many areas there was nothing to <u>impede</u> the terrible mud slides because the wildfires of 1993 had destroyed all the vegetation.

(TIME, Jan. 23, 1995, p. 28)

許多地方都沒有東西可<u>阻擋</u>可怕的土崩，因為1993年的數場野火摧毀了所有植被。

☐ 918 **indict** [ɪnˋdaɪt] (v.) 起訴

同 charge

Then last week Murayama got an agreement from the U.S. that American servicemen wanted in serious crimes can now be taken into Japanese custody before they are <u>indicted</u>, rather than afterward as was previously[73] the case.

(TIME, Nov. 6, 1995, p. 15)

然後，上週〔日本首相〕村山取得美國同意，往後所有犯下重大罪案而受通緝的美國軍人，都可在<u>起訴</u>前交給日本警方羈押，不必像以前一樣必須等到起訴後。

註 custody (n.) 羈押，監禁

☐ 919 **infringe** [ɪnˋfrɪndʒ] (v.) 侵犯（法律）

同 violate

The Indiana Democrat, who was worried that the ban[128] might <u>infringe</u> on the rights of law-abiding gun owners, had already voted against the bill.

(TIME, May 16, 1994, p. 40)

這名印第安那州的民主黨議員早就投票反對這項法案，因為他擔心這道禁令可能<u>侵犯</u>了那些合法擁槍者的權利。

□ 920 **inhibit** [ɪnˋhɪbɪt] (v.) 阻止，抑制

同 restrain

The highly popular Prime Minister is committed[510] to ending political corruption and trimming the vast web of economic regulations that <u>inhibit</u> imports, push up consumer prices and infuriate the U.S. (TIME, Feb. 14, 1994, p. 46)

這名極負衆望的首相承諾消滅政府貪污，削減經濟上綿密如網的管制規定，因爲這些規定<u>抑制</u>外貨進口、提高物價，且激怒美國。

註 trim (v.) 調整，削減

□ 921 **invoke** [ɪnˋvok] (v.) 引用，求助於；召喚，使…浮上心頭

He <u>invoked</u> the names of John's parents and said how proud they would have been; once again many of those present were brought to tears.
(TIME, Oct. 7, 1996, p. 42)

他<u>提起</u>約翰雙親的名字，以及他們會多驕傲之類的話，在場許多人再一次熱淚盈眶。

□ 922 **jolt** [dʒolt] (v.n.) 劇烈搖晃，衝擊

He added that a surge[643] in short-term rates could <u>jolt</u> the stock and bond market ....
(TIME, Jan. 10, 1994, p. 18)

他又說，短期利率急速上升可能<u>衝擊</u>到股市和債券市場。

□ 923 **languish** [ˋlæŋgwɪʃ] (v.)（在長久的困境中）受苦，受折磨

More than 40 Chinese dissidents[697] and their families who have <u>languished</u> hidden in Hong Kong will at last be granted asylum in the west.
(TIME, Feb. 10, 1997, p. 26)

四十多名躲藏在香港<u>捱日子的</u>中國異議份子及他們的家人，終將得到西方國家的庇護。

進階字
動詞

☐ 924 **leverage** [ˈlɛvərɪdʒ] (v.) 使（事情）變容易，使（事情）更順利進行
(n.) 手段，影響力

同 (v.) facilitate

We also try to energize the remaining people around increasing top-line growth, that is getting close to your customers, expanding[177] the business you're good at and looking for opportunities to use technology to <u>leverage</u> the work.

(TIME, Apr. 15, 1996, p. 28)

我們也鼓勵其他員工為公司創造更高的營收，如多多接近客戶，擴展專長的業務，以及找機會利用科技，<u>使</u>這項工作<u>進行更順利</u>。

註 top-line growth 公司常用的財務報表，不論是balance sheet（資產負債表）還是income statement（損益表），其第一行(top line)都是revenue（收入），最後一行(bottom line)則是純利。所以top-line growth指的是營收成長，bottom line則是指損益情形，引申為總結論。

☐ 925 **mimic** [ˈmɪmɪk] (v.) 酷似，呈現…的形象

同 imitate

A rapid expansion of hot gas would <u>mimic</u> a nuclear explosion. (TIME, May 23, 1994, p. 54)

熱氣的快速膨脹會產生<u>酷似</u>核子爆炸的效果。

☐ 926 **molest** [məˈlɛst] (v.) 騷擾，調戲

同 abuse

Don't <u>molest</u> crops, women or prisoners of war.

(TIME, Nov. 4, 1996, p. 41)

不<u>損壞</u>莊稼，不<u>調戲</u>婦女，不<u>虐待</u>戰俘。

☐ 927 **mushroom** [ˈmʌʃrum] (v.) 快速增長，快速蔓延

Faced with a <u>mushrooming</u> crisis, Yeltsin last week called for a new effort to stem[252] crime.

(TIME, Mar. 20, 1995, p. 54)

面對危機<u>快速惡化</u>，上週葉爾欽採取了一項新措施以抑制犯罪活動。

928 **negotiate** [nɪ`goʃɪ,et] (v.) 順利通過，成功越過

同 navigate

Trying to <u>negotiate</u> the curve around a sea of red ink, Amtrak announced that it would cancel more than a fifth of its service throughout the nation and trim 5,500 employees. (TIME, Dec. 26, 1994, p. 33)
為了安然度過虧損連連的危機，美國全國鐵路客運公司宣布將裁撤全國五分之一以上的營運業務，及5,500名員工。
註 a sea of 大量的；red ink 赤字，虧損；trim (v.) 削減

929 **nibble** [`nɪbl] (v.)（小口）咬

Rats and cockroaches <u>nibbled</u> at the torn flesh on his leg as he spent his nights in a bare brick cell, unheated even when the temperature fell to -7°C.
(TIME, June 24, 1996, p. 25)
晚上在空無一物的磚造牢房中，溫度降到攝氏零下7度也沒有暖氣，蟑螂、老鼠啃噬他腿上的傷口。
註 bare (a.)（屋內）沒有陳設的，空蕩蕩的

930 **nudge** [nʌdʒ] (v.) 輕推

Officials are trying to <u>nudge</u> the economy toward such higher-value goods as electronics and machinery. But so are competitors elsewhere in Asia. (TIME, Aug. 5, 1996, p. 42)
政府官員正試圖將經濟推向諸如電子及機械等更高價值的產品上，但是亞洲的競爭對手也都這麼做。

931 **override** [,ovɚ`raɪd] (v.) 使無效，推翻（決定）

同 overrule

Determined not to lose this battle, Lee's government announced Friday that it will dust off a little-used executive veto to save the project by getting around the Legislative Yuan. Opponents will need a two-thirds majority to <u>override</u> it.
(TIME, June 17, 1996, p. 54)
李登輝政府決心打贏這一仗，於星期五宣布將祭出極少動用的行政否決權，避開立法院的抵制，以挽回這個法案。反對者將需要三分之二的多數才能使否決權失效。
註 to dust off（將久藏的東西取出）準備重新使用

□ 932 **peg** [pεg] (v.) 斷定

Scientists <u>pegged</u> the age of the carbonate globules at 3.6 billion years, strongly suggesting that they formed in crevices of the rock while it was still part of the Martian crust.

(TIME, Aug. 19, 1996, p. 41)

科學家將碳酸球的年代認定在36億年前,這個年代強烈顯示,它們是在石塊仍屬於火星地殼一部分時在其裂縫中形成的。

註 crevice (n.)(窄而深的)裂縫

□ 933 **perch** [pɜtʃ] (v.) 使坐在…

Masayoshi Esashi is <u>perched</u> proudly on the cutting edge of technology. (TIME, Apr. 28, 1997, p. 46)

Esashi很驕傲自己<u>致力於</u>最先進的科技研究。

註 on the cutting edge of... 致力於最先進的…

□ 934 **precipitate** [prɪ`sɪpə,tet] (v.) 加速(壞事的來臨)

同 bring about
hasten

Castro is on the verge of collapse and should be squeezed even harder to <u>precipitate</u> his downfall.

(TIME, Feb. 20, 1995, p. 52)

卡斯楚即將垮台,因此應施加更多壓力,以<u>加速</u>他的垮台。

□ 935 **prescribe** [prɪ`skraɪb] (v.) 開藥方,規定

Oregon adopted the only measure[329] in the U.S. to allow doctors to <u>prescribe</u> lethal[434] doses of medication to terminally-ill patients.

(TIME, Nov. 21, 1994, p. 64)

奧勒岡州採取了美國境內僅見的一項措施,准許醫生<u>開立</u>致命<u>藥方</u>給病入膏肓的病人。

註 terminally (adv.) 末期地

□ 936 **pursue** [pɚˋsu] (v.) 走（路）

An increasing number of marital therapists believe it is their job to save the relationship rather than simply help each party <u>pursue</u> his or her chosen path. (TIME, Feb. 27, 1995, p. 48)
愈來愈多的婚姻治療師認爲，他們的職責是挽回婚姻關係，而非單單幫助雙方各<u>走</u>各的路。

□ 937 **rankle** [ˋræŋkḷ] (v.) 使憤慨，使痛苦

Not only have Washington's harangues on human rights <u>rankled</u>, but there have been other sources of friction[707]. (TIME, Mar. 25, 1996, p. 14)
華盛頓在人權上大作文章，<u>令中共不快</u>，此外雙方一直還有別的磨擦來源。
註 harangue (n.v.) 長篇大論的說教

□ 938 **ravage** [ˋrævɪdʒ] (v.) 破壞，蹂躪

UNICEF plans to use that time to step up public health and education programs in 14 war-<u>ravaged</u> countries. (TIME, Jan. 8, 1996, p. 13)
聯合國兒童基金會打算利用這段時間，加強14個<u>受戰火摧殘的</u>國家的公共衛生與教育計畫。
註 to step up 促進，提高

□ 939 **recede** [rɪˋsid] (v.) 後退

During the past 100 years, the sea level has risen 1 ft. along the U.S. Atlantic Coast, causing beaches to <u>recede</u> between 200 ft. and 300 ft. on average. (TIME, Mar. 14, 1994, p. 79)
過去100年，美國大西洋岸的海平面已上升1呎，造成海岸平均往陸地<u>後退</u>了200到300呎。

□ 940 **rehabilitate** [.riə`bɪlə,tet] (v.) 平反，恢復

Deng <u>rehabilitated</u> the individuals and restored[237] organizational life, but the damage to the party's authority was irremediable. (TIME, May 13, 1996, p. 26)
鄧小平<u>平反</u>這些人，並恢復黨機關活動，可是黨的權威所受的傷害已無法彌補。

□ 941 **reiterate** [ri`ɪtə,ret] (v.) 重述，重申

同 repeat

Even before Secretary of State Warren Christopher traveled to Brussels to <u>reiterate</u> U.S. commitment to the Contact Group plan ... the Pentagon was urging Clinton to cut his losses and compromise[138] with the Serbs. (TIME, Dec. 12, 1994, p. 30)
甚至在國務卿克里斯多夫前往布魯塞爾，<u>重申</u>美國對實行「接觸團體」計畫的承諾之前，國防部已在促請柯林頓減少美國損失，並與塞爾維亞人妥協。

□ 942 **relish** [`rɛlɪʃ] (v.) 特別喜歡（做…）

同 enjoy

They <u>relish</u> citing examples of overzealous enforcement (of federal regulation): the sheep rancher who was fined $4,000 for shooting a grizzly bear that was attacking him ....
(TIME, Feb. 27, 1995, p. 58)
他們<u>特別喜歡</u>引用一些聯邦法令被矯枉過正的例子，例如牧羊場主人射殺了一隻想攻擊他的大灰熊，結果被罰鍰4千美元。
註 overzealous (a.) 過份熱心的

□ 943 **rendezvous** [`rɑndə,vu] (v. n.) 會面，約會

同 (v.) meet

Leeson had left Kuala Lumpur to <u>rendezvous</u> with his wife Lisa in the Malaysian resort town of Kota Kinabalu, and there ... he boarded the plane in his own name. (TIME, Mar. 13, 1995, p. 40)
李森先離開吉隆坡，到馬來西亞的度假勝地Kota Kinabalu與其妻麗莎<u>會面</u>，然後在那裡以本名搭上飛機。
註 resort (n.) 度假勝地

☐ 944 **repeal** [rɪ`pil] (v.) 廢除（法律）

同 rescind

You can outlaw technique, you cannot <u>repeal</u> biology. (TIME, Mar. 10, 1997, p. 30)
可以立法禁止科技，但不能<u>廢除</u>生物學。
註 outlaw (v.) 宣布…為非法，禁止

☐ 945 **replenish** [rɪ`plɛnɪʃ] (v.) 補充，補滿

同 refill

The challenge for every prisoner, particularly every political prisoner, is how to survive intact[55], how to emerge undiminished, how to conserve and even <u>replenish</u> one's beliefs.
(TIME, Nov. 28, 1994, p. 52)
每一名犯人，尤其是政治犯，所面臨的挑戰，就是如何毫髮無傷地生存下來，如何保有原有的威望重出江湖，如何保住甚至<u>彌補</u>個人的人生信念。

☐ 946 **revile** [rɪ`vaɪl] (v.) 謾罵，痛斥

同 hate
despise

Meanwhile, the Bosnian Muslims <u>revile</u> them (peacekeepers) for standing by when women and children are shot. (TIME, June 12, 1995, p. 52)
在這同時，波士尼亞的回教徒<u>痛斥</u>和平維持部隊眼見婦孺遭射殺仍袖手旁觀。

☐ 947 **revitalize** [rɪ`vaɪtl͵aɪz] (v.) 再給予…活力，使復甦

同 revive
revivify

While the California company reported a healthy 10% gain in third-quarter profits, most of its toy lines are mature, and for them to grow, they must be constantly <u>revitalized</u>, particularly in the U.S.
(TIME, Nov. 11, 1996, p. 37)
這家加州公司在第三季的獲利仍穩定成長10%，但它大部分的玩具都已經到達市場成熟階段，若要再成長，勢必得不斷<u>賦予它們新生命力</u>，特別是在美國市場。

進階字
動詞

□ 948 **rig** [rɪg] (v.) 以不正當手法操縱（比賽、選舉等），作弊

In late February he came up with tentative[470] agreements on improved medical care ... , along with proposed reforms intended to make elections harder to <u>rig</u>. (TIME, Apr. 4, 1994, p. 32)
2月下旬他對醫療保健體系的改善方案和使選舉更難<u>舞弊</u>的建議改革方案，作出了初步同意。

□ 949 **scurry** [ˈskɝɪ] (v.) 急匆匆地走

Like an army of ants, Haitians by the hundreds <u>scurry</u> up and down the dusty banks of Massacre River with their gallon plastic jugs.
(TIME, Apr. 11, 1994, p. 55)
就像群螞蟻一樣，成百的海地人在馬薩克河塵土飛揚的岸邊<u>跑</u>上<u>跑</u>下，手中拿著一加侖容量的塑膠壺。

□ 950 **shell out** [ʃɛl aut] 付款

同 fork out

Before long, Meeks had <u>shelled out</u> more than $25,000 in legal fees. (TIME, Sept. 5, 1994, p. 15)
才沒多久米克斯已<u>付出</u>超過2萬5千美元的訴訟費。

□ 951 **simulate** [ˈsɪmjə,let] (v.) 模仿，模擬

Medic, an Osaka-based software company, is selling a popular video game in which players <u>simulate</u> the experience of AIDS from HIV infection until death. (TIME, Apr. 19, 1993, p. 15)
大阪一家叫Medic的軟體公司正販售一種極爲暢銷的電玩，玩者可以在遊戲裡<u>模擬</u>體驗到愛滋病患者從染上HIV到死亡的全部過程。

□ 952 **solicit** [sə`lɪsɪt] (v.) 請求，徵求

When the White House chose new Democratic National Committee members, it did not bother to <u>solicit</u> Jackson's opinion. (TIME, Mar. 13, 1995, p. 91)
白宮尋找民主黨全國委員會新委員的人選時，並未特別去<u>徵求</u>賈克遜的意見。

□ 953 **spawn** [spɔn] (v.)（大量）生產，引起

The result was one of history's headiest[422] corporate ascents, as the ubiquitous[859] Netscape Navigator browser helped <u>spawn</u> the world's startling online stampede. (TIME, June 17, 1996, p. 16)
結果是創下有史以來公司業績攀升速度最快的紀錄之一，無所不在的網景導覽器，<u>造成</u>爭先恐後的上網風潮，震驚全世界。

註 stampede (n.v.) 蜂擁上前，大量湧到

□ 954 **spearhead** [`spɪr,hɛd] (v.) 作…先鋒

同 lead

Both are <u>spearheading</u> the most adventurous, fascinating[179] movie movement of the '90s: Chinese films from the People's Republic, Hong Kong and Taiwan. (TIME, Jan. 29, 1996, p. 38)
由中國、香港、台灣通力合作製作華人電影，是90年代最勇於創新、最迷人的電影運動，而他們兩人〔陳凱歌和吳宇森〕都是這場運動的<u>先鋒</u>。

□ 955 **stifle** [`staɪfl] (v.) 壓制，遏制

同 repress

Critics charge that Gingrich is playing right-wing politics, trying to <u>stifle</u> funds for cultural projects that he and his allies[275] dislike. (TIME, Jan. 30, 1995, p. 52)
批評者指控金瑞契正在玩右翼政治的把戲，試圖讓他和他那一幫人都厭惡的文化計畫<u>籌不到</u>資金。

進階字
動詞

☐ 956 **synchronize** [ˈsɪŋkrəˌnaɪz] (v.) 使⋯同步，使⋯一致

Even Beijing agrees that reunification will not take place until some time in the future, when the societies on the two shores of the strait are more closely <u>synchronized</u>. (TIME, Mar. 25, 1996, p. 16)
就連北京也同意，統一不是現在，而是要等到海峽兩岸的社會更<u>趨於一致</u>之時。

☐ 957 **torpedo** [tɔrˈpido] (v.) 破壞

同 sabotage
wreck

Neither Israeli Prime Minister Benjamin Netanyahu nor the Arabs have <u>torpedoed</u> the search for Middle East peace. (TIME, Sept. 2, 1996, p. 23)
以色列總理內唐亞胡和阿拉伯人都未<u>破壞</u>追求中東和平的努力。

☐ 958 **tout** [taʊt] (v.) 吹捧，吹噓

Even fashion editors who <u>tout</u> couture's more fanciful currents on the pages of their magazines venerate Sander. (TIME, Nov. 7, 1994, p. 70)
即使是在自己雜誌上大力<u>吹捧</u>更奇巧服裝設計風潮的時裝編輯，也尊敬桑德這位時裝設計大師。
註 couture (n.) 時裝設計（業）；fanciful (a.)（設計等）新奇的；venerate (v.) 尊敬，崇拜

☐ 959 **traverse** [ˈtrævɜs] (v.) 橫越

同 cross

17 North Koreans recently found temporary refuge in Hong Kong, having taken a route to freedom that involved surreptitiously <u>traversing</u> much of China. (TIME, Feb. 10, 1997, p. 26)
17名北韓人最近在香港得到暫時性的庇護，他們投奔自由的路途還包括偷偷<u>越過</u>中國大陸許多地區。
註 surreptitiously (adv.)（因違法而）偷偷摸摸地

☐ 960 **trudge** [trʌdʒ] (v.) 步履艱難地走

As the Israelis and Palestinians <u>trudged</u> toward accommodation, hope for progress shone on another front as well. (TIME, May 9, 1994, p. 42)
當以色列和巴勒斯坦步履維艱地邁向和解，在另一個相互對峙的前線也亮起邁向和解的曙光。

☐ 961 **trumpet** [ˈtrʌmpɪt] (v.) 大力宣傳

In Los Angeles this week Sega will be <u>trumpeting</u> the arrival of a 32-bit version[372] of Sonic the Hedgehog, a soaring game called Nights, and a Net Link telephone hookup[1008] ....

(TIME, May 20, 1996, p. 60)
本週，世嘉公司將在洛杉磯推出32位元版本的「音速小子」、迅速竄紅的遊戲「暗夜」、以及名叫「網路連線」的電話連線裝置。

☐ 962 **underscore** [ˈʌndəˌskor] (v.) 強調

同 underline

To launch[203] his fall line—and celebrate 25 years in the business—he (Issey Miyake) put on an extravaganza in Paris, a long, lavish[433] show that <u>underscored</u> a strong reason for his enduring[36] career: complex technology made beautiful by artistry. (TIME, Oct. 9, 1995, p. 47)
爲了推出秋季系列的服飾並慶祝進入這行25年，三宅一生在巴黎舉行了一場盛大服裝秀，這場耗時且極盡奢華的服裝秀，正說明了他之所以能在服裝界屹立不搖的原因，即他有將複雜的科技產品美化的藝術才華。
註 line (n.) 系列產品；extravaganza (n.) 豪華的演出

☐ 963 **unravel** [ʌnˈrævl̩] (v.) 散開，瓦解

His struggle against his homosexuality was <u>unraveling</u> both his marriage and his academic post in a religious school. (TIME, Apr. 7, 1997, p. 36)
他與其同性戀傾向的掙扎，讓他的婚姻和宗教學院的教職雙雙亮起紅燈。

☐ 964 **usher in** [ˋʌʃə ɪn] 預告，宣告…的到來

同 herald

It may be an overstatement to suggest that without Deng, China will tumble into disorder. But his departure will <u>usher in</u> the greatest period of uncertainty since the death of Mao Zedong in 1976. (TIME, Jan. 23, 1995, p. 50)

沒有了鄧小平，中國將陷入混亂，這種說法或許言過其實，但他的去世將<u>宣告</u>自1976年毛澤東去世以來，最長的不穩定時期<u>的到來</u>。

註 tumble (v.) 跌倒

☐ 965 **vilify** [ˋvɪləˏfaɪ] (v.) 污衊，詆毀

同 malign

They branded her "an apostate appointed by imperial forces to <u>vilify</u> Islam." (TIME, Aug. 15, 1994, p. 26)

他們封她為「帝國主義者派來<u>詆毀</u>回教的叛教者」。

註 apostate (n.) 背教者，脫黨者

☐ 966 **vindicate** [ˋvɪndəˏket] (v.) 證明…為正確、合理，辯護

同 justify

Those who were responsible for the operation now seemed desperate[25] to <u>vindicate</u> their judgment in the face of overwhelming criticism. (TIME, Feb. 8, 1993, p. 38)

這次行動的各主事者，面對勢不可擋的批評聲浪，如今都急於想為自己的判斷<u>作辯護</u>。

註 overwhelming (a.) 壓倒性的，無法抵擋的

☐ 967 **wink** [wɪŋk] (v.) 眨眼，使眼色

Nintendo won't say anything about its Internet plans right now except to <u>wink</u> and say, as Lincoln does, that it "will be making announcements in the near future." (TIME, May 20, 1996, p. 60)

除了<u>使個眼神</u>，然後像林肯一樣說「會在不久的將來宣布」，任天堂目前還不願對於它在網際網路方面的計畫發表意見。

- advent 來臨，出現
- animosity 敵意，仇恨
- antecedent 前例，先聲
- aura 氣氛，光暈
- behemoth 龐然大物，組織龐大的機構
- bulwark 防禦工事，堤防
- bump （路面等的）隆起部分，喻困難
- carnage 大屠殺
- catalyst 觸媒，催化劑
- censure 責難
- charisma （使大眾信服的）群眾魅力
- chic 流行
- conglomerate 大型綜合企業
- contingency 突發狀況
- contraption 奇妙的設計
- corridor 人口密集地帶
- coup 大成功，大成就
- dearth 缺乏
- detractor 惡意批評者，誹謗者
- dominion 支配
- downsizing 公司裁員縮編
- episode 插曲，事件
- errand 差使，跑腿
- ethnic group 少數民族
- excursion 出遊，涉入
- fad 一時的流行，時尚
- feat 事蹟，成就
- fold 控制範圍，原意為「羊圈」
- forum 公開討論場所
- fray 爭論，爭吵，騷動
- gadget 精巧的小器械
- gambit 手段，招式
- geek 電腦狂，怪胎
- glut 過量，供過於求
- gorge 作嘔，厭惡
- hacker 駭客，電腦程式專家
- handler 處理者，經手人
- haven 避難所
- heretic 異端
- holdout 拒不合作者，拒不參加者
- hook-up 連線設施
- iconoclast 反抗或破除傳統者
- indignity 屈辱
- insurgent 叛軍
- interlocutor 對話者
- juggernaut 可怕、不可抗拒的力量
- lever 手段，方法
- minimalism 簡約主義
- nausea 噁心，反胃
- nostalgia 鄉愁，懷舊之情
- novice 初學者，新手
- omniscience 全知
- outlay 費用，支出
- paranoid 被迫害妄想狂者，偏執狂者
- pariah 被社會唾棄者
- pestilence 瘟疫
- pilgrimage 朝聖之旅，長途旅程
- ploy 策略，手法
- precursor 先驅，前輩；預兆，前兆
- prowess 好本事，英勇
- pundit 專家，權威
- qualm 良心不安
- rancor 怨恨，傷痛
- rebuke 斥責，申誡
- redoubt 避難所，庇護所
- remnant 殘餘物
- reprimand 斥責，申誡
- rigor 折磨，嚴厲
- scourge 天譴，災難
- shackles 束縛
- spin-off 副產品
- swap 交換，互惠資金
- tabloid 專報聳動新聞、配有大量圖片的小報
- thrall 控制，奴役
- traction 原意為輪胎抓地力，引申為攻擊的把柄
- trauma 創傷
- twist 創新之舉，新發展
- variant 變體，變種
- venue 會場，地點
- volatility 反覆無常，不穩定
- write-off （債務）勾銷

□ [968] **advent** [ˈædvɛnt] (n.) 來臨，出現

同 arrival
appearance

But with the <u>advent</u> of the drip-dry shirt and the frozen breakfast burrito, it became possible for any fellow, no matter how domestically challenged, to get out of the house on his own. (TIME, May 6, 1996, p. 53)

但是，伴隨著隨洗隨乾的免燙襯衫及冷凍的墨西哥餡餅早餐的<u>出現</u>，任何一個再不會做家事的傢伙，都能夠輕鬆靠著一己之力打點一切，出門上班。

□ [969] **animosity** [ˌænəˈmɑsətɪ] (n.) 敵意，仇恨

同 hostility

It is almost entirely the product of <u>animosity</u> between two men leading rival[358] parties who are deeply jealous of each other. (TIME, Mar. 27, 1995, p. 36)

這可以說全是兩個敵對團體的龍頭老大互相<u>仇視</u>所造成，這兩個團體都見不得對方好。

□ [970] **antecedent** [ˌæntəˈsidənt] (n.) 前例，先聲

同 precursor

In 1937, working in his kitchen, Stibitz cobbled together a primitive[75] adding device out of dry-cell batteries, metal strips from a tobacco can, flashlight bulbs and telephone wires. Many consider it the earliest <u>antecedent</u> to the digital computer. (TIME, Feb. 13, 1995, p. 23)

1937年史蒂比茨在廚房裡，以數個乾電池、香菸罐上取下的數條鐵片、數個閃光燈泡、數根電線，草草製成一部原始的計算機；許多人認為這是數位化電腦的<u>濫觴</u>。

註 adding device 計算機；to cobble together 草草製成

□ [971] **aura** [ˈɔrə] (n.) 氣氛，光暈

同 air

Redford's festival created an <u>aura</u> that welcomed young directors and persuaded Hollywood to do the same. (TIME, June 17, 1996, p. 45)

勞勃·瑞福的影展製造了歡迎年輕導演加入的<u>氛圍</u>，也說服了好萊塢效法。

☐ **972 behemoth** [bɪ`himəθ] (n.) 龐然大物，組織龐大的機構

同 monster

The deal may spur[635] more competition for Microsoft, but it removes the threat that the government will try to break up the <u>behemoth</u>.

(TIME, July 25, 1994, p. 13)

這筆交易或許會給微軟公司帶來更多的競爭，但也化解掉政府欲拆散這個<u>龐大公司</u>的威脅。

☐ **973 bulwark** [`bulwək] (n.) 防禦工事，堤防

One country's louse, of course, is another's <u>bulwark</u> against [fill in the ism: communism, nationalism, imperialism, capitalism].

(TIME, Sept. 23, 1996, p. 35)

當然，對一個國家來說是惡棍的人，對另一個國家可能是對抗〔什麼主義自己填：共產主義、民族主義、帝國主義、資本主義〕的<u>長城</u>。

註 louse (n.) 蝨，卑鄙的人

☐ **974 bump** [bʌmp] (n.)（路面等的）隆起部分，喻困難

Says Christensen of Thailand's progress from low tech to high: "It's a long journey. There will be <u>bumps</u> along the way." (TIME, Aug. 5, 1996, p. 42)

克里斯田森說，泰國由低科技提升到高科技的過程「是一條長路，沿路將會有許多<u>困難</u>。」

☐ **975 carnage** [`kɑrnɪdʒ] (n.) 大屠殺

同 slaughter

The once shabby alleys leading to Provincial Government Plaza, site of the worst <u>carnage</u> in 1980, are now lined with trendy boutiques, while a sprawling[463] shopping mall has just opened under the plaza. (TIME, Dec. 11, 1995, p. 20)

通往省政府廣場（1980年<u>屠殺</u>最慘烈的地方）的巷弄一度凋敝不堪，現在兩旁羅列著時髦的服飾精品店，而大型商場也剛在廣場地下開幕。

註 shabby (a.) 殘破的，破舊的；trendy (a.) 時髦的

□ 976 **catalyst** [ˈkætəlɪst] (n.) 觸媒，催化劑

But the innocence and trust of the young that most adults celebrate and nurture are powerful catalysts for the sexual fantasies[310] of pedophiles.

(TIME, Sept. 2, 1996, p. 41)

孩子的天眞無邪與對人的信賴，向來爲大部分大人所歌頌且悉心培育，卻也是刺激戀童癖人士產生性幻想的兩大誘因。

□ 977 **censure** [ˈsɛnʃə] (n.v.) 責難

同 (n.) condemn
(v.) condemnation

As he demonstrated[155] in the award-winning *This Boy's Life* (1989), Wolff knows exactly how to find and then walk the line between self-censure and self-pity. (TIME, Oct. 31, 1994, p. 81)

正如沃爾夫在1989年獲獎的《這男孩生平》一書中所展示，他清楚知道自責與自憐之間的界線，並懂得如何悠遊其間。

□ 978 **charisma** [kəˈrɪzmə] (n.)（使大眾信服的）群眾魅力

同 magnetism

Because of his high profile and charisma, and because of his own admission that he engaged[171] in numerous unprotected sexual encounters[304], Johnson has probably done as much to educate the public about AIDS as anybody.

(TIME, Feb. 12, 1996, p. 40)

由於他的高知名度以及獨特的群眾魅力，加上他公開承認有過數不清的危險性行爲，強森對教育大眾了解愛滋病的貢獻，絕不比別人來得少。

註 high profile 高知名度

□ 979 **chic** [ʃɪk] (n.) 流行 (a.) 時髦的

Now Chinese chic has become Hollywood's latest mania[741]. Ang Lee is an Oscar front runner for his first studio film, *Sense and Sensibility*.

(TIME, Jan. 29, 1996, p. 40)

好萊塢最近流行中國熱，李安第一次替製片公司拍的《理性與感性》就讓他成爲奧斯卡的熱門人選。

註 front runner 比賽中最有可能的奪標者；
    studio (n.) 電影製片公司

進階字
名詞

□ ⁹⁸⁰ **conglomerate** [kənˋɡlɑmərɪt] (n.) 大型綜合企業

Few American communities of any size have more than a single newspaper, which is frequently owned by a distant <u>conglomerate</u>.

(TIME, Feb. 10, 1997, p. 56)

美國鄉鎮不論大小，大都只有一份報紙，而且往往歸遠方的報業<u>集團</u>擁有。

□ ⁹⁸¹ **contingency** [kənˋtɪndʒənsɪ] (n.) 突發狀況

同 possibility
eventuality

The doctor, who is something of a gadget⁹⁹⁸ freak, was equipped for any <u>contingency</u>.

(TIME, Sept. 23, 1996, p. 43)

這位愛好小器械成癖的醫生備有因應任何<u>突發狀況</u>的裝備。

註 freak (n.)〔與修飾語連用〕（⋯的）愛好者

□ ⁹⁸² **contraption** [kənˋtræpʃən] (n.) 奇妙的設計

同 gadget

For quick acceleration and hill climbing, the turbine is linked to a flywheel, an energy-producing and energy-storing <u>contraption</u> that is at least as old as the first potter's wheel.

(TIME, Sept. 23, 1996, p. 41)

為了瞬間加速或爬坡，渦輪機還連接飛輪。飛輪是一種可以製造與儲存能量的<u>奇妙裝置</u>，其歷史與製陶器的轉輪一樣久遠。

□ ⁹⁸³ **corridor** [ˋkɔrɪdə] (n.) 人口密集地帶

It was for Asia the celestial event of the decade: total eclipses ... occur somewhere on the globe every one to two years, but rarely are they visible along such a densely populated <u>corridor</u>.

(TIME, Nov. 6, 1995, p. 21)

對亞洲來說，這是近10年來的天文盛事：全球每一兩年就會發生日全蝕，但很少像這樣發生在<u>人口稠密地區</u>。

☐ 984 **coup** [ku] (n.) 大成功，大成就

In an impressive <u>coup</u>, she was on the September cover of both *Vogue* and *Harper's Bazaar*.
(TIME, Dec. 26, 1994, p. 157)
她登上《時尚》、《哈潑》兩份雜誌的9月號封面，是她個人生涯一項令人讚嘆的<u>大成就</u>。

☐ 985 **dearth** [dɜθ] (n.) 缺乏

同 lack

And though Hou is proud of his films, he thinks the <u>dearth</u> of commercial films is hurting Taiwan cinema. (TIME, Jan. 29, 1996, p. 43)
侯孝賢雖以他的電影爲榮，但也認爲商業電影的<u>缺乏</u>正斲傷台灣的電影工業。

☐ 986 **detractor** [dɪˋtræktɚ] (n.) 惡意批評者，誹謗者

同 critic

Barbie may not be everyone's favorite companion—<u>detractors</u> love to hate her plastic perfection—but the fashion doll with the impossible figure has long been the most popular girl at Mattel. (TIME, Nov. 11, 1996, p. 36)
芭比娃娃也許不是所有人心愛的玩伴——<u>批評者</u>喜歡攻擊她塑膠製的完美造型——但這個身材只應天上有的時裝洋娃娃，長久以來一直是美泰兒公司最受歡迎的女娃娃。

☐ 987 **dominion** [dəˋmɪnjən] (n.) 支配

The deal immediately raised questions about whether Gates who has near monopoly[333] control of the PC software industry and is moving aggressively[379] into computer networking, is planning to extend his <u>dominion</u> into graphic images as well. (TIME, Oct. 23, 1995, p. 66)
這項交易立刻就引起了一些疑問，是否蓋茲在幾乎已獨占個人電腦軟體工業以及積極進入電腦網路領域之後，還打算<u>掌控</u>平面影像界？

☐ 988 **downsizing** [ˋdaʊnˏsaɪzɪŋ] (n.) 公司裁員縮編

He (Major) eased off on the giant welfare cuts and industrial <u>downsizing</u>. (TIME, May 12, 1997, p. 35)
在福利支出的大幅刪減和企業界的<u>裁員縮編</u>上，梅傑放慢了腳步。
註 to ease off 緩和

☐ 989 **episode** [ˋɛpəˏsod] (n.) 插曲，事件

Although civilian rule was restored[237] to South Korea in 1993, the wound inflicted[584] by the Kwangju <u>episode</u> has yet to heal.
(TIME, Dec. 11, 1995, p. 20)
南韓已在1993年恢復文人統治，但是光州<u>事件</u>所造成的傷痕仍有待撫平。

☐ 990 **errand** [ˋɛrənd] (n.) 差使，跑腿

His father, a carpenter, died when Paavo was 12, and the boy, eldest of five children, had to quit school and work as an <u>errand</u> runner, pushing a heavy wheelbarrow through the streets.
(TIME, June 24, 1996, p. 66)
帕沃的父親是位木匠，在他12歲那年就去世了，而他是家裡5個小孩中的老大，因此必須輟學並找份<u>跑腿</u>工作，推著很重的獨輪手推車在街上跑。

☐ 991 **ethnic group** [ˋɛθnɪk ɡrup] 少數民族

According to several statistical measures of intelligence, people of Asian and especially Chinese descent consistently[400] outscore other racial and <u>ethnic groups</u>. (TIME, Sept. 11, 1995, p. 60)
根據幾項智力測量的統計顯示：亞裔，尤其是華裔，在各項測驗裡領先其他<u>少數民族</u>，絕少例外。
註 outscore (v.)（表現）比…出色

992 **excursion** [ɪk`skɜʒən] (n.) 出遊，涉入

Crichton's other major <u>excursion</u> into cutting-edge science involves the trendy field of complexity .... (TIME, Oct. 2, 1995, p. 45)

科契頓所涉足的尖端科學領域還包括今日最風行的「繁複理論」。

註 cutting-edge (a.) 尖端的，最先進的；
trendy (a.) 最時髦的，走在流行尖端的

993 **fad** [fæd] (n.) 一時的流行，時尚

同 craze

Her legacy[732] can be seen in every thing from presidential candidates who discuss their marital problems on TV to the <u>fad</u> for crash diets.
(TIME, June 17, 1996, p. 27)

她的影響力所及，從總統候選人在電視上大談自己的婚姻問題，到風行一時的速成減肥無所不包。

註 crash (a.) 速成的

994 **feat** [fit] (n.) 事蹟，成就

同 accomplishment

It's worth noting that establishing growth at a company the size of IBM—with $72 billion in sales last year, it is the 18th largest on the planet—is no mean <u>feat</u>. (TIME, Nov. 4, 1996, p. 49)

值得一提的是，像IBM這種規模的公司——去年以720億美元營業額排名世界第18大企業——要創造成長絕非易事。

註 no mean 了不起的，不容易的

995 **fold** [fold] (n.) 控制範圍，原意爲「羊圈」

Mao Zedong, the leader of the communist revolution that forced Chiang Kai-shek and his Nationalist government to flee to the island of Taiwan in 1949, used to say he could wait 100 years to bring the province back into the <u>fold</u>.
(TIME, Feb. 12, 1996, p. 16)

當年領導共產革命而在1949年將蔣介石及國民政府逼到台灣的毛澤東過去常說，爲了收復這個省，等上100年也沒有關係。

☐ 996 **forum** [`forəm] (n.) 公開討論場所

She helped bring such topics as child abuse[113], homosexuality and marital dysfunction out of the closet and into the public <u>forum</u>.

(TIME, June 17, 1996, p. 27)

她把虐待兒童、同性戀與婚姻不和這些原屬私下密談的議題搬出來供<u>大眾公論</u>。

註 to bring ... out of the closet 把…從隱密狀態轉為公開；
dysfunction (n.) 機能障礙

☐ 997 **fray** [fre] (n.) 爭論，爭吵，騷動

Members of the NASA-led team arrived in Washington fully prepared to enter the <u>fray</u>.

(TIME, Aug. 19, 1996, p. 41)

由航太總署領軍的研究小組，有備而來抵達華盛頓，準備投入這場<u>論戰</u>。

☐ 998 **gadget** [`gædʒɪt] (n.) 精巧的小器械

同 appliance

To see about this technology for myself, I spent some time using one <u>gadget</u>, Philips Magnavox's WEBTV. (TIME, Mar. 10, 1997, p. 49)

為了親身體驗這項科技，我花了些時間使用其中一種<u>機型</u>，即飛利浦Magnavox牌的網路電視。

☐ 999 **gambit** [`gæmbɪt] (n.) 手段，招式

同 ploy
  tactic

Specter's pro-choice <u>gambit</u> may be less appealing when women are reminded of his role as Anita Hill's grand inquisitor during the Clarence Thomas hearings. (TIME, Mar. 13, 1995, p. 66)

在托馬斯聽證會上，史貝特曾是阿尼塔‧希爾的大審訊官，當有人提醒婦女他曾扮演這樣的角色，他所走的支持墮胎這<u>步棋</u>，其功效可能就打了折扣。

註 pro-choice (a.) 贊成墮胎的，相反詞是pro-life

□ 1000 **geek** [gik] (n.) 電腦狂，怪胎

Programmers who find the market for Windows software increasingly crowded and unprofitable see fresh opportunities to make their mark in Java. "The geeks are buzzed ... It's like a whole world just opened up to us." (TIME, Jan. 22, 1996, p. 42)

程式設計師發現，視窗軟體的市場愈來愈飽和，且愈來愈無利可圖，但在「爪哇」程式裡，他們看到了能夠攻占一席之地的新契機。「電腦玩家都為之瘋狂，就好像整個世界在我們眼前敞開一樣。」

註 to make one's mark 揚名，成功

□ 1001 **glut** [glʌt] (n.) 過量，供過於求

同 surplus

The House of Representatives last week passed a series of legal-reform bills intended to discourage frivolous lawsuits, of which there is alleged[380] to be a glut. (TIME, Mar. 20, 1995, p. 13)

上星期衆議院通過了一系列司法改革法案，以遏止人們打一些無關緊要的官司，據說人們打官司已到浮濫的地步。

註 frivolous (a.) 無意義的，不重要的

□ 1002 **gorge** [gɔrdʒ] (n.) 作嘔，厭惡

In the interest of participatory journalism, I swallowed my rising gorge and tried (*Doom* computer game) again. (TIME, Dec. 18, 1995, p. 60)

為了寫一篇親身參與後所做的報導，我硬是嚥下了那愈來愈強的厭惡感，再玩一遍「毀滅戰士」電腦遊戲。

註 in the interest of 為了；journalism (n.) 新聞寫作

☐ 1003 **hacker** [`hækə] (n.) 駭客，電腦程式專家

The transformation that has set Microsoft on the road to a Net-based future has also completed Gates' beatification as not just a great <u>hacker</u> but also a world-class CEO. (TIME, Sept. 16, 1996, p. 41)

讓微軟轉型，邁向以網路爲主的未來世界，此舉也完成了蓋茲個人的神化，使他不僅是超級「<u>駭客</u>」，更是世界級的總裁。

註 beatification (n.)（天主教）以教令宣告某死者因功德已升天列入「真福品位」，有資格受到大家的尊崇

☐ 1004 **handler** [`hændlə] (n.) 處理者，經手人

Some captured radio operators, ordered by the North Vietnamese to ask for more agents, managed to signal to their CIA <u>handlers</u> with code words that they were being held.

(TIME, June 24, 1996, p. 25)

有些被北越俘虜的無線電發報員，被北越命令發出增派情報員的要求，但他們成功地以密碼告知中情局<u>聯絡人</u>他們被俘的消息。

☐ 1005 **haven** [`hevən] (n.) 避難所

同 refuge

With the latest offers of asylum, human rights workers wonder what country can replace[232] Hong Kong as the chief political <u>haven</u> for refugees not just from the mainland but from elsewhere in Asia. (TIME, Feb. 10, 1997, p. 27)

在最近各國提供庇護之際，人權工作者懷疑有哪個國家可以取代香港，作爲政治難民（不只是從中國大陸逃出的，還包括亞洲其他地區）的主要<u>避難所</u>。

☐ 1006 **heretic** [`hɛrətɪk] (n.) 異端

He has been called a fascist, a <u>heretic</u> and shenjingbing, a lunatic. (TIME, Feb. 20, 1995, p. 61)

他一直被稱作法西斯分子、<u>異端</u>和神經病。

| hacker | handler | haven | heretic |

☐ 1007 **holdout** [`hold,aut] (n.) 拒不合作者，拒不參加者

The R.S.V.P.s are in, and 196 of the 197 nations invited to Atlanta have said yes. (Even <u>holdout</u> North Korea is wavering.) (TIME, Jan. 8, 1996, p. 13)
根據收到的回函，受邀的197個國家裡，已經有196個答應參加亞特蘭大奧運（連唯一說不的北韓也開始猶豫了）。

> 註 R.S.V.P. 法文répondez s'il vous plaît（請回覆）的縮寫，即「回函」之意；waver (v.) 意志動搖，猶豫不決

☐ 1008 **hook-up** [`huk,ʌp] (n.) 連線設施

MCI and the Japanese telephone company KDD donated an estimated $20 million to the cost of the 45-megabit-per-second data <u>hook-up</u>.
(TIME, Mar. 11, 1996, p. 35)
MCI公司和日本電話公司KDD捐贈了約2千萬美元來建設這條每秒可傳45百萬位元資料的<u>連線設施</u>。

☐ 1009 **iconoclast** [aɪ`kɑnə,klæst] (n.) 反抗或破除傳統者

Yet this unbending <u>iconoclast</u> lived a life of such relentless personal rectitude and brought such unmatched excellence to his many Olympic races that he won far more of our experts' votes as the greatest Olympian than any other athlete.
(TIME, June 24, 1996, p. 66)
但是這個個性不屈不撓、<u>打破傳統的人</u>，終其一生過著嚴謹的清廉生活，且在多項奧運比賽中表現出無與倫比的成績，所以獲得我們專家最多選票，榮膺「最偉大的奧運選手」。

> 註 unbending (a.) 堅定的，不屈不撓的；
> relentless (a.) 不屈不撓的；rectitude (n.) 操行端正，正直

☐ 1010 **indignity** [ɪn`dɪgnətɪ] (n.) 屈辱

同 humiliation

This son of a Georgia sharecropper endured unspeakable <u>indignities</u> and taunts to become baseball's first black player. (TIME, Apr. 28, 1997, p. 100)
這個喬治亞州某佃農的兒子，忍受了無法言喻的<u>屈辱</u>和嘲諷，才成為第一位黑人棒球選手。

> 註 taunt (n.) 嘲笑，奚落

☐ 1011 **insurgent** [ɪnˋsɝdʒənt] (n.) 叛軍

同 rebel

Politicians had no credibility[298] with slap-together committees of <u>insurgents</u>. (TIME, Mar. 24, 1997, p. 29)
政治人物在烏合之衆的<u>叛軍</u>委員會之前毫無公信力可言。

註 to slap together 草草拼湊，slap-together是其形容詞義

☐ 1012 **interlocutor** [͵ɪntɚˋlɑkjətɚ] (n.) 對話者

Without America, Great Britain and France cannot sustain[260] the political balance in Western Europe; Germany would be tempted[648] by nationalism; Russia would lack a global <u>interlocutor</u>. (TIME, Mar. 14, 1994, p. 73)
沒有美國，英、法無法維持西歐的政治均勢，德國將爲民族主義所誘，步入歧途，俄國將少了一位全球級的<u>對話伙伴</u>。

☐ 1013 **juggernaut** [ˋdʒʌgɚ͵nɔt] (n.) 可怕、不可抗拒的力量

Many Americans see Japan's economic <u>juggernaut</u> as a continuation of war by other means. (TIME, Dec. 2, 1991, p. 70)
許多美國人認爲日本<u>可怕的</u>經濟<u>力量</u>是以另一種形式延續的戰爭。

☐ 1014 **lever** [ˋlɛvɚ] (n.) 手段，方法

The U.S. has abandoned[111] the trade weapon as a <u>lever</u> to improve human rights in China.
(TIME, June 13, 1994, p. 31)
美國已不再以貿易武器作爲改善中國人權的<u>手段</u>。

☐ 1015 **minimalism** [ˋmɪnɪml͵ɪzm̩] (n.) 簡約主義

One could even argue that Klein's elegant take on <u>minimalism</u> has come to define the look of the late 20th century in the U.S. (TIME, June 17, 1996, p. 18)
我們甚至可以說，克萊對<u>簡約主義</u>的優雅嘗試，已經主宰20世紀晚期美國人的穿著。

註 take (n.)（俚語）嘗試，努力

□ 1016 **nausea** [ˋnɔʃɪə] (n.) 噁心，反胃

The FDA has approved the first-ever vaccine for hepatitis A, which afflicts[487] up to 150,000 Americans annually with fever, aches, <u>nausea</u> and vomiting. (TIME, Mar. 6, 1995, p. 25)

美國食品和藥物管理局已批准了有史以來第一個A型肝炎疫苗，美國每年有高達15萬人染上肝炎，產生發燒、疼痛、<u>反胃</u>、嘔吐的症狀。

□ 1017 **nostalgia** [nɑsˋtældʒɪə] (n.) 鄉愁，懷舊之情

Popular for its satirical tone, *All My Children* tried to capitalize[505] on viewer <u>nostalgia</u> last January, when it celebrated its 25th anniversary. The show spent a week reviewing in flashback its quarter century on the air. (TIME, May 29, 1995, p. 73)

以諷刺風格而備受歡迎的電視節目《我家小孩》，今年1月歡渡25週年，並試圖利用觀眾的<u>懷舊情緒</u>替節目造勢。該節目花了一星期播放過去25年的片段回顧。

註 review (v.) 回顧；flashback (n.)（小說、戲劇等）倒敘

□ 1018 **novice** [ˋnɑvɪs] (n.) 初學者，新手

反 old hand

While some nations immediately supported the idea, others completely missed the point of Malamud's vision: to make the fair a public-works project that focuses on what the Internet can offer expert or <u>novice</u>. (TIME, Mar. 11, 1996, p. 35)

有些國家二話不說就表態支持，有些國家卻完全沒有抓到馬拉末的著眼點：就是要使這個博覽會成為一個公共工程，此工程重點在網際網路能為專家及<u>新手</u>提供什麼服務。

□ 1019 **omniscience** [ɑmˋnɪʃəns] (n.) 全知

(Deep) Blue's <u>omniscience</u> will make it omnipotent. It can play—fight—with the abandon of an immortal. (TIME, Feb. 26, 1996, p. 42)

電腦「深藍」的<u>全知</u>將使它變為全能，它可以以不朽神祇的縱情而豪放嬉戲，盡情作戰。

註 abandon (n.) 放縱，無拘無束

☐ 1020 **outlay** [`aut,le] (n.) 費用，支出

But those hoping for new or even replenished[945] foreign-aid <u>outlays</u> should not hold their breath; there will be little money to throw at problems.

(TIME, Nov. 18, 1996, p. 33)

但是如果你希望有新的對外援助<u>經費</u>，甚或只是補足差額，你也不應該期望過高，因為沒什麼錢可用在這些問題上。

註 to hold one's breath（因焦急或興奮地等待而）屏息

☐ 1021 **paranoid** [`pærə,nɔɪd] (n.) 被迫害妄想狂者，偏執狂者

Andy Grove, the Intel CEO, ... has distilled the essence of competing in a high-tech world down to a single sentence: "Only the <u>paranoid</u> survive."

(TIME, Sept. 16, 1996, p. 41)

英代爾總裁葛羅夫把高科技界競爭的真締濃縮成一句話：「只有<u>神經兮兮的人</u>才能生存。」

註 distill (v.) 蒸餾，提煉

☐ 1022 **pariah** [pə`raɪə] (n.) 被社會唾棄者

同 outcast

For decades South Africa was an international sports <u>pariah</u>. (TIME, Aug. 19, 1996, p. 51)

數十年來南非一直是國際體壇的<u>拒絕往來戶</u>。

☐ 1023 **pestilence** [`pɛstələns] (n.) 瘟疫

同 plague

Soon the bikini was causing international incidents. France's Mediterranean neighbors reacted as if some <u>pestilence</u> were spreading. Italy and Spain forbade bikinis on their beaches.

(TIME, July 1, 1996, p. 54)

沒多久，比基尼惹出一些國際事件來。法國的地中海鄰國的反應彷彿當它是<u>瘟疫</u>。義大利和西班牙都禁止境內的海灘出現比基尼。

☐ 1024 **pilgrimage** [ˋpɪlgrəmɪdʒ] (n.) 朝聖之旅，長途旅程

His pilgrimage to an alumni weekend at Cornell University not only finessed a way through White House opposition but also created an international incident in which Taiwan came out looking like a winner. (TIME, Dec. 25, 1995/Jan. 1, 1996, p. 54)

他這趟康乃爾大學週末校友會之旅不僅巧妙避開了白宮的反對，還形成國際事件，而台灣在此事件中看起來像是勝利者。

註 alumni (n.) alumnus的複數，「校友」之意；
finesse (v.) 用巧計實現

☐ 1025 **ploy** [plɔɪ] (n.) 策略，手法

It was a familiar ploy for Sun's Joy, who helped foster[568] the growth of the Internet itself in the early 1980s by shipping free Internet Protocol software with every Sun computer.

(TIME, June 22, 1996, p. 44)

這個策略對昇陽公司的喬伊來說一點也不陌生，他曾在1980年代初期，在每部昇陽公司出產的電腦當中，灌入免費的網際網路所需的通訊協定軟體，藉此促進網際網路的成長。

☐ 1026 **precursor** [prɪˋkɝsə] (n.) 先驅，前輩；預兆，前兆

同 forerunner

Under the tutelage of Dan Leno, London's most beloved comedian and a precursor of Charlie Chaplin, Lizzie became a star ....

(TIME, May 29, 1995, p. 52)

李諾是倫敦最受喜愛的喜劇演員，也是卓別林的前輩，李濟就在李諾調教下，成為熠熠明星。

☐ 1027 **prowess** [ˋprauɪs] (n.) 好本事，英勇

Japanese corporations were quick to seize the chance of putting their technological prowess on show. (TIME, Mar. 11, 1996, p. 35)

日本企業搶先抓住機會，將他們的科技本領拿出來展示一番。

☐ 1028 **pundit** [ˋpʌndɪt] (n.)（常出現於媒體的）專家，權威

同 expert

Some <u>pundits</u> speculate that many computers are obsolete[61] before they're even designed, which goes a long way toward explaining why the ATM at my grocery store never works.

(TIME, Nov. 11, 1996, p. 16)

有些<u>專家</u>推測，許多電腦在被設計出來之前就已經過時了，這個原因頗能夠解釋為什麼我買東西的那些雜貨店的自動提款機從來沒有正常過。

註 to go a long way toward ... 對…大有作用，大有幫助

☐ 1029 **qualm** [kwɑm] (n.) 良心不安

They have no <u>qualms</u> about bestowing their inner life on a dozen members of the next generation.

(TIME, Mar. 10, 1997, p. 41)

他們對於將自己的內在生命贈與十數個下一代一點也不覺<u>良心不安</u>。

☐ 1030 **rancor** [ˋræŋkə] (n.) 怨恨，傷痛

同 bitterness

The nuclear material was made in Russia, and both Washington and Almaty (Kazakhstan's capital) knew they had to gain Moscow's approval for the unprecedented[104] transfer[267]. It did come, and apparently without <u>rancor</u>, in June.

(TIME, Dec. 5, 1994, p. 38)

這些核子物質是俄國所製，而華盛頓和阿馬提雙方都知道，這個前所未有的轉移行動，必須獲得莫斯科首肯；今年6月莫斯科眞的答應了，而且顯然答應得不帶任何<u>仇恨</u>。

☐ 1031 **rebuke** [rɪˋbjuk] (n.) 斥責

同 reprimand

To mainland communists, Taiwan's simple existence as an offshore rival[358] under the rule of Generalissimo Chiang Kai-shek's Nationalist heirs is an open <u>rebuke</u> of their legitimacy and a thumb in their eye .... (TIME, June 5, 1995, p. 18)

台灣在大元帥蔣介石國民黨繼承人的統治下，與中共隔海相對，是對中共政府合法性的迎面<u>譴責</u>，也是中共的眼中釘。

□ 1032 **redoubt** [rɪˋdaʊt] (n.) 避難所，庇護所

同 haven

In the past decade, an economic megaboom on this offshore Nationalist Party <u>redoubt</u> has produced one of the world's largest nest eggs of foreign-exchange reserves.

(TIME, Dec. 25, 1995/Jan. 1, 1996, p. 54)

過去10年，這個國民黨的海上<u>避難所</u>，經歷超級經濟繁榮，已創造出全球數一數二的外匯存底。

□ 1033 **remnant** [ˋrɛmnənt] (n.) 殘餘物

The setting [of the wedding] was one of the wild, unspoiled sea islands off Georgia—to visitors, they seem like <u>remnants</u> of the New World as it was before its discovery. (TIME, Oct. 7, 1996, p. 42)

喬治亞州外海有數座未遭人爲破壞的原始海島，婚禮的地點就在其中一座海島上；在訪客眼中，這些海島就像是新大陸還未被發現的<u>幾塊淨土</u>。

註 unspoiled (a.) 未喪失原有自然美的

□ 1034 **reprimand** [ˋrɛprəˏmænd] (n.v.) 斥責，申誡

同 (v.) admonish

The Navy claims[133] it punished Meyer with a letter of <u>reprimand</u> that effectively ended his career.

(TIME, Aug. 15, 1994, p. 37)

海軍當局聲稱已以一紙<u>申誡</u>函懲罰了梅爾，而且事實上梅爾也因這紙申誡函結束了海軍生涯。

□ 1035 **rigor** [ˋrɪgɚ] (n.) 折磨，嚴厲

A committee of Taiwanese curators and university scholars ... examined the works that were ready to be crated and requested that certain pieces considered too fragile[46] to withstand the <u>rigors</u> of travel be withdrawn. (TIME, Apr. 1, 1996, p. 47)

由台灣各博物館館長與大學學者組成的一個委員會，檢視這些即將裝箱的寶物，要求把其中一些被認爲太脆弱而不堪旅途<u>折磨</u>的作品撤下來。

註 curator (n.) （博物館等的）館長；crate (v.) 用箱子裝

☐ 1036 **scourge** [skɜdʒ] (n.) 天譴，災難

> Earlier this century, breakthroughs in antibiotics inspired[197] similarly confident predictions that the ancient scourges (infectious diseases) would soon be eradicated. (TIME, May 27, 1996, p. 67)
> 在本世紀稍早，抗生素方面的突破，引發了同樣樂觀的預測，以為自古以來人類認為是天譴的一些流行病即將被消滅。
> 註 eradicate (v.) 根除，消滅

☐ 1037 **shackles** [ˈʃæklz] (n.) 束縛

> As for Ted Turner, the merger liberates his lofty ambition from the shackles of cash-strapped[94] circumstance. (TIME, July 29, 1996, p. 43)
> 對特納而言，這次合併使他得以一展雄心壯志，不再受資金短缺的束縛。
> 註 merger (n.)（組織的）合併；lofty (a.) 崇高的

☐ 1038 **spin-off** [ˈspɪnˌɔf] (n.) 副產品

> The film, which links Michael Jordan with Bugs Bunny, Daffy Duck and the rest of the Looney Tunes stable, has generated[187] more than 200 spin-off items that Warner is hoping will eventually pull in $1 billion. (TIME, Dec. 2, 1996, p. 70)
> 這部結合了麥可・喬丹、兔寶寶、達菲鴨與華納「瘋兒調」卡通系列及其他動物的電影，已衍生出兩百多種副產品，華納公司希望靠這些副產品最後能賺進10億美元。
> 註 stable (n.) 屬同一主人的物品

☐ 1039 **swap** [swɑp] (n.) 交換，互惠資金

> Electronic Arts, a leading producer of games for personal computers and video-game machines, announced it will acquire[115] Broderbund Software in a $400-million stock swap. (TIME, Feb. 21, 1994, p. 15)
> 製造個人電腦和影像遊戲機所用遊戲軟體的主要廠商電子藝術，宣布將以總值4億美元的股票交換，買下「波德邦」軟體公司。

☐ 1040 **tabloid** [ˈtæblɔɪd] (n.) 專報聳動新聞、配有大量圖片的小報

反 broadsheet

But public male heterosexuality, like water seeking its own level, has settled down in the <u>tabloid</u> bottomlands, where it does its best to provide low entertainment. (TIME, Sept. 23, 1996, p. 60)
可是男性公眾人物的異性戀，如水之就下，已經沈淪到<u>小報紙</u>統轄的低窪地帶，在那兒大力提供低俗趣味的娛樂。

☐ 1041 **thrall** [θrɔl] (n.) 控制，奴役

Even as a sudden chill overtook Sino-American relations, and even as Beijing thundered that the traveler from Taipei was a traitor and schemer under the <u>thrall</u> of "political hallucinogenic drugs," Lee never flinched.
(TIME, Dec. 25, 1995/Jan. 1, 1996, p. 54)
即使中共與美國的關係突然變冷；即使北京激烈地譴責李登輝這位台北的出遊者是受了「政治迷幻藥」<u>擺佈</u>的叛徒與陰謀者，李登輝仍毫不退縮。

註 chill (n.) 寒冷，寒氣；overtake (v.) 突然降臨於；
thunder (v.) 厲聲發出（威脅、警告等）；
traitor (n.) 賣國賊，叛徒；flinch (v.) 退縮

☐ 1042 **traction** [ˈtrækʃən] (n.) 原意為輪胎抓地力，引申為攻擊的把柄

Dole has even been unable to find <u>traction</u> on defense spending. (TIME, Sept. 2, 1996, p. 23)
杜爾甚至一直未能在國防支出上找到<u>可大作文章的地方</u>。

☐ 1043 **trauma** [ˈtrɔmə] (n.) 創傷

What does seem clear is that pedophilia, like many sexual disorders, may have at its root some childhood sexual <u>trauma</u>. (TIME, Sept. 2, 1996, p. 41)
看來很清楚的是，戀童癖患者與其他許多種性失調患者相同，他們的病症可能都源於童年時的性<u>創傷</u>。

☐ 1044 **twist** [twɪst] (n.) 創新之舉，新發展

The 1996 world's fair is no exception, but it also has a decidedly eve-of-the-21st-century <u>twist</u>: the whole event happens in cyberspace.
(TIME, Mar. 11, 1996, p. 35)
1996年的世界博覽會也不例外，但這次確實有一項21世紀前夕的<u>創新之舉</u>：整個博覽會是在電腦網路上舉行的。

☐ 1045 **variant** [ˋvɛrɪənt] (n.) 變體，變種

Over the years, there have been women wrestlers, including a renowned[83] nun, and a <u>variant</u> so bloody that the sport was briefy banned[128].
(TIME, Sept. 30, 1996, p. 29)
漫長的歷史中曾有過女子相撲，其中還出過一位著名的比丘尼選手，及另一種極血腥的<u>變相相撲</u>，因而一度遭到短期的禁止。

☐ 1046 **venue** [ˋvɛnju] (n.) 會場，地點

Hong Kong films use mainland locations; Taiwanese companies co-produce P.R.C. films; Chinese and Hong Kong actors shuttle[631] from one <u>venue</u> to the other. It's a relatively free form of cultural exchange. (TIME, Jan. 29, 1996, p. 38)
香港電影在大陸拍攝，台灣電影公司參與製作大陸電影，大陸與香港藝人則穿梭於兩岸三<u>地</u>，形成相當自由的文化交流。

☐ 1047 **volatility** [ˌvɑləˋtɪlətɪ] (n.) 反覆無常，不穩定

同 instability

And the Kuala Lumpur stock exchange, though the world's 15th largest, is plagued[217] by <u>volatility</u> and frequent rumors of trading by politically linked parties. (TIME, Dec. 4, 1995, p. 26)
吉隆坡的股票市場雖是全球排名第15大，可是<u>變動太厲害</u>，而且時因政商勾結交易的傳聞而飽受傷害。

□ 1048 **write-off** [ˋraɪt͵ɔf] (n.) （債務）勾銷

In November 1994 the corporation (Sony) took a
$3.2 billion <u>write-off</u> for five years of studio
mismanagement. (TIME, Feb. 24, 1997, p. 42)
1994年11月，新力公司為電影部門5年來經營不善而償付32
億美元的<u>帳面沖銷</u>支出。
註 studio (n.) 電影製片廠

索引

309

315

單字進話論

啓發英語進「話」能力
輕鬆掌握日常會話

　　本書作者守誠，是日本著名的英語教學者，根據他長年的觀察，只要靈活運用國中英文的1,700個單字，就能應付日常生活所需的會話。換句話說，要治療「英語會話障礙」並不困難，重點在於「牢記基礎單字」和「靈活運用」，為了幫助讀者達到這兩個目的，作者萌生撰寫此書的構想。作者指出，隨著亞洲各國的經濟力提升，亞洲人開始利用英語參與世界的政治與經濟，「亞洲英語」的時代業已來臨。只要暫時拋開文法，全心感受溝通成功的喜悅，就能突破英語會話障礙，開口說英語了。

　　《單字進話論》分為九章，內容完全貫徹了作者「會話由簡易單字開始」的理念，從最基礎的單字開始，提供高明而有效的背單字技巧，循序帶領讀者進入現代生活各領域必備的單字，最後並列出聯考、留學考試、經貿、以及國際商業期刊上常見的字彙。在「靈活運用」方面，作者也將基本單字置入國外旅行的必備情境（如機場、參觀博物館、醫療）中，驗證他的「單字進話論」。全書每章都附有「休息小站」與「自我測驗」部份，前者以趣談的方式提出英文小常識，後者則提供讀者複習與檢測學習成果的效果。

■ 作者／守誠
■ 購書代碼 LE-005／定價 **280**元

TIME時代經典用字 政治篇
政黨政治、國際政治、經濟政策等TIME經典用字
旋元佑著　　　　310頁

chauvinism /ˈʃovˌnɪzm/ (n.)沙文主義
極端的、盲目的大國家主義，或者大男人主義。來自於人名Nicolas Chauvin，他是盲目崇拜拿破崙的一名法國軍人。拿破崙曾受歐洲知識份子矚目，認為是法國共和國的象徵、民主的鬥士。可是拿破崙稱帝之舉，再加上戰敗被囚禁，使他終於失去民心。然而Chauvin一本初衷，支持拿破崙到底。他的名字也逐漸成為「盲目的大國家主義」的代表……
——摘自第六章一般政治p. 196

TIME時代經典用字 商業篇
總體經濟、金融投資、證券、貿易等TIME經典用字
梁民康著　　　　312頁

IPR 智慧財產權
IPR是intellectual property rights的簡稱，財產權通常分兩類：工業財產權(industrial property)與著作權(copyright)。工業財產權又分專利權(patent)、「實用」新型權(utility model)、新式樣權(new design)與商標權(trademark)四項。著作權則主要指文學、音樂、藝術、攝影、電影、電腦程式等權利……
——摘自第七章商業p. 190

TIME時代經典用字 科技篇
電腦、環境、電機、生物、醫學等TIME經典用字
謝中天、顧世紅著　　　　296頁

anorexia nervosa & bulimia
/ˌænəˈrɛksɪə nɝˈvosə bjuˈlɪmɪə/ 神經性厭食及貪食症
anorexia是「厭食症」，加上nervosa則指由於精神方面的因素所引起的厭食症。相反症狀的病症就是貪食症了。anorexia這個字源自於希臘字首an-（表示without）加上orexia（appetite，食慾）；而bulimia源自於希臘文的boulimia(great hunger)……
——摘自第六章醫學p. 210

TIME時代經典用字 人文篇
影劇、文學、媒體、音樂／藝術等TIME經典用字
旋元佑著　　　　288頁

slogan /ˈslogən/ (n.)口號，標語
從前蘇格蘭高原一帶及愛爾蘭的住民，在戰場上發動衝鋒時，為激勵士氣而呼喊的口號(battle cry)稱為slogan。同時，這些地方的人民在召集人群集合時的呼喊(rallying cry)也是slogan。引申的意思可以解釋為政黨或其他團體的代表性口號或標語……
——摘自第三章媒體p. 90

本書附有 1 張精簡復習版、3 張完整版 CD 隨書銷售
由著名廣播節目主持人及專業美籍播音員
中、英雙語錄製

書＋精簡復習版 1CD　　　　　　　　　定價　600 元　特價 299 元
（錄音內容包括英文單字、中文字義）

書＋精簡復習版 1CD＋完整版 3CD 定價 1200 元　特價 599 元
（錄音內容包括英文單字、中文字義及英文例句）

國家圖書館預行編目

TIME 單挑 1000 / 編輯部 -- 初版 . -- 臺北市：經典傳訊文化，
1997 [民 86]
面；　公分 . -- (時代英語；1)

ISBN 957-99198-7-9(平裝)

1. 英國語言 - 詞彙

805.12　　　86002841

時代英語系列 01

TIME單挑 1000

資 料 來 源／美國時代雜誌集團(TIME Inc.)
英 文 審 校／Drew Hopkins
錄 音 人 員／S. Frued ・ Terri ・丹萱
責 任 編 輯／黃中憲

名 譽 發 行 人／成露茜
發 行 人／黃智成
總 主 筆／旋元佑
主 筆／梁民康
叢 書 主 任／陳瑠琍
執 行 編 輯／周健嬅
智 慧 財 產／陳湘玲
製 程 管 理／張慧齡・李祖平
行 銷／洪肇謙・張淑賢・王吟蘭・陳俊廷
網 路 讀 書 會／蕭怡雯・楊惟玲

發 行 所／經典傳訊文化股份有限公司
地 址／台北市 106 敦化南路 2 段 76 號（潤泰金融大樓）7 樓之 2
電 話／(886-2)2708-4410
傳 真／(886-2)2708-4420
E-mail／service@ccw.com.tw
製 作 中 心／台北市 116 文山區試院路（世新大學）傳播大廈
郵 政 劃 撥／18734890・經典傳訊文化股份有限公司
登 記 證／局版北市業字第 183 號

法 律 顧 問／國際通商法律事務所(Baker & McKenzie)
／陳玲玉律師・潘昭仙律師
製 版／大象彩色印刷製版股份有限公司
印 刷／科樂印刷事業股份有限公司
裝 訂／臺興印刷裝訂股份有限公司
總 經 銷／時代雜誌中文解讀版
服 務 電 話／(886-2)2754-0088
服 務 傳 真／(886-2)2754-0099
零 售 經 銷／農學社　電話／(886-2)2917-8022　傳真／(886-2)2915-7212

定 價／320 元
特 價／250 元
海 外 售 價／亞洲、大洋洲　　US$ 19
歐美非　　　US$ 21

ISBN　957-99198-7-9
出 版 日 期／1997 年 8 月 1 日初版
2001 年 9 月 25 日初版三十五刷